THE TIME OF THE
REAPER

THE TIME OF THE
REAPER

ANDREW BUTCHER

www.atombooks.co.uk

ATOM

First published in Great Britain in 2007 by Atom
Reprinted 2008

Copyright © Andrew Butcher 2007

The moral right of the author has been asserted.

A CIP catalogue record for this book is available from
the British Library.

ISBN 978-1-904233-94-7

Typeset in Baskerville by M Rules
Printed and bound in Great Britain by
Clays Ltd, St Ives plc

Atom
An imprint of
Little, Brown Book Group
100 Victoria Embankment
London EC4Y 0DY

An Hachette Livre UK Company

www.atombooks.co.uk

For Darren Nash

PROLOGUE

Six Years Ago

The day his father died began like any other.

Travis was sitting in front of the Cartoon Network, munching his way through a bowl of cornflakes. His mum was calling from the kitchen for him to hurry up or he'd be late for school (she made the same dire prediction every morning but he was always on time). His dad was pacing the hall as if he was already on his beat. Everything was normal, safe, comforting, the way it always had been, the way it always would be, Travis assumed. He was ten years old.

'Bye, love.' His dad's voice.

'Bye.' Mum's.

The wet smack of their kiss. Then the hand, strong and protective, ruffling his shock of brown hair.

'Dad!' Travis complained with a grin, gazed up at his father.

'You be a good boy at school today.'

'I will.'

'That's if he ever *gets* to school,' his mother groaned in the background. 'Look at the *time*.'

'Catch loads of crooks,' Travis said.

And his father smiled. 'I'll see you tonight,' he said.

1

But he never did.

Mrs North, the Head's secretary, came for Travis that afternoon while they were writing about Best Things and Worst Things. She whispered to Miss Bruton at the front of the class and then Miss Bruton approached Travis almost as if she was suddenly afraid of him and touched him lightly on the shoulder. 'Travis, could you go with Mrs North, please. Mr Shelley would like to see you. You're not in any trouble.' Which was the usual reason for a pupil's school day to be interrupted by an unexpected summons from the headmaster.

Even so, long afterwards Travis remembered how worried he'd felt, leaving the classroom with Mrs North, and all the kids' eyes on him, certain mouths twisted into anticipatory gloats. He remembered the tears pricking at his own eyes as if their time was near.

They walked in silence along the corridors and from behind closed doors he could hear the lessons going on without him, could glimpse the children through the windows not thinking about Travis Naughton or why Mr Shelley wanted to see him, engrossed by the intricacies of their own lives. Mrs North was leading him away.

When he entered the Head's study his first thought was that Dad had arrived to fetch him home for some reason. The man with his back to the room, staring out across the sunlit car park, the man in the uniform of a police officer – at a glance and from behind it could have been his father. 'Ah, Travis,' Mr Shelley began awkwardly. 'You're here. That's . . . come in. Please. Sit . . . take a seat.'

And then the other man turned to face him and it wasn't his dad after all but Uncle Phil.

2

What was Uncle Phil doing here when he should be out patrolling with Dad?

'I'm afraid,' Mr Shelley said, frowning down at his desk, 'I'm afraid, Travis . . .'

Uncle Phil with eyes red as blood, eyes that might have been stabbed.

'. . . I've got some very bad news . . .'

But, of course, it wasn't Uncle Phil who'd been stabbed.

And even long afterwards, Travis fought hard *not* to remember how he'd felt then, that day and the many days that followed. Days of silence and sobs. Days of darkness. Grief. It was as if he'd fallen into a bottomless pit, a void of unutterable blackness, consuming, all-enveloping, suffocating. It was as if he was alone, with no one to help him, no one to hold him, and alone he was falling for ever.

His dad had found him crying once, in the lounge, the TV's remote in his hand. 'Travis?' the man had said. 'What's the matter?'

'I've turned the telly off.'

'That's not worth getting all upset about, is it? You can always turn it back on again.'

His father hadn't understood. At first. 'There was this pro-gramme. There was a policeman in it. And a Bad Man. The Bad Man had a gun. He shot . . . he *killed* . . .'

'I see.' Travis's dad had nestled onto the settee alongside him, eased a reassuring arm around his shoulders, squeezed. 'You mustn't worry, Travis. It was only a programme. Nothing like that is ever going to happen to me. I won't let it.'

'Promise?'

'I promise.'

Travis had been heartened only partially. 'But the Bad

Men. They're not only on TV, are they? Some of them are real. Some of them have got guns. Why do you have to go after them?'

'Because I'm a policeman.'

'Why are you a policeman?'

His father's expression, usually so gentle around him, had grown graver, more serious. 'I'm a policeman *because* of the Bad Men, Travis. You're right. There are criminals out there, too many of them, people who break the law, greedy, violent people who don't care what they do or who they hurt. Dangerous people. Which is why those of us who believe in rules, in justice, in right and wrong, why we have to fight for our beliefs. Because the simple truth is this, Travis: unless good men are prepared to stand up for what's right, evil men will have their way.'

Travis recalled those words while Uncle Phil and some other police officers bore his father's coffin down the aisle of the church. Grandma was gripping Travis's hand so tightly as they followed behind, was guiding him every step of the way as if he was suddenly blind and in need of the assistance. Grandad was supporting Mum. Her feet dragged and trailed along the stone-flagged floor like they'd forgotten how to walk. Travis couldn't bear to look at his mother that day. It hurt too much, almost stopped him breathing. It was like watching someone drowning, but you couldn't help them because you were drowning too.

Funeral. That was the *real* F word.

He didn't sing any of the hymns or recite the prayers, even though he knew most of them. There was no voice in him. But he could hear.

'. . . a terrible thing, tragic . . .'

'. . . that poor little lad. Losing your father when you've

4

grown up is traumatic enough, but how old is he? Ten? Eleven? And what *happened*. I can't imagine how he must be feeling . . .'

'. . . brave of him to come – but then, his father was brave. *Too* brave . . .'

Travis's father was talking to him, too. Inside his head. 'Unless good men are prepared to stand up for what's right,' he was saying, 'evil men will have their way.'

I know, but I won't let them, Travis vowed silently. *I want to be like you, Dad. I'll do what's right. I'll make my stand. I promise.*

Later, the smoke from the crematorium chimney darkening the sky – like a premonition of the horrors to come.

But none of that had happened yet. It was morning once more: Travis was chomping cereal as usual and from the kitchen Mum was warning him about the time as usual and Dad was pacing the hall, alive again. Travis could hear him. If he got up, popped his head around the door, he'd see him.

The boy's heart surged. He was dreaming, he knew, but what if that didn't matter? The dream had whisked him back in time to that fateful, terrible, grievous day, like a character in a science fiction film, and to a point in that day before his father had left the house, before he'd . . . The dream had granted him a second chance. He could save his father. He could keep him alive. *Alive*. He could change reality.

He wouldn't let Dad down.

'Dad!' And he was on his feet and milk from his bowl was splashing on the carpet like drops of white blood but he didn't care and he was darting into the hall and his dad was at the door. About to open the door. 'Wait!'

His father paused. 'Travis?' He turned to face his son. 'What's the matter?'

5

Something. Something was the matter. Dad was wearing his uniform now but previously Travis was pretty sure he hadn't been. He seemed to remember that Dad used to change into his uniform at the station, travelling to and from work in his own clothes. Or maybe he'd got that wrong.

And he looked pale, his father. Maybe just a little pale.

'Don't go, Dad.'

'What are you talking about, Travis? I have to go or I'll be late.'

'Call in sick. Stay at home today. Don't go into work. Please.'

'I don't understand.'

'Something . . . something bad is going to happen to you today if you leave, Dad. I know it is. I've seen it. Stay with Mum and me.' Travis threw his arms around his father's neck, pressed himself against his father's body.

The cold took his breath away.

'Dad?' Instinctively, Travis recoiled. He hated himself for it.

Pale. Definitely pale. Like frost. Like ice. Lines scored across the man's brow like furrows in snow.

'Dad?' And what was this on Travis's neatly pressed white school shirt, this dark, damp stain? He smeared his fingers with the substance and rendered them deep red. Blood, of course. But how could it be blood? Travis wasn't bleeding.

The same could not be said of his father. How come he hadn't noticed earlier the evidence of Dad's punctured chest, spreading incriminatingly across the front of his uniform, soaking the cloth? Travis stared aghast. His father frowned as he looked down too, as if he himself had only now noticed his wounds. The wounds that had killed him.

6

Travis was too late.

Because the door was open already. It had opened of its own accord. And beyond the house lay darkness, not day, and the hallway seemed longer than it should, elongating itself to separate son from father, the living from the dead. And Travis's heart ached. He could change nothing. His dream was mocking him.

'Oh, God, Dad. Please don't go. Please don't leave us. Please. Stay.'

But his father was shaking his head, resignedly, mournfully, and the weariness of the departed was in his voice. 'I *have* to go, Travis. I know you want me to stay but I can't. I don't belong here with you any more.' A bleak wind blew across the night-world beyond the door. 'Goodbye, son. You have to go on without me.'

'I can't. I can't.' Clutching for his father again but not reaching him, unable to touch him.

'You must. For your mother. For yourself.' The man was disappearing through the doorway. The wind was snatching at him, gusting him away. 'Travis, I was your father and I loved you. Remember that.'

'Dad, I don't want you to go . . .'

But the dream wasn't listening to him. It was over. It was morning – for real.

Travis lay still and gazed into the empty whiteness of his bedroom ceiling. He didn't need to feel his pyjama jacket to know that he'd find no trace of blood there. Nightmares tended to leave little by way of tangible legacy. Yet the vision had driven home a difficult lesson, finally and irrefutably. His father was gone for ever.

Once something was lost, it could never be regained.

7

Six Days Ago

Captain Gavin Hooper hated the desert. He glowered down at its arid, rocky expanses through the helicopter window and he knew: the desert was his enemy.

Hooper felt more than qualified to comment on the topic of enemies. During his career as a member of Her Majesty's Armed Forces he'd faced – and defeated – many of them. Some had taken the form of men rushing at him with a curse on their lips and a gun in their hands – they'd been the easy ones to dispatch, even when, from time to time, the men had turned out to be little more than boys or, once, a young woman. Others had come composed of steel and wire and dynamite, and had lurked in parked cars on dusty roadsides, and they'd been more difficult to defend against. Hooper's own lacerated body and footless left leg testified to that. The most lethal, most dangerous enemies, the soldier's experience had taught him, were those that stayed hidden, secret, biding their time, those you couldn't see until it was too late. Or, he'd begun to think since his latest posting, those that were all around you, seemingly innocent, apparently harmless, but which sucked you in and wore you down, which killed you slowly by sapping your will to live. The desert, Hooper mused grimly. The desert was like that. The desert was his enemy.

'Sir.' The pilot alongside him, still young enough for serious acne. 'Sandstorm's picking up behind us.'

'How far to the base?'

'Twenty klicks, sir.'

Hooper nodded approvingly. 'We'll be on the ground before it closes in, son. Any contact from the base yet?'

'Still nothing, sir.' With a note of tension in his voice.

'Keep trying. You're doing a good job,' the captain added reassuringly.

The young pilot flushed at the compliment. *Too* young, Hooper considered. Like a lot of the lads he'd fought alongside in Iraq, like those he'd seen die. Not that politicians back home ever seemed to lose sleep over the average age of those they packed off to risk their lives in their foreign wars. Hooper remembered the two who'd been killed in the same incident that had lost him part of a limb, the boy who'd lingered screaming for a mother he'd never see again. *Politicians*. Should be put up against a wall.

Iraq had finished him as a front-line soldier, too. A man with a prosthetic foot was not to be subjected to combat. So he'd been transferred out here, made military liaison officer to one of the few Arab states in the Gulf still on friendly terms with the United Kingdom. Friendly enough to welcome her military assistance and technology, at any rate. Friendly enough in exchange to permit the establishment of the occasional scientific installation in the middle of nowhere, such as the one Hooper and his little squadron of three troop-carrying helicopters were approaching now.

Of course, that raised the question, *why* should the British government choose to exile groups of its scientists out in the trackless wastes of the desert rather than employ them more cosily in some state-of-the-art laboratory complex in the shires? What were they doing here? Apparently that was classified, even to somebody permanently maimed in the service of his country. But whatever the work entailed, Hooper doubted it was legal. 'Legal' tended not to require solitude and secrecy. New weapons technology, he suspected – that was what the boffins were developing in the desert: new ways to kill young soldiers more ruthlessly, more efficiently. Ways that a soldier wouldn't see until it was too late.

Scientists. Should be put up against a wall.

'Sir!' The pilot's tone brightened. He was pointing ahead with something like relief.

The camp.

'Take her down, son,' said Hooper.

Though quite frankly, bottom line, he didn't really care *what* a bunch of geeky guys in white coats and spectacles got up to on their mysterious bases so long as it didn't impinge on his own existence, and until three hours ago it hadn't. But three hours ago was when all communications between the base and the outside world had come to a summary and inexplicable stop. None of the installation's personnel had been contactable since. Hooper and his men had been assigned to find out why.

Odd that this should happen now, though. Only yesterday a new contingent of scientists had been flown out to supplement their colleagues already resident here. At least, that was the official line. Hooper had glimpsed the team waiting for their ride, however, and he doubted any one of them had ever so much as slipped on a lab coat. Dark glasses. Darker suits. There was more of MI6 than Ph.D. about these latest recruits. Which matched up with a rumour he'd heard from a mate in air-traffic control that some kind of object had been tracked falling to earth in the base's vicinity. A fragment of a decaying satellite that had failed to burn up in the atmosphere, most likely, and, given that the newcomers had obviously arrived to check it out, not British in origin. Maybe the government was worried that others besides itself were taking an interest in the work being done in this godforsaken place.

Hooper was frowning as the chopper descended into the camp's compound. From this perspective, everything appeared normal, peaceful. The ranks of prefabricated huts and larger buildings, all single-storey, stood silently and respectfully like troops awaiting inspection: nothing out of order there. The camp's trucks and jeeps were also lined up in a neat row, its own helicopter in mint condition on its launch pad. The perimeter fence – rather a superfluous security measure, one might think, given the location's remoteness – remained serenely unbreached. Of human beings, however, there was no trace. The entire scene was as still as a photograph, and maybe that was what bothered Captain Gavin Hooper. There was no life in a photograph. As for the base . . . Just because you couldn't see an enemy, that didn't mean he wasn't there. Hooper felt his muscles tensing.

The pilot's landing was exemplary, even as the first winds of the imminent storm whipped across the open desert. Hooper patted the boy's shoulder and told him to stay where he was.

'Sir? With respect, sir, it wouldn't be a good idea to take off into this storm.'

'Hopefully we won't have to,' said Hooper. 'Now radio HQ and inform them that we've reached the base.'

The three choppers disgorged their occupants, six soldiers from each, all of them armed with automatic weapons.

'What do you make of this, sir?' said Corporal Kent, joining his superior officer. 'A bit *Marie Celeste*, if you ask me.'

'You think there's nobody here?'

'I think if anybody *was* here, sir, they'd have heard us coming in and somebody would have come out to investigate.'

'Looks like somebody has, corporal,' said Hooper, pointing.

A dog, a mongrel, suddenly ventured into view around the

corner of one of the nearest huts. Its tail and ears were drooping and it was whining.

'Here, boy, here,' coaxed Kent, but the dog only cowered away from him. When the corporal took a cautious step forward it fled.

'Hm. You obviously have a way with animals, Kent,' observed Hooper.

'Something's frightened it,' the corporal said. 'I wonder what.'

Hooper squinted up at the sky. It was the colour of jaundice. Dust and sand were beginning to lash at the soldiers in the compound, which perhaps explained why the men were instinctively clustering together. Whatever they might or might not discover in the base over the next few minutes, it occurred to Hooper, they were stranded with it.

'All right, let's do our job.' His voice, hardened by years of soldiering, cracked like a gunshot. 'Buddy teams.' He reeled off names. 'Start at this end of the camp.' More names. 'Start from the far end. Search each building in turn. Be thorough and be careful. Corporal Kent and I will meet you in the middle.'

'Where are we going?' Kent asked.

The mongrel had appeared again. Now it barked, apparently torn between fear and a need to make some kind of urgent canine communication with the new arrivals. 'We're going wherever the dog leads us,' said Hooper.

The soldiers penetrated deeper into the base, gradually losing sight of each other among the silent buildings. Men slipped inside one hut or another and did not reappear. Hooper watched them vanish. Perhaps they'd never truly existed in the first place.

'*Sir.*' Kent had been focusing on the dog. The animal had

insinuated itself through the narrow gap of a partly open door and into one of the larger constructions, perhaps a lab. Corporal and captain followed its lead.

'Hello?' Hooper shouted on the threshold. 'Anyone there? Dr Lansburg? Professor Fielding?'

If they *were* there, then they weren't answering. And it wasn't a lab into which the two men stole with all the wariness of seasoned burglars. It was a recreation room. There was a bar and a canteen, pinball and one-armed bandits, pool and table tennis. Nobody was playing just now, but they had been. The soldiers could tell because one guy was still at the pinball machine, only he wasn't likely to rack up much of a score slumped across it like that; and they could tell because a man and a woman were still holding table-tennis bats, though they wouldn't be very effective wielded from recumbent positions on the floor. The half-dozen other occupants of the rec room had obviously come here just to take it easy, which must have been why they were sat in two groups at the long tables in the centre of the room. Maybe it was also why they seemed to have fallen asleep, lolling back in their chairs or resting their tired heads on the table.

Only they weren't actually asleep.

Hooper stiffened, his eyes burning with alertness. There was another presence here as well, belonging to an entity as yet unseen. The most ruthless and implacable enemy of all.

'Dead,' Kent gasped. 'They're all dead.'

No mark of violence. No sign of struggle. No visible wounds. It was as if the base's staff had simply and collectively decided to die and had carried out the operation with the minimum of fuss.

'What the hell happened here?'

13

Hooper shook his head. No visible wounds? Not in the sense of gaping holes and dripping blood, but even from the doorway there seemed to be a redness about the deceased scientists' faces, as if they'd been boiled. Hooper glanced down. Their hands, too, where he could see them. The dog was licking at one that dangled listlessly from the arm of a bearded man whose head was thrown back with his mouth wide open as if expecting a dental examination in the very near future.

From outside, Hooper could hear the squalling of the sandstorm. The dog turned to look at him and barked.

Hooper advanced towards the corpses.

'Sir, do you think we ought to . . . ?' Kent held back.

'We don't have a choice, corporal.'

Hooper neared the body of the man who'd presumably been the dog's owner. At closer quarters, the scientist's heightened colouring made a grim kind of sense. Hooper felt his gorge rise. The man's skin was ravaged with a profusion of crimson circles, as if a lunatic had carved rings into the flesh with a knife. Or it was like he'd been tangled and suffocated in a scarlet net and its meshing had cut into him savagely.

It was disease. Infection had killed him.

Hooper moved on to the next body, despite the whimpers of the dog. Sightless, staring eyes, white in a mask of red. He didn't feel the need to check further. They'd all have perished the same way, that much was obvious.

'Sir . . .'

He ignored Kent. It must have come quickly for them, death. At once. In a moment. As they played and laughed and talked and drank coffee. Death had joined them and made himself at home.

'Sir . . .'

14

But how? Stealthily. In deadly and innumerable armies of bacteria. Invading through the nostrils, through the pores, conquering from the very air its victims breathed, murdering from the inside out. Some kind of fearsome viral agent, perhaps? A biological weapon? One that affected human beings only? The dog's continued survival proved that. Maybe new strains of disease were what the scientists had been working on out here, far from innocent population centres. Maybe there'd been an accident. Maybe the poison had been released into the base like cyanide capsules spilled.

Maybe it was still active.

'Sir . . .'

'Kent, call the men. We've got to evacuate im—'

And it was as if Corporal Kent had contracted a bad case of sunburn from somewhere. He was swaying unsteadily on his feet. 'I don't feel so . . .' He dropped his gun. He tried to reach down for it, but as he stooped he crumpled forward onto the floor and neither spoke nor moved again.

'Kent!' Hooper stretched out his hand towards his fallen comrade. It was blotched with the faintest of scarlet circles. 'My God . . .'

The enemy was close now, just as it had been months ago on the roadside in Iraq. But Captain Gavin Hooper had cheated death then and he'd cheat death now. Discretion had always been the better part of valour.

Striding towards the door he snapped into his radio, 'Rogers, Smith, Barnard – can you hear me?' It seemed not. 'Can anyone hear me?' Only the dog, yelping from behind him as though begging him to stay. 'If anyone can hear me, get back to the choppers now. We're pulling out.'

If the sandstorm would let them. It smashed into Hooper like

15

a boxer as he burst out into the compound, buffeting, staggering him. He raised his hand to protect his eyes. The red rings were bolder now, more deeply ingrained, as though they'd taken root.

Death was in him. He could feel it, corrupting his cells, attacking his organs. He could feel contagion brimming in him. But he could fight it. He could hold it back. The will was stronger than the flesh. He'd always believed that. Hooper waded through a blizzard of sand as through deep and drowning waters. No sign of any of the others. They must be dead, all dead. Like Kent. He was the last. But he would live. The huts were fading shapes around him. Ahead, like charcoal smudges, the choppers. That young pilot waiting. He'd fly him, Hooper, back to HQ. The doctors would save him, cure him. He'd stay alive if he had to cut off his own arm. But if his commanding officers *knew* that treacherous biological experimentation was going on here, why hadn't they properly equipped Hooper and his men with gas masks? Didn't they care?

Commanding officers. Should be put up against a wall. They were as bad as the politicians, as bad as the scientists. Up against a wall. All of them. Every damn one. The whole damn world.

Hooper's skin was burning. He felt like he was on fire. But he was almost there. Groping through the whirlwind of sand and grit. The chopper. The pilot where he'd left him, at the controls. Kid deserved a medal.

He heaved open the door. 'Quick, get us airborne.'

Unlikely. Dead men don't fly helicopters.

Captain Gavin Hooper cried out then. He tottered backwards and the gale of the storm spun him round as if he was nothing, as if he was dust, and he cried out in rage and frustration and despair.

But not for long.

16

ONE

At just after eight on what he later considered to be the last night of the old world, Travis Naughton stood on the doorstep at the Lanes' house and rang the bell.

His finger had scarcely applied its pressure before the door swung excitedly open. Light and music and chattering voices spilled out in an animated jumble. 'Travis!' Jessica had been poised to greet her guests, of course. She'd probably been hovering by the door all day in case someone arrived early. 'You're *late*.' Initial delight tempered with feigned reproof.

'Yeah, I know. Sorry about that. Thought I'd better start looking at those past papers old Thompson gave us. Went on the internet and kind of lost track of time.'

'No,' huffed Jessica, folding her arms. 'I don't want excuses, especially not if they involve school or work. Two words absolutely banned on my birthday. The invitation did clearly state seven-thirty, Travis.'

'How about I compensate you for those tragically missing thirty-five minutes?' Travis offered up his card and present like one of the three kings at Jesus's crib. 'Happy birthday, Jess.'

'For me?' She grabbed them with a gasp of exaggerated pleasure.

Travis hoped she wasn't going to be disappointed. He'd only been able to afford chocolates. 'So am I forgiven? Can I come in?'

'Yes, you are and yes, you can,' said Jessica, beaming. 'On one condition.'

'Does it involve self-humiliation?'

'That depends whether your definition of humiliation includes kissing girls on their birthday.'

'You know, I *think* we're all right.'

They held each other. They kissed. Travis was reminded of all those other birthday kisses he and Jessica had shared over the years. The embarrassed pecks on the cheek at four and five, both participants close to tears. The first brushing of the lips at eleven and twelve, mouths resolutely closed as if to protect against germs. The parting of the lips at thirteen; a meeting of tongues at fourteen. At fifteen, the issue complicated by dates and pressure and then the break-up. At sixteen, tonight, an almost innocent gladness at being together, at being friends with the stirring mysteries of life still ahead of them.

'What's that old song?' Travis said. '"Happy Birthday, Sweet Sixteen"? It's a milestone year, Jess.'

'If you say so.' Jessica turned and finally closed the door behind Travis. He thought that her head seemed to bow a little but he might have been wrong. When she looked at him again, she was still smiling exuberantly. 'What do you think of my dress? Do you like it? It's new.'

Of course it was new. Jessica *always* had a new dress for her birthday party. Each year, though, there seemed to be less of it. This one was traffic-light red and left all four limbs rather bare – shoulders, too. Jessica's shoes, lipstick and nail varnish matched it, the colour fetchingly complementing her sweep of strawberry-blonde hair.

'Do I like it? Yes,' Travis conceded. 'It's very nice.' And Jessica Lane was very gorgeous, he realised, as her green eyes sparkled at his appreciation. 'Wouldn't wear it myself, though. Don't have the legs for it.'

'Oh, *Trav*.' She hugged him again.

Maybe it had been a mistake to agree to the split. Maybe he should have tried harder.

'So what's the scene?' Though it wouldn't be fair to complicate things for Jessica tonight.

'Music in the family room. Chill-out area in the lounge. Nibbles in the dining room . . .'

'Could be nibbles in the lounge as well if people get lucky,' Travis noted, a remark which his hostess chose to ignore.

'Drinks in the kitchen.'

'Including your dad's famous non-alcoholic punch?' Travis grinned.

'Absolutely.' This time Jessica grinned back. 'It's still with us, same as ever, even if Dad – and Mum – aren't. Not until eleven, anyway.'

'Parents have done a runner, huh? Excellent. While the adults are away . . .'

'So whether it *stays* non-alcoholic between now and then . . .'

'Might have to taste it and see. You coming, birthday girl?'

'In a minute. I'm just . . .' Jessica gestured towards the door. 'In case there's anyone else still on their way.'

'Might be. I thought I saw a *Hello!* photographer along the road asking for directions to the party of the year. I nearly told him . . .'

'Really?' The blonde girl blushed at Travis's good-humoured laughter. But she could get her own back. 'Mel's here,' she said with sly simplicity. 'You'd better just hope she's not in one of the rooms with the lights switched off or you'll never find her.'

She certainly wasn't in the kitchen. Trevor Dicketts and Steve Pearce were there, carrying on the same interminable discussion about football which had seemed to occupy them since the age of ten. And Cheryl Stone was there, too, pouring herself some punch. And Simon Satchwell. *Simon Satchwell?* Not exactly a name that featured high on most people's guest list – though Travis remembered that Jessica's parents knew Simon's grandparents somehow. The birthday girl herself probably hadn't invited him. Cheryl Stone for one evidently would have preferred it if *nobody* had. In heroically volunteering to help her with the punch, the bespectacled Simon had only succeeded in splashing the front of her dress with the liquid. Producing a handkerchief and dabbing at the subsequent wet patch, he was merely exacerbating his original offence.

'Simon, what do you think you're *doing*? Hands. *Off.*'

'Sorry, Cheryl, I just . . . sorry.' Wiping his nose with the handkerchief. 'Sorry.'

Travis's sentiments precisely, though in a slightly different context. He felt sorry *for* Simon Satchwell. He wasn't exactly Brad Pitt Junior himself, never had been. His undistinguished brown mop of hair was as unruly as ever and his features, while pretty much the right size and in pretty much the right places, hardly qualified as 'Hunk of the Month' material. He'd been told before that his blue eyes were kind of piercing, but they didn't smoulder: they were unlikely ever to gaze out

20

at adoring female fans from the pages of a teenage magazine. Still, Travis conducted himself with confidence, earned respect from boys and dates with girls. In all his life, to Travis's knowledge, Simon Satchwell had experienced neither.

It wasn't just the body, the angular awkwardness, the boniness, the colourless hair, the vapid expression, the glasses – though that was a lot. Appearance only ever set up certain expectations, like the opening chapters of novels. It was down to the individual to prove first impressions right or wrong, and in Simon's case, sadly for him, it was always the former. Had he been American, he'd have numbered among the nerds, the kind of guy whose photo you'd see in newspapers and on TV after he'd shot twenty of his classmates during a high-school rampage. Travis refused to apply the word nerd to him: Simon Satchwell was simply one of life's losers. And Travis recalled what his peers seemed to have forgotten, that Simon had lost a lot, more even than *he* had, and at a younger age, too – ample reason by itself why he didn't deserve the thinly disguised contempt of people like Cheryl Stone.

Who was scowling at him now. 'Simon, will you just get out of the way? Don't you think you've done enough damage already?'

'Sorry, Cheryl, but I was . . . I was just wondering . . . there's music playing in the other room and I was wondering if you wanted to . . .'

'No. I don't want to. Ever.' At which point, the girl noticed Travis. She cried out his name as if calling for help, lunged for him as for a lifeline. 'Travis, how *are* you? It's so good to *see* you.'

'Cheryl.'

21

'Dance with me. Dance with me.' Virtually dragging him away. 'In the family room. In the hall. Outside, if you like. *Anywhere but here.*'

'Actually, I was planning on getting a drink.'

'Have mine. Take mine. Come on, let's go.'

Cheryl Stone didn't glance back but Travis did. Simon hadn't moved. He was staring at the floor.

By the time they'd reached the family room – lights off, sound system in fine voice – Cheryl's ardour had cooled considerably. Thirty seconds. That was good for her.

She was grateful, though. 'Thanks for saving my life, Trav. That Simon Satchwell . . .'

'What? You think he might have been aiming to drown you in the punch bowl or something?'

'Why not?' Cheryl thrust her chest forward, jabbing at the fading stains. 'He made a start.'

'You were maybe a little unfair on him,' Travis suggested. 'Simon's not so bad, is he?'

'Not so bad?' Cheryl snorted derisively. 'Wait till he asks *you* out. "Not so bad" – way I hear it, he's running out of girls to pester so it could be soon. Let me tell you, the world'll have to end before I spend time with Simon Satchwell.'

'Well, I think you've stated your position clearly enough, Miss Stone,' said Travis. He'd never much liked Cheryl Stone. 'I guess I was glad to be of assistance.' Backing away from her.

'Don't you want to dance, Trav? Now that we're here, I mean.'

No. I don't want to. Ever.

'Maybe later,' he said. 'I'm looking for Mel, really.'

'Last I saw her, she was in the lounge.' Travis thanked Cheryl for the lead. 'No,' she stressed. 'Thank *you.*'

And Jessica had had a point about needing the lights on to see Mel. In the crowded lounge, at the other end of a sofa to Alison Grant and Dale Wright who were engaging in mouth-to-mouth as if practising for a life-saving class, Melanie Patrick sat like an ink stain, with her legs curled up beneath her. Black boots. Black tights. Black skirt – long. Black shapeless sweater kind of thing several sizes too big for her but which success-fully swathed and hid her entire upper body – possibly her intention. Where any part of her could be glimpsed, a tide of dyed black hair, black nails, black lipstick, black mascara, black pretty much everything except her skin, which was quite the opposite in complexion. Funnily enough, though, the sight of Melanie Patrick always seemed to bring colour to Travis's life.

'Hey, Mel,' he grinned. 'So it's past chucking-out time at the morgue, huh?'

The goth girl smiled sarcastically. 'Beginning to think you weren't coming. Beginning to think it might turn out to be a good night after all.'

'Sorry to disappoint you.' Travis tried to slot himself onto the sofa between Mel and the lip-locked lovers. 'Evening, Dale, Alison. Any chance of you shifting up a little bit?'

'Mm *mm* mm mm *mm*' from the couple, which evidently constituted an affirmative since the sound was accompanied by a movement towards their end of the seat.

'Any chance of you guys getting a *room*?' Mel added dis-gustedly.

'What? There are men in long raincoats who'd pay good money to watch that,' said Travis.

'Yeah.' And, somewhere concealed by her voluminous sweater, Mel might have shuddered. 'Men have got a lot to answer for.'

23

'Present company included?'

'Present company honourably excepted.' Mel breathed in as if in slight but sudden pain. 'I'm glad you're here, Trav.'

'We aim to please. Actually, I wasn't sure you'd be on your own tonight, or even here at all.'

'Let Jessica down? Why would I want to do that?'

'I heard Kev Meade was going to ask you out.'

'Who told you that?'

'As in Kev "Gandalf" Meade,' Travis teased.

'It's not funny. Who told you? Don't laugh like it's funny, Travis. He *did* ask me out.'

'Excellent. Where to? A wizards' conference? A special screening of all three director's cut versions of *Lord of the Rings*? You'll have a magic time.'

'Travis . . .' Mel warned.

'You said yes, of course.'

'I said *no*, of course. What do you take me for?'

'Actually, Mel,' Travis reflected a little more thoughtfully, 'someone who it seems to me has loads in common with Kev Meade. You like the same things. You like the same look. He's a good bloke, really. I'd have said yes if I were you. If you were lucky he might have let you hold his wand.'

Mel curled her upper lip derisively. 'Just as well you're not me, then, isn't it? Though if you find Gandalf *that* attractive I happen to know he's free tomorrow night.'

'So poor old Kev joins the list, does he?'

'What list?'

'The list of guys who've asked you out only to have their best efforts thrown back in their faces. Where Mel Patrick walks, she walks alone – is that it?'

'I don't know what you mean, Trav,' Mel retorted frostily. 'Kev Meade's a loser.'

'They can't all be losers. The entire male sex can't be losers.'

'Says who?'

'People are going to start talking if you're not careful, Mel.' And just then, Travis wasn't sure whether he was being serious or not.

'What? 'Cause I haven't got a boyfriend? Where does it say in the Teenagers' Charter that you have to have a boyfriend by sixteen or be accused of, well . . . You don't have a girlfriend, Big Guy.'

'Not right now, maybe, but I've had my moments. You were in some of them, remember? Briefly. And Jess and I were an item for a while, weren't we? We just decided in the end that being good friends was more important than being boyfriend/girlfriend. Same way we did.'

'Yeah, yeah.' Mel didn't sound convinced. 'Jessica was just too good for you, Travis Naughton.'

'Maybe.' And maybe it was time to change the subject. 'So, not dancing, then?'

'To that boom-boom dance crap they're playing?' Mel scoffed. 'You're kidding, right? I outgrew that when I gave up believing in Father Christmas and happy endings. Should have brought my Fractured CDs along – they'd have added a little bit of class to the proceedings.'

'Fractured? Never heard of them.'

'Ah, Travis, my sweet musical innocent' – Mel tapped his lower lip with a long, slim, black-tipped finger – 'you have now. And this party sure needs something to give it a kick-start.'

Mel wasn't wrong. All the required elements for a good time were in place, Travis felt, with the possible exception of a few cans of lager. But the celebrations seemed slightly reserved, somehow, the atmosphere strangely muted, almost as if there was a sense among the party-goers that enjoying themselves tonight was for some reason inappropriate, even indecent. It was as if, in the midst of all their frivolity, someone was dying in a room upstairs. Several people whom Travis had expected to be present he hadn't seen yet.

Mark Doyle entered the room, carrying a drink and looking lost. 'All right, Mark,' Travis called across. 'No Jilly? What, she's wised up and left you?'

Doyle came over, shrugging. 'She's had to go to Derby for the weekend to see her dad. He's got this flu-bug thing. Laid up in bed, Jilly says. Whole family's gone.'

'Think that's why Carrie's not here, either,' piped up Janine Collier from the other side of the lounge. 'Phoned me this afternoon to say both her parents are coming down with it. She's having to look after the little ones.'

'It's going to be an epidemic,' predicted Jon Kemp alongside Janine. He was top of the year in science, so whatever he said on related matters came heavy with the weight of authority.

'I reckon it's already that,' said Mark Doyle. 'I mean, look how many supply teachers we're having at school. Half the staff out sick and us a couple of weeks from taking our GCSEs. This bloody flu thing could end up putting our futures at risk.'

Alison Grant wrestled her way out from under her boyfriend to prove that she'd been listening. 'I had my riding lesson cancelled today because the stables are understaffed due to the flu.'

'Don't worry, Allie,' Mel reassured her. 'Dale'll make up for it.'

'But what do you think it is?' worried Janine. 'My mum says it's the wrong time of year for normal flu. She reckons it's something like that bird-flu scare we had last year. My dad reckons it might be the start of a biological attack on the country by terrorists.'

'Cheerful parents you've got there, Jan,' grunted Mark Doyle.

'According to the news,' said Travis, 'it's not just happening here. It's everywhere. A *pan*demic.'

'Well, it's not avian flu,' proclaimed Jon Kemp. 'Not unless a new strain's mutated that can make the leap from birds to humans without us having to be living in close proximity to them. And it's difficult to believe terrorists are involved in something that's so widespread. Besides, the government has already denied either possibility.'

'Then it's probably both,' scoffed Mel. Jon Kemp's credibility on issues scientific did not extend to his utterances on politics. 'And it'll get worse, let me tell you.'

'Will it? And on what evidence are you basing this pessimistic forecast, Melanie?' challenged Jon Kemp in a huff.

'On the evidence of my life so far,' said Mel. 'It'll get worse because it always does. It'll get worse because everything gets worse, because this whole sad world is run by adults with no subculture. And if you think I'm all doom and gloom, there's your solution. Get rid of the adults, put kids in charge, things'd soon get better.'

'Put *you* in charge,' sniffed Jon Kemp, 'things would certainly get *blacker*.' And he earned a laugh for that from some people.

Jessica joined in with it as she darted into the lounge, despite not having the faintest clue what was supposed to be funny. It was just that, being Jessica, she wanted to hear laughter at her party. 'What's everybody doing in here? Talking? When you could be dancing? What are you all talking about?'

'Actually, the flu,' admitted Janine Collier.

'Ah-ah. No, no. Off-limits.' Jessica's smile was fixed and frozen on her face. 'Nobody mentions illness on my birthday. I declare this party a flu-free zone. Now, what are you sitting around for? You can do that at home. Come on. Let's dance.' She started walking about and clapping, like a teacher hurrying her class to assembly.

'Don't think so, Jess,' said Mel. 'Sorry, but this party's also a good-music-free zone.'

'Travis.' Jessica seized him with both hands. 'You'll dance, won't you? You'll dance with me.'

'I thought you'd never ask,' he said, grinning as he allowed her to pull him to his feet.

'That's good. That's better. Come on,' exhorted Jessica. 'Let's have a good time.'

'You heard her, Mel,' Travis said, looking back at the goth girl over his shoulder. 'Come on. Just imagine it's Fractured.'

'Maybe later,' Mel negotiated. 'I'll be in in a minute. Just let me finish . . .' From the floor she lifted a drink which she'd not so much as sipped since Travis's arrival.

He followed Jessica to the family room, the birthday girl managing to usher most of her other guests in, too. It wasn't so much dancing that ensued as a kind of rhythmic shuffling. The loudness of the music ended all prospect of conversation, whatever the topic. Travis noticed Simon Satchwell trying to catch a girl's eye from the margins of the room – any girl. They were all turning away.

And then, rather later, someone put on a slow record, prompting the usual pairings-off. Alison Grant and Dale Wright, obviously. Jon Kemp and Janine Collier, perhaps a little more unexpected. Cheryl Stone and Mark Doyle, a liaison the latter might have trouble explaining to Jilly on Monday morning.

Travis and Jessica.

He ought to have been pleased, the way she clung to him. He ought to have been flattered that this gorgeous blonde girl should choose to press herself against him so unaffectedly, so artlessly, and he supposed he was, kind of. But he sensed her priority wasn't so much to thrill him as to comfort herself. His arms around her were, he felt, protective rather than passionate. Despite the revealing dress and the irrefutable fact of her age, Jessica seemed very young tonight, and despite virtually forcing her guests into having a good time she suddenly didn't appear inordinately happy herself.

'You all right?' He wanted to sound tender but the CD player's volume counted against him.

'I'm fine,' Jessica claimed. 'It's my birthday. Why shouldn't I be?'

'Because' – Travis's turn to take the lead, drawing her into the dining room where it was quiet enough to speak without shouting – 'you're not. Are you?'

Jessica gazed down at the floor. 'I'm sixteen, Travis. May the twelfth. Today. My birthday.'

'And?'

'And tomorrow I'll be sixteen and a day, and the day after that sixteen and two days . . .'

'I can see where the maths is going, but the sense . . . ?'

'And next year I'll be seventeen and then eighteen and I'll have decisions to make and we'll all be going off to different universities or getting jobs and nothing will be the same again. There'll be change, Trav. Everything will change.' She lifted her eyes again and fear flickered in them.

'There's always change, Jess.'

'Why?'

'Because that's what life is. Time passes and we grow older. It's inevitable.' Travis didn't know quite what else to say. For a second he thought Jessica was going to stamp her foot as she'd used to do on those rare occasions as a little girl when she hadn't got her own way.

'But I don't *want* things to change. I like them the way they are. I want them to *stay* the way they are. Like tonight – *now* – wouldn't it be wonderful if a single moment could last for ever?'

'Possibly, but not possi*ble*,' Travis commiserated. 'And anyway, look on the bright side. You can come close. You get older, get a job, you buy your own house, you can hold a party like this every night, alcoholic punch included, and nobody can stop you.'

Jessica seemed unconsoled. 'Did I ever tell you my parents were originally going to call me Wendy, after Wendy in *Peter Pan*? That was the first book I ever remember being read to me. But I never wanted to be Wendy. Wendy grew older. I wanted to be like Peter and never grow older. I'm not sure I like the world outside my home, Travis. I'd be happier – I'd feel safer – staying just where I am.'

At the heart of her own little world, Travis thought, at the centre of her parents' world, an only child like himself. But he knew more than most that you couldn't rely on your parents for ever. Sooner or later, you had to learn to rely on yourself. It was a lesson that he hoped would come *much* later for Jessica.

'Well, some things won't change,' he said emphatically. 'Ever. For one, I'll always be around for you if you need me, Jessie. I'll always be your friend. When you're sixteen. When you're sixty. It'll make no difference to me.'

'Travis.' Jessica threw her arms gratefully around his neck and kissed him again. On the cheek.

'Sorry, am I interrupting something?' Mark Doyle stood in the doorway. From the family room, the tempo of the music had quickened again. 'Only, with my Jilly not here, I was wondering if the birthday girl wouldn't mind – ah – sharing herself around a bit.'

'Sensitively put, Mark,' commented Travis.

'Dance?' Doyle asked Jessica.

Who glanced at Travis almost as if she was asking for permission. 'A good hostess always keeps her guests happy,' he said. 'Go ahead. Time I forced Mel onto her feet anyway.'

'Thanks, Trav.' Jessica squeezed his hand in parting. 'I mean it.'

And Mel hadn't moved from the sofa, even though her only companions in the lounge now were Trevor Dicketts and Steve Pearce and their ongoing debate concerning the relative merits of 4-4-2 and the Christmas-tree formation. The glass she nursed in her hands was still half full – or, no doubt, from Mel's point of view, half empty.

'OK, no more excuses,' Travis said briskly. 'And before what's left of your leg muscles wastes away entirely through lack of use, you and me, Miss Patrick, are going to show the others how it's done.'

'You're still talking dancing, Trav, right?' Mel clarified. 'In which case . . .' She raised her glass to him like a shield.

'The reason you still haven't finished your drink is that you haven't worked up a thirst. That,' Travis insisted, 'is going to change. Like I said, no more excuses.'

Except for one, maybe. When Travis reached out for Mel – playfully, not violently or in a cruel way. When his hand closed around her left arm just below the elbow, the limb, even padded by the bulging folds of her sweater, feeling stick-thin. When he squeezed ever so slightly.

When she winced in pain.

Suddenly, Travis's face blanched almost to the paleness of his companion's. Suddenly, dancing seemed to lose its attraction, even its meaning. He released her as if his fingers had been scalded.

'Upstairs,' he whispered, his tone brooking no dissent.

'I thought we were supposed to be just good friends.' Mel's attempt at humour was lame, weak.

'Jess's room.' They couldn't talk down here, not about this. With all the others around, even the quietest corners might have ears.

As it turned out, nobody seemed to pay them any attention as they sidled upstairs to Jessica's bedroom. Travis turned on the light and closed the door behind them. There was a pink-ness and an innocence about Jessica's bedroom: stuffed toys sitting on shelves, posters of ponies and pop stars on the walls. Mel looked uncomfortable.

'OK,' Travis demanded coldly. 'What's been going on?'

'Nothing's been going on, Travis.' But Mel couldn't meet

32

the boy's penetrating blue gaze. 'I don't know why you've bundled me up here. Bedrooms are out of bounds at Jessica's parties – you know that.'

'He's hurt you again, hasn't he.' It wasn't a question.

'No.' On Jessica's bedside table, Mel noticed a framed photograph of the blonde girl with her parents and Mickey Mouse, all of them smiling, all of them happy.

'You're lying, Mel.' Travis caught hold of her left hand with his own, with his right yanked up the baggy sleeve of her sweater. He exposed her skinny white forearm. '*This* is telling the truth.' The skin purple with bruises in places.

'Travis, please.' She shook off his grip. 'Don't look.' Covering herself as if he'd seen her naked.

'That's it, Mel. I told you that if your dad hurt you again I'd report him to the authorities.' Gerry Patrick, Mel's father. The name was like an obscenity to Travis. He couldn't think of or visualise the man without being seized by loathing and disgust. And a feeling even darker, even worse when he thought of his own dad, six years dead.

'You can't, Trav,' Mel protested bleakly. 'You mustn't report him. I know he deserves it – that's the *least* the pig deserves – but think what it'd do to Mum if she ever found out. She wouldn't be able to bear the shame of it, Trav. It'd destroy her.'

'I'm sorry about that but I'm thinking of you, Mel, what your dad's done to you, seems is *still* doing to you.'

'I know. Don't think I don't – appreciate . . .'

'Abuse is wrong. Full stop. The only right thing to do is to report it and put an end to it. If we don't make a stand, the perpetrators – bullies like your dad – they'll think they've got away with it and simply carry on.'

'I know. I know.' Mel had heard Travis speak like this before, often. She longed to be able to say the same sort of things, to be as certain and as strong. 'But it's easy for you, Trav. It's not your family involved. It's not your dad who . . .' She trailed away, remembering that not all wounds were visible on the body. 'Sorry.'

'No, you're right,' Travis said. 'It's not my dad who hits his child when he's drunk. Neither would it have *ever* been.' There was a long, awkward pause. 'I thought you said he'd stopped. I mean, that was how you persuaded me not to go to the police the last time. You believed his promises that he'd stop.'

'He had. I honestly thought he had.' Mel's voice was earnest. 'Things at home haven't been too bad for months. This was just – he lost a lot of money on a horse – this was just a one-off, Trav. I'm sure.'

'Your dad won't change, Mel,' Travis sighed. 'He might give up knocking you about for a bit, but abuse is an addiction, you know? Your dad's an addict. All the while you live in that house . . .'

'But that's just it.' Mel clasped his hand eagerly. 'I won't have to live there much longer. We've got our exams next month and then I can leave school and get a job. And *then* I can find somewhere nice to rent for Mum and me and we can both move out and be safe' – her expression became as black as her clothes – 'and then my scumbag of a father can rot, for all I care.' Her tone turned to pleading: 'So please, Travis, I know you want to do the right thing but – just this once – please don't.'

'Mel . . .' Doubtfully.

'A few more months and I'll be out of there. By Christmas.

34

No more Dad. So for Mum's sake. For mine. Don't tell anyone.'

'I ought to at least warn your dad that I know, that someone knows, and if he doesn't control himself . . .'

'No. Travis. Please. Don't. *Please.* Just let me deal with it in my own way. OK?'

'I shouldn't.'

'*OK?*'

'Mel.' Gently, stroking her hair. It was like caressing night. 'OK, but if he even so much as *touches* you again . . .'

'He won't. I promise. Thank you.'

Mel would have kissed him then, only the moment was interrupted by an explosion of shouting from downstairs. Hard, humourless male laughter.

'What's that?' she frowned.

A girl's scream.

Travis was at the bedroom door in an instant. On the landing, Simon Satchwell almost seemed to be cowering.

'Simon? What's going on?'

'I think we've got gatecrashers,' Simon whined. 'Richie Coker.'

'Coker.' Another name that tasted like filth in Travis's throat. He strode for the stairs.

'Travis, wait.' And Mel following.

And it *was* gatecrashers. And it *was* Richie Coker. Even partially concealed by his baseball cap and the hood of his sweatshirt, the thug's heavy, sullen features were unmistakable to Travis. Coker daring to come here, to Jessica's house, on Jessica's birthday. Not alone, of course – flanked by his usual mob of morons, more fists than brain cells between them. They were wedging open the front door. Most were

35

still outside. Only Richie and a couple of his loyal lieutenants had forced their way in as yet.

And Richie had his paws on Jess.

'Come on, babe, like what's the problem?' he was slobbering. 'One little kiss. One birthday kiss.'

'Please, let go of me.' Jessica struggled. 'You shouldn't be here. Someone . . .'

But no one was making a move. The majority of her guests – her *friends* – were cramming into the hallway, but at the same time they seemed to be intent on keeping their distance, like random bystanders. Travis, halfway down the stairs, was dismayed. He could understand the girls not daring to tangle with Richie Coker and his cronies, fair enough (and with the likely exception of Mel). Maybe Simon Satchwell, too: victim in school, victim out of school. *Maybe* even the likes of studious Jon Kemp. But Mark Doyle? Steve Pearce? Why weren't they standing up to Coker and his goons? Why were they allowing brutishness and bullying to prosper without protest?

Well, Travis wasn't tolerating it. 'Do as she says, Coker,' he snapped from the stairs. 'Let her go.'

'Travis!' Jessica cried with relief.

Richie Coker grinned. 'Hey, Naughton, thought you must be around somewhere. So why don't you just push off somewhere *else*? There's no problem here. Just being friendly, aren't we, lads?' The lads grinned too, as though they'd recently been lobotomised. 'Nobody else sees a problem here, do they?' Challenging the other guests. The other guests didn't appear to see anything. 'Yeah? Maybe *you*'re the one with the problem, Naughton.'

'You'll be the one with the broken face if you don't leave

Jessica alone, Richie,' threatened Mel from the shelter of Travis's shoulder, clenching her fists into little balls.

'Been up in the bedrooms with Morticia, huh, Naughton? What's she like?'

'I'm going to say this once, Richie.' Travis targeted the gate-crasher with his eyes. 'But I'm going to say it slowly and clearly 'cause I know you have difficulty in understanding English sometimes.' His voice and gaze were steady but his heart was racing. He felt Mel's fingers twisting his shirt. 'Take your hands off Jessica, take your idiots with you, and get lost. Now.'

The idiots in question *ooh*ed mockingly in high-pitched voices.

'Or what?' goaded Richie Coker.

'Or I'll make you.'

The bully bawled with laughter. His hangers-on joined him. Somehow, the ridicule only gave Travis strength. He felt his heart swell with a kind of pride. He felt empowered. He felt inspired. 'Or you'll *make* me? Look around, pal. Apart from Morticia, you're on your own. Me, I've got mates.'

'I don't need anyone else to put scum like you in their place,' said Travis.

Richie Coker stopped laughing. He regarded Travis curiously. 'Watch your mouth, Naughton, or you might end up with fewer teeth than you started with.'

'If you're not out of here in, shall we say, fifteen seconds, Coker,' vowed Travis, 'you, too.'

'*Rich*.' One of his lackeys tugged nervously on Richie Coker's sleeve. '*Car*.' A sleek dark shape nosing into the drive, headlights stabbing towards the house.

It appeared Mr and Mrs Lane were returning home a little earlier than expected.

Threatening kids his own age was one thing. Taking on adults, however . . . Too many complications. 'This is a shit party, anyway,' sneered Richie, letting Jessica go. 'You losers deserve each other.' He joined his cronies stampeding across the lawn and towards the street.

'Yeah?' Mel yelled after him. 'You'd know about losers, you low-life piece of . . .' It was probably just as well that Richie Coker was already too far away to hear the rest. Mel watched the gang vault the garden's low wall and charge out into the road. If a bus had chanced by and ploughed into each and every one of them, she'd have been delighted.

Travis only had eyes for Jessica. 'Jess, are you OK? Are you sure?' His arms were pretty much fully occupied with her, too.

'I'm fine now. I'm fine.' She strove almost physically to regain control of herself; it wouldn't do for her parents to see her distraught. 'But Travis, it was . . . I thought it must be Carrie or someone at the door but it was Richie and his mates and I tried to shut them out but they forced their way in. I wanted them to *go*.'

'It's OK. It's OK,' Travis soothed her. 'They're gone now and they won't be back.'

'Unlike your mum and dad, Jess,' said Mel. The Lanes had parked the car. Its lights and engine had been turned off.

Travis wasn't listening. He'd turned accusingly to his fellow guests. 'And what did you lot think you were doing – or not? You know Coker's a thug. So you just thought you'd stand around while he terrorised Jessica, did you? When were you going to object? After he'd smashed the house up a bit or what?'

At least, Travis thought, nobody had the gall to look him in the eye. Now that the crisis was over, there seemed to have settled over the party-goers a general atmosphere of sheepish embarrassment. Simon Satchwell peeped over the banister at the top of the stairs like a besieged soldier raising his head above the battlements.

'Travis, Trav,' Jessica said, pulling at his sleeve as her parents clambered out of the car. 'It doesn't matter now. Like you said, they've gone. I don't want Mum and Dad knowing they were here, OK? They'll get angry and phone the police or something and I don't want my party spoiled, OK?'

'But they *saw* them,' Travis pointed out.

'Leave that to me,' winked Mel. She waved cheerfully from the doorway. 'Hi, Mr Lane, Mrs Lane. You're home early.'

'Hello, Melanie. We thought we'd better get back after all,' said Jessica's father.

'It seems as well we did,' said her mum. 'Who were those hooligans running around in our garden just then?'

'No idea,' lied Mel with vigour. 'They were looking for someone called – uh – Mikey. Wrong address, so they just kind of took off.'

'Rampaging through decent people's gardens like that.' Mrs Lane glared in the direction the culprits had taken. 'Do you think we should call the police, Ken?'

'They'll be long gone before the police get here,' discouraged Mel.

Mr Lane concurred. 'Melanie's probably right, dear. Best to leave it now. Let's not get involved. Hello, Travis, how are you? Jessica, sweetheart.' He kissed his daughter on the forehead. 'Are you having a nice time?'

'Yes, thank you, Dad,' Jessica said dutifully. 'Absolutely. Aren't we, everyone?'

And everyone *was*. The verdict was unanimous. A really, *really* nice time.

Because, in the end, Jessica's sixteenth birthday party was practically identical to her fifteenth, as that had been to her fourteenth. *At* the end, particularly. In the Lane house, continuity was everything and security was found in routine.

The traditional finale involved everyone gathering in the dining room for the singing of 'Happy Birthday' and the cutting of the cake, for the toast in honour of the birthday girl herself. Once it had been celebrated in squash or lemonade. Tonight was the second year for a swig of non-alcoholic sparkling wine.

And everyone was smiling, everyone laughing as Jessica's mum lit her daughter's candles and Jessica's dad filled the guests' glasses. Even Simon Satchwell. Even Mel. Travis too, though hollowly. Had they all so soon forgotten Richie Coker? He hadn't. Could Mel alongside him put what her father had done to her out of her mind so easily? He couldn't. He thought of Gerry Patrick and he thought of Richie Coker grabbing Jess and nobody even attempting to intervene.

Travis was afraid he wouldn't be able to keep his word to Mel after all.

Someone turned off the dining-room lights. The singing started. The yellow flicker of candles danced across Jessica's face as she leaned forward to extinguish that, too. In the temporary darkness, everybody cheered.

'May I ask you to raise your glasses, please,' urged Mr Lane when artificial light was restored. 'I'd like to propose a toast. To Jessica, our beautiful daughter, and to the wonderful future she has and that *all* of you have in store for you.

40

Jessica and the future!'

And if the birthday girl harboured any secret misgivings concerning the second part of her father's sentiment, she was careful not to betray them.

While around her everyone whooped and applauded and joined together in unison. 'Jessica and the future!' they chorused. Even Simon. Even Mel. 'Jessica and the future!'

TWO

The Children of Nature assembled in the clearing as usual to greet the dawn. 'The appearance of each new day must be cherished and celebrated,' Oak always said. 'It is like the birth of a baby, the beginning of a life, and what it might promise no one can know.'

But sometimes you can have a good idea, thought Linden Darroway. Like this morning, for example, with the thirty or so Children of Nature congregated in their waterproofs beneath dripping foliage and slate skies. If today was an infant it was likely to grow up sulky and miserable. At times like these, and increasingly of late, Linden felt herself longing for a normal life. But 'Isn't it beautiful?' her mother was sighing, so perhaps Linden was in a minority.

She slipped away from the ceremony as quickly as she could, trudged back towards her own tent among the motley collection of shelters pitched and heaped and strung between the trees here on the site chosen by Oak for the Children of Nature. Several campfires had already been lit for the preparation of breakfast; smoke groped greyly and arthritically upwards through the drizzle.

A normal life, yeah. A house built of bricks and mortar, on solid foundations, that stayed where it was. An address to which postmen could deliver mail and friends pop round to

42

chat and gossip and listen to CDs and watch rubbish programmes on TV (she hadn't even *seen* a TV during the eighteen months they'd been with the Children). A place where she was known; a place where she belonged.

Linden vaguely remembered living in a house when she was a very little girl – or, at least, she imagined she did. She thought it must have had a backyard because she could picture herself tricycling around a flat concrete square in an endless circle, going nowhere, herself and her closest companion, a fraying rag doll she was certain she'd named Daisy after the flowers Mummy used to make her such beautiful necklaces. On one disastrous occasion, Daisy had fallen from the tricycle and Linden, not noticing at first, had blithely continued with her time-honoured route until during her next loop she'd run over the poor doll's head, had probably broken it and killed her dead. She recalled sobbing uncontrollably with the lifeless body of Daisy cradled against her chest.

Even now, Linden *hoped* the memory was true because it concluded with her daddy asking her what the matter was in a voice far softer than when he talked to her mummy. She'd told him, of course, mournfully, without hope, and he'd chuckled as though killing someone dead was nothing to worry about. She recalled gazing up at him for consolation though his features had faded from her mind many years ago. But she remembered his hands – strong, sprouting little black hairs, his fingers yellowing at the tips – as he gently eased the doll from her grasp and told her that he'd better examine Daisy to see if something could be done to make her better again. And Linden had wept that once you'd been killed dead you couldn't be made better again but had to go and live with God and Baby Jesus.

But Daddy had said that everything could be made better again if you really wanted it to be, everything, and he'd said that Daisy wasn't really killed dead in any case, simply sleeping – and now she was awake again. And it was true. And Linden remembered being so happy that she hadn't only rained kisses on Daisy's stitched brow but on Daddy, too. Later, she was glad she'd done that. It turned out to be one of her last opportunities. Not long afterwards, her father had moved away and she never saw him again.

It seemed in Linden's mind that little further time had elapsed before she and her mother had moved away as well, packed up and left the house with the backyard for ever. Their wanderings had begun.

Though, actually, 'journey' was the word her mother used to describe what their lives became, that or 'quest'. And the accompanying pronoun was pluralised by necessity rather than choice. Linden entertained a sneaking suspicion that *their* journey was in reality her *mother*'s journey, a quest, the woman often declared with visionary pride, to 'find herself'. Not an easy task, it appeared, given that they'd trailed across the country for years now, transferring from commune to camp, migrating between one New Age or traveller community and another, seeking, searching for the true Deborah Darroway, and they hadn't quite located her yet. The chances of her being among the Children of Nature, however, seemed encouragingly high. Deborah had become Fen, in keeping with the group's habit of renaming themselves after the glories of Nature as proof of their allegiance. (Linden's given name, of course, luckily exempted her from a similar rebranding.) The new Fen Darroway had also recently taken to composing poetry, mostly in homage to Nature and to women who were courageous enough to leave their past behind them in order to 'find themselves'. Regardless of the consequences to their children, Linden assumed.

The way she was feeling these days, she herself would be doing a little leaving behind of her past before too long.

She crawled into her tent and zipped it down, as much to keep people out as the weather. The trouble was, who could she *talk* to about her feelings, her fears? Not Mum, that was for sure. The only emotions that concerned Fen Darroway lately were her own. One of the other adults? They were satisfied out here in the woods; they wouldn't understand anyone who might want more. Oak? No chance. The first day they'd arrived at the Children of Nature's settlement Linden had asked him what about food? What about clothes? And medicine? And money?

'O you of little faith,' Oak had responded, not unkindly. 'Look at the animals and birds who share this forest with us. Which of them worries about such matters? Yet Nature in Her bounty tends to them all. Let material things fetter material minds. Liberate yours to revel in the beauty that surrounds us. Mother Nature knows Her children's needs and She will provide.' The benefits cheques that the community cashed at the post office in Willowstock came in handy, too, but Oak never mentioned those. He seemed to be in constant rehearsal for the role of John the Baptist in a remake of *Jesus of Nazareth*. He looked the part as well: shaggy, bearded, wild, convinced he was always right. No, Linden would get nowhere with the self-appointed father of the Children of Nature.

But with his son? Ash was sixteen like her. As the only two kids of that age in the settlement, they'd grown close over the

45

last year and a half. Sometimes, Linden thought Ash might like to get closer still, and sometimes she thought she'd like to let him. But that aside, if she could confide her inmost troubles and hopes to anyone it would be Ash. Coincidentally, it was her and Ash's turn to make the morning's three-mile trek to Willowstock for provisions. Maybe they could talk on the way.

Linden inspected herself in the small mirror she kept among her meagre belongings. The light in the tent was still dim but sufficient to determine that the drizzle had not made her bedraggled as yet, though it could probably afford to bide its time. She ran a comb through her russet hair anyway. Once she'd worn it long, but not now. The rigours of the outdoors and the limited supply of super-model-endorsed grooming products in the camp had persuaded her to crop it short. The effect had been to make her hazel eyes seem larger, her lips redder, and to accentuate the naturally elfin appearance of her face: maybe she belonged in the forest after all. Or maybe she didn't. Either way, she was the one to make the decision.

A hand patted the canvas of the tent. 'Linden, you in there?' It was Ash. She said she was. 'Fancy some breakfast before we head for the village?'

'Coming.'

Porridge and coffee. Both in plentiful supply but both pretty tasteless. Linden often claimed that if you closed your eyes and somebody else fed you, you wouldn't be able to tell whether you were sampling the porridge or the coffee. She'd have probably restated the claim to Ash this morning had not their customary banter been tempered by self-consciousness. Oak himself elected to eat with them.

46

'I happened to notice you leave the dawn greeting this morning a little – hurriedly, Linden,' the Children's leader observed, 'and without your usual smile. Are you unwell?'

Those beady eyes don't miss a thing, do they, Linden thought ruefully. 'No, I'm fine, thank you, Oak. Bad night's sleep, that's all.'

'Ah.' Oak nodded sympathetically. 'Troubled sleep is often the product of a troubled mind, did you know that, Linden? Perhaps you have something on *your* mind?'

'No, I . . .' And then yes. The question about her state of health had suddenly reminded her. She was surprised she'd been able to forget the subject until now. 'Actually, maybe Ash and I had better visit the surgery when we go to Willowstock later, talk to Dr Parker.'

'So, you *are* unwell?' Oak said.

'No.'

'What's the matter, Lin?' Ash chipped in, concerned.

'No, I'm fine,' Linden declared again. 'But I think it's a good idea for all of us if somebody sees the doctor.'

'Why, Linden?' Oak asked mildly, as if he already knew.

'To find out more about this flu outbreak, of course. To check if it's spreading. They told me in the post office on Saturday that it's really taking a grip in the cities and yesterday, when Rainbow and Sky came back, they said there'd been three cases reported in Willowstock itself.' Annoyingly, Oak merely stared at her in benign superiority. 'We might need to take precautions.'

'We *have* taken precautions, Linden.' The man smiled tolerantly. 'We have stepped from the path of so-called civilisation. We have left the road and entered the forest. We are the Children of Nature.'

47

'Yes, I know,' Linden conceded. 'But I don't see how that's going to stop us getting sick. Actually.'

'Do you not?' Oak sounded almost sorry for her.

'Listen to Dad, Linden,' advised Ash (not a *good* sign).

'This disease, this virus,' Oak stated, 'whatever it is, it is clearly not of Nature. It is *un*natural, if what we are beginning to hear is true, a punishment sent to plague those who abuse Nature in their lives and who have turned from Her in their hearts. It will infect the materialists only, not the Children of Nature.'

'But they say people are dying,' Linden found herself protesting. 'You mean it's their own fault?'

'Nature has bestowed upon us the gift of choice, young Linden,' Oak pointed out, 'and we bring upon ourselves the consequences of our choices. We can reject Nature or we can embrace Her.'

'So you think we're going to be immune.'

'We live at one with the forest, in harmony with Nature Herself.' Oak half closed his eyes and lifted his face to the louring skies. 'This sickness cannot harm us.'

'Let's hope you're right,' muttered Linden.

'I don't know why you bothered trying to get through to my dad about this flu outbreak,' Ash said as he and Linden strolled through the forest towards Willowstock. 'He never listens. It's a lot easier if you just say what he wants to hear to his face and then do whatever it is you really want behind his back.'

'Some people might call that kind of behaviour a little dishonest, though,' said Linden, with a laugh. She wasn't quite sure whether Ash was serious or not.

The boy shrugged burly shoulders. 'A little bit of dishonesty never hurt anyone.'

'So we'll drop by the surgery after all? You obviously don't believe that being a Child of Nature is as good as a vaccination, then.'

Though it did seem strange to be talking about illness and epidemics amidst the peace and tranquillity of the forest. The early drizzle had abated; more encouragingly still, the cloud cover was beginning to break, forecasting the unexpected bonus of a pleasant day ahead. Maybe Oak had a point. Right now it seemed that nothing bad could reach them here.

'I don't believe a word my dad says,' grunted Ash. 'He's full of it.'

'What?' So her companion *was* serious. Linden glanced at his thickset frame curiously. His lank brown locks were as unkempt as his father's, though he boasted rather less facial hair; his features were swarthier and could be interpreted as sullen until he smiled.

Which he did now, though some might have termed the expression a sneer. 'Come on, Lin, you're not a sucker like the rest of them, are you? All that living in harmony with Nature Herself crap? *Nature*'ll look after us like She tends to the animals and the tiny little birds?' Very much *not* like father, like son. 'Most of the animals would *eat* the tiny little birds if they got half a chance, and each other. A lot of caring there – I *don't* think. Nature's about blood and death, not goodness and mercy like Dad says and he knows it. So who's *really* being dishonest?'

'You don't think we can learn anything from Nature then, Ash?'

'Oh, sure we can. One lesson. The only one that matters.

The strong survive. The weak don't. That's all. You've got to learn to be strong.'

'If you feel like that,' Linden ventured, 'why do you still stay with the Children? Why don't you just leave? You're old enough to get a job or something.'

'Why don't *you*? I know you're not happy in the settlement. I can tell.'

'Can you?' Linden sounded forlorn but, well, she'd wanted to broach the topic anyway. 'Ash, it's just that ... sitting around in the forest all day, living – existing – from hand to mouth, I can't go on like that indefinitely. There's got to be more. I think I deserve more. A challenge. A purpose. Something to test out what I'm really capable of. I don't know. I mean, yes, Rainbow and Sky teach us stuff, I've attended school on and off over the years. I don't envy the kids our age having to take GCSEs this summer. I think I've had as good an education as any of them, but in a way I guess I *am* jealous, because at least their exams'll open up options for them, take their lives in new directions. That's what I want. Some way of proving myself, of making my life mean something. Living with the Children, it's too blinkered, too restrictive. I want to see further. I want to travel beyond the trees.'

'You think your mum'll miss you if you go?' said Ash.

'I don't think she'll even notice.' And now Linden sounded unhealthily bitter.

'So what's keeping you, then?'

'Fear, I suppose. Striking out on my own. It's a big step, daunting. I want to take it but' – Linden sought the words to articulate what she felt only amorphously – 'there's safety in numbers, isn't there, and security. If I stay with Mum and your dad and the others that's what I get. If I leave, there'll just be me. I'd be alone and I don't want to be alone. Ever.'

'So don't be,' Ash said.

Linden stopped in her tracks, held out her hand to halt him, too. 'What do you mean?' She searched his face for his intentions. 'You mean you'd come with me? We'd go together?'

'Saying goodbye to this shit-hole doesn't bother me. I'm just waiting for the right moment. Could be the right moment's arrived.'

'Would it work, Ash?' Linden said. 'You and me?'

'Oh, I reckon it would,' said Ash. 'I reckon we'd be good together – in lots of ways.'

He stroked her cheek and neck with his fingers. They were warm and strong. Linden thrilled at the touch.

'Then let's do it. Together.' She laughed at their audacity. Her heart raced. 'There's no reason for us not to.'

Ash leaned forward. He was going to kiss her. The act would seal their bond and Linden wanted that. She moved towards him, too.

But they didn't kiss.

A frantic crashing in the undergrowth startled them. Someone was coming. Someone in a panic, bearing down on them. One of their own? A villager, perhaps? Linden didn't think so. A dark figure in the foliage.

'Ash . . .' She gripped his hand more tightly.

A man burst into view, blundering from among the trees. Man? He looked barely older than the two teenagers and his face was contorted with the irrational terror of a child haunted by nightmares. But he wore the combat fatigues of a soldier. He carried a rifle.

51

And he pointed the weapon at Linden and Ash.

'Don't move,' he warned. 'Don't move or I'll shoot.'

Certain aspects of Travis's breakfast routine had not altered with time. He still tended to sit in front of the television munching his way through a bowl of cornflakes. Mum continued to call from the kitchen for him to hurry up or he'd be late for school. But there was no more cartoon fodder for Travis. For the past six years he'd switched on *Breakfast News*. He watched the news at six o'clock as well, and again at ten, and more often than not dipped into the satellite news channels between times for good measure. It was important – vital – for him to keep up to date with what the Bad Guys were doing. In fact, it was pretty much an obsession with him, and had been since the loss of that other major element of mornings in the Naughton household. His father.

Today, *Breakfast News*'s Natalie Kamen was wearing her serious face. '. . . The latest developments as the flu outbreak continues to sweep the country,' she was saying. 'The government's Chief Medical Officer will be in the studio and we'll have reports from hospitals across the nation. We'll also be travelling further afield, to Europe, the United States and China, to find out how they're coping with what is rapidly becoming one of the most far-reaching global pandemics in history. But if you're already suffering with the snuffles at home, we've got just the tonic for you: coming up a little later, Melody Summers with this year's British Eurovision Song Contest entry, "Wake Up To The World".'

Travis thought he'd rather wake up to Natalie Kamen if that was OK. Somehow, though, it didn't seem right that news presenters should be so *hot*. They should be like librarians: bookish, prim, big glasses, and kind of grey. How was he supposed to concentrate on the headlines with Natalie Kamen's legs to distract him?

'She's too old for you. She's too rich for you. She's too pretty for you.' Jane Naughton poked her head around the sitting-room door. Travis often wondered whether all mothers were in possession of psychic powers or just his own. 'And if you don't get to school, Travis, she'll also be too well educated for you.'

'You ever thought of going into motivational speaking, Mum?' grinned Travis.

'I have enough to do making sure you're fit to leave the house in the morning,' his mother said. 'Let alone . . .' The phone rang. 'Who's that calling at this hour?'

'Natalie Kamen,' predicted Travis. 'She *wants* me.'

Actually, he didn't really have time to care *who* was on the phone, not if he wanted to get to Mel's early enough for what he intended. Travis gulped coffee.

'It's Grandma,' Jane Naughton announced. 'She wants to know if we're all right. Are we showing any symptoms of the Sickness.'

'The Sickness? Like with a capital S?' On the television a reporter was standing in a hospital corridor in Leeds somewhere. 'It's only some kind of flu, isn't it? It's not the Plague. How are *they*?'

'We're both fine, Mum,' certified Jane Naughton. 'How are *you*?'

'. . . The number of patients overwhelming,' the reporter was saying. 'Every ward in the hospital has been full since last night but still the sick arrive, to be left on trolleys in corridors like this one because there is simply nowhere else to put

53

them.' Coughing, groaning patients in white smocks and languishing on wheeled beds shunted up against the walls provided graphic testimony to the correspondent's words. Medical staff rushed in and out of camera shot behind him, harassed and confused. 'And it's the same increasingly chaotic story in every hospital in the city.'

'Grandma says they're both well,' Jane Naughton supplied. 'They've had their flu jabs. It seems Grandad doesn't think the jabs will do any good, though. He reckons this isn't a flu epidemic at all.'

'Some of my mates' parents think the same,' Travis mused. 'What does Grandad think it is, then?' The *Sickness*.

'What does Dad think it is, Mum?'

Breakfast News had cut back to the studio. The luscious Natalie was questioning an expert in communicable diseases about the illness.

'Grandad thinks this is all the result of an accident or something in some secret government installation for the development of biological weapons.'

'Does he?' Travis said without humour.

The expert in communicable diseases was talking death rates.

'Mum, where does he get these ideas from?' Jane Naughton scolded amusedly. 'Tell Dad he should read fewer science fiction books and maybe help you out with the housework a . . . I know he does his share, Mum, I was only . . .'

There were deaths. People were dying. Not just in countries where people were always dying in disasters of one kind or another but here, in British cities, on British streets. A small number only, the expert in communicable diseases was explaining. A *small* number. The luscious Natalie seized on that as if viewers should be reassured. Travis knew better. It didn't matter how insignificant the total was statistically speaking if you or someone you loved were among the fatalities. Take the annual casualty rate for serving police officers, for example . . . That was the trouble with experts. They saw information, not people.

'Mum, I don't think that's necessary. I told you we're both fine. Not even a runny nose between us.'

Deaths. To the Sickness. In every country in the world.

Apparently, the government's plan to administer vaccine from huge centralised stockpiles protected by the police from possibly over-eager citizens was in full swing. Apparently, entertainment was being laid on at their locations because the queuing might take a while, though there was certainly plenty of vaccine for everyone.

Travis, rather uncomfortably, thought of the band playing 'Nearer My God To Thee' as the *Titanic* went down.

'Trav,' his mother hissed across the room, 'Grandma and Grandad want us to go to Willowstock.' The small village a hundred-plus miles away where they lived. 'They think we'' be safer there.' She shook her head tolerantly. 'Don't th worry over nothing.'

'Sure, Mum,' said Travis.

Apparently, the cheering prospect of Melody Summers and 'Wake Up To The World' was having to be postponed. Apparently, Melody was a little under the weather just now. The luscious Natalie hoped she'd feel better soon.

'We'll leave it at that, then, Mum.' Jane Naughton strove valiantly to bring the call to an end. 'If the situation gets worse, we'll think about it, but I really don't . . . Yes. Travis? Do you want a word with Grandma?'

55

Sadly, there was someone else he needed a word with first. His heart hardened inside him. 'Can't. Sorry. Got to get to Mel's.'

'Now?' his mother marvelled. 'But it's still only—'

'Yeah. Sorry. Tell Grandma I'll call her tonight.'

'Travis . . .'

He turned off the TV on his way to the hall. Natalie Kamen blinked out of existence. Travis didn't know it then, but that was the last he'd ever see of her.

'I mean it.' The soldier's eyes stared wildly at the teenagers. 'You move. I fire.' His finger trembled on the trigger. His whole body shook.

'OK. All right. Take it easy,' Ash soothed. 'We're not moving. See?' Linden for one felt herself frozen to the spot. 'Take it easy.'

'Good. That's good. I don't want to hurt anyone.' The soldier's lips quivered like those of a little boy on the brink of tears.

Linden felt her fear receding. 'Why don't you put the gun down? That way—'

'No. *No.*' A feverish urgency seized the young soldier again. He waved the rifle at them more threateningly.

'Oh, nice one, Lin,' muttered Ash.

'If I put the gun down you'll run and if you run you won't listen and you have to listen to me. Everybody has to listen to me.'

'We're all ears,' confirmed Ash.

The soldier's voice was racked with sobs. 'It's coming. We won't be able to stop it. It's coming for all of us. It's coming for *you.*'

'What is?' Linden said. 'What's coming?'

'If they knew I was here . . . But people have to listen to me. It's coming and it'll mean the end.'

'The end?' A chill deeper even than that of being held at gunpoint by a clearly mentally unbalanced soldier frosted Linden's heart.

'Of everything. Of *every*thing.' The soldier sagged where he stood as if stricken with grief. 'I've got to get home. I need to find my way home before it's too—'

'Lin!' said Ash, warningly.

The soldier's head snapped up and a cry of despair rose from his throat as other soldiers materialised among the woodland shadows, seeming to solidify only as they stepped forward to surround their younger colleague and the two Children of Nature. They were maybe a dozen strong and twice that number of metres away and Linden hadn't heard their approach at all. Combats. Automatic weapons. Faces blanked out by what looked like gas masks. Guns levelled at a trio of targets.

'Listen, we . . . we don't know this guy.' Ash appealed to the silent soldiers. 'We don't want any trouble.'

'Don't let them take me,' the young soldier begged Linden desperately. 'I want to go home. I don't want to go back. It won't do any good. *Tell* them.'

But Linden was speechless.

The soldiers moved in.

'Remember what I said!' the young man entreated. 'It's *coming*!'

And as he swung his rifle Linden felt sure he was going to fire on the masked soldiers, go down in a blaze of glory. Then she realised what he was really about to do. He thrust the barrel of the gun under his chin. He squeezed the trigger. A single shot reverberated through the forest.

Followed by Linden's scream, Ash's cry of shock.

The masked soldiers made no sound.

The teenagers clasped each other and Linden was glad she'd closed her eyes at the last moment. But she didn't dare to keep them closed now. Better that they were open if she was going to have to plead for her life. Which looked likely. While some of the soldiers attended to the body of the suicide, others kept their weapons trained on her and Ash.

'Please,' she begged, 'don't kill us. We're nothing to do with . . . any of this.'

Maybe they believed her. Possibly that was why, when the young man's body had been lifted from the ground and carried into the forest out of sight, the rest of the soldiers backed away too, still without a word, as though their tongues had been removed along with their faces. They melted into the undergrowth. They vanished like ghosts. In seconds it was as if they'd never been there, as if the entire incident had been a grisly dream.

'My God,' breathed Ash.

Mel's mum opened the door, a little nervously, it seemed. But then, everything Mel's mum did was nervous. She was a singularly pale, bloodless woman who appeared to have been made out of paper. 'Travis,' she said with the twitch of a smile.

'Morning, Mrs Patrick. Monday's here again.'

'Come in,' the woman invited. 'Mel's almost ready.'

'No, she is not!' Mel was on the stairs, heading up. Her school clothes were as black and as baggy and as smothering as the most liberal interpretations of the uniform code would allow. 'What time do you call this, Trav? School starting early this week or something?'

'I couldn't stop thinking about you,' Travis quipped.

'Urgh. Excuse me while I go vomit.' Mel bounded up the remainder of the stairs.

Good, Travis thought. That was her out of the way for the next five minutes. Five minutes were all it would take.

'Would you like to . . . come through to the kitchen, Travis?' asked Mel's mum.

'Could I wait in the living room if that's all right with you, Mrs Patrick?' Travis said.

'Gerry's in the living room,' the woman mentioned, as though this was not a recommendation.

'Yeah.'

In the living room. In his armchair. Watching satellite sport. A bottle of lager in one hand. Fresh butt-ends in the ashtray in front of him. Unshaven and overweight. If ever one man could provide the definition of slob, that man was Gerry Patrick. He was living proof that all clichés were founded in truth. Living proof.

And Travis remembered a line from Shakespeare that his English teacher had raved about once. From *King Lear*, she'd said. The old king mourning over the corpse of his favourite daughter: 'Why should a dog, a horse, a rat have life, and thou no breath at all?' For once, Travis had known what the Bard was getting at. The unfairness of existence, the injustice of life and death. His own dad dead, killed struggling to bring order to society, murdered trying to do good. Filth like Gerry Patrick alive, prospering, abusing the very concept of fatherhood. It was almost more than he could bear.

59

Only with difficulty could he keep the contempt from his face.

Patrick himself didn't bother. 'You again,' he grunted as Travis entered the living room and shut them both in. 'Still sniffing around our Melanie, I see.'

'Morning, Gerry,' Travis said through tight lips.

'Gerry? It's Mr Patrick to you, boy. Where's your respect?'

'Respect has to be earned these days, haven't you heard, Gerry? And you ain't earned it.'

'Why, you cheeky little . . .' If the man's intention had been to leap to his feet, he failed. The blubbery ballast bulging at his waist restricted him to a lumber rather than a leap, like an irate walrus.

Travis wasn't impressed. Neither did he retreat. 'What, you want to hit me, Gerry? Like you hit Mel?'

The man paused. 'I don't know what you're talking about.'

'Yes, you do. We both know. I've seen the bruises.'

Gerry Patrick sneered squalidly, an 'I bet you have' sneer. 'She walked into a door. She's always walking into doors. She's clumsy.'

'Yeah? Well, why don't you sit back down? We haven't got long but I just thought we should have a quick chat about Mel's "clumsiness".'

Gerry Patrick glared at Travis but he did resume his seat. He might have been a brute, but he wasn't stupid. 'Get on with it, then, and then get out.'

'A pleasure, on both counts. You see, Gerry,' Travis said, 'I kind of want Mel to become less clumsy, as you put it. For her own good. I don't want to hear about her walking into doors from now on, or falling down the stairs, maybe, or off a chair. I want health and safety to be a big issue in this house, and I expect you to take a lead. Because.' – Travis felt his anger building – 'if I see any more marks on Mel, any more bruises, any more evidence of any kind of her being knocked about and hit, as *I* put it, then I'm likely to report the guy responsible to the relevant authorities, and I don't think you'd like me to do that, would you, Gerry?'

Patrick stared expressionlessly at Travis for a few seconds. Then he gave a short, harsh laugh. 'I couldn't care less what you do, boy. Report me if you like. I *dare* you. Nobody'll believe you anyway and you want to know why? Because Melanie'd never tell tales against her old dad. Nor would my darling wife. I know that. You probably know that. You'd never get any charges to stick.'

'We'll see. You want to take that risk?'

'And Melanie'd never talk to you again. You want to take *that* risk, Travis, boy?' Gerry Patrick evidently felt that the whip hand belonged to him. 'I bet she doesn't know you're trying to threaten her old dad in your prissy, self-righteous little way, does she? Course not. She wouldn't like it.'

Travis sought to ignore the truth in Patrick's words. He had to focus on what was right. 'I want you to stop . . .'

'Little boy,' scoffed Patrick. 'Meddling in matters that don't concern you. Just like your old man, PC Plod. And look what happened to him. Stuck his interfering nose in where it wasn't wanted and got a knife between the ribs for his trouble. Shame and all that but—'

'Shut up,' Travis gritted through clenched teeth. His eyes blazed blue fire. 'You're not fit to mention my dad.' The bitterness, the rage, they were still in him, they were part of him now, and sometimes it seemed his fury and his grief would overwhelm him. '*Why should a dog, a horse, a rat have life, and thou no breath at all?*'

Gerry Patrick chuckled coldly, swigged beer, changed channels on the TV.

But Travis steadied himself, controlled himself. To become consumed by loss, to be crushed by grief, to rail against a past that could not be reversed or to fret for ever over what could not be understood, that way madness lay. His father's death had been a senseless tragedy, an affront to justice, but Dad wouldn't want it to destroy Travis, too. And Travis would not be destroyed. He would survive. He would be strong.

He wouldn't take crap from the likes of Gerry Patrick.

'You might be right . . .' he admitted.

'What? You still here, boy?'

And gaining in confidence. 'You might be right: Mel and her mum won't testify to what a piece of filth you are, Gerry. You've had years to scare them and intimidate them and I'm not going to blame them for that. I'm blaming *you*. And I'm promising you this, if you *ever* touch Mel again, I mean *ever*, I won't inform the social services or report it to the police officially, I'll go and have a quiet word with some of my dad's mates who are still on the force. And they don't like scumbags like you, Gerry, and they'll like you even less when I tell them what you think of my dad and his sacrifice, and I reckon that between them they'll be able and more than happy to fit you up on some other charge, where Mel won't need to give evidence. And then you can say goodbye to your armchair and hello to a prison cell. I'll do it. I promise.'

Gerry Patrick glanced into Travis's eyes and saw something

62

there, a steel, a commitment. Fearlessness. He wasn't chuckling or sneering or scoffing now. 'OK,' he capitulated grudgingly. 'OK. I get the picture.'

'One finger on her and you go down.'

'Whatever.'

'And I don't want Mel to know about our little exchange of views.'

A terse nod of the head from Gerry Patrick.

As Mel rushed into the living room, shoes and jacket on. Her gaze darted tensely between Travis and her father as though she'd anticipated trouble. 'You all right, Travis?' she said cautiously.

Travis turned to her and grinned. 'Never better,' he said.

The school bus was late. Then it was very late.

'Looks like it's not coming,' Mel observed.

'Looks like it,' said Travis, still in truth a little preoccupied by his confrontation with her father. *Had he done enough? Had he succeeded in putting an end to Gerry Patrick's abuse? Or – and here was an unsettling possibility given that it was now too late to do anything about it – had he only made the situation worse?*

'I guess the driver might have the flu and hasn't turned up.' Mel looked around her. 'Maybe he's not the only one.' The gathering of students at the bus stop was sparser than normal, even for a Monday.

'Maybe.' An odd thought suddenly occurred to Travis. 'But you know, Saturday night, the others were talking about people's parents and the owners of Alison's stables or whatever, teachers, coming down with the bug, but no kids. All adults. That strike you as weird?'

'Kids are healthier than adults,' Mel stated. 'It's that high-fat, high-sugar, no-portions-of-fruit-and-veg-a-day diet we're not supposed to have keeping us going.'

'Seriously, Mel,' Travis said. 'Do we know anybody our own age or younger who's caught this flu?'

'What about the kids who aren't here now?'

'Looking after sick family. Skiving. Using the flu as an excuse.' The *Sickness*. 'Anyone we know for *sure?*'

Mel shrugged. 'Ask me one on pop music.'

'Mel . . .' Travis shook his head in exasperation.

'OK. Well, the real puzzler is, do we discuss your far-out theories while we walk to school like good, eager little students, or do we do it – discuss your theories – at your house over coffee and CDs because the system's let us down and stranded us at the bus stop and—'

'Neither,' said Travis. 'We're being rescued.'

A car was indicating before pulling into the bus stop's lay-by. Mr Lane's car. He was driving; Jessica, in a school uniform that could have been bought new that morning, occupied the front passenger seat.

She activated the electric window as Travis and Mel crossed to the vehicle. 'Bus not turned up? Fancy a lift?'

They climbed into the back, said their thank-yous and good-mornings to Mr Lane, repeated how much they'd enjoyed Jessica's party.

After all of which, 'Don't expect to see too many buses on the road today,' their chauffeur warned. 'It's been on the radio. Service cut down to the bone. Drivers phoning in unwell. This flu bug. Good excuse for lazy employees to throw a sickie.' Mr Lane was a director of a company that made disposable containers. Sometimes it showed.

'Dad,' disapproved Jessica.

'I think it might be more than that, Mr Lane,' said Travis. 'If you listen to the news it's hitting pretty hard. Everywhere. There've been some deaths.'

Jessica winced at the word. Death was a change unthinkable.

'I reckon it's going to get worse before it gets better.'

'That's what everyone seems to be saying, Travis,' agreed Mr Lane. 'Though I'd still be a little sceptical if I were you. Governments have a habit of preparing us for worst-case scenarios so that when things don't turn out to be *quite* as bad as predicted the same governments can then take the credit. Having said that,' he conceded as he nosed the car from minor to major road without the usual wait for a kindly fellow motorist to flash him out, 'there *does* seem to be less rush-hour traffic this morning.'

'Dad's paper's started to call the flu the Sickness,' said Jessica, with a shudder. 'It starts like flu – coughs and aches and a temperature and stuff, those are the first symptoms – but it isn't flu. Not according to Dad's paper. After a while you develop these disgusting crimson circles all over your body, like a kind of rash. According to the paper. I don't fancy that much, do you?'

'I don't know where the paper is getting its information from,' said Mr Lane sceptically.

'*Breakfast News* hasn't said anything like that,' Travis frowned.

'Exactly. Probably a total fabrication.'

'Or the truth they'd rather we didn't hear.' Not that Travis liked to think the luscious Natalie had been holding out on him.

'Chill, anyway,' shrugged Mel. 'Say it's true. A red rash.

65

We've all had those, haven't we? I mean, what I *mean* is it could be worse. Could be like the Black Death. Stinking, suppurating buboes – swellings – in your armpits and, well, other places. Catch that and it was pretty much all over for you. People thought the arrival of the disease meant the end of the world, the time of the Reaper, when the Grim Reaper, Death himself, would walk among them and punish them for their sins. The Black Death, 1348–50. Wiped out half of Europe.'

'I wasn't aware you were a history buff, Melanie,' Mr Lane remarked a little frostily.

'Only the gross parts,' Mel admitted. 'Which is most of them.'

'Well, I seriously question the relevance of the Black Death to the present situation,' said Mr Lane. 'You're broadly right about the depopulation that happened in the fourteenth century, Melanie, but this is the twenty-first century now. Medical science has moved on. We have drugs. We have cures. We have preventative measures that can be called upon in public-health emergencies. It is simply inconceivable for any disease in this day and age to cause the number of casualties for which the Black Death was responsible. Impossible.'

Travis hoped so. But what about AIDS? As he was a guest in Mr Lane's car, he thought it best not to mention the spread of AIDS. And for another, what about that guy on the bike they'd just passed? He was wearing a mask. All Travis saw of his face were his eyes. Frightened eyes.

Medical science might well have moved on since the 1340s. But what if disease had as well?

That evening the Naughtons received an unexpected but welcome visitor. 'Phil!' Jane Naughton exclaimed, delighted, opening the front door wide. 'What a lovely surprise. Come in.'

'How are you, Jane?' Phil Peck hugged her, kissed her in the way of old friends. 'Good to see you, too.'

'Come on through. Is this a flying visit or have you got time for a coffee? It's been a while.'

'Yeah, I'm sorry about that. Things have been busy, particularly lately.' Phil Peck's brow creased involuntarily. 'But yeah, I'd love a coffee.' He stood in the lounge and glanced around uneasily, almost as if he hadn't been there at least once a month since Keith had been killed. 'Is Travis around?'

'Upstairs. Supposed to be doing homework. Probably playing computer games. I'll call him. He'll be pleased to see you. Phil, chairs are in their usual places, you know.'

Travis *was* glad to see Uncle Phil. Phil Peck wasn't his biological uncle, of course, no blood relation at all (unless it counted that he'd had Dad's blood all over him that terrible day, that he'd held Dad at the last, cradled him in the street while he died). He'd been Dad's long-term partner in the police and was still on the force now. He always took care of his appearance, did Uncle Phil, always kept his beard and moustache neatly trimmed, but tonight Travis thought he was looking haggard, worn, as if he hadn't slept for a week. He also seemed to have little patience for the niceties of conversation, taking his coffee from Mum with scarcely a thank-you.

'This isn't exactly a social call,' he said. 'I suppose you could say I've come to warn you.'

'Warn us?' Jane Naughton said blankly. 'About what?'

Travis studied Uncle Phil's face. It was set in the same

67

expression he'd worn six years ago in Shelley's study, the emotion of being the bearer of unimaginable tidings contained and controlled by training.

'It's the Sickness,' he said.

'That's what it's being called officially now?' Travis asked.

'You mean the flu.' His mother preferred to use a more familiar term, one that seemed somehow safer.

'Sickness. Flu. They don't know what to call it because they don't know what it is,' said Uncle Phil grimly. 'Nobody does. Doctors. Scientists. The government's long line of experts. They know what it does, though.'

'Phil, are you all right?' Jane Naughton was growing concerned.

'What I'm about to tell you, both of you, it's off the record, you hear me?' Glancing pointedly from mother to son and back. 'I shouldn't be telling anyone this, not even Marion. But I owe it to you to give you a chance. If – well, if the situation had been reversed, I know Keith would have gone to Marion with the same information.'

'Uncle Phil' – Travis leaned forward – 'what does the Sickness do?'

'It kills you,' said Phil Peck simply. 'If you contract it, you die.'

'Phil, really,' Jane Naughton objected, startled. 'I don't think there's any need to talk like that with Travis in the room.'

'*Mum.*' Travis clearly felt otherwise.

'And besides, isn't that what's called scaremongering? Have they been working you too hard, Phil? You don't look . . . I mean, on the news they've acknowledged some deaths, but surely . . .'

'If they told you the truth, the whole truth and nothing but

68

the truth,' Phil Peck said, with a brief ironic smile, 'there'd be greater unrest than there already is. The authorities don't want that, especially with coppers going down with this infection as quickly as everyone else. What the media are being allowed to report, Jane, let me tell you – I've seen it – the reality is ten times worse, and the situation is deteriorating by the day. Soon they won't be able to cover up the truth, there'll be too many bodies to hide in the mortuaries and the funeral homes, and then the brown stuff will definitely hit the fan.'

'But surely, even if things *are* bad, like you say, Phil,' argued Jane Naughton, 'they'll find a cure, a treatment, *something*. They always do, don't they? Surely they can learn from those who've recovered from the Sickness.'

'To my knowledge, Jane,' and Phil Peck shook his head darkly, 'nobody *has* recovered from the Sickness. As far as I know, the mortality rate is one hundred per cent. So if they're going to find a vaccine, let's hope they do it soon.'

'I don't – I can't believe it,' persisted Jane Naughton defensively. 'What about the vaccine they're already distributing? The stockpiles at hospitals and medical centres?'

'It doesn't work,' Peck said. 'It's a placebo, a pretence. It allows the government to look like it's doing something, like it's got everything under control. It hasn't. It just doesn't want people to realise it hasn't and panic. Keep people ignorant and they're less likely to take to the streets.'

'Take to the streets?' Jane Naughton looked worried. 'What for?'

Her late husband's partner declined to answer. 'There's something else that's not been announced officially,' he pursued. 'Something else that'll soon be obvious, though. The Sickness only seems to affect adults.'

69

'I *thought* so.' Travis's heart thumped. 'I was talking about that with Mel . . .' He trailed off awkwardly. Uncle Phil was looking at him and he couldn't tell whether it was with envy or pity.

'Again, as far as I'm aware, and I've been in all the local hospitals at one time or another over the past few days, not a single sufferer has been under eighteen. Not one. Looks like the Sickness is shaping up to be an adults-only experience.'

'I don't understand,' said Travis's mother. 'How is that possible?'

'DNA. Genes. Cell development. I don't have a clue. How is *any* of this whole bloody nightmare possible?' sighed Uncle Phil. 'It just *is*. Still, maybe we shouldn't be surprised, the mess we've made of the world. Maybe it's all we deserve.'

'That's not fair, Phil. Some of us have tried our best to live right,' Jane maintained. 'You have. Keith did.'

'Yeah. Sorry. It's just a little bit hard to take, that's all.'

'Grandma and Grandad phoned this morning, Uncle Phil,' Travis said. 'Invited us to Willowstock while the Sickness is still spreading. What do you think?'

Phil Peck shrugged defeatedly. 'What do I know? Maybe you should consider taking them up on their offer. Disease spreads more rapidly in areas of high population density, that's for sure. And the government's only operating Stage One of its emergency plan at the moment: reassurance, however hollow, making a play of carrying on as normal. Stage Two'll be with us soon. In some areas I hear it's already starting. Scapegoating. Pointing the finger of blame at minority groups. Terrorist suspects. Anarchists. Activists. Muslims. All fair game. They'll all be rounded up – while we've got the manpower to round anyone up. Maybe they'll deploy the

70

army, if they can fetch them back from Iraq and Afghanistan and God knows where else in time. Yeah, they'll need the army for Stage Three.'

'What's Stage Three?' Travis prompted.

'Anarchy. Chaos. The total breakdown of order. The collapse of society. Martial law. What your mum and dad said, Jane? I'd give it serious thought if I were you. Out in the country you might be safer. But if you're going to go, do it quickly before the curfews and the quarantines start to be imposed. I know I'd go if I could.'

'If you could?' ventured Travis.

'I'm still a police officer,' said Uncle Phil. 'I'm needed here, to protect the public. Besides, Marion hasn't been feeling too well today. Seems she's got a touch of the flu.' Neither Travis nor his mother could meet the man's gaze. 'Listen, I'd better be off. I've said too much already but I thought . . . well, anyway, I could be wrong. Probably am. You were right, Jane. I've been under a lot of stress lately. Police leave cancelled. Covering for absent colleagues. They've probably found a cure already and the world'll be back to normal by the end of the week. I just thought you should know . . . it might not be. And listen, here's my police mobile number. You know my other, don't you? Call me if you need anything, if anything happens . . . You look after yourselves, all right?'

'All right,' said Travis. But he had a sinking feeling it wouldn't be.

THREE

To begin with, Mel wasn't at home when Travis called for her again before school the following morning. 'She's already left, Travis,' said Mrs Patrick, snuffling into a handkerchief as though her daughter's premature departure brought her great sorrow.

'Without me?' Travis and Mel had been walking to the bus stop together since their first day at Wayvale Community College.

'I don't know why,' said Mrs Patrick. 'Have you two had an argument or something?'

'Not that I know of.' Travis's brow furrowed. 'Are you OK, Mrs Patrick?'

'Of course, dear. I'm fine.' The woman smiled wanly, her eyes red. 'Just the sniffles, that's all. Not the flu. Just sniffles.'

'Yeah,' Travis said.

He hastened towards the bus stop. He didn't share Mrs Patrick's diagnosis. It seemed that the Sickness had reached the streets surrounding his own home. It was coming closer all the time. So why was he even bothering to go to school today? On Mum's insistence. Because Mum was stubbornly clinging to the belief that everything would turn out well in the end, like the resolution to a fairy story, and so was refusing to alter or amend her daily routines.

Such behaviour was how his mother coped with disaster, Travis knew. She'd been the same after Dad had died. For weeks she'd continued to press his shirts as if one day he might magically appear in the doorway requiring them again. Several months had passed before she'd finally mustered the courage to bundle Dad's clothes up and donate them to an Oxfam shop – several months before Mum could bring herself to face reality. Travis wondered how long it might take her this time.

'We'll give it to the end of the week,' she'd decided in the wake of Uncle Phil's visit. 'If things aren't back to normal by then, we'll go to your Grandad's. But they will be. Phil said so.' Travis could have pointed out that Uncle Phil's optimism hadn't been *quite* as emphatic as that, but whatever kept his mother happy was fine by him. He could stay watchful for both of them.

'Mel.' Together with a smattering of other students, standing at the bus stop. 'You left without me.' In hurt recrimination.

The girl glanced around airily. 'Looks like it.'

'You want to tell me why?'

'No reason.' Squinting up the road in the direction from which the bus should soon appear.

'You want to tell me that to my face? Mel, what's the matter with you?'

'The matter with *me*?' Her black-ringed eyes blazed fiercely at Travis then, but she said no more, if only because Mr Lane and Jessica chose that precise moment to pull up by the bus stop once again.

No chance of the school bus this morning. Normal service suspended due to massive driver illness. The Sickness

73

bringing public transport to its knees more effectively than any industrial action. Would Travis and Mel like to avail themselves of the Lane and Daughter taxi service?

Mel was in the car in an instant. Throughout the journey to school she kept as much distance between herself and Travis as possible, pressing her body against the far door as if several invisible passengers of considerable girth had been shoehorned between them. She looked only out of the window. She spoke only to Jessica and her father.

'Stephanie's going to pick Jessica up this afternoon,' Mr Lane said when they'd arrived at the school gates. 'She'll be happy to give you two a lift as well. Unless you prefer Shanks's pony. And tomorrow, why don't you call round to ours first thing? Save you a wait for a bus that won't be coming.'

'Thanks, Mr Lane,' Mel said hurriedly. 'Must go. Got to be somewhere. See you for registration, Jess.' Wherever it was that Mel needed to be, evidently she needed to get there swiftly.

'What's with her?' a puzzled Jessica asked Travis.

'I've got to dash too, Jess. Sorry.' Setting off in hot pursuit of Mel.

'What's with *him*?' Jessica Lane muttered to herself.

Travis caught up with the goth girl by the lockers. Almost. 'Mel, wait.' She wouldn't. 'Mel, *wait.*' His hand clamped down on the girl's shoulder.

She wheeled in anger. 'Don't touch me. Get that hand off of me. Who do you think you are, my father?'

Travis winced. 'Is that what this is about? Your dad? Has he – he hasn't hurt you again?'

'No, he hasn't,' Mel snapped. 'But *someone* has.'

'I don't follow.'

'Dad *told* me, Travis.'

'Told you?' Now it was his turn to look away. Guiltily.

'That nice little conversation the two of you had – about me.'

'I don't . . .'

'But you must do, Trav. It only happened yesterday morning and that's just twenty-four hours ago. Course, on the other hand, maybe you are developing problems with your short-term memory, 'cause it was only – oh – thirty-six hours before *that* that I insisted in no uncertain terms that I didn't want you talking to my dad about me. And then you go right ahead and do it anyway. So either you're making history as the youngest-ever sufferer of Alzheimer's, Trav, or else you don't actually give a toss what I want. Which is it?'

'I told him not to say anything. He said he wouldn't.' Travis was aware that his fists were clenching.

'But you can't trust my dad – didn't you know?' Mel laughed at the boy's naivety – it wasn't a pleasant sound. 'And now I can't trust *you*, either. Thanks for that, Trav.'

'You *can* trust me.'

'Who? My do-gooding, self-righteous, interfering boyfriend? That's what Dad called you. He got three out of four right, didn't he? That was before he started ridiculing me for getting you to fight my battles for me, for being a whining, pathetic little girl. I told him, though, I made it clear, I don't need Travis Naughton to stand up for Mel Patrick. I can stand up for myself. I don't need Travis Naughton at all.'

'Mel, you mustn't be like that. I know what I promised you . . .'

'Yes, Trav,' accused Mel bitterly. '*Promised.*'

'. . . But I couldn't just say nothing, do nothing. If you do nothing, the bullies win, your dad wins, the Bad Guys win.' The old certainties gave Travis the passion to justify himself. As always, they gave him strength. 'I understand why you're angry with me but your dad had to know he'd been found out. He had to be warned off. I had no choice, Mel. It was the right thing to do.'

'Yeah?' Mel shook her head and her raven locks shivered. 'Then I hope you and the Right Thing are going to be very happy together, Travis. Without me.' She turned her back on him.

'Mel . . .'

But she was already stalking away.

'Is this a joke?' The duty sergeant peered incredulously across the interview room's table at Linden and Ash.

No joke, the russet-haired girl thought with a shudder. *Just a total waste of time*. The sergeant didn't believe them.

'You said you wanted to report an attack.' His gaze flickered between the seated teenagers and their respective parents standing behind them. Oak, resembling Robinson Crusoe freshly retrieved from his desert island; Fen, sandy hair dreadlocked, freckled flesh pierced, clothes colourless from perpetual wear, looking as if she might have mistaken Fordham's modest police station for Glastonbury. 'You said you wanted to report an attack and you come up with *this*?'

Linden detected it in the policeman's eyes, that frost of disapproval bordering on hostility that she and her fellow Children of Nature were accustomed to encountering virtually every time they left the settlement to venture among the civilised population. People, she remembered hearing many times at the many different schools she'd attended, should not judge others by appearances. Yet that was always precisely what people did.

The sergeant didn't believe them.

'The young people have told you what they told us yesterday, sergeant,' said Oak. 'That is what happened.'

'That's what they *say* happened,' replied the policeman. 'Though, as I understand it, neither of you were actually present at the apparent . . . incident. Is that correct?'

'My Linden's a good girl,' asserted her mother. 'She doesn't tell lies.'

'Surely, sergeant,' added Oak, 'one does not have to witness an occurrence personally if somebody else was there whose word – and therefore whose information – one trusts.'

Linden smiled inwardly. Mum standing up for her – that was a first these days. And Oak, he might be as full of it as Ash suggested, but at least he believed in those around him. He hadn't questioned their account of their adventure with the soldiers in the slightest, hadn't even registered shock or surprise. Perhaps displays of paranoia, irrational suicides and mysterious military operations were just what he expected from the materialists, as he termed those who spurned a life in harmony with Nature. Oak would probably have ignored the entire episode if he could have but there did exist, as Linden had stressed, the possibility that the masked soldiers would come back. Hence this early-morning trek to Fordham, the nearest town with a police station, to report the matter.

A total waste of time, just as Linden had predicted.

'In principle, sir – Mr Oak . . .' began the sergeant.

'Just Oak,' the bearded man said.

'Yes. In principle, sir, what you say is right, but the details of the youngsters' story, well . . . Quite frankly, they're unbelievable.'

'They are,' granted Oak. 'But their unlikelihood does not necessarily also render them untrue.'

The sergeant tutted exasperatedly as if he'd rather be dealing with a good, honest, *decent* citizen who paid his taxes and who therefore had a *right* to take up valuable police time. These hippie types . . . 'But soldiers in masks . . . There are no permanent military bases within a hundred miles of Willowstock woods, not even an encampment, and we've been notified of no manoeuvres, either. Even if this was some kind of war game the kids chanced across, we'd have been informed about it in advance.'

'This wasn't a game.' Linden sat forward. 'A man shot himself, killed himself. It wasn't a special effect. There was blood everywhere.'

'Yes,' said the sergeant, which sounded more like the opposite. 'A young soldier who stumbled out of the forest and said little that made sense apart from "It's coming." What's coming, I wonder?'

'I don't know,' said Linden. 'The guy blew his face off before he could tell us. But, bearing in mind that the prospect of it clearly drove him to take his own life, I don't reckon he was referring to Christmas, do you?'

'Linden,' cautioned Fen.

'Well, really, miss,' objected the sergeant. 'There's no need for sarcasm.'

'What about some action, then?' Linden retorted. 'We've told you what happened so why don't you do something – send somebody out to the forest, look for clues, find out who those guys were?'

'I'm afraid it's a matter of priorities,' the sergeant said officiously. 'Whatever your alleged suicide soldier allegedly warned, the only thing that's "coming" at the moment is the Sickness, which is why the Fordham and District Constabulary is having to operate with significantly reduced manpower just now. Which is why myself and my officers do not have time for wild goose chases in the woods on the say-so of – well, at the risk of sounding blunt – possibly unreliable witnesses.'

'I knew it,' Linden said, bridling. 'If we lived in a nice semi-detached in the next street you'd believe us, though, wouldn't you? If we were conventional. If we conformed. Then you'd take us seriously.'

'Linden, anger will not advance our cause,' Oak advised placidly.

Maybe not, but maybe Linden didn't care, either. 'What, you reckon we were smoking dope or something and hallucinated the whole thing? 'Cause that's what drop-outs like us do, isn't it? Smoke dope all day?'

The police sergeant was impervious to her outburst, however. In fact, he even seemed to smile slightly, as though he'd anticipated such a performance all along and was gratified to have been proved right. 'Thank you for bringing this matter to our attention,' he said. 'It will be investigated further when appropriate personnel become available. Good day to you.'

'Linden,' said her mother when all four Children of Nature had vacated the premises, 'I'm proud of you. You only said what the rest of us were thinking, didn't she, Oak? That policeman was prejudiced against us from the start. The whole system is.'

Oak studied the concrete beneath his feet critically. 'Let us return to the settlement,' he said.

'For now, huh?' Ash whispered in Linden's ear.

Though her experience in the interview room had made the girl wonder. What if, after all, the big wide world should turn out to be not so very much better than the narrower horizons of the Children of Nature? And her fury had cooled to a kind of fear. What if the sergeant had accidentally happened upon the truth? What if the terrified soldier *had* been referring to the new flu, the Sickness? She thought of his pursuers, masked as if to protect themselves against a gas attack – or a more subtle but equally lethal biological assault.

What if it was the Sickness coming for them all?

Simon Satchwell slunk through the corridors of Wayvale Community College and wondered why he'd bothered coming into school today. Course, he wondered *every* day why he bothered coming into school. For Simon Satchwell attending school was like being landed behind enemy lines in the war and having to stay secret and out of sight if you wanted to make it back home alive. Though he'd had plenty of practice, Simon's survival rate was not good. Almost every day he was caught and suffered for it. Almost every day the bullies got him.

So why did he lay himself open to torment and humiliation with such regularity when there was always the option of hanging around at the Marlin Centre with the rest of the skivers? He did it because of Nan and Grandpa. If he skipped school the authorities would track him down, as sure as Richie Coker would fleece him of his last penny. If the local truancy officer found nobody else, she'd find *him*. There was never a hiding place for Simon Satchwell. And then Nan and Grandpa would have to be told he wasn't in school when he should have been, and why. And they'd be crushed. They'd be heartbroken if they knew about the bullying, the loneliness, which was why he'd told them he'd had such a great time at Jessica's party, danced with that nice Cheryl Stone and everything. Simon didn't have much power in his life, but he had enough to spare them the dismal truth, at least. He'd sooner hurt himself than Nan and Grandpa.

Ironic that they'd inadvertently helped to start the whole wretched process, though, wasn't it? Years and years ago. Simon going to live with his grandparents after Mum and Dad had been killed in a car crash. He could hardly remember them now. He'd been four at the time. Nan and Grandpa, they'd taken him in willingly, gladly, and they'd done their best for him, always, Simon knew that. But their idea of how little boys should be dressed on their first day at school (and, indeed, on subsequent days) didn't quite accord with the views of parents thirty years younger. It tended to err on the side of the old-fashioned. So Simon had stood out from the crowd from the very beginning, and not in a good way.

There were also the glasses, of course, the kind you saw in photos from the 1930s. And Simon burst into tears quite often back then, seeing the other children with their mummies dropping them off at the school gates, collecting them at the end of the day, knowing that his own mummy was not in a position to perform either service for him. The occasional nervous not-quite-getting-to-the-toilet-in-time incident didn't help, either. And the other kids, they didn't know him, they didn't know his grief: school was a vast and belittling experience for them all, a frightening novelty, and they hid their insecurities by identifying someone who was finding it even harder to cope than they were. And making his young life hell.

Over time it became like smoking. A difficult habit to break.

Simon had vaguely hoped today might be different. The Sickness, or whatever people were calling it. Some kids might have been kept off school because of it. Better yet, Richie Coker and his cronies might have *caught* it. That'd be a cause for celebration. Particularly if they died.

Disappointment had swiftly dashed Simon's hopes, however (the story of his life). Coker was still around, swaggering about as if he owned the place as usual. The close-cropped hair like black bristles, exposed now due to the enforced absence of the baseball cap; the pugnacious jaw and the unhealthy skin, sprinkled with acne like the decorations on a peculiarly inedible cake; the pale, malicious, unforgiving eyes. A lot of kids *were* away, but nobody whose loss was to Simon's advantage. And, worse, teacher numbers were radically down. That meant fewer sources of protection for Simon, especially at break and lunchtime. Breaks and lunchtimes were the worst, when the system almost wantonly turned its back on the victims of bullying, retired behind closed staffroom doors, abandoned the weak to fend for themselves, sanctioned the strong to do as they pleased.

Simon had cowered through break in a store cupboard that had, luckily, been left open. Come lunchtime, he wasn't so fortunate.

'If it isn't my old mate Simon.' Coker and his mob were blocking the classroom door before he could get out. He backed away and collided with a desk. Even the furniture was against him. 'Mind how you go, though, Simes,' said Richie Coker in mock concern.

'Sure, Richie. Good to see you, but can I just . . . if I can just squeeze . . . I've got to . . . I need to . . .' Simon bobbed to either side of the impassable bully, his stare fixed on the door like a man in sight of heaven who was being dragged off to hell.

'You sound like you want to go, Simon,' Richie noted. 'But we haven't had a chat all day, have we, lads?' The other lads, three of them, agreed as one that they hadn't. 'It's always a shame when we don't get to have a chat with our old mate Simes here, isn't it, lads?' Shame? It was tragic. 'My day just isn't quite complete without one of our little . . . *chats*, Simes, old mate.'

An outbreak of giggling could be heard. There were still some other kids present whose form room this was, interpreting Simon's ordeal as free lunchtime entertainment. Certainly, they did nothing to stop it, were prepared to tolerate it (at least it wasn't happening to *them)*. Simon wasn't surprised. His experience had taught him that there was very little people *wouldn't* do to keep themselves out of the firing line. Intervention was unlikely. *They should* all *contract the Sickness*.

'Leave him alone, Richie, why don't you?'

Except maybe Melanie Patrick. Who was huddled over by the windows with Jessica Lane, engrossed in a quiet, earnest and obviously very private conversation with the blonde girl but who now, miraculously, seemed prepared to speak up for Simon.

'Shut your mouth, Morticia,' responded Richie gallantly, 'unless you want a black eye for real.'

'Charming.' And Melanie turned back to Jessica.

So that was it. No wonder Simon didn't believe in miracles. Hot tears of helplessness welled up from within. 'Please, Richie, I've got to go. Mr Clancy's supposed to be giving me some extra maths tuition. If I'm late . . .'

'Clancy's not here today,' Richie said with a cold smile. 'So there's no need to waste your time looking for him, is there? But don't look so worried, Simes. We won't keep you long. Just that we're a bit peckish, what with it being lunchtime and all. Wondered what *Nanny*'s packed in your lunch box today.'

Simon produced the article from his school bag in seconds, presented it to his persecutor like an offering. 'Here. Take it. You can take it if you want. I'm not hungry.' If Coker stole the box itself, Simon could always tell Nan he'd left it at school and/or lost it.

But maybe the lie wouldn't be necessary. Richie had opened the container and was peering inside with a mixture of pity and revulsion. 'Actually, Simes,' he grimaced, 'on second thoughts your lunch box isn't up to much. Not exactly gifted in the *lunch box* department, know what I mean, lads?' General amusement at their leader's wit. 'Not much there at all.' Richie grinned. 'You can have it back.' And he emptied the box's contents into Simon's bag. 'Cheese-and-pickle flavour exercise books. Lovely. Don't say I never give you nothing, Simes.' Richie wagged an admonishing finger. 'And now I have, it's your turn to give *me* something. *Us* something. It's only fair, right?'

'How much do you want?' Simon was familiar with the routine. He was gouging his pocket for money already.

'How much have you got, Simes?'

'Nothing.' A new voice spoke up. 'Nothing for *you*, Coker.'

84

Richie and his cronies swivelled their necks. Behind them. Who *dared*?

'Keep your money, Simon,' Travis said from the doorway.

Richie frowned. 'Naughton? Again? What are you doing here now?'

'I've come to have a word with Mel if that's all right with you.' Glancing pointedly towards her.

'What if it's not all right with *me*?' Mel huffed. Travis saw that Jessica was clasping one of the goth girl's hands in both of hers, as though she was comforting her.

'You're welcome to Morticia, Naughton.' Richie relaxed his frown. For a moment.

'Yeah? And you're welcome to stop bullying Simon, preferably now.'

'What?' Richie didn't understand. Did Travis Naughton have a death wish or something? 'You calling me a bully, Naughton?'

'If you don't like it, don't be one.'

Richie drew himself up to his full height – intimidatingly, he imagined. Only Naughton didn't appear to be intimidated. And he kept staring at Richie with those unsettling blue eyes of his. 'This is the second time you've got in my face, Naughton, and that's not a good idea. It's not a *healthy* idea.'

'Is it not?'

'Trav . . .' Travis heard Jessica's worried voice from across the room. Mel remained silent, but she was watching him and there was concern on her face, too – he thought.

'I'll give you the one at Barbie's party 'cause that was like home territory for you and I'm a generous kind of guy. But this school is mine and while we're in it I do what I like.'

'I can't let you take Simon's money, Richie,' Travis said simply. 'It's not right.'

'*What?*' Richie. Baffled.

Simon, too. He adjusted his glasses as if the lenses were suddenly not to be trusted. Why was Travis Naughton putting himself on the line for him? Travis was a good sort, sure, always had a passing word for the poor sap at the bottom of the teenage food chain, had never victimised him. But they'd never been friends or anything, either. Simon didn't have friends as such. Then he remembered that Travis had lost a parent too. His father, stabbed to death in the street. Simon felt a surge of sympathy and gratitude towards his unexpected defender.

'You know who you're talking to, Naughton?' Richie Coker glared. (If only the damn loser wouldn't stare at him with those *eyes*.)

'Oh, I think so.'

'I ought to smash your face in. I should have done it Saturday.'

'You should have. You had three times as many idiots to help you out on Saturday.'

'You're asking for it.'

'Then what are you waiting for? You want to make a move, Coker, make a move.'

Silence in the classroom, more silence than during lessons, and tense, expectant. As if nobody was daring even to breathe. Richie found his own hard-man stare locked into the other boy's blue gaze – and Naughton wasn't blinking, wasn't bluffing.

'I'm waiting,' he prompted.

'Get him, Rich.' Nudged advice from Lee.

He should do. Travis Naughton had overstepped the mark this time.

'Let's roll him over.' Reinforcements in the tones of Wayne and Mick.

And he should do. It was about respect. And there was no car coming this time, no adults to interfere.

'*Rich*,' muttered the lads, spurring Coker on.

There was nothing external stopping him. He could do what he liked.

Richie Coker looked away.

The suspense was broken. Simon felt himself shivering. Jessica darted to Travis's side. Mel made no move at all. She was staring down, almost shamefacedly.

'Nah,' Richie said, as if little of importance had been at stake. 'You're not worth it, Naughton. Neither's Simes here. I get into trouble in school again, I get suspended. I can do without the hassle. Let's go, lads, there's a funny smell in here.' The bully and his cronies shoved their way past Travis and Jessica. 'This isn't over, though.' Richie's sallow face thrusting close to Travis. 'Watch your back, Naughton.'

Then he was gone.

'Next time you want to risk your life like that, Trav,' Jessica advised, 'do it when I'm not around to see, will you? Richie Coker could have done you serious damage.'

'He didn't, though, did he?' Hugging Jessica reassuringly. 'Simon, how are you?'

'Better off by four pounds fifty,' Simon said. 'Thanks for that, Travis. Richie Coker seems to have a problem with me. I don't know what I've done to deserve it, really, but – they *could* have beaten you up. I mean, you don't *owe* me anything – why did you . . . ?'

87

Because Dad would have done. 'Bullying's wrong,' Travis said. 'And when it comes down to it, morons like Coker are cowards. They rule by fear. All you have to do to beat them is show them that you're not afraid.'

'That's all, is it?' Simon laughed hollowly. 'What if you *are* afraid?' And had been for years, terrorised in school for long years, your whole life.

Travis sensed the appeal in the other boy's voice. He thought of the outsider at the party. 'Coker gives you any more trouble, Simon, let me know. You want to talk, we can talk. If you ever want help . . .'

Mel suddenly, sheepishly appeared at his shoulder. 'Hey, Sir Travis, can the knight in shining armour climb down from his trusty steed for a minute? There's a damsel in distress here who's ready for that word you wanted with her. In private?'

Travis nodded gratefully. 'Jess, do you mind? Mel and I . . . And Simon, I mean it. If you ever need a friend, you've got one.'

Simon watched Travis and Mel leave the room while Jessica drifted back towards her original seat. She didn't want to be around him any longer but he didn't mind. He had a champion now, a chance. Simon watched Travis go with a feeling he'd experienced towards only two people before in his entire life.

Loyalty.

Out in the corridor. 'Sir Travis?' The recipient of that title was mulling it over. 'Are you taking the mick, Mel?'

'Actually, it's kind of an apology. Just not a very good one.'

'Well, let's see if I can do any better, then. I'm sorry.'

'Travis, what have *you* got to be sorry about?'

'I shouldn't have spoken to your dad behind your back. I should have kept my promise to you. I was wrong.'

'Oh, Trav,' sighed Mel with a kind of admiring resignation. 'You don't *do* wrong. You can't. You're incapable of it. Standing up to Richie Coker just then, for Simon Satchwell of all people, that just proves it. You always do the right thing. You can't help yourself. I should know that by now which is why *I*'m apologising and you needn't. I shouldn't have sounded off at you like I did this morning. It won't do Dad any harm to know that I've got people looking out for me. Friends.'

'Always.'

They paused in the middle of the corridor and Travis put his arms around Mel, held her protectively close.

'People'll talk,' she warned, grinning.

'That's what mouths are for.'

'One of the things.'

But they didn't kiss. They never kissed *like that* any more.

'So am I forgiven?'

'Am *I*?'

'What do you think?' Travis laughed. '*Lady* Melanie.'

So by the end of the school day things were back to normal. At least, they were between Travis and Mel (much to Jessica's relief – she didn't like friends to fall out, it disrupted her sense of security). Their lift home, however, turned out to be provided by Mr Lane rather than his wife.

'Closed the office early,' he explained. 'Not enough people in to get any proper work done. This wretched Sickness. What's attendance like at school? They'll be having to close those down too if things go on like this, I shouldn't wonder.'

89

'There *is* a God,' said Mel.

'But what about our exams?' Jessica asked, worried. 'We've got GCSEs in a few weeks.'

'Now, now, princess.' Mr Lane soothed her as if addressing a child ten years younger than his daughter. Travis and Mel exchanged amused glances. 'There's nothing to fret about. I'm sure they'll keep the exam classes going.'

Stage One, Travis thought, *making a play of carrying on as normal.*

But not in Trafalgar Road.

It was fortunate that Mr Lane had already slowed the car in order to take the left turn safely – lucky, too, that he was a driver who believed in keeping alert behind the wheel at all times. Otherwise the man running at them head-on and slamming into the radiator might have been even more of a problem than it was. The man spreadeagling himself across the bonnet, grasping for both wings with wide arms as if trying to halt the car without the aid of the brakes that Mr Lane had automatically applied. The man whose eyes bulged with terror, whose mouth gaped wide.

The Asian man.

'What the hell . . . ?' Jessica's father shouted as his daughter squealed.

'Help me. Help me!' The man pounding with feeble fists on the windscreen, pleading through the glass.

Beyond him, some kind of disturbance seething in Trafalgar Road. Police cars. Police vans. An abortive attempt at a cordon. Members of the public in angry scrums and pressing rowdily towards what seemed to be the entire law-enforcement community of Wayvale. Travis glimpsed officers in flak jackets, officers armed.

'Can't you see what's happening here? *Help* me!' The man was sobbing, desperate.

'Lock your doors. Lock your doors, kids. Now.' Mr Lane would have reversed but the traffic backed up behind him made it impossible.

The Asian man glanced over his shoulder, was further terrified by what he saw in the street. Glares of unreasoning hatred turning towards him. 'They'll be coming for you next!' He bolted across the road. Blaring its horn, an Audi nearly killed him. The man obviously thought it had been worth the risk. He raced on.

'What was that about?' Mel wondered, her nervous laugh weak and uncertain.

'I don't care. Let's get out of here, Dad. It looks dangerous.'

'Absolutely.' Mr Lane thrust the gearstick into first, preparing to perform a U-turn and avoid Trafalgar Road altogether.

Travis unbuckled his seat belt and shoved open the door.

'Trav, where do you think you're going?' Mel demanded.

'Travis!' Jessica sounded panicky.

'Ah, Travis, we need to . . . I don't think it's very wise to get out.'

'I'll only be a sec,' Travis reassured them, exiting from the car anyway. 'I want to find out what's happening. My Uncle Phil might be here.' Though he hoped not.

And as he jogged along the pavement towards the focus of unrest, he had a pretty good idea what was going on. *Scapegoating.* He remembered the policeman's words. *Pointing the finger of blame at minority groups. All fair game.* Trafalgar Road was the centre of Wayvale's small Asian community – its Muslim community.

Looked like the round-up had begun.

People were being arrested, it appeared. Certainly they were being removed from their homes and escorted towards the vans, the kind used to transport criminals to court or prison. Some of those selected for an outing evidently didn't want to go. Some of them were yelling, swearing, sometimes in English, sometimes not, protesting. Some of them were having to be physically restrained by police officers. Others were even having to be dragged kicking and screaming into the street in the first place. The fear and fury disfiguring a blurring succession of Asian faces found paler reflection in those of the continually swelling, increasingly unruly crowd, by now on the brink of becoming a mob. Insults and ignorance spitting from a hundred mouths like stones flung by louts to smash a window. Fists clenching, shaking, punching at the air. When one Muslim man fell to the pavement an approving cheer went up. When a woman, possibly his wife, tripped in the same way, the same response.

'This isn't right,' Travis muttered under his breath. 'This is insane.'

He thought of Sanjay Rahman, a boy from school, a boy Travis had known since primary days, a boy whose football team he'd played on countless times, who'd partnered him in science experiments with litmus paper and Bunsen burners. Sanjay wanted to be a doctor, not a terrorist. How could he be a terrorist? But he was a Muslim and he lived in Trafalgar Road. He was going the same way as all the other Muslims who lived in Trafalgar Road – into custody.

Like the young mother, manhandled, her two wailing children clinging onto her skirts as they were bundled in a family group towards and into a van. Like an elderly woman and a younger man, hauled into view in their nightclothes, dragged coughing and wheezing from their sickbeds, clearly afflicted with the very disease for which they seemed to be being held responsible, too ill to put up much of a struggle.

But some people were prepared to defend them. A small group, younger than the majority of the crowd, protesting at the naked persecution they were witnessing, condemning the mob, condemning the police. Travis could hardly catch their words above the hostile roar of those who *didn't* want to hear them, but 'innocent' was in there, and 'irrational', and 'ashamed'. There might have been something about tolerance, too, which was ironic. The principal dissident, a girl in her twenties with pierced lips and nose, was suddenly struck above the eye by an object hurled from the mob. Blood flowed brightly. Like an animal maddened by the sight and smell of it, the mob surged forward as one, overwhelming the protesters. Shouts became screams. Fists that had punched air more satisfyingly battered flesh. The police waded in, too, in an anarchy of violence. Turmoil spilling in further bloodshed across the street.

In Trafalgar Road a full-scale riot was breaking out.

'Travis.' The teenager jumped as Mr Lane's hand gripped his shoulder. Mr Lane, ashen-faced. 'I think it's best if we get back to the car, don't you?'

'But they're arresting everyone who's a Muslim, just for being a Muslim. It doesn't make sense. There's no reason for it.'

'The police must have a reason, Travis,' Mr Lane said. His brow was shiny with perspiration. 'They're the police. Back to the car.' Tugging on the youngster's arm.

'We have to *say* something.'

'It's none of our business. Let's not get involved. Back to the *car.*' Virtually pulling Travis along.

'None of our . . . ?'

'Back,' insisted Mr Lane, oblivious, 'to the car.' And Travis went. Truth to tell, he had little choice.

The girls were pale, although with Mel it was difficult to tell. Jessica looked on the verge of tears. Violence in the streets. Not in some distant, godforsaken inner-city slum that she'd never have to visit. Here, where she lived.

'What's going on, Trav?' asked Mel.

Travis's blue eyes were bleak. 'Stage Two,' he said.

Contrary to popular belief, his typical academic performance, and his usual appearance, Richie Coker was not stupid. It was just that his intelligence found forms of expression different from those traditionally favoured by society. The lessons he'd learned were on a curriculum not taught at school.

For one thing, he sensed more perceptively than most what the British education system was all about in the early twenty-first century. Achievement? Excellence? Like hell. It was about making kids feel good about themselves. It was about piling their plates with stacks of qualifications that reached higher than the heaps of junk food the dinner ladies served in the canteen. It was about rising pass rates and plunging standards, prizes for all. It was about churning out half-baked kids for half-baked jobs. Half-baked jobs that paid a pittance and expected you to turn up to earn it. Richie Coker wasn't having any of that. First lesson: his mum hadn't worked a day in her life but she was still better off than loads of idiots who had; a bumper package of benefits every week brought in more than many wage slips. So don't play the game, play the system. Fail happily at school and be supported for the rest of your natural by those with their puny pieces of paper who'd succeeded.

Then there was his dad. A son should always learn from his father, Richie believed that. He was eternally grateful for the lesson his father had taught him in his absence, an absence that was six years long and counting, an absence caused by that tart who'd used to live next door and who'd always been asking Dad to go round and help her knock up some shelves or something. Wasn't only shelves he'd knocked up. But fair enough. Richie had learned. Second lesson: do what the hell you like – don't care about anyone but yourself and take what you can get. It was the takers who were the winners in this world, who were strong. Richie liked to win.

Which was why today had been a bit of a nightmare. What had Travis Naughton been up to, crossing him a *second* time like that? And for a worthless, whining four-eyes like Satchwell. What was he getting out of it? Maybe he was queer for Satchwell. Nah, not with babes like Jessica Lane and even Morticia following him around. He had to have an angle somewhere, though. Nobody did anything for nothing. He, Richie, ought to have battered Naughton this time for sure, if only to reassert his authority. Lee, Wayne and Mick – maybe he was imagining it – but he felt they were looking at him differently since, with, like, less respect. You couldn't be strong without respect.

But the way *Naughton* had looked at him had been worse. It was like he hadn't looked *at* him so much as *into* him. Richie had felt something bad then, the way he'd felt when Dad had caught him chucking snails at the garage wall that time, their frail shells splintering and the grey meat splattering. Uneasy. Guilty. Richie'd had to turn away from Naughton's stare. There was an intensity in those blue eyes, a strength that he couldn't comprehend and he didn't like.

But so what? Naughton wasn't here now. It wouldn't take much to remind his mates who was boss. And it was dark outside and the streets were waiting for one of their own. Richie was ready. Combats. Designer trainers. Baseball cap. Hooded sweatshirt in grey with the word *Warrior* stencilled across the chest in red. He had a lot of tension he needed to work off tonight.

'Richie, where are you going?' His mum was huddled up on the settee with a blanket wrapped around her.

'Out.'

She was bony and shivering. She was feeble and pale. 'Not tonight, Richie, please. You can't go out tonight.' And she bleated like Satchwell, his own mother. 'I'm not well. I think I've got the Sickness.'

'So what do I look like to you? A doctor? Take an aspirin.'

'Richie, I'm really not well. I feel bad. I think I need an ambulance.'

'Call one. You know how to use a phone. I've got things to do.' Raising his hood.

'Couldn't you do it, Richie, love? Please? Tell them I've got the Sickness.'

'I told you I've got things to do. Stop going on.' Slouching towards the door.

'Richie, no.' His mother's voice was pleading, desperate. 'Don't go. Not tonight. I don't want to be on my own tonight. Stay with me. I'm sick.'

'Me, too. Of your non-stop moaning. Get off my *case*.'

Mrs Coker rallied briefly, stung into a moment of outrage. 'Don't you talk like – how dare you talk to me like that, Richie Coker. What kind of a son are you?'

'What kind of a mother are *you*?' Richie retorted. 'An old woman, making out you're at death's door or something. It's a touch of the flu, Mum, that's all. Sometimes I can see why Dad left you.'

'*Richie*.'

'No, Mum. I'm leaving too, OK?'

Evidently not. His mother was still calling after him as with callous disregard he shut the door on her and made off towards the comfort of the night.

'Are you all right, Mum? Can I get you anything else?' Mel tried to sound cheerful and in control as she looked down on her mother confined to bed like an invalid. The older woman was panting quietly, sweat dampening her nightclothes and the sheets.

'No, Melanie, you've done . . . Did you get your father's tea?' Mrs Patrick suddenly seemed anxious.

'Yes, Mum, don't worry about it.' Soothingly. 'He didn't go hungry.' Coldly.

'You're a good girl, Melanie. When is the doctor coming?'

'I told you, Mum, I couldn't get through. Line's engaged. I could try calling an ambulance.'

'No, no. I don't want to cause anybody any trouble. I think I'm feeling a little better anyway. I think a good night's rest and . . .'

'That's right, Mum.' Mel brushed a stray strand of hair from her mother's face, squeezed her hand. It was wet and limp. 'You try and get some sleep now. I'll look in on you again before I go to bed.'

'Sleep, yes.' Mrs Patrick closed her eyes gratefully. 'You've been such a good girl.'

'I wish, Mum,' Mel whispered.

Downstairs, Gerry Patrick was on to his third can of the evening. His mood, never exactly characterised by sunshine and light, had been darkened further by a spate of unadvertised changes to the television schedules.

'How is she?' he grunted unfeelingly as his daughter entered the living room.

'Why don't you go up and see? Top of the stairs, take a left . . .'

'Don't get clever with me. I'm asking *you*.'

'Well, I'm afraid I'm not qualified to practise medicine, Dad, so I don't know for sure how Mum is. But she could be bad.'

'Didn't you call the doctor? I thought I told you . . .'

Mel explained, briefly and with barely restrained contempt, why medical assistance was not at the present moment forthcoming. 'Of course, if you'd driven Mum to the hospital maybe she could have seen someone there.'

'She don't need no hospital.'

'They have drugs there, special vaccinations against the Sickness.'

'If you believe that, my girl, you'll believe anything. What they're saying isn't fooling anyone.'

'And in any case, we certainly wouldn't want you having to interrupt your telly or your drinking, would we, Dad, eh? Not for something as trivial as Mum's health.'

'Sarky bitch.'

'What did you call me?'

'You heard, unless that black stuff you drench your hair in's clogged your eardrums.'

Tears of disgust and loathing and rage stung Mel's eyes. She blinked them back defiantly, refused to let them be seen. Her father. Dad. There he slumped in all his fat, balding, bullying glory. Without him she wouldn't exist. She was what in old books they'd termed the fruit of his loins. The thought made her want to heave.

'Well, I can see the standard of conversation's likely to be as high as ever,' Mel said through gritted teeth, 'so I think I'll pass and go up to my room.'

'You'd be better off going out to the kitchen and practising how to cook a decent meal,' recommended her father with a sneer. 'Delia you ain't, Melanie. That slop you served up tonight wasn't fit for a pig.'

'No? Shame. It was intended for one.'

'Why, you . . .' Gerry Patrick made a fairly token grabbing gesture which Mel avoided easily.

'Careful, Dad,' she cautioned from the doorway. 'Or I might have something to tell Travis.'

Pursued by several anatomically unlikely suggestions that her father also seemed to want passed on to that meddling Naughton kid, Mel bounded upstairs to the sanctuary of her room.

At one time, she remembered as she closed the door and threw herself across her bed, she'd believed that all fathers were like hers. In those days she'd imagined that beatings and brutality were routine elements in the daily discourse between dads and daughters. Gradually, however, she'd learned otherwise. Travis's dad, when he'd been alive – how wisely and gently and lovingly he'd brought up his son (and when he'd died, how Mel had wished the loss had been hers). Jessica's father, too, he might still want to treat his princess as if she was a *little* princess, might have difficulties coming to terms with her growing up, might be a little stuffy and strait-laced, but he'd do anything for his daughter, anyone could see that. Yet she, Mel, was cursed with Gerry. But not for too much longer. She meant every word she'd said to Travis at Jess's party, about getting a job and a flat or somewhere absolutely as soon as possible, smuggling herself and her mum out of Dad's nicotine-stained clutches.

If her mother would come. Sadly, incredibly, there was no guarantee of that. Whether Mum loved her husband or not – and surely, rationally, it had to be not – she was blindly loyal to him despite everything, even though he was a total scumbag. The wedding ring her mother wore might as well be a shackle. She was a slave, not a spouse, and the law consented.

Marriage? For Mel herself? Never.

Men.

And boys. She pretty much kept her distance from boys in a *relationship* sense. Travis hadn't been wrong there. Actually, Travis was the only boy she'd ever gone out with, and that had been – what? – three years ago? Well before he'd dated Jess. And she'd only done it because she trusted Travis. And it had all been pretty innocent, in any case. Holding hands and hugs. They'd tried the kissing thing after a while but it hadn't quite worked out. They'd known what to do and everything but it hadn't felt right, somehow. It had felt like trespassing. Maybe they'd known each other too long. Maybe what they felt for each other – and Mel was pretty sure that it was love – was a brother-sister kind of love. Which suited Mel fine. She and Travis had stopped going out but they'd remained close, more faithful as friends than most married couples.

She hadn't been unduly upset when Travis had broken up with Jessica, either.

Glancing over her shoulder first to check unnecessarily that she *had* closed the door, Mel opened the drawer of her bedside table. Out of it she drew the photo of herself and Jessica. It had been taken at a party last winter. One arm around each other's shoulders, a glass of something alcoholic flourished in their free hands. Both girls laughing as if life held no dangers for them. Mel darkness; Jessica light. Mel lingered over the photo as she'd done many times before. A proud smile teased her lips.

Jessie was lucky. She had everything. Family. Home. Talent. Looks.

And there was more she could have, too, even more.

In its most secret centre, Mel's heart stirred.

Jessica lay in bed with only the table lamp for illumination and listened to her parents' voices from downstairs. She couldn't hear their precise words, of course, but that didn't matter and never had. It was the sound that was important, the security it confirmed, the continuity, the love. All the while that her days closed to the music of her parents' voices, Jessica knew that nothing could harm her.

She'd come up to bed a little earlier tonight than usual. The goings-on in Trafalgar Road had disturbed her, though oddly the mass arrest of Muslims they'd witnessed hadn't even made the local news – such as it was this evening. There were lots of shorter news bulletins instead, interspersed with all the wrong

101

programmes and a series of little films like adverts fronted by smiling celebrities reassuring viewers not to worry about the Sickness and telling them that the authorities had the situation well in hand. Not a single politician appeared. Dad noticed that. Mum said at least the blessed Sickness was good for something. But Jessica still didn't enjoy being reminded of infection every few minutes, so she'd said goodnight.

She'd sooner think about the people in her room. Crystal with the flowing blonde locks on which she'd modelled her own. Andy from the Heartbreakers, whom she could adore from afar and never have to worry about actually getting physical with. Lucinda Digby-Smythe and Gossamer. The others. The friends who were always smiling for her, who'd always been there for her in two brightly coloured dimensions. Who never grew older, never changed. Blu-Tacked to the walls as proof of a perfect world. Where the Sickness couldn't touch her.

Jessica glanced around the room one final time, as if to check that everyone was present and correct. They were. She smiled approvingly.

Drowsy, warm, safe, Jessica Lane turned out the light.

Richie Coker returned home a little before midnight. He was feeling considerably better than when he'd gone out. That was the effect of a night roaming the streets with the lads, supplemented by four cans of strong beer, half a bottle of cheap cider and a few puffs of an illegal substance. That was what such jovial pastimes as setting a stolen car alight on the Old Rec and chasing a wino halfway across the park did for the self-esteem of Richie Coker. He felt powerful, magnificent, a winner.

He was even prepared to make generous inquiries into his mother's health.

There she was, exactly where he'd left her, huddled on the settee in a blanket. The lights were on. The telly was on. She hadn't moved.

Or, actually, she had. Sort of. Her head. It had sort of nodded forward. It was sort of sagging, like her shoulders. And her fingers were no longer gripping at the edges of the blanket.

His mother had fallen asleep. That was what she'd done. That was why she hadn't reacted to her son's entrance. 'Mum, I'm back.' Or to his voice. '*Mum.*' Even when it was quite loud.

A deep sleep, then.

'It's no good ignoring me, Mum. You can't ignore me. How are you? Are you feeling better?' Richie stumbled towards the settee. '*I* am. Come on, I'm sorry for earlier. I am. I shouldn't have spoken to you like that. You were right. Come on.' He reached out. He shook her shoulder. 'After all, you are my—'

The woman slid onto her side. Her mouth gaped open, but not to respond to her son's words of reconciliation. Her eyes were open, too, and they were staring, so she wasn't sleeping.

Not the kind of sleep from which you woke.

Richie issued a sound somewhere between a groan and a scream. All of a sudden he wasn't feeling so powerful. He'd noticed the crimson circles mutilating his mother's face, infesting her flesh, the rims rising to break the skin like welts. 'M-mum . . .' And he wasn't feeling so magnificent now, either, or such a winner. The Sickness has sliced its rings into her hands, her neck. The woman was blotched with scarlet.

103

And she was dead. Dead beyond resuscitation. Dead beyond question.

'Mum?' Richie staggered backwards. The alcohol he'd guzzled churned in his stomach, wasn't going to stay there. The room was swirling. The world was reeling. He lurched to the bathroom and was copiously, violently sick.

Rather later, he dared to venture back into the lounge, as if he wanted to start again, as if he longed to start afresh. It didn't do him any good.

His mother was just as dead.

FOUR

No Mrs Patrick answering the door. Mel herself, and for once all ready to leave for school. Travis recalled her mother's symptoms yesterday. 'Your mum, is she . . . ?'

'She's fine, Trav. Well, she's not actually entirely fine but it's nothing serious. She's in bed with a cold but she's a lot better than she was last night. I told her to stay in bed anyway today, take it easy, really knock it on the head. You know.' Mel's bright-eyed optimism (anxious-eyed, Travis thought) wasn't convincing either of them. 'By the time we get home, she'll be up and around and doing housework and stuff, believe me.'

'Of course she will.' Artificial smiles seemed to be contagious this morning.

'It's not the Sickness. Just a bit of a cold.'

'Course.' Travis tried to forget Uncle Phil's grim prognosis for anyone who contracted the disease. No survivors he knew of. None. 'What about your dad?'

'Oh, there's nothing wrong with him,' Mel said resentfully, 'other than the obvious . . .'

'Well, listen, maybe you shouldn't bother with school today. Half the teachers'll be out anyway. Maybe you'd be better off staying home and looking after your mum.' *Being with her while you can.* Travis was only grateful that his own mother had shown no sign of the Sickness as yet.

'Mum said I've got to go,' Mel explained. 'Got to carry on as normal. "Can't miss school with your exams coming up, Melanie." So you're stuck with me, Trav.'

'I can think of worse people to be stuck with. If you give me a minute . . .'

Mel slapped him playfully. 'Lead on, Macduff, or Jessica will have left without us.'

They made their way to the Lanes'.

'Actually,' Travis mused, 'we might be wasting our time anyway. Heard it on the news. The government's likely to bring in some major movement restrictions. There's going to be an announcement at eight o'clock. If people have to stay in one place, so will the Sickness – at least, it might help limit the rate it's spreading at. That's the theory. They reckon people'll only be allowed to undertake journeys if they're essential, or in an emergency. They also reckon public buildings will close for the duration – and that includes schools. Could be our last day for a while.'

'What about our exams – as Jessica would say?'

'Who's going to be fit enough to mark them?'

Mel frowned. 'Why don't they just lock us up in our houses and have done with it?'

'Maybe they won't have to.' Travis glanced up and down the street. 'Looks like some people have got there already.'

No movement. No indication of life. Dwelling after dwelling solitary and silent. No cars speeding down the road. No children cycling to school. Nobody out walking their dog. Only closed curtains in more houses than not provided the slightest suggestion that they were occupied. Travis remembered how when his nana had died they'd drawn the curtains – in the middle of the day they'd drawn them with the hearse pulling up outside, as a mark of respect. In daylight, he'd imagined ever since, drawn curtains meant death.

Mel's fingers brushed his own, warm as he began to feel cold. 'Lot of people sleeping in today,' she said, speaking quietly as if not wishing to disturb them.

At least the curtains were open at the Lanes'. Everything else was shut, however – windows, garage, door – a condition which seemed to have about it a worrying permanence. The bell echoed emptily inside the house, sepulchrally. Repeatedly.

'Sounds like no one's home.' Travis stated the obvious, pressing his face to the lounge window. 'Looks like it, too. Must have forgotten we'd arranged for a lift and gone without us.'

'No. Jessie wouldn't forget. Mr Lane wouldn't. And anyway, Mrs Lane should still be in.'

'She could have gone shopping or something . . .'

'Before eight o'clock in the morning? I don't think so.'

'So . . .'

'. . . Where are they?' Mel produced the mobile she technically wasn't allowed to take to school on pain of confiscation. 'I'll call her.' But Jessica's phone was turned off. Puzzlement began to transform itself into concern. 'She's all right, though, Travis, don't you think? Jessica. She can't have caught the Sickness, can she? I mean, you said kids can't catch the Sickness. What if something's wrong?'

'Nothing's wrong.' He hoped. 'Jessica's fine.' He hoped. 'She's probably at school and her mum's gone into work with her dad 'cause other people are off ill.' God, he *hoped*.

They walked quickly, urgently towards Wayvale Comp, as though they were being timed. Through residential streets that were as identically and eerily deserted as those around

107

their own homes. Through the town's commercial centre and occasional pockets of frantic, almost irrational activity (though at least there were *people*): a traffic jam in front of a green light, every single driver pounding down on their horns except the first, the woman causing the hold-up, who sat hunched over her steering wheel, sobbing; clutches of people clamouring at the doors and windows of shops closed for business, yelling to be let in, milling around and shouting as if they were drunk; a man with a Bible held high and an entourage in tow, calling – between racking coughs – on sinners to repent because the Day of Judgement was upon them, and half his followers crying 'Hallelujah' and the other half just crying.

When some people saw Travis and Mel they pointed, they glared. Youngsters' inexplicable but apparently universal immunity to the Sickness was now, according to *Breakfast News*, an established fact. A fact envied by those potential victims of the contagion, Travis knew, particularly as even official figures reported the number of fatalities to be rising steeply. Desperate people could not be guaranteed to behave in a civilised way. Mel and he had seen no hint of the police nor an ambulance nor any other sign of official authority.

Travis hurried the goth girl on.

Trafalgar Road had been entirely depopulated. Graffiti of the foulest kind was daubed like excrement on the walls. Some windows had been smashed and a number of doors broken open. If a man's home was his castle, Travis thought, this keep was crumbling. He was beginning to feel as he had after his father's death, as if he was going through the motions of a life that no longer made sense.

He'd never been so glad to see the grey, ugly buildings of Wayvale Community College.

Mr Greening stood at the main entrance like a sentry. Short back and sides, moustached as if auditioning to play Hitler, 'Gestapo' Greening was the school's deputy head in charge of discipline, and he took his responsibilities seriously. The little kids feared him, the older ones respected him, and one or two students, if they were being honest, had confessed to actually quite liking him. 'Gestapo' brooked no nonsense, not from kids, not from colleagues and not, Travis was relieved to observe, from the Sickness, either.

'Naughton. Patrick.' A terse nod of recognition as the teenagers approached. 'Gestapo' was the only teacher in the school – including Dr Shiels – who knew every student by name, and the only one to retain the formality of surnames when addressing them. 'What time do you call this? Any later and it might qualify as being early for tomorrow.'

'Sorry, sir. We had to walk.' Mr Greening's normality seemed unreal to Travis.

Neither did it last. 'Well, it seems that lessons are cancelled today, in any case. Cut along to the hall with everyone else. Dr Shiels will be making a short but important announcement at 0900.'

'What about registration, sir?' asked Travis.

'Registration?' Mr Greening's moustache twitched. 'Not today, Naughton.'

'Everyone else' had been something of an exaggeration. Probably only about a hundred students clustered in small, nervous groups in the assembly hall. The chairs had not been put out. Members of staff scarcely made it into double figures. Jessica was not present. Neither were Richie Coker or

Simon Satchwell. Or Alison Grant or Dale Wright or Jon Kemp or Janine Collier or Cheryl Stone or Mark Doyle or his girlfriend Jilly, who'd never in fact returned from Derby. (Apparently her mum had caught the Sickness from her dad during their weekend mercy mission, thus stranding the whole family miles from home.) Trevor Dicketts was around, though, on his own for once, desolately scouring the hall for Steve Pearce so that they could discuss whether the forth-coming FA Cup Final was likely to be postponed.

'I'm calling Jessica again.' Mel doubted anyone would care if she used her mobile. They didn't, but the instrument once more proved useless. She was still vainly sending text mes-sages when Dr Shiels made her entrance.

Travis sucked in his breath. The headmistress had the Sickness. That much was obvious. Her eyes were rimmed with red as if by way of preparation, she was visibly feverish, shaking, and she wheezed like an asthmatic. She could hardly muster the strength to walk, stumbling towards the stage aided by Mr Greening. The other adults kept their distance, perhaps understandably. The woman's complexion seemed pinker than usual. Dr Shiels shouldn't be out. She should be in bed. She should be in hospital. *For all the good it might do her*, Travis thought bleakly. It occurred to him that this woman, his headteacher, was the first indisputable casualty of the Sickness he'd seen. Chillingly, he doubted whether she'd be the last.

'Gestapo' Greening helped her up the steps to the stage, to the lectern. No mike today. The students crowded closer to attend to the headteacher's words. A funereal silence had descended on the hall.

Mel gripped Travis's hand tightly.

110

'Good morning, everyone,' said Greening, his voice ringing out strongly. 'Dr Shiels has an announcement to make.'

The headmistress could hardly be heard. 'Good morning, students. How few you are today. How few we all are.' A weak and rueful smile troubled her lips. 'Because of that, I'll try not to keep you, but there are certain matters about which you need to be informed. The government . . . as of eight o'clock this morning, the government has declared a state of emergency . . . a state of emergency has been established throughout the United Kingdom in order to check the further advance of . . . advance of the Sickness and to assist in combating its . . . effects.'

Too late for some, Travis feared. He'd never had much time for Dr Shiels, who was the kind of Head who led from behind her study desk and her deputies rather than from the front, but he could see courage in her now, could discern the effort of will necessary to carry out her duty and conduct her final school assembly.

'Curfew . . . curfews will be imposed between the hours of six in the evening and six . . . six in the morning. Towns and cities are to be quarantined and these new arrangements will be enforced by the authorities. Schools will . . . schools will close forthwith until the period of the emergency has passed. Let it be soon,' the headteacher murmured in an undertone. 'But until then, this school, our school, will close.'

If anybody felt like cheering, they didn't show it. Some of the Year Seven girls seemed to be in tears.

'You must all . . . must all return to your homes. Go quickly home. Go safely home.' Dr Shiels briefly became more strident. 'Stay in your homes. Stay with your families, with those you love . . . Government advice is to stay in your homes. Mr

Greening and I will keep the school open for as long as anyone needs . . . needs to be collected, but then . . . Take care, all of you. My best wishes go with you at this difficult . . . this difficult . . .'

She groped for Greening with her right hand as if suddenly unsure of her balance, and though the deputy head seized it he could not prevent her collapse. Dr Shiels pitched forward heavily, toppling the lectern and sending it thudding to the boards. Her convulsing body followed it down.

Most of the students cried out in shock. Some screamed. Somebody laughed with shrill hysteria.

Only Travis bounded up the steps to the stage. And Mel, who didn't really want to get too close to Dr Shiels but who didn't relish being too far from Travis either.

Mr Greening was kneeling, supporting the stricken woman's head and trying to raise her into a sitting position. 'Dr Shiels. Dr Shiels, can you hear me?' She seemed barely conscious.

And it was the Sickness. Travis failed to keep instinctive revulsion from his expression.

Across every inch of skin that he could see, the headmistress was scarred with scarlet circles.

'And I am only too aware of what this means.' In the clearing by the camp, Oak regarded the gathered Children of Nature knowingly, wisely. 'The speed with which the police dismissed Linden and Ash's story, their utter refusal to take any immediate investigative action, persuade me to just one conclusion. They knew about the incident already. They know precisely what is going on. Our so-called forces of law and order are part of it. The cover-up. The conspiracy.'

Murmurs of agreement from the bearded man's followers. A firm assent from Fen and a burst of spontaneous applause from a fulsomely admiring Ash. Even Linden had to concede that Oak might have a point, but in her mind the issue wasn't really what kind of mess the authorities had got themselves into. It was how the Children of Nature were going to protect themselves from its consequences.

'The soldiers our young people saw, the terrible event they witnessed, they are linked to the Sickness, that much is certain.' And if Oak had stopped there Linden would have been in total accord. But, of course, he didn't. 'And the Sickness itself is symptomatic of all that has gone woefully wrong in the world. The authorities are striving to keep the truth hidden, but we can see past their lies and their obfuscation. This contagion infecting the materialists is the result of their own madness, their own science, society's twin obsessions with technology and death. Biological weapons, brothers and sisters, biological experimentation. The materialists chose to tamper with the purity of Nature Herself, to desecrate Her in the name of progress. They believe that they can bend mighty Nature to their will, mould and manipulate life to their own sick and savage ends, but their sheer vanity blinds and deceives them. This new pestilence can only be the product of biotechnology gone wrong, a plague of their own making. I have said this before, and I know that some of you have doubted me' – Linden didn't have to meet Oak's eyes to guess that the leader was referring to her – 'but now that the origin of the Sickness is plain, I am more convinced of it than ever. We who are pure, we who are Nature's Children, have nothing to fear from this disease. It is none of our concern.'

No, Linden groaned inwardly. They had plenty to fear.

They ought to be concerned, and more than concerned. Their lives could be at stake.

'The Sickness may strike down the materialists, but we who shelter in the loving arms of Nature will be spared. This, brothers and sisters, I promise you.'

'You've got to talk to him, Mum,' Linden urged her mother when the meeting was over and the Children had dispersed.

'Oak? Why?'

'Because he's *wrong*.' The teenager knew that her own chances of persuading their leader of that were nil. But Fen, on the other hand . . . 'Mum, disease doesn't discriminate. Beliefs aren't vaccinations. We have to stop hiding our heads in the sand – or maybe, in our case, it's in the trees. The Sickness will infect us the same as anyone else.'

'Linden, Linden,' Fen said, shaking her head tolerantly. 'Oak isn't wrong. He's never wrong. You must trust him as the rest of us do.'

'On the best place to pitch camp, yes. On which mushrooms are safe to eat, fine. But this is life and death, Mum. Oak's closed his mind to the reality of what the Sickness means.'

'I don't think Oak is the one whose mind is closed,' Fen said archly.

'What – what do you mean by that, Mum?' But as she defied the woman's condescending, almost pitying gaze, Linden saw little of a mother behind it.

'You know what I mean, darling. Even with the way you stood up to that police sergeant in Fordham, sometimes I feel that you're not yet quite one of us. Sometimes I feel you have yet to fully appreciate the marvellous simplicity of life here,

114

the peace of mind, the fulfilment that can be found by communion with Nature. Open your mind to Nature as I have, Linden. Be one with the world.' Fen's eyes were glazed like those of somebody brainwashed or in a trance. Her smile was as inane as an idiot's. Deborah Darroway had led Linden to the Children of Nature, but she was gone now. Only Fen remained.

'So you won't . . . talk to Oak,' Linden said dully, dispiritedly.

Fen stroked the girl's hair, an automatic gesture from years past. 'I'll send Oak to talk to you,' she said, and walked away.

A sudden, irrevocable sense of bereavement overpowered Linden then. She felt helpless, weak, her legs like water. She slumped against a tree. It kept her from falling (score one for Nature). But she could hardly breathe. Her mother was gone. She had no mother. She was alone in a settlement of lunatics. She felt blackness surging at the edge of her consciousness.

'You OK, Lin?' Ash appeared at her side out of nowhere, or perhaps out of the undergrowth that could have screened his presence throughout the previous dialogue with the now departed Fen. Together the teenagers stood on the margins of the camp.

'Sure, I'm . . . I'm fine, I . . .' Defeated, Linden exchanged the rough support of the tree for the more responsive embrace of the boy. 'No, I'm not. I'm really not.'

'Lin, don't upset yourself.' Following her mother's lead with the hair stroking. Actually, taking a few more liberties with his fingers than a parent would. 'Everything's going to be good. Trust me.'

'But what are we going to do? About the Sickness?'

'We might get lucky. We *do* live apart from other people, after all. That might help.'

'But they won't listen. My mum. Your dad. Any of them. They won't listen. They won't think. They won't help themselves.'

'I know. It's all right.'

Linden was grateful that Ash seemed prepared simply to let her express her anxieties, pleased that he seemed to concur with them – not that she'd ever marked Ash down as a deep thinker. She didn't mind that he was still hugging her, either, and his hands were kind of roaming over her back as if the two of them were in a nightclub and that song from *Titanic* was playing instead of them standing beneath a canopy of branches with the only music the piercing yet remote melodies of the birds. And it was more than that she didn't mind. She was actually enjoying Ash's attentions. She needed something like this right now. Human warmth. Human contact. Lucky Ash had been around.

'We're on our own, Ash,' she said mournfully. 'I'm on my own.'

'You don't have to be. I'm with you, you know that. I *want* to be with you.'

His words comforted and consoled her. She held him more tightly and in that moment Linden felt closer to Ash than she had done to anybody else in her whole life. 'It's not fair, that the Sickness should strike now, in our lifetimes, while we're young. Everything could change. The soldier said that everything was going to end. Ash, what if he was right? If the end is coming . . .'

Ash's eyes gleamed with determination, and something else besides. 'Then let's live while we can.'

'I don't . . .' began Linden hesitantly. But a blush suggested she pretty much did.

'I like you, Lin. I always have. You must know that. I mean, I *really* like you.'

'Ash.' Her heart thudded. Excitement stirred. A breeze rustled through the trees and above them the May sun was shining innocently.

'You want to know how much I like you? You want me to show you? I can show you, Linden, if you like. If you're ready. Just say you want me to show you . . .'

And she was vulnerable right now, she knew that, and sleazier guys might just have been after taking advantage of her, but she trusted Ash, and the paper they'd bought in Fordham claimed that teenagers and children appeared to be immune to the Sickness, but if that turned out to be wrong, and if the worst was to happen, Linden Darroway didn't want to die without first having . . . well. And Ash was so very, very— 'Show me,' she said.

He grinned. He took her by the hand and he led her deeper into the forest. And Linden went with him freely, willingly.

She couldn't bear to be alone.

They managed to move Dr Shiels to the medical room where there was a bed, the woman's arms slung limply around the shoulders of Mr Greening and Travis respectively. Mel rather unnecessarily led the way. The remainder of the head teacher's erstwhile colleagues, people she'd worked with – some of them for years – were conspicuous only by their absence; it was likely that they were no longer even within the school's grounds. This was why disease made such a deadly

117

enemy, Travis thought, how it conquered: those who should be united in common cause it turned against each other; it divided by fear. Yet disaster and tragedy did not so much *change* people as strip away the image they liked to present of themselves, their façade, their public front, probing beneath the surface to expose with cold ruthlessness the individual's true nature. It wasn't always pleasant to behold. Crisis shone a spotlight into the soul.

Dr Shiels was shaking violently but her skin felt as though it was roasting and she was drenched with sweat. Her lips and eyelids fluttered; her fingers fumbled at invisible tasks. Mr Greening covered her with a blanket.

'Shall we give her something?' Mel said, guiltily conscious of her close proximity to the medical room door.

'There's nothing to treat the Sickness here, Patrick,' said Mr Greening. 'I'll try 999. She needs an ambulance.' He rang the emergency number on his mobile. When his brow almost immediately furrowed, as Travis had seen it do many times prior to the deputy head's renowned castigations of recalcitrant pupils, the boy assumed bad news. 'I'm on hold,' the teacher said in astonishment. 'I've been put on hold. 999. Incredible.'

'Let me try.' But Mel's phone yielded the same unsettling result.

'They must be swamped with calls,' Travis said. 'Inundated until they can't cope any more. An emergency on every street.'

'Maybe the operators are sick, too,' Mel added.

'Well, it looks like I'll have to drive Dr Shiels to the hospital myself,' decided Mr Greening. 'Or home, or somewhere. She certainly can't stay here in her condition.'

118

'Do you want us to come, sir?'

Mel almost screamed at Travis's serial generosity of spirit. She didn't wish poor Dr Shiels any harm, of course not, but she had other priorities now that school was finished for good – like taking care of her mum.

'No, Naughton. Thank you, but you've already done more than enough.' And she could almost have kissed old 'Gestapo'. 'School matters are my responsibility. You'd better get home yourselves, I think.'

'Mr Greening's right, Trav.'

'OK. If you're sure, sir.'

The teacher was sure. 'One thing, though, before you go, the two of you. Be careful,' he warned. 'There are dangerous times ahead. I don't think you can yet comprehend *how* dangerous.'

'You? Don't you mean *we*, sir?' Travis said.

'I listen to the news, Naughton. I know the Sickness doesn't seem to affect young people – at present, anyhow. Everybody else, on the other hand, the adult population, the adult population of the *world* . . . I appear to be healthy now, but for how long, I wonder?'

'Long enough for government doctors and scientists or somebody to find a cure.' Travis tried to sound positive. His hope sounded as hollow as Mel's had earlier.

'Perhaps.' Mr Greening's moustache twitched. 'But I doubt we can rely on it, which is precisely my point. Have you studied *Lord of the Flies* in your English lessons, either of you?' Both of them had. 'Good. Then you know what can happen when adult authority is removed, when young people are left to fend for themselves. Those boys marooned on that island started with the best of intentions. They tried to come together as a

119

group, to organise, to form a society with rules, responsibilities, order, the strong taking care of the weak, working as one for the common good. They tried to preserve their civilised values, their sense of right and wrong – dare I say their sense of duty? But they failed. Ultimately, they failed. One by one the trappings of civilisation fell away like the rags of clothes they had outgrown. Gradually, the memories of their parents and the world in which they'd lived, the boys who once they'd been, faded and were lost. The slide into superstition and savagery began. The descent into darkness.'

'Not for everyone, sir.' Travis had been both disturbed and moved by *Lord of the Flies*. 'Not Piggy. Not Ralph. They stayed true. They never forgot.' He'd read Ralph's dialogue as though it had sprung from his own heart. Ralph had remembered his father.

'True,' Mr Greening conceded. 'But what happened to them in the book? Piggy was killed. Ralph was hunted through the jungle like an animal, the island burning. If it hadn't been for the sudden and fortuitous arrival of the ship at the end, the adults' return . . .'

'But this time the adults won't be coming back.' Mel shuddered. 'That's what you're saying, Mr Greening, isn't it?'

'I'm saying that real life is not a novel where sanity can be restored at the stroke of an author's pen. The Sickness will change the world, perhaps for ever.'

'But it won't change us,' Travis asserted. 'It won't change me. I won't let it.'

'I hope you're right.' The teacher's gaze strayed again to the shivering form of Dr Shiels. 'But I've delayed you too long already. Just – there *will* be chaos and there *will* be anarchy, and they will start first in the cities. I can't leave – I have nowhere to go – this school has been my life – but if you *do* have a place to retreat to, somewhere far from here, I recommend that you make your way there quickly. While you still can.'

'Yes, sir.' The teenagers spoke in unison. For the second time in virtually as many minutes Mel felt an urge to kiss Mr Greening. She sensed that she would never see him again.

'And Travis, Melanie,' the teacher said. 'Good luck.'

Jessica was woken into nightmare.

Mum, shaking her by the shoulder. 'Jessica. *Jessica.*' Her first thought was that she'd overslept, but she hadn't. It wasn't even six. 'Your father . . . isn't very well.'

'What?' Rousing herself, sitting up in bed, blinking at her mother whose own eyes seemed wide and staring. Fearful.

'He's got a temperature, a fever. He . . . I've tried to call an ambulance but I keep getting put on hold. I'm sure if we were asylum seekers or on benefits they'd soon . . . we need to get your father to hospital.'

'Hospital?' Jessica caught the fear from her mother. How could Dad possibly require hospital attention? How could he be ill at all? Parents didn't become ill – they stayed inviolably healthy in order to tend to their children when *they* fell sick, to prop them up with pillows on the sofa, to wrap them in a blanket, to buy them Lucozade. That was the natural order of things. 'Mum . . .'

'I've dressed your father. You get dressed, too, love. We have to go.'

It was the Sickness. Jessica didn't need to be told. Somehow it had invaded the impregnable fortress of their home; not even Mum and Dad had been able to keep it out.

121

Nightmare. Around her room as she scrambled into jeans and top, Andy and Crystal and the others smiled on, as though amused by the whole situation. None of them even bothered to glance after Jessica as she rushed out.

Dad was in a bad way. His eyes were pits of red, like blisters, and his hot, perspiring skin was tinged with crimson. 'There's no need . . . darling. I'm just . . . no need for any fuss.' Wife and daughter assisted him down the stairs, outside and into the car. He slumped along the back seat and Jessica sat with him and held his hand for comfort and that was wrong, too. Ought to be the other way round. Everything was wrong.

'It's all right, Ken. We're taking you to the hospital.' Mum seemed to be driving without reference to the speed limit.

'Princess,' murmured her father. He tried to smile at his daughter until a coughing fit contorted his face in pain.

Jessica felt his fingers gouging into her flesh. She winced but not just from that, and she couldn't see too clearly because tears tended to have a blurring effect on vision. But were those scarlet circles developing on Dad's brow, on his neck, as if red-hot rings had been cruelly pressed against his skin? 'Mum,' she pleaded, '*faster*.'

But there was no way they were even going to get close to the hospital. The streets surrounding Wayvale General were clogged, suffocated with traffic, much of it unoccupied, abandoned. Some vehicles in their desperation to inch nearer to the building had run into the backs of the cars in front; several had struck lamp-posts or collided with walls as they'd tried to bypass their rivals by mounting the pavements.

People who'd either left their cars or never arrived in one wandered mindlessly, like sleepwalkers, like zombies, only they wailed or they moaned or they cried for help while children shrieked, and their relentless cacophony of human misery fought with the strident blast of a thousand car-horns for possession of the air.

People were in groups, in families, clutching at each other, bearing up those among them who were stricken with the Sickness, or they were alone, lost and desolate. Some had collapsed in doorways or on kerbs; nobody paid them any attention. The infected were converging on the hospital in the hope of a cure as, in the days of the Black Death, sufferers had sought succour from their church. They seemed likely to meet with equally little success.

'We can't stay here.' Stephanie Lane reversed violently before they were boxed in by the vehicles already arriving behind them.

'But Dad needs a *doctor*,' Jessica urged.

'Princess, I don't want to be . . . any trouble . . . I'm just . . .'

'We can't stay here. We'll take him to the Woodhurst.' A local private hospital. 'About time we got something back for the astronomical amounts of health insurance Ken pays. There won't be this kind of confusion at the Woodhurst.'

But there was. Fewer cars, yes, fewer people, but the clamour and the despair were the same. The hospital was surrounded like a castle under siege.

It was a nightmare. A kind of whimper rose in Jessica's throat. Why did this have to be happening? How could it be? How could all this be real?

'Come on.' Tight-lipped, Stephanie Lane acted, because this time, at least, she could see evidence of somebody trying to keep order. The entrance to Woodhurst itself was cordoned off by a series of low timber barriers manned by several police officers who appeared to be armed. A white-coated doctor and a uniformed nurse stood with them. All wore masks covering their noses and mouths. While the police seemed to be principally engaged in preventing anyone from actually going inside, Stephanie Lane was certain that could only be because the rabble didn't possess private health insurance and so did not deserve access to private medical care. She, Ken and Jessica did. The Woodhurst staff could check on their computers if they wanted to.

She hauled her husband out of the car, helped him forward. He leaned on her heavily, dragging his feet. Jessica wasn't a lot of use. 'Come on. Keep up with us, Jess. Let's get your father to a bed.' They forced their way through the crowd. 'Let us pass. Excuse me, let us through, please. *Please*. We're entitled to use this hospital. Let us through.' And, oddly, the mass of bodies *did* part to provide a passage for the Lanes – grudgingly in many cases, with a few surly expletives. But the conviction and authority in Stephanie Lane's tone proved as powerful as a passport.

Until they reached the police.

'Sorry, madam.' The officer's voice behind his mask might have been a little muffled but his eyes above it were as hard as stone. 'You can't go in.'

'I think you'll find that *we* can, officer.' Mrs Lane begged to differ. 'Unlike – well. We're entitled. We're members of – we have private health insurance.'

'Maybe you have, but I'm afraid under present circumstances that doesn't make much of a difference. Nobody is being permitted entry to the hospital.'

'*What?*' This unanticipated obstruction seemed to shock

124

the woman more dramatically even than her husband's illness. 'But this is preposterous. It's *outrageous*.'

A nightmare, Jessica thought. It *isn't* happening.

'I *demand* that we be allowed access to medical care. I *demand* my husband be admitted. We pay a lot of money for the right to be treated here. We're *entitled*.'

Jeers and taunting laughter from others close by. Yells of 'Shut up, woman' and 'Go home' and 'Who does she think she is?' Some more sympathetic, directed perhaps at the police: 'Who does he think *he* is? . . . Shame on him . . . We're all bloody entitled.' A restlessness in the crowd, a hardening of hearts.

The doctor intervened. 'Madam,' he said to Stephanie Lane, 'I'm Dr Laker and I'm afraid I have to tell you there's no *point* in us admitting your husband. We have no beds. We have patients in the corridors, on trolleys, on the floor. We have no one to treat them even if . . .' He checked himself. 'We're awaiting more colleagues from neighbouring hospitals but due to the Sickness at the moment Nurse Tindall and I are the only medical staff here. I'm sorry.'

'But you have the vaccine, the vaccine the government told us about. You could give Ken that.'

Dr Laker shook his head. 'The vaccine proved . . . ineffective. We don't have any left in any case. You're better off going home, making your husband as comfortable as you can . . .'

'What about the other doctors? The ones you're expecting? Perhaps they'll be more helpful. I think we'd sooner wait and see one of them. Inside.'

'There's no *room*, madam. It's impossible.'

'. . . No trouble . . . don't want . . . a burden, Stephanie . . .'

125

'Madam, listen to what the doctor's saying . . .'

'The people inside, the ones taking up the beds – have they a *right* to those beds? This is not an NHS hospital that will admit just anyone.' A mixture of amusement and offence from the 'just anyones' pressing around the Lanes. 'Have they paid their private medical insurance as *we* have? Are they entitled to treatment at the Woodhurst?'

'Madam, these issues are irrelevant, given the levels of clinical need at this moment in time.'

'But now is surely when they're *most* relevant. What have we paid for but to be given priority at times like this? It's only fair. You *have* to admit my husband.'

'Go *home*, madam.' Dr Laker widened his entreaty. 'All of you, go home.'

Jessica tried not to listen to her mother's continued protests, to the intractability of the doctor and the police, the escalating frustration and anger of the crowd. As a very little girl, she remembered sometimes feeling overwhelmed by the noise and bustle of the streets when she'd been out shopping with her mother. She remembered how – holding tightly on to Mummy's hand, of course – she used to squeeze her eyes shut and block her ears and shut out the reality of her surroundings. She used to dream herself elsewhere, to imagine herself in a magical, marvellous place all her own, peaceful, perfect, impervious to harm.

As the crowd began to jostle, as the doctor raised his arms futilely for calm, as the police instructed everyone to leave the area, to disperse – and they *were* armed – as her mother finally, forlornly conceded defeat and backed away, Jessica wished with all her heart that she was there now.

*

Jane Naughton must have been packing when she collapsed. Travis found her slumped across her bed with the open suitcase, half stuffed with clothes, at its foot. She was conscious but breathing shallowly and with difficulty. She managed a weak, apologetic smile for her son.

Rushing to her side: 'God, Mum, what happened?' He'd only been gone a couple of hours. He'd been gone scarcely longer than a football match or the average running time of a movie, yet within those brief minutes the Sickness had struck, almost as if it had been watching, waiting for him to leave the house. He scrutinised his mother's skin for the telltale marks of scarlet. No trace of them as yet. That was something. That was good.

And there wouldn't be, Travis forced himself to think. Mum didn't have the Sickness. She was somehow immune. Or if she did have it, she would somehow recover.

She *had* to recover.

With Mum's assistance he shifted her position until her head rested on the pillow and she looked more comfortable. He clasped her hand: her flesh had turned to fire.

'Travis, why aren't you in school?' Her voice little more than a whisper.

'School's closed, Mum.' And when he took his uniform off, would he ever put it on again? 'Now you just lie here and relax. I'm going to get some help.'

'No. No time to waste. We have to – we have to go to Grandma's. Safer at Grandma's. We have to pack and then we have to go. Long drive. If only – I'm so tired. Travis . . .' Straining to lift herself from the bed. Failing.

'It's all right, Mum. Don't move – lie still.' Even if she was well enough to travel, which was debatable, she certainly wasn't competent to drive. In any case, Travis doubted that they'd get farther than the outskirts of Wayvale. The quarantine that Dr Shiels had spoken of must already be in effect. There'd be roadblocks to prevent citizens from fleeing to the countryside. And police.

Travis felt a wild and sudden hope. Just as well they knew a policeman, then.

'Mum, I'm going to phone Uncle Phil. He'll be able to help us.' No point in even attempting the emergency services. 'Do you want anything? I'll fetch you some water. I'll be downstairs.' He didn't want her to hear him. 'It's going to be all right, Mum.'

Astonishingly, he got through to Phil Peck on his mobile first time. The police officer sounded exhausted and fatalistic. 'It's falling apart like I told you it would, Travis. Stage Three.'

'Uncle Phil, I think Mum's got the Sickness.'

'Not her too. Not Jane too.' There was a long silence. 'Marion died last night.'

'What?' Travis's turn for horrified speechlessness. Aunt Marion. She'd put her arms around him at Dad's funeral. She'd kissed his hair and told him that if he ever wanted to talk, ever . . . And now she was dead. 'I'm sorry, Uncle Phil, I'm so . . .'

'I know. Me, too, but what I'm seeing, Travis . . . Marion is one person in millions. One in millions of dying and dead. We can't help them. They're beyond help. I put on my uniform but what good does it do? I can try but there are so few of us left.'

'Uncle Phil.' Travis tried to concentrate the man's mind on his mother. 'Mum's alive. I'm alive. We need you. Like we've needed you ever since Dad . . .'

'Keith, yes. Yes.' Phil Peck's voice became more controlled, more decisive. 'Listen, Travis, I'm at Wayvale General. *Guarding* Wayvale General, do you understand? The hospitals are in turmoil, people demanding medical treatment that no longer exists. There could be a riot here. Don't even think about trying to get Jane to a doctor.'

'No. I'd already worked that one out. But if we can get out of town, to Grandma and Grandad's, Mum might stand a better chance.'

'You too, Travis. The young might not contract the Sickness, but with too many bodies to be buried – do you hear what I'm saying? – the cities will become charnel houses, breeding grounds for diseases that you *are* vulnerable to.'

'Yeah, but Mum's in no state to drive,' Travis said. 'And I've heard there are quarantine restrictions.'

'I can sneak you through those. Just stay where you are for now. Stay at home. It's – there's no point me being here. The General's had it. We're only delaying the inevitable. Stay at home, Travis, I'll come for you both. *I*'ll drive you to your grandparents'.'

'Thanks. Oh, God, Uncle Phil, thanks.'

'Stay put. I'll be with you as soon as I can.'

But he hadn't appeared by evening. Mel had phoned, to report that her mum was worse and her dad was also now beginning to show the first symptoms of the Sickness. Jessica had phoned and told Travis her whereabouts earlier that morning: she and her parents were now back home and she was tending to her father while her mother decided their next move. Even Grandma had phoned, tearfully, panicking, though Travis had put her mind at rest a little with news of their imminent departure and perhaps a misleadingly optimistic assessment of his mother's health. But there'd been no communication from Phil Peck. Travis was trying his mobile every quarter of an hour. Each time, turned off. There seemed to be nothing to do but wait.

And waiting was the official advice, too. It was broadcast on every TV channel and all radio stations. No charade of a normal service any longer. Even the soaps had been cancelled – a state of emergency indeed. And the usual presenters, newsreaders, reporters, the faces and the voices that the British people had grown up with and come to trust, or at least to recognise, almost like old friends, they had also vanished. (Did Natalie Kamen have the Sickness? Travis wondered. Was someone caring for her if she did?) But familiarity didn't seem essential now, anyway. The remote, expressionless men on the airwaves repeated the same single message over and over, like a prayer mouthed by a robot.

Members of the public should remain indoors, safe in their own homes, until paramedics or other representatives of the emergency services arrived with special inoculations against the Sickness, freshly prepared after a breakthrough in government labs.

Travis didn't believe it, of course. It was sheer propaganda, designed to pacify, to offer a spurious hope that many would probably cling to unquestioningly. And why not, really? The alternative was despair. Even if some kind of medical breakthrough *had* been made, how – logistically – could a drug be delivered house by house and street by street in every village, town and city in the United Kingdom? In the *world*? Because, reading between the lines of the bulletins, it was clear that the Sickness was continuing to devastate every country on the planet, that this was a global catastrophe of apocalyptic proportions. And yet the Great British Public were expected to sit back in their armchairs and await a knock on the door and a smiling man in a white coat to administer them life through the needle of a syringe.

It wasn't going to happen.

At one point Travis tried to access the internet, to see if there was any more that he could find out from that traditionally fertile source of intelligence. The internet was off-line; cyberspace was off-limits. Of course. Information was being controlled and denied, knowledge rationed and reduced. The man in the street – and the woman, and the child – they were not being trusted with the truth. Which meant the truth was bad. Which meant, Travis sensed grimly, darkly, the end. Of the world he'd known. Of the life he'd led. Of everything he'd loved. He heard his mother coughing softly upstairs.

He went back into the lounge. And he waited.

Simon drew the curtains well before dark. They were about the only thing left that he could hide behind, the only defence he had from the cruelty and mockery of the outside world.

His grandparents had both developed the Sickness overnight. Simon had looked after them as best he could. There'd been an answerphone at the medical centre and he'd been put on hold when he'd tried for an ambulance. Maybe they somehow knew it was him phoning and because it was only Simon Satchwell they were ignoring his call and attending to worthier cases first, leaving losers till last. Which was why, though his heart was breaking when he saw his grandparents frail and feverish in their bed – helpless, looking older than they'd ever been – he felt a certain resentment too and was ashamed. But they'd promised to protect him. After his parents had been killed, he remembered them promising to care for him and to raise him in their place. To *protect* him. How could they do that from their sickbed? They should have resisted the Sickness more staunchly, for his sake.

They'd failed him.

And now it was night. Simon sat alone in the living room and watched TV. Plenty of people dying now, evidently – not that he cared about casualties. When had anybody beyond these four walls ever cared for him? They couldn't expect his sympathy. And at least the schools were closed for the time being. Let it be a *long* time being. Coker and his mates couldn't bully him outside of school. They didn't know where he lived. *Every cloud* . . ., thought Simon, gnawing at his fingernails. He was still so afraid.

The doorbell rang. *Who?* For a moment Simon was prepared to let it ring, to stay silent, but then it occurred to him who. One of the promised members of the emergency services. A saviour with a Sickness jab for his grandparents. He felt tears of gratitude and relief prickle his eyes. He rushed to the door.

Before he touched it, that second of doubt nurtured by years of persecution. 'Who's there?'

'We're doctors. We've got your vaccinations.'

Simon chose to believe the voice. He had to trust someone. He opened the door.

They burst inside at the first sliver of light, whooping with success. Four of them. Violent eyes under raised hoods. Feral. Male. Older than Simon but not old enough to be infected by the Sickness. None of them were doctors.

And he tried to put up a fight. 'Hey, what do you – who . . . ?' But the lead intruder slammed him against the wall and was laughing in his face and the reek of alcohol was on his breath and he wasn't Richie Coker but in a way he was. They *did* know where he lived, after all.

'Shut up. Shut up, Four Eyes. We're looking for booze. You got any booze in this shit-hole? You got any fags?'

The others were ransacking the downstairs rooms, scattering photographs, smashing ornaments, sweeping books from bookcases and crockery from cupboards, yanking drawers out like teeth and spilling them onto the floor, disfiguring Simon's home.

'Why are you doing this?' he whined pathetically – he knew he was pathetic. 'We haven't done anything to you.'

'Why?' The question seemed scarcely to have occurred to the gang's leader. 'Because there's nobody to stop us, Four Eyes. Because we *can*. The Sickness. Every cloud and all that. Now: booze. Fags. Where?'

Simon gave in, of course. He always did. 'There's a drinks cabinet. In the living room. But it's not very well stocked . . . And no cigarettes. Nobody smokes.'

'Who else lives here? Mumsy? Dadsy? Brothers and sisters? Anybody else here?'

'No. My grandparents. But they're not well. They—'

'Where?'

'They're in bed. Upstairs. But—'

'Pete, check out the fogeys.'

Another of the thugs stomped upstairs.

'No!' Simon protested. Outrage gave him strength. 'You mustn't! Leave them alone. They're ill!'

'Then they'll be glad to have a visitor. And stop *squirming*.'

133

A fist jabbed hard into his belly – once, twice – put paid to Simon's struggle. He doubled up against the wall and the tears came. He saw the contempt in the lout's eyes but he didn't care and he couldn't stop. From his grandparents' room, an old man's indignant cries, an old woman's feeble screams. An intruder's hoot of callous glee.

'We're not gonna hurt 'em. Just want to see if there's anything medicinal by the sickbed, if you know what I mean.'

'I hope you die,' Simon spat. 'I hope someone kills you.'

'If anyone does,' sneered the thug, 'it won't be you.' He brought his knee up, savagely, between Simon's legs. The younger boy dropped to the floor, clutching himself, writhing in agony, retching as if about to be violently sick. His attacker stepped back just in case.

'Nothing,' Pete reported, descending to the hall empty-handed.

'*Better* than nothing.' The other two gang members emerged from the living room with the frugal contents of the drinks cabinet bagged. 'But not by much.'

Their leader sniffed. 'We'll see if they're more like party people next door. But let's thank Four Eyes for his hospitality first.' Lashing out at Simon's tender parts once more with his boot. His accomplices queued up behind him to take their turn. 'And you never know, mate.' His tormentor winked. 'We could be back tomorrow.'

But for now they ran howling with laughter from the house. Simon mastered his pain sufficiently to kick the door shut. Then he subsided to the carpet again and sobbed. *Bastards*, he cursed silently. *Evil, ignorant bastards.* But what could he do? Nothing would change for him. Nothing would ever get better. The sign of the victim must be branded on him like the mark of Cain.

He could hear Grandpa calling his name. There was fear in the old man's voice but Simon didn't reply. What was the point?

The future that stretched before Simon Satchwell seemed as dark and unforgiving as the grave.

It startled Richie when the lights he'd not turned off at dawn began to be necessary again as night returned like the tide of a black and despairing ocean. He'd sat beside his mother the whole time, twenty hours, holding her cold, dead hand, and he hadn't moved. His physical needs – for food, drink, sleep – seemed frozen, his mind and his ability to act paralysed. He was like one of those marble statues carved to keep a lonely vigil by a tomb, except that cemetery sculptors tended to model their figures on angels and Richie Coker was no angel.

His mum had used to say that, when he was a very little boy and had smashed a neighbour's window or yelled naughty words at the girl from down the street. 'My Richie's no angel,' his mum had used to say, 'but he's a good boy at heart.' It occurred to him, through the numbness of his brain, that she'd ceased to express such sentiments towards him for a long time now, for years. As though she'd changed her mind.

It occurred to him that most kids would have been crying by now. If he hadn't been Richie Coker, with a reputation as a hard man to live up to, he might even have cried himself.

What did you do when you came home to a dead person? Who did you call? How did you dispose of the body? Did it get taken away in an ambulance or in a hearse? When you arranged a funeral, did you have to choose a coffin, and if so, did you have to make a selection from a catalogue, like the catalogues from which once upon a time he'd picked what he wanted for Christmas?

He couldn't stay here. He had to find a place where he could think, away from his mother's accusing sightless eyes. Somewhere he felt safer, stronger. The streets.

Richie disentangled his fingers from the stiff and icy clutch of his mother's hand. Should he sit her up or at least stretch her out and cross her hands over her chest like he'd seen dead people lying in pictures? No, best to leave her on her side. Best not to touch her again. Not even a kiss goodbye? Raw red rings encrusted her brow and cheeks.

Richie pressed his lips against his mother's hair. 'Sorry, Mum,' he whispered.

Outside, the night had changed. He felt the transformation in the air. The town seemed darker as he ventured through its streets, and it *was*. Fewer lights from private dwellings. Row upon row of houses shrouded in black, as if mourning some terrible loss only they knew about. How many of them concealed corpses now? How many had been visited by the Sickness? Richie lifted his hood and slunk along furtively beyond the pools of light cast by the street lamps. He'd seen no news today but it seemed obvious that things had got worse – much worse. He'd need his wits about him if he wanted to remain a winner.

The screaming started as he topped the brow of Canter's Hill. The streets swept down towards the Old Rec, its lightless expanse like an obsidian lake. Not a place for the faint of heart or the law-abiding of spirit to visit after dark, but the screaming wasn't coming from there. Instead, it seemed to originate from one of the furthest, the lowest of the streets themselves, as from the bottom of a mine shaft or a pit, and it began in solitude. A single voice – male or female, adult or child? Impossible for Richie to tell. The pain and the horror expressed by that sudden shocking utterance rendered all other considerations obsolete. And it spread, like a black flame of sound leaping from house to house, igniting every one. Other voices joined it, disembodied, ownerless, shrieking, howling, multiplying, a dismal choir of grief. And it grew, the screaming, a shattering crescendo of hysteria and rage and terror, lunatic, inarticulate, beyond language, swelling and rising from the lower streets, crashing into Richie and engulfing him where he stood.

He wanted to scream, too. He wanted to combine his voice with the many and join them. But on the crest of the hill he felt as if he was teetering on the brink of a precipice. If he submitted to the screaming, if he allowed his own trauma to tear from his throat without restraint, he doubted he'd be able to stop. He'd fall. He'd be lost. There'd be no coming back.

A less shrill, more mechanical sound drew his attention to the skies. The insect drone of helicopter rotor blades. Three of the machines, flying low above Wayvale, powerful searchlights stabbing at the streets below, prowling, probing.

Richie hadn't realised the word 'curfew' existed in his vocabulary.

He set off down Canter's Hill at a pace, plunged into the screaming, and whether it was fear of the helicopters spotting him or fear of the tumult itself, by the time he reached the Old Rec he was hurtling along as if his life depended on it. Beneath his feet, the hard earth and scabrous grass gave him

137

hope. He felt more confident on the Old Rec. He knew who he was here, what was expected of him. As the choppers scudded overhead and passed him by without the slightest interest after all, he felt stronger again.

His own kind would be waiting for him.

They were, by the emaciated clump of poplars where they traditionally met, though they were depleted in numbers tonight. Just Lee, Russ and his three mates, a handful of others, including a few groupie chicks. Of the older regulars only Terry Niles was there, leather-jacketed as ever, sitting with his back both to a tree and to his nominal companions. He was swigging methodically from a bottle, not his first.

'Hey, Coker, where's the fire?' Russ laughed like he'd said something funny. The groupie chicks evidently thought so, too.

'What?' Gasping as he slowed to a standstill. He was *way* out of condition.

'No need to rush. We've got loads of time from now on. Here, get a drink down you. Looks like you need one. Pete, intro Richie to the bar.'

Under Richie's nose Pete opened a plastic bag that was full of bottles of wine and spirits. No magician could have produced a rabbit from a hat with greater pride.

'Been "borrowing" from the offie again, Russ?'

'Nah. Offies have all been cleared out already. You'd never believe it. Every single one of 'em looted, while decent people are dying in their beds. It's not right, is it? Some people are treating the Sickness like it's a licence to steal.' Russ chuckled. 'Nah, me and Pete and the lads, we've been doing a little bit of house-to-house.'

'House-to-house?' Richie helped himself to a half-empty

bottle of vodka – a good brand – and a cigarette offered by Pete. To steady his nerves.

'Yeah. Like a collection. We collect booze and fags from houses where they're not wanted any more – you know, on account of people catching the Sickness. We take 'em off their hands. It's like a public service. Actually, most places we could have taken whatever the hell we liked, couldn't we, lads? That's what I meant by no need to rush, Richie, mate. If you don't have to worry about the Sickness – and we *don't* – you don't have to worry about *nothing*. Cops are gone. No law. Nor order. World belongs to us now. Pretty good, huh?'

'What about—' Richie decided he didn't want to appear soft or sentimental. 'So what's happening with your family?'

'Oh, who gives a toss about them?' Russ gulped some brandy. 'Don't even talk to me about them. I don't need family now. No one does. Families are done with. We've all got to find new relationships now, right, girls?'

The girls seemed to think so. They allowed Russ to empty the bottle into their mouths and only two of them vomited the liquid back up again.

'Rich.' It was Lee, tugging the sleeve of his sweatshirt.

'Lee. You all right?' He looked petrified.

'I went round Wayne's. His parents are dead. They were in bed and he's covered them up with a sheet. He was – sobbing and stuff. His sister was there, too. Gemma?' Richie knew Wayne's sister's name. She was fourteen and fanciable. One night he'd planned on getting to know more than her name. Wouldn't happen now. 'She was bawling her eyes out like she was crazy or something. I didn't know what to say. I didn't know what to – I came here. But my old lady's got the Sickness too and there's the twins to think about. I should be

139

at home, maybe. Should I be at home, Richie? What should I do?'

'How the hell should I know?' Didn't Lee realise that Richie had problems of his own? 'What the hell are you asking me for?'

'I don't know.' Lee looked crestfallen. 'I just thought you might . . . How's *your* old lady?'

'She's fine,' Richie lied. 'What's it got to do with you, anyway? Do what the hell you like. Just – get out of my *face*.' He walked away from Lee, took a long, burning draught of vodka. It might be better tonight to be drunk than sober. (Actually, in this shitty world it was *always* better to be drunk than sober.) But Richie sensed his system was going to rebel against his wishes, that he could probably guzzle the whole of Russ's haul and suffer no after-effects whatsoever, no sweet and abiding oblivion. And what did Lee think he was doing, anyway, trying to burden him, Richie, with issues that were not his responsibility? He'd had no option but to turn his back. You didn't get anywhere in this life by helping other people. You helped yourself, that was what you did if you wanted to be strong and respected. Like Russ. Like Terry Niles. Whom he found himself alongside now. 'All right, Terry?'

'What do *you* think, shithead?' Niles glared up at Richie from his position at the base of the tree. His skin, unhealthy at the best of times, bore the scarlet mark of the Sickness. Terry Niles was twenty-one years old.

Richie took an involuntary pace backwards. 'God . . .'

'Looking good, huh, Coker?' The ridges of several of the crimson circles had broken through the young man's flesh and were bleeding, dribbles of blood on his brow, the backs of

140

his hands. Only now did Richie realise how much Terry Niles was shaking.

'Terry, shouldn't you be – I don't know – seeing someone? A doctor? Getting some treatment or something instead of—'

'There ain't no treatment, shit-for-brains. Get real.' The snort of Terry Niles's contempt implied he wasn't looking for sympathy. 'For all I know, there ain't no doctors left now either. That's why we've got curfews. That's why we've got national quarantines. I don't need to go to no hospital, whether I want to or not.' He raised his bottle to Wayvale. 'The hospital's come to me.'

'Quarantine?'

'Ain't you heard? What you been doing all day?'

'What are you going to do, more to the point?' said Richie evasively.

Terry Niles chuckled with bleak relish. 'I'm gonna carry on drinking until I pass out, that's what I'm gonna do. Won't be the first time. Probably be the last, though. I want to see which is gonna get me first, the booze or the Sickness. Want to place a bet, Coker?'

'Terry, you can't just give up. There must be something . . .' Richie remembered Terry and his mates allowing him to tag along to football with them when he'd been only thirteen, to the match first and the rucks after. Good times. Gone now.

'There *ain't*.' Niles was emphatic. 'And don't waste time feeling sorry for *me*, Richie Coker. I didn't want to get old anyway. Old people smell and forget their own names. Feel sorry for yourself. You might be – what? – sixteen now. Gives you a bit of time. But in four years or so, if you last that long, you'll be *me*.'

One of the girls suddenly screamed. Richie snapped round

141

to look at her. She'd staggered away from the group and the trees so she was scarcely visible, but she seemed to be standing stock-still and pointing into the deeper darkness of the Old Rec as though she'd seen something sinister there. Or maybe heard it. Now Richie could hear it, too. An oily, grinding sound like the tracks of a heavy vehicle in motion. Absurdly, Richie thought of a tank.

He wasn't far wrong.

The spotlights blazed on first, brilliant, blinding. The girl wasn't screaming alone. Richie dropped the vodka bottle, covered his eyes.

'Stay where you are! Stay where you are!' A voice more machine than human, amplified to an assault on the eardrums. It seemed to be booming from all around them. 'You are in breach of curfew regulations. You are to be taken into custody.' Disorientated, Richie steadied himself against a poplar, blinked furiously. He had to be able to see. 'Stay where you are. Make no attempt to resist. You are in breach of curfew regulations.' He had to be able to see if he was going to get out of there.

Armoured vehicles. Three of them, stationed at fairly even intervals and surrounding the young people. As Richie's eyes adjusted, he could make them out beyond their spotlights. The kind of armoured vehicles you saw suppressing riots or in science fiction films of police states in the near future, patrolling frightened streets, intimidating innocent citizens. Three. Same as the helicopters, Richie thought. In collusion with the helicopters. Identifying curfew-breakers. Arresting them.

They needed state-of-the-art military-style hardware for that?

142

'Repeat: make no attempt to resist. You are to be taken into custody.'

From inside each of the vehicles they emerged. Riot police? Soldiers? Men in silver protective suits that covered their entire bodies, their faces, too, masks embellished with electronic insect-like eyes and a filter for a mouth. Men who moved remorselessly, silently into position, encircling the offenders. Men armed with guns the glittering likes of which Richie had never seen before. And all to deal with a bunch of half-drunk kids?

Lee was whimpering. Pete was darting to and fro, going nowhere. Russ had fallen to his knees. Some of the others were hugging each other as though preparing for a final farewell.

Only Terry Niles remained defiant. He was on his feet, smashing the bottle against a tree to make it into a jagged weapon. 'You want me?' he roared. 'You want me, arseholes? Then you'd better shitting well *take* me!'

It crossed Richie's mind to shout 'Terry, don't!'. But then the thought also struck him that if Niles unwittingly created a diversion it might be more helpful to Richie's own cause. He shut his mouth. Terry Niles didn't listen to anybody anyway.

Swinging his bottle, yelling abuse, Niles charged the soldiers.

Who raised their guns and shot him.

The pellets slammed into the young man's body, throwing him back with such force it was like somebody jerking him back by the collar. Terry Niles spun in the air before thumping to the ground, unconscious. Not dead. No blood. They wanted the curfew-breakers alive. Which was why their

143

weapons fired pellets, not bullets. Richie thought of rangers on the wildlife programmes that his mum had liked to watch, tranquillising animals with darts before transporting them to their labs – 'You are to be taken into custody' – for tagging or surgery or some other operation. For *experimentation*.

Richie gulped. That explained the overreaction of armoured cars and soldiers. The authorities needed to learn why kids didn't contract the Sickness. Maybe they needed a few young bodies to analyse, to work on. Human guinea pigs. And who better than the kind of kid who wouldn't be missed? No way they could know that Terry Niles already had the Sickness. The rest of them didn't have it.

If the soldiers arrested them, Richie suddenly knew with steely clarity, that was the end.

'Run!' he bellowed. 'They're not the cops. They're gonna cut us open!'

Panic. Like a herd of animals aware of a predator among them, the teenagers scattered. The soldiers opened fire at will.

But, at this crucial juncture, their discipline let them down. They became too eager to farm their specimens; they behaved too much like men distracted by thoughts of loved ones suffering the Sickness. They wanted to get this done so they surged forward and broke their lines. Darkness gaped like a gateway beyond them.

Richie fixed his gaze on it and ran. The girl who'd first glimpsed the armoured vehicles saw nothing more as a spray of pellets felled her. 'Lee! Lee!' Richie grabbed at his fleeing companion's sleeve. 'Keep with me!' And Lee glanced at him gratefully – poor sucker. Pete's backwards-and-forwards tactic was interrupted by the impact of the pellets which dashed him against the trunk of a tree. Russ squealed like a girl

144

before he was cut down: his next house-to-house undertaking would have to be postponed, indefinitely. The soldiers closed in.

But Richie and Lee were still free. Richie's heart was pounding, not just from exertion. The line had parted ahead of them as several soldiers moved to retrieve their already fallen quarry. One man blocked their path, calmly lifted his weapon, took aim. Couldn't miss. But one soldier and two targets. Richie could have kissed himself for his foresight.

He cut across Lee, deliberately barged into him, propelled his friend stumbling directly towards the soldier. If the man had been undecided who to shoot first before, he wasn't now and both he and Lee knew it. 'Richie!' Time for a frenzied, accusing cry, but nothing else.

And what was Lee's problem anyway? Self-preservation was more important than loyalty. Betrayal was just a word. Nobody was going to cut Richie Coker open to see what made him tick.

So Richie raced across the Rec, and its darkness consumed and concealed him, and he wasn't pursued – he reckoned that the soldiers had collected sufficient guinea pigs for their present purpose without him. But he didn't pause. He didn't slow down. Not until he'd regained the relative heights of Canter's Hill. He collapsed then, from sheer physical and nervous exhaustion. He crouched in the porch of somebody's house and if anyone had seen him there they might have identified the foetal position. But nobody did.

And Richie's dazed mind asked, *Where to now? Where to?*

Still there was screaming in the night, but in isolated out-breaks now. And the helicopters were back, scouring the streets to aid their faceless allies on the ground. Sirens split the sky. Fires bloomed like a new and savage species of flower against distant, dark horizons.

Where to now? Where to?

Home? Where his dead mother lay. Lee's house? Lee wouldn't be there. Wayne's? Mick's? Who could help him survive? Who could keep him strong? Tears came at last to Richie Coker and, to be fair, they weren't all shed for himself. He closed his eyes and he pulled his hood down tight over his face and he shuddered.

Where to?

FIVE

There were thirty-two members of the Children of Nature all told, including Oak. Fourteen appeared at the day's dawn greeting ceremony. Only nine of those were adults. Linden knew what the numbers signified.

The Sickness had infected the settlement.

'Wait. Linden!' Oak called after her as she promptly turned on her heel and hastened from the clearing. 'Where are you going? You can't . . . we have yet to give thanks for the new day.'

'I don't think this is going to be one we'll be feeling too thankful *about*,' Linden returned over her shoulder. 'You know what's happened, Oak. I'm going to check on Mum.'

Ash glanced from his father to his girlfriend, made his choice. 'I'm with you, Lin,' he declared, following.

'Ash, come back. Come back, both of you.' The prophet's voice of Oak reverberated beneath the trees but it made no difference. The several small children in the clearing with him started sobbing. 'There is no Sickness here.' The adults in attendance drifted away. 'There is no Sickness here!'

Linden found Fen still in her tent. Crawling under the canvas was like entering a warm and fetid bath but the girl had little choice. To talk to her mother she was forced virtually to lie alongside her. The woman was soaked with sweat,

147

burning with fever. 'Mum, can you hear me?' Fen's eyelids were fluttering and sometimes her eyes rolled up inside her head, exposing the whites like twin tokens of surrender. 'It's Linden, Mum.'

'Linden.' Her voice a breath, barely audible. 'What time is it?'

'Don't worry about that, Mum.' Linden smoothed the woman's hair from her eyes. On the skin, faint pink circles.

'But we must . . . greet the day . . . the day Nature has given us . . .'

'Don't worry about that.'

'Linden, I feel . . . different . . .'

'You're not well, Mum. Lie here and get some rest, OK? Try to get some rest.'

'I'm so thirsty.'

'I'll fetch you some water. Then I'll fetch you some help. I promise, Mum.'

Mere hours ago, Linden reflected, she'd been ready to leave the Children behind, Fen included, without a backward glance, to fashion a new life for herself elsewhere. No longer. Not now. How could she? Whoever Deborah Darroway had become over the years, however hard it had been for Linden to understand, she was still Linden's mother. In the end that was all that mattered.

Ash was waiting outside the tent. 'Is it the Sickness?' When Linden nodded, he added, 'I'm sorry.' But he didn't offer to hold her.

'I'm going to get Mum something to drink. Then I want a few words with your father.' Linden's expression suggested they were unlikely to be supportive.

Oak hadn't moved from the clearing. He seemed almost

148

incapable of movement. His arms drooped limply at his sides and his shoulders slumped; his head hung forward. He looked like a broken man. He looked, with his ragged beard and his wild hair, a hundred years old.

'Oak,' Linden said stonily, 'we need to go into Willowstock. Ash and me, and anybody else who wants to come. We need to get some help out here.'

'Help?' Oak might have smiled ruefully beneath his beard. 'Nature is our help.'

'Mum's got the Sickness,' Linden stated. 'I haven't gone round tent by tent but it's obvious the others have it too. More than half of us in one night. We need proper medical assistance – if it's not too late already.' A barb directed mercilessly at the Children's leader.

'Rainbow. And Sky,' Oak said. 'They can cure us with the healing touch of natural remedies. We don't need potions. We don't need pills.'

'Rainbow and Sky didn't show at the dawn greeting, did they? That means Rainbow and Sky are sick in their tent. Don't you get it even now, Oak? We can't cope with this ourselves.'

'You're wasting time, Lin,' Ash intervened. He looked at his father disdainfully. 'Let's just go.'

'Yeah.' Linden sighed. 'Keep everyone together, Oak. Keep them strong. We'll be back.'

She was on the point of leaving but Oak's hand suddenly shot out to grasp her arm. 'This isn't Nature's doing,' he said. 'This dreadful punishment befalling us is not of Nature, Linden. Don't delude yourself by believing that. We ourselves are to blame. We ourselves have brought plague into the wood. Because though we call ourselves the Children of

Nature we still have been the sons and daughters of society. And though we strive to be pure and walk in Nature's way, the corruption of materialism yet clings to our souls and we are lost. Our own imperfections will destroy us, Linden. We are not worthy to survive.'

'Yeah.' Linden shook off Oak's restraining hand. 'Whatever. Like I said, we'll be back.'

'Dad's really lost it, hasn't he?' Ash commented as they hurried from the camp.

Linden said nothing. At the last she'd seen a terrible fear in Oak's eyes, but it wasn't fear of the Sickness. It was fear of being wrong.

Somehow Travis had fallen asleep. He stirred stiffly on the settee, consulted his watch. Nearly seven. The entire night had passed and Uncle Phil still hadn't turned up.

What if he wasn't going to?

That ominous possibility dragged Travis to his feet, forced him to think. What had happened to the television, the lights? He'd left both on to help keep him awake and now neither appeared to be working. It required only a few seconds to ascertain why. No electricity. Electricity, the lifeblood of modern civilisation. Travis doubted that it was just a temporary power cut. Something rather more permanent had terminated the supply. The Sickness.

Things were falling apart.

Mum.

He leaped up the stairs two at a time. (He wondered about three but then it occurred to him: what if he slipped and fell? What if he broke his ankle – or worse? Who'd be there to set and mend any broken bones for him? It was senseless to take chances in this bleak new world that was being born.) 'Mum. Mum! Are you . . . ?'

Alive. She was alive. Semi-conscious. With his mother's feeble assistance last night, Travis had undressed her and put her to bed. Strangely, perhaps, he'd felt no embarrassment. Under the present circumstances, caring for Mum was a task he simply needed to accomplish to the best of his ability, one he carried out with love. Her fever appeared to have abated somewhat – a good sign (he kidded himself) – but Jane Naughton seemed distant, confused. She sensed another presence in the room but she didn't seem to recognise it as her son.

'Keith?' she said.

'No, Mum.' The boy's heart heaved with grief. 'It's Travis.'

'Keith, what's happening to me?'

The circles had inscribed themselves on her body, lightly as yet, a preliminary pattern that would be completed later at the Sickness's leisure.

She was worse. She was dy— She was worse.

Travis couldn't afford to wait any longer. Waiting was wasting time. He tried Uncle Phil on his mobile. Still no reply. He tried his grandparents. A similar lack of response from Willowstock. He didn't wish to dwell on the implications of either silence. Better to occupy himself. Better to do something. But what? *Whatever he could.*

Maybe if he went to the hospital himself. He might have better luck than the Lanes. Maybe Uncle Phil was still there after all. Maybe *somebody* was, somebody who could do something. Maybe. Where else could he go?

Travis left his mother with a jug of water by her bed and some bread – not that she looked capable of eating anything.

He didn't expend energy pointlessly by trying to explain to her where he was going. He did promise to be back as soon as possible. He did beg her to stay alive.

Silence outside. A hush as of horrified awareness of the catastrophe unfolding. Wayvale felt like a morgue as he half walked, half ran towards Mel's place. How many houses had been transformed into tombs by now? Streets of mausoleums. Cities of the dead. *Necropolis*. That was the old word for it.

Travis cried out in alarm as a dog barked manically at him from a house he was passing. An Alsatian, butting its head against the window. Maybe an *unfed* Alsatian. How many pets would starve to death because their owners had perished? How long would it take for domesticated animals to revert to the wild? Was that blood smeared on the glass, from around the dog's muzzle? The window shook as the beast threw itself against it. Travis didn't loiter to see if the glass would break.

And there were some kids up ahead, a group of kids, maybe half a dozen badly dressed under-fives being shoved along, slapped and struck along, by a couple of girls who were nearer ten. The little ones were crying; their older guardians were shouting something Travis couldn't quite catch but which sounded like abuse.

'Hey, you kids! Hey!' He waved, made towards them. He had some idea about helping them. But as soon as they saw him the children ran off, disappearing down a street in the opposite direction to Mel's. 'Hey, wait! Don't . . . I didn't . . . I want to . . .' No good.

He had better luck at the Patricks'.

'Trav. God.' Mel threw her arms around him. 'I'm so glad you're here.' She was struggling to hold back the tears. For once, Travis thought sadly, her customary midnight garb seemed appropriate.

He returned her hug with vigour, almost with desperation. The human contact didn't just feel good. It felt necessary, like breathing. They stood in the hall entwined and for long moments neither of them spoke. But for his mother, Travis knew, time was of the essence.

'How's your mum?' he asked cautiously.

'Not good. What about . . . ?'

'The same. Your dad?'

'Getting worse. The power's gone off.'

'Yeah.'

'So what's happening? I mean, out there.'

'I don't know.'

'They said, last night, that paramedics would come and give us a jab.'

'Yeah.'

'They won't, though, will they? Nobody's coming.'

'I'm going to the hospital. That's why I've left Mum. Maybe I'll find something out. It's worth a try. Do you want to come?'

'Travis, I'd go with you, but I can't.' Mel's gaze strayed towards the stairs.

'That's OK. That's OK.' Travis stroked her hair. 'If I can find help I'll bring it here, too.'

'For Mum. Dad doesn't deserve it.' Bitterness curled Mel's upper lip.

'He doesn't deserve the Sickness, either. Not even your dad. Nobody does.'

'No.' Mel cast her gaze down. 'Travis!' Lifted it again. 'What about Jessica?'

153

Travis hadn't forgotten her. 'I'll call there as well. I'll let you know. Try to ring her if you can.'

'OK. Call *me*. From the hospital. If there's, like, good news.'

'Sure.'

'Trav?' Mel smeared wetness from her eyes. 'Do you think there'll ever be good news again?'

He squeezed her once more. 'I'll see what I can find.'

Only when Mel had closed the door behind him did she allow herself the freedom of her tears. She leaned her head against the jamb and she wept as she hadn't done since she was a little girl.

'Melanie, that you blubbing?' Her father, shuffling about on the landing in his dressing gown and pyjama trousers. His voice was bleary, slurred, and not – for once – through drink. 'You can pack that up. And who was at the door? I thought I heard someone at the door.' Swaying like a man on a ship in a storm, clinging fast to the banister, Gerry Patrick staggered down the stairs. 'Who was it?'

'It was Travis, if you must know.' Loathing of her father dried Mel's eyes better than any tissue.

'He doesn't give up, does he?' Gerry Patrick wheezed and sweated to the hall. He was clearly ill, but the Sickness had yet to fully enmesh him in its crimson net. 'What did he want? Thinks he's got more chance of having his wicked way with you with your old dad laid up, does he?'

'You're disgusting.' Mel grimaced. 'Let me past. I'm going up to see how Mum is.'

Her father wouldn't let her by. 'What did your little hero want? If it *was* him.' Patrick's bloodshot eyes narrowed craftily.

'What are you talking about?'

'It was paramedics, wasn't it? The paramedics they promised on the box.'

'You're out of your head, Dad. The Sickness is messing with your brain – what there is of it.'

'No, no.' Patrick groped for Mel, caught her at the second attempt. 'Paramedics. What would Hero Boy want to come round here for? Paramedics with our cures. That's why you sent them away. You sent them away when they could have saved me. Because you want your old dad to suffer.'

'I don't have time to listen to your mindless ranting, Dad, so get your hands off of me.' Mel pushed him away from her easily. He seemed to be finding it difficult to keep his balance. She started up the stairs.

'Don't you dare turn your back, miss.' He snatched for her again but this time he missed. 'I want you to explain yourself, why you sent those paramedics away.'

'There *were* no paramedics. It was Travis. *God*. How many times?'

'I'm talking to you.' Stumbling up the stairs in unsteady pursuit. 'Come back here.' Lunging forward. 'You'll talk to me, goddamit.' By chance, damp hand clamping Mel's right wrist. 'I'm your father.'

'I said get your hands *off*!' And Mel swung round, lashing out with her free arm, wrenching the captive one from her dad's grasp. But as she shook him off she also sent him tottering backwards. His own arms windmilled crazily – comically, in a way. Only Gerry Patrick wasn't seeing the joke. He seemed unable to grab the banister which might have saved him. Gravity became an irresistible force. He was a tree chopped down by an axe. His slippered feet lost their grip on the carpet.

With a cry of stupid disbelief, Gerry Patrick crashed backwards down the stairs.

'Dad!' Mel was horrified in spite of everything. Not least because she saw how he was lying.

Again, under other circumstances the ungainliness of his sprawl – limbs ludicrously askew, one slipper on, one off – might have been amusing. But his neck made a cartoon angle, too. It was broken. And at the moment of impact with the floor he must have bitten off part of his tongue, because blood bubbled from his mouth. His eyes stared at his daughter in blank and sightless astonishment.

'Oh, my God. Oh, my God.' Mel sank to her knees on the stairs.

Even if Travis returned with an army of paramedics and the cure for the Sickness besides, they couldn't help her father now.

They would find no salvation in Willowstock. That much was disturbingly obvious to Linden as soon as its lone street of shops and houses came into view. The village had never exactly been a hub of activity, but lives had been lived there, quietly, modestly. Now the place had about it an air of obsolescence, like an exhibit in a museum no one ever visited.

Linden and Ash walked down the middle of the road with impunity.

'Looks deserted,' observed the boy. 'You don't reckon it's been evacuated, do you, and everyone's moved out? Somewhere safe.'

'The villagers are here.' Linden scanned the closed doors and windows warily. 'We just can't see them.' *Will never see them again*, she thought.

'Let's not waste our time, then.' Ash regarded the silent buildings as though personally insulted by their redundancy. The post office. The village shop. The pub. Useless, all of them. Relics. 'What about trying Fordham? Might be survivors, someone who knows what they're doing, in Fordham.'

'We might as well check the surgery since we're here.' Linden headed for the cottage that functioned both as Dr Parker's place of work (on the ground floor) and his home. 'We might be able to find something out even if . . .'

'Whatever,' grunted Ash without enthusiasm. His gaze was drawn to the sweep of the road as it passed through the village and left Willowstock behind.

The surgery door bore a brass plate with Dr Parker's name, qualifications and consulting hours engraved upon it. According to those, the doctor should be available to see patients right now. How Linden prayed that would be true, that all she needed to do was to push open the door and Dr Parker would be there, lounging back in his chair to reassure them with his booming laugh and his cheery manner that everything was going to be fine, that the Sickness was under control. That there was nothing to fear.

'Are we going in, then, or what?' Ash prompted surlily. 'No good standing around.'

Linden turned the handle and the door opened obediently. For a moment her pulse raced with hope: someone was ensconced behind the desk in the waiting room.

It wasn't Dr Parker.

The receptionist must have been sixty, though she seemed to have dressed herself with as little skill as a child less than a tenth of that age: her hair, dramatically uncombed, stuck up on her head in grey peaks as if in perpetual shock. The woman seemed to notice neither of these incongruities. She was shuffling sheaves of what looked like medical records in front of her to no apparent purpose. The anxiety in her face, however, brightened into pleasure when Linden and Ash entered.

'Ah, good morning, good morning. Have you come to see the doctor?'

'Uh, kind of.' Linden was taken aback. Her relief at the sight of an adult seemingly unaffected by the Sickness was tempered by the woman's idiosyncratic appearance.

'Is it both of you or just one?' Her smile was brisk, businesslike, efficient.

'Both, I suppose, but . . .'

'Do you have an appointment?'

'Appointment?' Ash scoffed, pushing past his companion. 'Are you for real?'

'*Ash*,' scolded Linden, slipping in front of him again.

'I'm afraid you can't see the doctor without an appointment. Doctors are busy people. Busy, busy, busy.'

'So is Dr Parker – well, is he all right?' Linden ventured. 'Are *you* all right, Mrs – ah – Wilson?' Managing to read the woman's name badge. Which had been pinned on upside down.

'But you're in luck.' The receptionist was smiling so hard she risked straining the muscles of her face. 'We have a cancellation. Miss Tillotson. She's . . . We have a lot of cancellations today.'

'Listen, can we just see Dr Parker?'

'I'm afraid Dr Parker is indisposed today. Indisposed. I'm afraid he won't be able to see any patients today. Not one.'

Linden leaned across the desk. 'Where is he?'

The receptionist's smile froze and became a rictus of fear,

and her eyes were glassy with terror. 'He's upstairs,' she whispered, her voice suffused with dread. 'Dr Parker. He's upstairs. You can't see him.'

'Has he got the Sickness? Mrs Wilson, is Dr Parker still alive?'

'He's upstairs. You can't see him. He's upstairs.'

Linden felt Ash's hand on her shoulder. 'This is rubbish, Lin,' he said. 'The doc's dead and the old dear's crazy, can't you see? We're wasting our time here.'

'OK, just – in a second.' Linden felt a sudden sympathy for the traumatised receptionist. 'Mrs Wilson, don't you think it might be better if you went home? There's no reason for you to be here.'

'I can make you an appointment for tomorrow.' The woman's eyes might as well have been blind for all she saw. 'Or the day after, if you'd rather. I can make you an appointment for next week. Would you prefer that? I can do that.'

'*Lin*,' urged Ash.

Linden nodded, sighed. 'I know.'

'If you just tell me your names I can make you an appointment.'

'No, that's fine,' Linden said hollowly. 'We've got to . . . Thank you for your trouble, though, Mrs Wilson. Be well.'

Before the teenagers had even left the waiting room the receptionist had returned to her file-shuffling.

In the street again, Linden ran her hands through her short russet hair, appalled. 'Ash, the poor woman's had some kind of breakdown. Can't we help her? I don't know. There's got to be something . . .'

Ash shrugged. 'If she doesn't have the Sickness yet, she'll have it soon. Nothing we can do.'

'Don't say it like that, Ash,' Linden reproached him, though she knew of course that he was right.

'Like what?'

'Like you don't really care.'

And Ash grunted. 'I *don't* really care. Why should I? Old dear's nothing to me. She's nothing to you, either, Lin, don't pretend otherwise. No need for pretences now. Not any more.'

'What do you mean?' She'd wanted Ash to put his arms around her, to comfort her. All of a sudden she wasn't so sure.

'The Sickness, of course. It'll strip us down to the basics, get rid of all the crap and the play-acting and the pretending. The lies. That's what it's doing. None of the rules we're supposed to live by'll mean anything in a week's time. Maybe they'll have vanished by tomorrow. All the laws'll be gone, except one. Nature's law.'

'The strong survive,' Linden remembered distastefully. 'Survival of the fittest. I'm not sure that's a world I want to live in.'

'We won't have a choice,' Ash said, 'if we want to live at all.' He seemed almost to relish the prospect. 'Now let's go. We've spent too long in this shit-hole as it is. Fordham?'

'Hadn't we better go back and check on the others first, tell your dad there's nobody in Willowstock to help us?'

'I reckon he'll be able to work that one out for himself.' Ash regarded his companion with something like disappointment. 'Lin, haven't you realised yet? And I thought you were supposed to be the one with the brains.'

'I don't . . .'

'This is it. Now is now. I'm not going back. Ever.'

'What?' He was smiling at her, but the expression seemed

160

to Linden now like a wolfish, predatory clenching of facial muscles and there seemed to be no tenderness or affection or love in it.

'Get real, Lin. They're all going to die, aren't they? My dad. Your mum. Rainbow. Sky. The lot. They've lived in the forest. They'll die in the forest. I reckon most of 'em'll be more than satisfied. It's certainly not gonna make a difference whether we go back to hold their hands or not.'

'Ash, I can't believe . . .'

'We planned on getting out, didn't we? No time like the present.'

And it was Ash in front of her but it wasn't, couldn't be, or it was a different Ash. *The real Ash*. 'But we can't just abandon them. It wouldn't be right. I can't just run out on Mum when she needs me.'

'I thought you said she wouldn't even notice if you left. You *did* say that.' Almost taunting her. Almost cruel.

'But it's different now. Mum's sick.'

'So she'll probably slip into a coma or something. She won't even know.'

'*I*'ll know.' Linden felt her eyes sting with fierce, hot tears. 'I can't leave yet, Ash.'

'Suit yourself. See you around, maybe.' Ash stepped out onto the carless road.

'Wait!' In disbelief. 'You're not actually *going*? What about your dad? What about *me*?'

'Dad'll have to take care of himself, or get ol' Mother Nature to lend a hand,' Ash said dismissively. '*You*, Lin, you can come with me if you like. You said you wanted to. Here's your chance. But it's your only chance. It's got to be now. Or else – it's have a nice life.'

Linden remembered Ash's kisses on her skin, the wetness from his tongue drying in the sunlight. She remembered his hands roaming. 'I don't . . . how can you talk to me like that? Like you're giving me an ultimatum, Ash. After . . . how can you be so clinical? What we did, I thought that meant something. I thought we were special, that I was important to you. I thought . . .'

'You thought what you wanted to think, Lin. I didn't make any promises. We had a good time, though, didn't we? And we still can. I like you, sure. That's what I'm saying. I'm not saying you can't come with me . . .'

'No,' Linden snapped coldly. 'But *I*'m saying it. I can't go with you, Ash.' Because she'd reluctantly acknowledged the truth. She'd been cheated. She'd been deceived. She felt soiled and cheap and dirty. She'd given Ash what she could now never give to another, and for nothing. 'I don't want to.'

The boy at least had the decency, at the moment of parting, to look vaguely apologetic. 'Pity, but have it your own way. I got you all wrong, Lin. Thought you were somebody else.'

'I thought you were, too. Bye, Ash.'

'Yeah.' He turned. Then, one last pause: 'Tell my dad – nah, tell him what the hell you like.'

Linden watched Ash walk away, from Willowstock, from the Children of Nature, from her. She gazed after him until he vanished in the distance. Then she closed her eyes and listened to the silence. She was alone.

There was no sign of life at Jessica's place, which, after what she'd told Travis over the phone yesterday, seemed a little strange. Particularly as Mr Lane's car was erratically parked in front of the house as if it had screeched to a frantic halt rather than slowed and stopped sedately. Of course, the family might have since departed in Mrs Lane's car, but it didn't feel that way. It felt as though someone was home. The curtains were drawn in what Travis knew to be Mr and Mrs Lane's bedroom but nowhere else. He circled the house, peered through the windows into vacant downstairs rooms, called Jessica's name through the letter box. Nothing. And yet . . . But, short of breaking in, that was all he could do for the time being. He had even more pressing matters to attend to.

The closer he drew to the hospital, however, the less chance there seemed to be that his journey would ultimately prove worthwhile. He was hurrying through a town transformed. Overnight, Wayvale seemed to have been transported from the peaceful heart of England to a war zone in Bosnia or Chechnya or the Middle East. Shattered windows. Looted shops. Burned-out cars, some of them overturned in the middle of the road or crashed through fences or walls into unobjecting gardens. Other fires still blazing unchecked. Streets that could have been in Beirut or Baghdad or on the Gaza Strip. And a total absence of adults. No sign of officialdom.

But Travis wasn't entirely alone even so. More kids on the streets, appearing furtive, somehow, as if they thought they shouldn't be, and keeping together in small groups like the one he'd seen before, wary of others. Some were running, though whether they knew where to or why Travis doubted. Most were his own age or a few years younger, a fact which, despite the morning's pleasant warmth, chilled him to the bone. Did that mean that *everyone* over eighteen was either dead or stricken with the Sickness? And what about the *very* young, kids of four or five, the toddlers, the babies? What would happen to the children who simply weren't old enough to fend for themselves? The Sickness was ruthless. It could kill even those who couldn't contract it. The catastrophe that had befallen the human race was almost too monumental, too staggering in its scope to comprehend, the concept of death on such a scale too harrowing to contemplate.

Then don't think about it, Travis ordered himself. *Focus only on the immediate* – the present moment, the people he loved, what he had to do now and for whom.

The glass of Wayvale General glittered in the sun.

Jessica hadn't been wrong about the numbers. Hordes of people had made a pilgrimage to the nearest of the modern world's new cathedrals in order to save their lives. Those who remained in the hospital's environs had been failed.

Travis didn't want to believe it at first – obviously. The great, now silent mass of vehicles jamming and cramming and clogging every road that led to the General – he tried to convince himself that the drivers and the passengers still slumped inside them had only fallen asleep through inaction and long hours of waiting. But he couldn't because they hadn't.

They were dead, every last one of them.

As he mazed his horrified way between the cars, every face he glimpsed (he didn't dare stare) through windscreens or side and rear windows was ravaged with the crimson mark of the Sickness. The man whose wife's head inclined restfully on his shoulder while he gazed stupidly in front of him. The old woman in the back seat, pressing her cold face against the window with the eagerness of a child off on holiday, her jaw hanging open slackly. The solitary driver who seemed to have been attempting to change the CD in his in-car entertainment system before music became a very secondary consideration. All of them dead. Every last . . .

Except one. Travis's heart surged.

A girl – seven, eight years old, maybe – clinging to her driver mother whose head nodded forward over the steering wheel. She was alive. Travis could see her moving, constantly altering the contours of her embrace as if she might eventually happen upon a hug that brought with it some magical revivifying power.

He couldn't leave the girl there.

'Hello?' he said, rapping on the passenger-door window. 'Little girl?' As she didn't respond he tried the handle and the door opened. 'Little girl?'

She turned her head towards him then. Before terror and grief had scarred it, the girl must have been pretty.

'My name's Travis,' he said gently. 'What's yours?'

'Laura,' the girl said. 'My mummy's asleep.'

'Yes. Yes, she is.' Travis extended his hand palm upwards into the car. 'Maybe we'd better leave her alone for a bit then, Laura, huh? What do you think? Let your mummy have a nice long sleep all by herself.' He paused. The little girl seemed to be considering. 'Why don't you come with me, huh?'

She shook her head, mournfully but emphatically. 'I want to wait for Mummy to wake up.'

'Yes, but that might take a while yet. Your mummy looks like she really needs her sleep. It's all right, Laura. You can trust me. Why don't you . . .'

He touched her. Not good.

The little girl screamed with a hysteria so raw and shrill

that Travis recoiled instinctively. As he did, she slammed the door shut with one hand, still keeping hold of her mother with the other. But she kept on screaming. And she was shaking her mother now. Shaking her mother and screaming.

It was more than Travis could bear. Forcing down his own cry of despair, he broke into a run. The hospital. There might still be hope at the hospital itself.

And once, it seemed, there might have been. Why else would armoured cars, military vehicles, stand sentinel in its grounds? Why else would a cordon of barriers have been placed around its buildings? To keep order. To prevent a panicking public from stampeding inside and overwhelming the medical staff who might possibly have been able to help them. But if hope had ever existed at all, it was gone now. Like the soldiers who'd abandoned their vehicles. Like the police officers who'd no doubt manned the barricades. Like the mob which had obviously charged the defences at some point, because many of the barriers were broken and one of the armoured cars was on its side and the bodies of those who'd been shot and killed in the assault still littered the ground.

Shot and killed. Outside a hospital. In England.

At least there was nobody around to deny Travis access to the wards.

He didn't get any further than reception. Didn't need to. There were enough corpses there to confirm beyond doubt what in reality he'd known since before he left home. Corpses on trolleys. Corpses on truckle beds. Corpses heaped against the walls like drunks. Corpses in white coats. Corpses in nurses' uniforms and in the uniforms of police officers – not Uncle Phil, though, thank God. But they all told the same grim and fatal story.

The Sickness could not be cured.

Oddly, however, it wasn't the panorama of the dead that launched Travis into headlong flight from Wayvale General. It was the sign on the wall pointing towards 'Maternity' – and the half-imagined, *had*-to-be-imagined distant, drifting wail of crying newborn babies.

He ran through desolate streets he barely noticed, in directions he hardly registered. He ran until his lungs and the muscles in his legs burned, until every breath was an agonising rasp. He probably would have kept on running even then had it not been for the car almost knocking him down.

Stupid, really. Travis had known how to cross a road safely since the age of four. His dad had taught him. And one thing you didn't do was dart out from the pavement without first looking both ways for traffic. It appeared that even in the days of the Sickness some elementary rules were worth remembering.

The screech of tyres. The flash of a blue bonnet in the sun. Travis froze, flung up his arms in self-defence. But the car had stopped in time. Just.

'Travis?' Someone riding in it *knew* him? She was scrambling out of the front passenger seat. Cheryl Stone?

'You stupid bastard. You trying to get yourself killed, Naughton?' He recognised the driver, too, who was switching off the engine before stepping from the vehicle himself, all bone and brawn. Joe Drake, who'd been in their year at school until his expulsion for starting a fire in the science labs.

Other kids packed along the rear seat. Teenagers. No adults.

Cheryl Stone was giggling but her eyes were wide and frightened and flickered from side to side like those of an animal in dread of a hunter. 'Trav, we stole a car. Actually, Joe stole it.'

'Don't put yourself down, doll,' grinned Joe Drake, who did not radiate fear. 'You picked it out. You picked all of 'em out.'

Because Joe's vehicle was not unaccompanied. Several others – three, four – had pulled up behind it. Hoodies at the wheel. Drake's dodgy mates. Vandals and yobs. Travis was mildly surprised not to see Richie Coker among them.

'What are you doing?' he said, gasping, heart and head still thudding from his exertion. 'If you're thinking of heading for the hospital . . .'

'Why'd we wanna go there?' grunted Joe Drake. 'We ain't sick.'

'My parents – they died, Trav,' said Cheryl Stone, and then, rather disturbingly, she giggled again. 'I'm with Joe now. He'll look after me, won't you, Joe?'

'Sure, doll. I'm gonna give you a real good looking-after,' promised Joe Drake, with a conspiratorial wink to Travis.

Who felt his flesh crawl. Even Cheryl deserved better than that. 'So where are you going?'

'To school. To *school*,' Cheryl tittered.

'What?'

'Yeah. To finish what I started before they kicked me out.'

'What?'

'We're gonna burn it down, Naughton,' Joe Drake drooled. 'To the ground. Wayvale Community College is for the torch.'

SIX

'You can't be serious,' Travis gasped. 'Burn the school down?'

'I *can* be serious.' Joe Drake moved to the boot of the car. 'You want to see how serious I can be, Travvy?'

He opened the boot. It was full of petrol cans. The petrol cans were also full. Drake sloshed one around to prove it.

'Same in the others.' He indicated the companion vehicles. 'More than enough to start a nice little bonfire, don't you reckon, Naughton? With all the desks and the chairs and the books and the lockers and the registers and all those essays and every last scrap of school shit dumped on top of it. Yeah, the bastard place is gonna make a bonfire worth seeing. You want to come?'

'Yes, come with us, Travis.' Cheryl Stone laid coaxing hands on his shoulders. 'You can hang with us.'

'I don't think so. You shouldn't be part of this either, Cheryl.' Travis appealed to her. 'It's not right. It's arson.'

'Not right?' Joe Drake guffawed. 'Who do you think you are, Naughton? Some kind of shitting saint? And arson doesn't exist any more. Who's gonna arrest me for it? No cops means no crime. We can do what the hell we like now and no one can stop us.'

'*I*'ll stop you,' Travis declared automatically – and for once, perhaps, rather prematurely.

He didn't see Joe Drake's bricklike fist until it had smashed into his jaw and he was staring at it from the ground. The lout's lackeys roared with amusement.

'You can't stop *nothing*, Naughton,' Drake sneered. 'It's out of your hands now. It's out of control. What I'm gonna do, see, is make it so everyone knows. The school is gonna burn.' Barking to his cronies: 'Gentlemen, start your engines!' Slamming down the boot lid.

Travis struggled to stand but he could scarcely sit. To her credit, Cheryl knelt beside him.

'Are you OK, Travis? You shouldn't have made Joe angry. He can't help himself when he's angry.'

'Don't go with them, Cheryl.' He'd never liked her but he went on: 'Stay with me. Come with me. I'll make sure you're safe.'

'But I'm with Joe now. Joe's strong.'

'Joe's a thug. He'll drag you down.' The girl's eyes widened helplessly. 'Cheryl, what would your parents say?'

'My parents are *dead*,' cried Cheryl Stone, and Travis realised that he'd made a mistake. She stood and he realised she was lost.

'Wait. *Wait*.' Heaving himself up. '*Drake*, you piece of—'

'You want to continue this discussion, Naughton,' said Joe Drake, clenching both fists, 'you know where we'll be.'

'Wait . . .'

But they didn't. Joe and Cheryl piled back into their car. The entire convoy sped off, horns blaring and hoots of ridicule directed at Travis, finally staggering to his feet.

Was this what it was going to be like from now on, after the Sickness? Violence and brutality? Ignorance and fear? The disintegration of order, the corruption of good? Already. It

170

had started already. While the body of the old world was still scarcely cold in its coffin. For the degeneration to have commenced so quickly, how close must society have been to anarchy and decay in the first place, how thin the line between law and lawlessness. As thin as the blade that had pierced his father's chest and robbed him of his life. And now that line had been crossed for the whole world. Who was there to restore it?

Maybe he ought to simply retreat home, Travis thought. Mum would need him. He didn't want her to be alone *if*. And in the great scheme of things, what did it matter what crimes Joe Drake and his army of cretins committed? But he had to see. If the school was to be burned like a martyr at the stake, he had to be there to witness the execution for himself.

The blaze had begun by the time he arrived. The science block. The music block. P Block, where the junior classes had their form rooms. All alight. Black smoke belching through smashed windows and wrecked doors, flames like vandals at liberty to destroy. Some of the buildings' inanimate inhabitants had, however, escaped, though not without injury. Desks and chairs hurled through gashes in the glass nursed snapped limbs. Books writhed in the wind with broken spines and flayed skin. Books, Travis thought. The starting point of education. The cornerstone of civilisation. Tossed away like garbage now. Pages of knowledge and learning as worthless as autumn leaves crackling and curling on garden bonfires.

He might have been alone in seeing things like that, Travis mused. Most of the scores of kids capering around the school grounds seemed to be having a high old time of it, if the fixed, almost fanatical frenzy of their expressions, their shrieks and howls of hysterical laughter were to be believed.

But there was a craziness about the scene as a whole and its participants, a chaos, a lunacy, as if nothing that was happening was real any more.

Cars driven by those who'd never sat behind a wheel before tore over the playing fields. One of them shot into the goal on a football pitch and ripped the net clean away from the posts, became like a glass and metal fish trawled from the sea.

But Joe Drake's car was parked. Joe Drake and his cronies – and Cheryl – were converging on the three-storey Main Block with the remainder of their petrol cans. A small army of dazed, disturbed kids followed in their wake. One last building to burn. The biggest of them all. Where the Head had her office. Where the staff sipped their coffee at break. One final statement to be made.

Mr Greening emerged through the double doors.

His appearance was like the stopping of time. Everyone was stilled, everyone suddenly and sensationally silenced. 'Gestapo' Greening. Alive. Unchanged. He'd obviously meant it when he said he had nowhere else to go. A cowering of younger kids behind him. Perhaps they'd sought sanctuary at the school. Perhaps it was the only safe place they knew apart from their homes. They trusted Mr Greening to protect them and he was doing it.

He was trying to do it.

'Drake. I should have known.' 'Gestapo''s voice snapped as briskly and authoritatively as in any weekday morning assembly. His moustache twitched. 'And Roland. And Stanley. And Collins. And – *Stone*? What do you think you're doing, all of you? What do you think you've *done*? You should be ashamed of yourselves. You're behaving like savages, like beasts. It ends *now*. Your childish little tantrum finishes here. Break up this gang of yours at once and go home. Turn yourselves around and leave the school's premises immediately.'

And, incredibly, it seemed they might. Travis nearly shouted with triumph. Among the younger, less hardened members of the mob one or two heads dropped, one or two pairs of feet shuffled nervously, sheepishly. Some kids blinked as if they'd awoken from a dream into a more familiar reality. Even Joe Drake faltered, uncertain momentarily what to do, how to proceed. Mr Greening spoke like a man who was accustomed to being obeyed. He stood tall and unassailable before them, the physical embodiment of the past, of the world of teachers and students and adults and children and structure and limits and rules that had existed so recently. The last scene of *Lord of the Flies*, Travis thought.

But the school buildings still were burning.

And Joe Drake was not to be dissuaded. 'You can't – you can't order me around any more – *Gestapo*.'

'How dare you address me in that way, boy?' The teacher stepped forward. The mob cringed back. 'My name is Mr Greening. *Mr* Greening. You know who I am and you'll do as I say. Now disperse at once and go home.'

'Or what?' Joe Drake rebelled again. After all, his own authority was also on the line here. 'Or what – Gestapo?'

And for a fraction of a second, the teacher had no answer to that question. And *in* that fraction of a second, Travis realised sickeningly, Mr Greening had lost. The entire way of life he represented had lost.

Joe Drake sensed it too, the way predators do when their prey can resist the teeth and claws no longer. 'Gestapo,' he growled, trying to build a chant. 'Gestapo. Gestapo.'

Roland took it up. And Stanley. And Collins. And Stone. While the school blazed around them. 'Gestapo. Gestapo! *Gestapo!*'

'Stop this! Stop this at once!' The children behind him sobbing, wailing, Mr Greening raised his hand, raised his voice. 'Think what you're doing! Behave like human beings!' But it was too late now. No one could hear him. No one was listening.

'Burn it!' screamed Joe Drake, and his youthful followers swarmed towards the Main Block. Towards Mr Greening.

'No!' Travis was rushing forward too, with the urgency of desperation. 'Don't! Stop!'

They didn't stop. Drake's hordes were like a wave, like the tide. They swept over the teacher and into the school with the unopposable inevitability of the future. Travis saw Mr Greening go down, might have heard a strangled cry from the man – difficult to tell as a chilling cheer went up – and he lost sight briefly of the deputy head. Then the mob helped him out. Mr Greening was hoisted high by numerous teenage hands, bobbing above half as many teenage heads as if he was floating on a restless sea, as if he was a trophy. Or a sacrifice. He struggled uselessly but fearlessly. Defiance still burned in his eyes. But other flames were stronger today.

The teacher was borne unwillingly inside.

As he vanished, so did the last of Travis's resolve. He managed only to wade on after a fashion for a few metres before sinking to his knees on the lowest step of the Main Block. He could accomplish nothing. He was too little, too late. Superfluous. Irrelevant. The younger children, those who had sheltered with Mr Greening, were wandering around him, distraught. Others, drawn by the commotion and the crowd's charge, gazed up at the building, whooping like an audience waiting for the show to begin.

Joe Drake didn't disappoint them.

The windows of the first floor burst outwards almost as one. Screams and shrieks from those assembled below as a jagged spray of glass like crystal rain sliced through the air. *Get back. Get out of the way.* Travis knew how he ought to be warning the onlookers, but he had no voice. Neither could he take his own advice. Stray splinters of glass lodged in his hair, sparkled on his sweatshirt like a kind of dew. Small cuts on the back of his hand.

Then the tables and chairs came falling, hurled from within. Travis scrambled to his feet at that point, which was just as well. He'd barely darted out of range before a metal locker unit plunged to the concrete and smashed on the spot where he'd been kneeling. The doors, ruptured at the hinges, swung open. Books spilled out like internal organs. Somebody's pencil case. A car magazine. A dirt-caked pair of football boots.

Desks and lockers tended to shatter where they landed. The chairs bounced a bit more. The watching kids cheered the chairs.

Heads were thrust through the holes where windows had been. Fists punched the air. The Revolution was well under way.

It came to the top floor just as explosively. Windows. Tables. Lockers. Chairs. The routine repeated. And something else. Something else planned for the top floor of the Main Block. Kind of like a climax, maybe, the Big Finish. Why else would Joe Drake be leaning out as far as he dared, resembling a dictator on a balcony, yelling something to the masses gathered below? What was he saying? Travis could hardly hear him. Mr Greening? Something about Mr Greening? '*Shout if you want him. Shout if you want Gestapo.*'

Eyes glazed as in a trance, existing in a nightmare, most of the onlookers shouted.

Not Travis, though. If he was aware of uttering any sound at all, it was a groan. Of realisation. He'd guessed where the hurtling violence of the scene was leading Joe Drake, the only way it could end. He didn't want to see it. He couldn't bear to see it. He was turning away even as Joe Drake's head disappeared back inside the classroom.

Was he betraying himself as he broke into a run? Worse, was he betraying the memory of his father? Hadn't he, Travis, promised to do what was right, to make a stand?

His feet were pounding the school drive as a strange, unsettling ululation issued from the crowd in front of the Main Block, a primitive howl of horror and fear and, somehow, loss. Above that, a lone note of protest. Even now, even at the last, unbowed.

And something made Travis slow down despite himself. Something made him look back at the burning school and the mayhem and the chaos. He wasn't sure what. Maybe the need to witness. Maybe the same deep, powerful impulse that racked his body with sobs and blurred his sight with tears.

So he couldn't quite see *who* had been thrown from a top-floor window. But then again, he didn't have to see to *know*.

And later, from the surrounding streets, he could still see the flames rising from the Main Block like a funeral pyre for one man whose life had been the school, for the institution itself.

By now Travis's expression was grim, his eyes dry again.

He'd had time to think and had come to some unpalatable but unavoidable conclusions. Realistically, there was nothing he could have done to stop Joe Drake and the mob. When they were outnumbered even the good could be overwhelmed. He could not have saved Mr Greening. Wayvale Community College was finished. Wayvale itself was finished, that was obvious. But Travis wasn't. He would only be a traitor to his father, a coward, if he gave up, if he accepted what was happening to the world. He didn't. He wouldn't. And if a stand for order and for good could not be made here, in the town where he'd grown up, Travis Naughton would pursue his responsibilities somewhere else.

Time to move on.

'Travis?'

'That's right, Mum. It's me.' His mother recognised him. That was something. The *only* thing, unhappily. The crimson rings had dug more deeply into her flesh. Deadened, numbed by their tightening and possessive grip on her, the boy knew it wouldn't be long now.

'Where have you been, Travis?'

'I went to the – to try to find some help.'

'Is there any, love? Help?'

'Sure,' Travis lied comfortingly. 'It's on its way. It'll be here soon. Really soon. Just – try not to worry, Mum.'

'I'm not worried, darling.' Jane Naughton smiled dreamily in her bed. 'While you were out, I had a visitor.'

'What?' An intruder? If anyone had *dared* . . .

'It was your father, Travis,' the woman said with quiet adoration.

'Dad? But . . .'

'It was him. It was Keith. He was standing over there.' The sick woman's hand gestured weakly towards the bedroom door. 'He was standing in the doorway. He was wearing his uniform and he was alive again.'

'Mum . . .' *Oh, God, if only.*

'He was there, Travis. He was smiling. He was perfect, golden. And I called out to him to come in, to sit by my side, to hold me again after all these years. I wanted him to hold me again. But he said he couldn't. He said he couldn't stay here because he didn't belong here any more. But he said that if I wanted to, I could go with him. Oh, and I *wanted* to go with him, Travis, to be with my own darling Keith again. And I tried, I tried to get out of bed and cross to the doorway, but I didn't have the strength. Keith was waiting for me and I couldn't reach him.' She grew agitated, tossing her head helplessly from side to side on the pillow.

'It's all right, Mum.' Travis tried to calm her, held her hand. 'Maybe Dad'll come back.'

And Jane Naughton's anguish immediately left her at the prospect. She sighed, relaxed. 'Oh, he will, love. He told me. He said he'd come back for me and next time, he said, my darling Keith promised, I'll be able to join him for certain. I'll be able to go with him.' Her eyes shone with an inner vision. 'Your father and I together again, reunited. Isn't that wonderful, Travis?'

But her son could say nothing.

Simon hoped he was doing the right thing. Not that he had a great many options about now. (Ah, but when did he ever?) He certainly couldn't stay at home with the bodies of his grandparents.

They'd died during the night, together, as they'd lived. Simon almost wondered whether, in the end, it hadn't been the Sickness that had killed them but the shock of having their house broken into by a gang of thugs. His grandparents had always believed in old-fashioned values such as honesty and integrity and self-restraint. Maybe they simply hadn't wanted to survive into the harsh new world being born. Simon couldn't blame them. He'd pulled the blanket up to cover their faces and he'd been relieved they'd both perished with their eyes closed. He couldn't have touched the lids himself.

All morning he'd agonised over what he should do next, where he should go, who he could rely on. He'd dismissed the authorities out of hand – if there were any authorities left, they'd only be interested in important people, not the nobodies of the world. He'd been able to think of just one possible ally, someone who'd promised to be there for him if ever he needed help.

So long as Travis could be taken at his word . . .

Simon knew where the Naughtons lived, the street and the house if not the number. He negotiated the route between his home and theirs in the same way that he'd stolen through the corridors at school: warily, his senses alert to any threat from anywhere. His extensive experience of victimhood might finally come in handy. He was used to making himself invisible.

Only when he'd pressed the bell until his finger ached, without response, only after thumping on the door for several minutes with his fist (imagining the oak panels were Richie Coker's face kept him going), only then did he begin to ask himself what he should do if Travis couldn't be found. The possibility filled him with an awful dread. He realised how much faith he was investing in Travis Naughton. He *had* to be there. He *couldn't* let Simon down.

He didn't. At last Travis opened the door.

'Simon.' The identity of his visitor couldn't have been predicted but Travis seemed beyond surprise. His intonation was dull, drained of emotion, his features ashen and drawn.

'Am I . . . I hope I'm not . . . I had nowhere else to go. Nan and Grandpa, they're . . . It was the Sickness. You said if I needed a friend . . .'

'You'd better come in.'

Gratefully, Simon followed Travis through to the lounge. There was a fully packed rucksack on one of the chairs. 'Are you – going somewhere, Travis?'

'Yeah. I'm sorry about your grandparents, Simon.'

Who realised that he ought to reciprocate. 'Travis, what about your mum?'

'She passed away, maybe a couple of hours ago. She's upstairs.'

'Sorry.' Simon shuffled, embarrassed.

'She's with Dad now. All her worries are over.' Travis sighed deeply: it wasn't that he couldn't cry for his mother but he had no tears left in him. More would come in time. 'Mum's gone and I'm going. I've got no more ties here. It's too dangerous to stay in Wayvale in any case.'

'I know. Last night a gang of yobs forced their way into our house and ransacked it for drink.'

'That all?' Travis gave a bitter smile. 'Today they burned the school down.'

'Say again?'

'And the hospital's full of corpses. The *town's* full of corpses, and I know it's horrible to think about it but those corpses will soon start to rot. I don't want to catch cholera or typhoid or whatever. Besides, there's a more important reason to leave.'

'What's that?'

'The adults are gone, Simon. Nobody's coming to put things back the way they were. It's up to us now. Those of us who are sixteen, seventeen. We're the oldest now. It's up to us to take the lead, to organise, to form new communities and start again. And we can't do that in the cities.'

'Will we be able to do it at all?' Simon asked doubtfully.

'We don't have a choice,' Travis stated flatly. 'If we don't at least try, we're surrendering to anarchy, to the likes of Joe Drake and Richie Coker. I'm not prepared to do that, Simon. In memory of all the good people no longer with us, we're going to try – and we're going to succeed.'

There was passion in the boy's voice again, and in his burning blue gaze Simon saw the old Travis once more, and he was convinced, inspired. He believed in Travis Naughton. 'So where are you heading for?'

'Willowstock. Where my grandparents live. It's a village in the country. A good place to build. Maybe – even – my grandparents could still be alive. Can't get through to them on my mobile.'

'Batteries'll start running out soon. Systems'll break down. Mobiles'll be useless.'

'We managed without them before. We will do again. We'll just have to *adapt* – in lots of ways.'

'Travis, have you thought how difficult it's likely to be to start up any kind of community with just kids? I mean . . .' Simon blinked helplessly behind his glasses.

'I know what you mean. Cross each bridge as we come to it. One problem at a time.' *Or we'll go mad*, Travis thought. He feared that in the post-Sickness world there might be little dif-ference between sanity and madness. 'First thing, getting to Willowstock. I've been trying to call Mel and Jessica. No luck so far. So I'm going round to their houses myself, try to per-suade them to come with us.'

'Us?' asked Simon.

'Or is it just me?' The invitation was frank. 'Up to you, Simon.'

'It's us. It's us, Travis. *Thank you.*'

'OK. Then you need to go back home and pack some things. You got a holdall or a rucksack or something? Pack clothes, stuff like can openers, knives and forks, matches, can-dles if you've got them – things that we can't make ourselves and might need on the journey. We'll be able to stock up when we get to my grandparents' place and set up a base, so keep it light. But I don't want to take chances. Perishable foods. Bread. Cheese. Cooked meats. Pack all that. We might as well eat that first before it goes off. Cans we can leave till later. OK?' Travis reached into his pocket. 'Here's a front-door key so you can let yourself back in. I'll use Mu— the spare. You might be back before I am. We're not setting off until dark, though. After what I've seen today, it might be safer to move about at night.'

'How far away is Willowstock?' asked Simon. Travis told him. 'A hundred miles? So how are we planning on getting there? I can't drive. Can you?'

'We're going to keep well off the beaten track,' said Travis, 'and we're going to walk. So after you've got your things together, Simon, maybe you should think about grabbing yourself some sleep.'

*

182

Travis found Mel huddled on the doorstep outside her house. Her shoulders were hunched forward and her head was in her hands. Her black hair tumbled down, increasing the appearance of sorrow. She looked small and alone and afraid. Travis longed to put all that right.

'Mel,' he said. She hadn't even been aware of his approach.

'Trav?' She looked up and took her trembling hands away from her eyes, which were dark and grieving smears. They told him, he thought, everything he needed to know.

'I'm so sorry.' He opened his arms and enfolded her in them. The teenagers held each other so tightly, so emotionally, they could scarcely breathe.

'What are we going to do, Trav? What are we going to do?'

'I don't know. Try to keep living.'

'Our poor mums.' Evidently something in Travis's expression had revealed his loss, too. 'I liked your mum, Travis. I'll miss her like I'll miss mine.'

A strange note of alarm sounded in the boy's mind. 'What about your dad, Mel? Is he . . . ?'

'He's gone too, Travis.' Mel's voice was cold as she looked her companion unflinchingly in the eye. 'The Sickness took my dad as well.'

Travis nodded. Gerry Patrick was not a subject he wished to dwell on. 'Listen, I did try to call you before like I said I would but obviously . . . There's something we need to talk about now, something that can't wait. Can we . . . ?' He indicated the house.

'*No.*' The vehemence of Mel's refusal startled him. Her hands encircled his wrists like fetters. She interposed herself between Travis and the house.

'Mel?'

'I can't go back in there. Not with Mum and – and with Dad – like that. I can't. Let's stay out here. We can stay out here, can't we?'

'Sure. If you want to. I know it's difficult . . . I don't want to upset you unnecessarily, Mel, that's the last thing I want.' Her grip on him relaxed. 'But if you want to come with me, you're going to have to go back inside to collect some clothes.'

'Come with you? Where?'

Travis explained. He also told her about the burning of the school. She was clearly moved by the final fate of Mr Greening. But, encouragingly for the boy, her most visible emotion seemed to be relief, almost eagerness, at the prospect of leaving Wayvale. He felt pretty much the same way himself when she declared: 'I'm in. But are we really lumbered with Simon Satchwell?'

'Don't be like that, Mel,' Travis chided her gently. 'We'll need all the people we can get for any kind of community to work. And Simon's OK. We can trust him. He probably knows stuff. Give him a chance.'

'If you say so, Trav,' conceded Mel. 'So are we going to try to find Jessie?'

'After you've packed. It'll save time, not having to come back. Actually, it'll be quicker if I help you.'

'No. Travis. Wait.' Stopping him again. 'It'll be *quicker* if I pack and you go on and then I'll meet you at Jessie's.'

Travis saw the sense in that. 'Are your parents . . . covered up?' he asked cautiously. 'If they're not, might be a good idea. It's tearing me apart to think we're just going to leave them in their beds but I can't see any alternative. Do you think they'd understand, Mel?'

'They'd want us to do whatever's best for *us*, Trav,' Mel assured him. 'They'd want us to live.'

Travis seemed heartened by her words and she was glad. It made her feel a little better about lying to him earlier. She waited until he'd disappeared towards the Lanes' place before returning indoors. Her father was not, of course, stretched out lifelessly but peacefully on his bed. Gerry Patrick was still heaped crookedly at the foot of the stairs where he'd fallen and where he would remain, his daughter too squeamish, too revolted to touch, let alone move him. And symptoms of the Sickness did not include broken necks. *She*'d been the cause of her father's death, and though it had been an accident, and though Gerry Patrick would surely have died soon afterwards anyway, it also had to stay a secret. Mel's secret. She could share it with nobody. Not even Jessica. Not even Travis.

The burden of her deed was hers alone.

This time Travis didn't just stand around. When he found the situation at the Lanes' place identical to what it had been before, the house as mute, he felt he had no choice. Jessica might not be inside. On the other hand, she might. Maybe she'd suffered some kind of accident and couldn't answer him. He had to be sure.

It took half a dozen juddering karate kicks before the front door gave way.

'Jess? Jessica!' Travis hastened through the downstairs rooms. The lounge where he'd sat with Mel only days ago. The dining room where they'd sung 'Happy Birthday' to Jessica. The family room where they'd danced. The kitchen where Mr Lane's famous non-alcoholic punch had been served up – for the last time. All empty now. A pervasive sense

185

of absence. The party was over. The guests were gone. They wouldn't be coming back.

Travis stood at the bottom of the stairs, called up. 'Jessie? Are you up there? Mr Lane? Mrs Lane?'

There was no point in delaying. He'd have to find out for himself.

At first he thought Jessica was dead. She was curled up on her bed, fully dressed apart from her shoes, and she was silent and still. He couldn't tell if she was breathing. 'Jess?' And even if she'd been asleep his voice should have woken her. But she wasn't asleep. Her eyes were open. As Travis knelt anxiously on the floor beside the bed he could see her eyes were open. They just weren't seeing him.

They weren't seeing anything.

'Jessie, can you hear me?'

If she could, she gave no indication. Her thumb was so close to her lips that it looked as if she had more than half a mind to suck it self-comfortingly like small children do, like unborn babies do in the womb. She was in the womb again.

'Oh, God. Jessica, what's happened to you?' Aghast, Travis reached out to her, stroked her beautiful thick strawberry-blonde hair, ran his hand over the soft curve of her shoulder and arm. He could have been caressing a stone, such was her lack of physical response.

He sat back on his haunches in dismay. For the first time he noticed the posters around Jessica's room. Someone had ripped them to shreds. The chick with the hair been cruelly scalped. The unfairly handsome face of the singer with that crappy boy band Jessie liked had been slashed to ribbons as if by a music-loving serial killer. Even that pony poster that Jess had loved for years had been mutilated beyond reclamation.

Yet she must have committed the atrocities herself. Travis couldn't imagine why.

But there was something else he needed to check on. 'You wait here, Jessie,' he soothed. 'I'm not going far. Across the landing. I'll be right back.' He leaned over her and kissed her tenderly on the cheek. 'I'm here for you now. I'm not going to leave you.'

Mr and Mrs Lane were in their bed. Travis knew they were dead even before he pulled the curtains back. Their skin was encrusted with the livid circles of the Sickness. Incongruously, the adults were both fully clothed – Stephanie Lane still wore her shoes – Travis saw them peeping out from beneath the duvet. From their expressions, it seemed that Ken Lane had faced the inevitable with humility, unobtrusively, as if even in his dying he hadn't wanted to make a fuss. His wife had not given in to the Reaper with such grace, however: her arms were flung wide and her body was twisted to the left like someone desperately seeking to evade an object on a direct collision course with them.

Gently, respectfully, Travis eased Jessica's mother onto her back, crossed both her parents' cold hands over their chests. He slipped off the woman's shoes and placed them on the floor. 'I'm sorry.' Fresh tears trickled down his face. 'I'm sorry you're dead. I know you wouldn't have wanted to leave Jessica on her own like this, but I want to tell you, if you can hear me, wherever it is souls go, you don't have to worry about that. You don't have to worry. I'll look after her for you. I'll make sure she's safe. I promise.' He gazed at the bodies of the Lanes. 'Goodbye.' And he covered their faces with the duvet.

He stayed there staring down at the shrouded shapes of Jessica's parents as a great weariness seemed to wash over

187

him, and gradually it seemed to him that he could understand Jessica's reaction to the unfolding horrors of their lives.
How tempting it was to deny them simply by not thinking
about them, by emptying the mind of all thought and focus,
allowing oneself to drift away into blankness and oblivion.
Just let the world and its troubles slip away. Let yourself slip
away . . .

A girl's cry roused him. It had come from Jessica's room.

Travis swore under his breath as he darted back across the
landing. What was wrong with him? He had no right to even
consider seeking refuge in oblivion. He had responsibilities.
People were depending on him. Jessica. Simon.

'Mel?'

She was kneeling where, minutes or however long before,
he'd knelt himself, by Jessica's side. The blonde girl hadn't
moved. 'The door was broken in. I didn't call out in case it
wasn't you who'd done it. Travis' – looking up in anguished
bewilderment – 'what's the matter with Jessica?'

The boy ran his hands through his already tangled brown
hair. 'I don't know. I'm not – I *think* she's gone into some kind
of withdrawal.'

'Withdrawal from what?'

'From everything. From reality. Mel, I found Mr and Mrs
Lane.' Travis's implication was clear. 'Jessica – I don't think
she can cope with what's happening so she's denying it. She's
opting out, retreating into a sort of trance, I guess, like a
coma only she's conscious. I think I read somewhere that they
call it catatonia, a catatonic state.'

'OK. A catatonic state. Sounds medical. So how do we get
her out of it? Travis' – imploringly – 'how do we wake her up?'

'I don't know.'

'You don't know? I thought you knew everything.'

'That's not fair, Mel.'

'*This* isn't fair, Trav.' Mel hugged the motionless form of Jessica possessively. 'Jessie reduced to this – *catatonic state*. A vegetable. I guess that's the *un*medical word for it, huh? Well, can she see us? Can she hear us?' Travis shook his head helplessly. Mel shook Jessica. She shouted into her ear. 'Hey, Jess, are you in there? Come on, wake up. It's only us. Travis and Mel. Wake up, Jessie!'

'Mel, don't. I don't think . . .' Crossing to the bed.

'You don't have to retreat from us. You don't have to withdraw from us.'

'It's not a good idea. Mel . . .'

'We love you. Can you hear me, Jessie? Listen to me. We *love* you. *I* . . .'

'No more, Mel. That's not the way.' Travis seized her firmly, pulled her away from the blonde girl. 'Outbursts won't help you and they won't help Jessica.'

Who, her protective foetal position having been disturbed by her friend's agitated attentions, demonstrated she at least still retained the power of movement by immediately curling up again.

'So what are we going to do, Travis?' Mel challenged. 'Tell me that.'

'She might come out of it herself. Given time.'

'Might?'

'Will.'

'How much time?'

'Mel, who can say? Come on, we just have to be patient and hope Jessica's strong enough – in the end – to come back to us.'

189

'All right. All right. You can let go of me now. I've just had an idea.' Mel shrugged free of Travis. 'Jessie loves myths and fairy tales, doesn't she? Has done ever since I've known her. It's why her dad calls – used to call her "princess", isn't it? Well, what about those stories of sleeping princesses – maybe they couldn't face the world either, not alone. Maybe that's why they slept for a hundred years until somebody came to be with them, somebody who'd love them, a handsome prince. Maybe that's why it always took a kiss to wake them. Well, Jessie,' Mel said, 'the world's out of handsome princes these days but if a kiss is what it'll take to bring you back . . .' She leaned down and pressed her lips against the other girl's. 'Come back to us, Jessica.'

No reaction.

'So much for fairy tales and happy endings,' Mel sighed. 'What now?'

'We take her with us, of course,' Travis said. 'We look after her until she recovers. Did you bring your things?'

'Downstairs.'

'Good. We'll have to pack some clothes and stuff for Jessica too. OK.' He addressed the girl on the bed like a nurse jollying along a patient. 'All right, Jess, we're going to sit you up now and then we're going to my house. You remember my house? You can help us. Sit up. That's it. Good.' He coaxed her into a sitting position and, though Jessica moved with robot stiffness, without expression, she did what Travis told her. He and Mel exchanged hopeful glances.

'That's excellent, Jess,' the black-haired girl encouraged her. 'But Trav? You're going to be the boss man for our little group, the leader. Nobody's going to dispute that, which means you're going to have to look out for all of us, and Jessica needs – she's going to need special attention all the while she's like this, isn't she?'

Travis had to admit that was true. 'Your point being?'

'Let me look after Jessica, Trav. Let her be my responsibility. I won't let either of you down. Please?'

He looked at Mel curiously. 'Sounds like it'd mean a lot to you.'

'I know Jess is important to both of us, Travis, but yes,' confessed Mel, 'it *would* mean a lot.'

The Lanes had liked Mel Patrick. Travis knew that. 'OK, then,' he consented. 'Jess is in your charge. Now let's get moving. I want to be on our way as soon as it's dark.'

'I'm dying, aren't I?' In the dimming light of her tent, Fen Darroway's precise expression was difficult to discern. Maybe that was just as well. Linden was troubled enough by the calm, accepting tone of her mother's voice. 'That's OK. That's fine. Don't be sad, Linden.'

'Somebody still might come, Mum. The police. The army.' Though, after Willowstock, she didn't believe it. 'You have to fight.'

'I don't think so.' Was the woman actually smiling? 'Fighting is wrong, Linden. You still have so much to learn.'

'Fighting against – against the Sickness,' Linden protested. 'That can't be wrong.'

'Death isn't the end, darling,' breathed Fen. 'It's part of the journey. It's an experience to be embraced. When the time comes, Nature will take me to Her and all that I am will return to the soil. I will become one with Nature at last, truly. I will have found my purpose after all these years of searching.

191

From the remains of me new life will grow and so I will live on, too. For ever.'

'What about everything you're leaving behind, though?' Linden said. 'What about me, Mum?'

'You should be glad for me, Linden, and be thankful. Nature is good. I love Nature.'

More than you ever loved me, the girl thought bleakly, but she didn't say so. She didn't want to mar her last hours with her mother by arguing. But Nature wasn't good. Not if it could allow an evil like the Sickness to exist and to spread unchecked among the human population. By the time she'd returned alone from Willowstock, all the previously unaffected adults in the camp bar two were exhibiting symptoms of the infection. Including Oak. When she had told him – as tactfully as she could – why his son was not with her, the effect on the Children's leader had seemed more devastating than the disease itself. Almost literally, Oak was felled. He was dying in his tent now, like the others. Like Fen.

'Don't be sad, Linden,' the woman said again. 'Be happy.'

Which was something Linden couldn't manage, not even as a pretence for Fen's sake. Her mother might be looking forward to becoming one with Nature, but Linden wasn't and never would. In a world of death, she wanted to *live*.

Simon was already at the Naughtons' house when Travis himself and the two girls arrived back. From his nervous manner, he'd evidently been there some time.

'I was beginning to think you weren't coming. I was beginning to think you'd gone on without me.'

'I said I'd be back, Simon, didn't I?' Travis was vain

192

enough to be a little hurt that Simon should have doubted him.

'You did. Yes, you did. I should have – sorry. Hello, Mel.' Half offering her his hand.

'Simon.' Wholly ignoring it. Mel had always entertained the vague notion that Simon Satchwell's skin would feel cold and clammy like a frog's.

'Hello, Jessi—' Behind his glasses, Simon's eyes widened. Jessica Lane was a zombie. It was as though she'd had a lobotomy or something. She was staring dully ahead, focusing on nothing, and her mouth was kind of hanging open. She could walk and sit down and everything but Mel, who held her hand as securely as if the two of them were glued together, had to guide her. 'Is there something the matter with Jessica?'

'We found her like that,' Travis said. He recapped.

'It's temporary,' Mel insisted. 'She'll be all right again – soon.'

'Yeah, but . . .' Simon's mind raced. He'd sought out Travis because he trusted Travis to protect him. He had nothing against Melanie Patrick – she was one girl who could proba-bly take care of herself – and he actually *liked* Jessica Lane, the only schoolmate ever to invite him to her parties – he'd had *dreams* about Jessica Lane – but with her in her present sorry state, would even Travis Naughton be able to defend them all? 'Until Jessica is, you know, better, won't she be a bit of a, you know, liability?'

'Hey, Simon,' Mel flared up instantly. 'If we're talking lia-bilities, there's only one of us here who qualifies that I can see. You want to guess at his initials?'

'I'm not being personal. I'm not saying anything against

193

Jessica. I'm just saying, won't she slow us down and stuff? It'll be like taking an invalid along.'

'I'll invalid you if you don't shut up,' said Mel, glaring.

'I'm just saying, mightn't it be better if we left her somewhere she might get some proper help?'

'OK, both of you,' Travis intervened. 'Enough.'

'Are you gonna let him talk about Jessie as if she's nothing but a handicap, Trav?'

'*Enough.* Nobody's leaving anybody anywhere. Jessica comes with us. She's one of us. If that means we travel more slowly, then we travel more slowly. No arguments. We're a group. We're a team. We've got to be able to trust each other and rely on each other. Who knows? Our lives might one day depend on that, so it might be wise if we made some kind of effort to get along. If *four* of us can't manage it, how the heck are we going to cope when we've got a community of fourteen, or forty?'

'All right, Trav, you can stop the sermon,' Mel grumbled. 'I get the point.' With an effort, she added: 'Sorry, Simon.'

'Me, too. My fault. I'm just edgy, that's my excuse.' He smiled the ingratiating smile he'd developed over the years in his attempts to deflect bullies. 'I'll help you with Jessica if you like.'

'No, that's all right,' Mel said promptly. 'Thanks, but . . .'

'More like it,' Travis said.

Simon offered his hand again to Mel, more forthrightly this time, and this time she actually took it. And she'd been wrong about him all along. Simon Satchwell's skin was as warm and as human as her own.

When it was too dark to see each other inside the house they

194

set off. Travis went to his mother's room one last time but he didn't pull back the sheet to look at her. She was in his mind now, in his memory, and in his memory she would always be alive. He didn't lock the front door behind them but, absurdly, he took his key with him, and his wallet, containing all the money that had been in the house. Habit, he supposed. He wondered if he'd ever spend money again.

All four teenagers wore practical clothing – jeans and trainers, Travis and Jessica had denim jackets in blue, Mel a leather version in black. Simon had on a chunky grey sweater which his nan had probably devoted several weeks of her life to knitting. Apparently, he had a cagoule in his holdall in case it rained between Wayvale and Willowstock (Mel had half expected him to have packed an umbrella). Travis and Jessica walked with rucksacks strapped to their backs; Simon and Mel's holdalls swung from their shoulders.

The plan, Travis explained, was to get out of town as quickly as possible, then keep going until morning before finding somewhere to rest up and reduce the provisions they'd packed. They'd eaten as much as any of them had an appetite for before nightfall. Mel had had to feed Jessica, who had at least chewed and swallowed for herself, albeit like an automaton.

Nobody disagreed with Travis's intentions, particularly not the first of them. The cloudy night sky above Wayvale was blistered with the ghosts of countless fires below. Sometimes the group could hear screams or shouts or smashing glass or screeching wheels – disturbing, violent sounds. The baying of dogs – hardly ordinary barking now, but something wilder, more rabid. Sometimes, glimpsed in the anaemic glow of a distant street light, a number of which were still stolidly carrying out their duty, figures flitted by like thieves. Travis thought of Joe Drake, Simon of Richie Coker, and both boys instinctively increased their pace. Although Mel was doing her best to hurry Jessica along after them, it was like leading a blind person and the girls soon fell behind.

'Travis, wait!' Mel complained with a mixture of exasperation and accusation. 'What happened to "if we need to go more slowly we'll go more slowly"?'

Travis hesitated. 'We need to keep moving,' Simon urged in his ear.

'We need to keep together,' he replied. 'All right, Mel.'

Travis tracked back to the girls. Simon frowned before reluctantly following. His own finely tuned sense of self-preservation was warning him that delay meant danger, but he was part of a group now. For the first time in his life he had a chance to belong. He supposed he'd have to learn to take others into account.

Mel had stopped Jessica. The blonde girl was breathing more quickly but beyond that continued to show no awareness of where she was or what she'd been doing. 'I think this is going to be harder than we bargained for,' Mel admitted.

'You're not suggesting . . .'

'*No*, Travis, of *course* not.' The goth girl's eyes flashed. 'I'm just *saying*. If I'm suggesting anything, maybe it's that we need to reconsider our transport options.'

'You mean steal a car?' Simon guessed.

'No good.' Travis dismissed the idea. 'No keys and I don't know how to hot-wire. I guess we could go back and use Mum's car after all. I could *try* driving us. I mean, I broadly know how.'

'Steering. Gears. Clutch. If the kind of morons who spend their evenings doing handbrake turns on the industrial estate can drive without killing themselves,' said Mel, 'we should be able to manage it.'

'But Trav,' said a worried Simon, 'go *back*?'

'I don't know.' Travis was suddenly aware of both Simon and Mel looking to him for a decision. 'I don't know.'

And then something else sudden. A vehicle's engine. A car's headlights sweeping into the street where they were, exposing the teenagers' presence by their brightness. Everyone but Jessica shielded their eyes and backed away – Mel dragged the blonde girl with her.

'Wait! Don't run!' A voice through the vehicle's open window. 'We want to help you.' A woman's voice.

'Travis,' Simon gasped with wild relief, '*adults*!'

A dark green people carrier pulled up, the kind of vehicle more normally associated with the school run or family outings. The woman who'd hailed them stepped out. She was middle-aged, bespectacled, looked like she grew her own vegetables and attended church every Sunday. The driver and another passenger remained in the car. They were of the same sort of age and obvious respectability as their companion but both were male. All three were smiling at the teenagers.

'How lucky – how lucky we are to *find* you,' the woman gushed, thrilled. 'My name's Daphne. That's Colin driving and that's Nigel. We've been looking for you.'

'For us?' Travis was baffled.

'For poor children like you. We've been driving around searching. Some ran away but some we've been able to help. Have you lost your parents?'

'If you mean are they dead,' replied Mel, grimacing, 'yes.'

'Oh, you poor things,' lamented the woman. 'You poor, poor, orphaned things.'

'You're the first adults we've seen in a while,' Travis said. 'Do you . . . have the Sickness?'

'Thankfully, not yet – and perhaps we won't.'

'You mean – there's a cure?'

'Trav, she said they can help us,' Simon reminded him excitedly. 'Didn't you, Daphne? I'm Simon, by the way. You said you can help us.'

'That's right, Simon,' the woman smiled. 'We can help you.'

'How?' Mel demanded bluntly.

'There's a group of us, a small group – uninfected adults. We've gathered in the local Conservative Club. We have a working radio there and we're receiving broadcasts from the authorities. There are medicines that have been developed, treatments for the Sickness. What's left of the army is mobilising. We've been able to get in touch with the local command and they'll be coming to evacuate us to safety by morning. By *morning.*'

'Travis,' Simon exulted, 'we're going to be all right.'

'That's why we've been roaming the streets, looking for young people to join with us, to come with us and wait for the army. Quickly, there's no time to lose.' She slid open the people carrier's side door. 'Climb inside.'

Simon was already on his way. For some reason, Travis remembered a kids' film he'd seen years ago. *Chitty Chitty Bang Bang.* The Child Catcher. *Lollipops today. Lovely lollipops. And all free.* And hope was even more seductive than sweets. 'Simon,' he snapped. 'Hold on.'

198

'Is something wrong?' the woman asked.

'Trav,' said Mel, 'when the army comes, maybe they can help Jessica recover.'

'Is pretty Jessica a little traumatised? One can hardly blame her. But yes, dear, I'm sure the medics will soon have her right as rain again.'

'Come *on,*' Mel urged, though Travis still stood firm.

'We have a police officer in our little group,' revealed the woman. 'At the club. If you're concerned about coming with us.'

'My dad was a police officer. What's this guy called?'

'It's – I'm not sure I can remember exactly,' sighed the woman. 'I only met him a few hours ago. I think . . .'

'Is it Peck?' Mel asked. She was keen to get Jessica inside the people carrier.

'I do believe it is,' recalled the woman cheerfully.

'Your Uncle Phil, Trav!' Mel said gleefully. 'He's alive!'

'Yes, that's right. Phil Peck. That's his name. Is he your uncle, Travis?'

'A family friend.' Why was he bothering with biographical details? The scene was becoming surreal, *un*real. But if Uncle Phil *was* alive . . . God, how he wanted to believe that. Something to hold on to. Someone to connect him to his own past. *And all free.*

'What a coincidence, Travis. What a wonderful coincidence,' the woman was saying delightedly. 'Your Uncle Phil. He's alive and he's waiting for you. Quickly, we can't waste time.'

'Come *on,* Trav.' Mel with Jessica, following after Simon.

'OK. OK.' And Travis clambered into the people carrier too. Why not? His shapeless suspicions were ludicrous, had to

199

be. Paranoia. Daphne and Colin and Nigel were pillars of the community, anyone could tell that simply by looking at them. He and the others were being escorted to the Conservative Club, where nothing more threatening than a game of darts or a debate over government economic policy ever took place. The authorities were on their way. Uncle Phil was waiting.

'All aboard,' chuckled the woman.

And slammed the door shut.

SEVEN

Wayvale Conservative Club was housed in a Georgian building that had survived unscathed through two centuries of social turbulence and change. It looked as if it might well outlast the Sickness, too. The large elegant windows and porticoed entrance appeared unaffected by events in the wider community. Glimmers of light flickered from within, the only illumination in a street otherwise entirely dark.

Stepping down from the people carrier, Travis thought he glimpsed blacker shapes slinking around in the night. But, like the niggling doubts still lurking at the back of his mind, they were unverifiable.

'Inside,' the woman called Daphne said, urgency in her tone. 'Quickly. Quickly.'

Colin thumped on the door and called out his name. The door opened. The teenagers were bustled inside.

Into a bar lit by an array of gas and paraffin lamps placed on tables and along the bar itself. Nobody was drinking. The eight or nine people present, all adults, slumped listlessly on stools and chairs like refugees whose spirits had been broken by unendurable experiences. When they saw the new arrivals, however, when they saw the youngsters, their mood changed. Dramatically. Glee suddenly glittered in their eyes. Slack lips twitched into expressions of pleasurable anticipation. They sprang to their feet. Those that could. Several were unable to move, were evidently already suffering in the advanced stages of the Sickness.

Travis scanned the occupants of the bar. Uncle Phil was not among them.

The smile that had been on Simon's face seemed to congeal there. Mel glanced behind her: Colin and Nigel were blocking the exit.

'You found some more. You found some more.' A bearded man in his forties, the early signs of the Sickness reddening his cheeks, stepped forward to study the teenagers with unsettling intensity. 'Well done, Mrs Spears.'

'Trav . . .' Mel sounded nervous.

'Oh, hi. We came because we were told there was a policeman here,' Travis said. To giggles from some of the adults. Who had them now pretty much surrounded. 'We were told that you were in touch with the authorities.' The adults' eyes told a different story. The bearded man shook his head and grinned. 'My Uncle Phil was supposed to be here,' Travis said.

'He isn't,' said the bearded man. 'But he left you a message.'

For the second time that day, Travis didn't see the punch coming.

And he must have blacked out. Maybe he'd struck his head against the bar or the floor as he'd gone down. He had to be unconscious or dreaming or something because he was sitting at home on the settee with his dad and his dad was wearing his uniform and the front of his shirt was sticky with his blood. Travis was pleased to see him, even so. 'You're back,' he said, but his father said, 'You can't go back, Travis. What's lost once is lost for ever. It can never be regained. You have to go forward. You have to go on.' And Travis said, 'But what if

202

I can't? It's so hard.' And his father said, 'You have to or *you*'ll be lost. Go forward, Travis. Go on.'

And that was when the ache in his skull dragged him back to awareness.

'Travis. *Travis.*' Mel's voice, sounding agonised.

'Here he is.' The bearded man.

'All right, Mel. I'm . . . OK.' *Relatively speaking.*

They were still in the bar. They were tied to chairs, backs to the wall in a row, Mel, Jessica and Simon to Travis's left. Their bags were in a pile nearby – not that it looked like the teenagers would be needing them any time soon. The adults were hovering over their captives, leering, rubbing their hands together. There was a hunger in them, an excitement. Faces that a week ago could have passed as those of stock-brokers or bank managers or politicians' wives, faces that would have defined respectability and moral rectitude, here now corrupted by a disease more fundamental even than the Sickness. By hatred. By malevolence. By envy. By fear.

It was doubtful whether Wayvale Conservative Club had played host to such a scene very often in its previous long history.

Travis struggled against his bonds but knew in an instant that he wouldn't be able to break them. He needed a knife.

'Nigel used to be a Scout Leader,' the bearded man said, 'when there were still young people of sufficient decency and discipline to want to be Scouts. He knows how to tie a knot. I wouldn't waste your strength if I were you.'

'What the hell is going on?' Travis attempted to disguise his own fear with fury. 'Why the hell are you—? Who *are* you people?'

'Let Jessica go, at least,' Mel pleaded. 'Whatever you do to us – can't you see she's not well?'

Jessica, though bound like the others, sat as uncomplainingly as she'd done when her arms were free.

'Please. We've done nothing. *Please*.' Simon's victim's whine was in full voice at the far end of the row. 'Let us go. I'll do *anything* . . .'

'Silence!' ordered the bearded man. 'Mindless prattle. Typical of teenagers today. So many words. So little to say. Do you not agree, Mrs Spears?'

'We could always cut out their tongues, Mr Hoskiss,' suggested Daphne Spears. 'I brought my kitchen scissors with me as well as my garden shears.'

'Perhaps . . . later,' considered the bearded man. 'We have yet to vote, remember.'

'Look, *look*,' said Travis, 'I don't know who you think we are or what you think you're doing, but there's no need for any of this. We're no threat to you if that's what you reckon. Just untie us and we'll be out of here. We won't even look back.'

'Let you go?' the bearded man mused. 'After all the trouble Mrs Spears and Colin and Nigel went to, luring you here in the first place? Oh, I don't think so.'

'They lied.' Travis's piercing eyes narrowed. 'There are no medicines. There are no troops arriving before morning. Are there?' And no Uncle Phil. Uncle Phil was dead. 'The whole thing was a trap and we fell for it.'

'You asked who we are, young man,' said Mr Hoskiss. 'I'll tell you. We are what used to be called the Silent Majority. We are the people who strove to lead honest, decent, law-abiding lives. We paid our taxes. We worked hard. We did our duty. We never complained or asked for anything from the state but the freedom to carry on our lives in peace and quiet.

And for so long we have been denied even that. For so long our lives have been blighted, ruined by the anti-social activities of the likes of *you*.' An accusing judgemental finger jabbed at Travis.

'You don't *know* me,' he protested. 'You don't know any of us.'

'I do. We do,' asserted the bearded man to a chorus of agreement. 'You're all the same. All of you. With your hooded sweatshirts and your baseball caps and your foul manners and your foul language and your wretched music blaring out and your contempt for everyone and everything except yourselves. *Kids*. Slouching, ignorant kids. Louts, vandals, hooligans, thugs, making the lives of respectable people a misery, leaving decent people too frightened to walk the streets at night, reducing the elderly to prisoners in their own homes while you rampage around in feral gangs, dealing drugs, creating havoc.'

'I tried to move on a group of you young yobs from outside my garden,' Daphne Spears put in bitterly. 'But you came back and you trampled all over my flower beds and you tore up my begonias.'

'That wasn't us,' Travis cried. 'Can't you understand?'

'You were kicking a ball against my car,' a man said. 'When I objected, you yelled abuse at me and ran off but later you smashed my lights and mirrors and scraped a key along the side of the car.'

'You broke the windows of my shop. Soon as I had them fixed, you broke them again . . .'

'You hang around in a gang on the corner of my street, drinking and swearing all hours of the night . . .'

'You attacked me and stole my pension as I was walking

home from the post office. I don't dare collect it myself now . . .'

Travis shouted above the clamouring voices. 'This is madness. You're all mad.'

'No,' snapped the bearded man. 'We *were* mad, perhaps, for tolerating it, the tyranny of the teenager. We might have been mad for allowing our neighbourhoods to decline into decay and despair. But we were given no support, remember. Our so-called representatives, the weak-willed authorities, they wouldn't help us, didn't care about us. They were always too busy making excuses for the monsters who were destroying our quality of life, too busy protecting the rights of criminals and thugs to worry about the sufferings of the Silent Majority. Because however pathetically little the likes of you learn in school these days, the hooligans always know their rights. Ah, and there were times when I thought things would never change,' sighed Mr Hoskiss. 'But they did. They have. The Sickness has come and the Sickness has made us sane.'

'Man,' said Travis, 'I don't reckon.'

'The unfairness of it brought us together, helped us to see what we should do, the sheer injustice of a disease that slaughters those of us who have behaved ourselves and led blameless existences while sparing the lives of *you*, the teenagers, the troublemakers, who steal and swear and run riot. Well, we may be dying, our values and our way of life may be coming to their end, but before we and they are gone we intend to fight against that injustice, to redress the balance, just a little.'

'What,' Travis asked, dreading the answer, 'do you mean?'

'No do-gooders to help you now,' the bearded man said, with mock sadness. 'No sociologists and psychologists and apologists to make excuses for you now.'

206

'What are you going to do?'

'Young man,' said Mr Hoskiss, 'we're going to make you suffer as we have suffered, as we made the *others* suffer.'

'Others?' Mel's voice was cold with foreboding. 'You've done this before?'

'Oh, yes, we're really quite practised at it now. We should have started a long time ago.'

'So where . . . ?' Mel wasn't sure she wanted to know.

'. . . Are they?' The bearded man lifted his eyes to the ceiling. 'Upstairs, of course. When we've finished with them, we put them upstairs. And they've plenty of room for company.'

Which was more than Simon could bear. He screamed, babbled incoherently, though words such as 'no' and 'please' and 'I'm sorry' seemed very much to the fore. He thrashed against his bonds, toppled the whole chair sideways, crashed to the floor. The ropes loosened but did not come undone. He and his chair were heaved upright again by several of the more helpful members of the Silent Majority. Nigel even settled Simon's glasses firmly back on his nose. 'You don't want to break these,' he advised. 'You want to be able to see what's happening.'

'Sufficient explanation, I think, Mr Chairman,' said Daphne Spears. 'I propose we move to the vote.'

'Mrs Spears has proposed a vote,' announced Mr Hoskiss. 'Do we have a seconder?' The man whose car had been vandalised. 'Very well, then the newly elected committee of the Wayvale Conservative Club will vote on the matter before us: should these young hooligans in our charge be made to suffer?'

'Wait. *Wait*,' implored Travis desperately. '*Listen*. I understand your feelings, your fear . . .'

207

'This one never shuts up, Mr Chairman,' observed Colin. 'Perhaps for the next group we capture we should consider gags.'

Ignoring him, Travis persevered. There had to be some part of the adults' brutalised minds that still responded to reason. He had to reach it. If he couldn't, then he and Mel and Jessica and Simon were going to die. 'I can understand your resentment. The Sickness *isn't* fair. It hasn't been fair to us, either. We've lost parents, people we love. But abducting kids, looking for some kind of revenge, this isn't the way. There were – are – bad kids, sure, I don't deny anything you've said. How can I? But there are good kids, too, kids who believe in the same values you do, who want to work hard and make something of their lives. We're not all the same.'

'You all look the same to me,' said Mrs Spears icily.

'We can help you. You can help us. We have to come together to build, not to destroy. If we don't we're finished, all of us.' One final appeal: 'We have to be *better* than this.'

Travis's gaze bored into the chairman's, but Hoskiss's eyes were as emotionless as glass. 'How does the committee vote?' he said.

'Make them suffer,' snarled Mrs Daphne Spears.

'Suffer.' And Colin.

'Suffer.' And Nigel.

And, in turn, the others.

'I vote for suffering, too,' concluded Mr Hoskiss, 'which makes the decision unanimous. Fetch the implements, please.'

From behind the bar, snooker cues, some of which were already cracked or split, an assortment of household cutlery, stained with what might have been rust, two sets of darts, minus their flights, a pair of garden shears.

'My God, this is real.' Mel fervently wished otherwise. 'This is really happening. *Trav*.'

'I know. I know.' Flexing his muscles, failing to make any impression on the ropes. Out of the corner of his eye, a chalk-written notice reminding patrons of the 1960s and 1970s disco to be held at the club on Saturday night – get your tickets early. Simon wailing thinly. Jessica thankfully oblivious.

'Who first, Mrs Spears?' the chairman asked politely.

'What about the blonde girl? Perhaps a little attention will help her find her voice.'

'Don't you touch her!' Travis raged, straining forward. 'Touch her and I'll—'

'You'll what, young man?' chuckled Mrs Spears.

It was then they heard the revving of a powerful engine from the street outside. Approaching. More than a dozen pairs of eyes shot to the window. As the metal frame of a Land Rover smashed shatteringly through it, showering the bar with glass and demolishing half the wall. The vehicle appeared to be driverless, but it wasn't hard to guess the likely owners.

Maybe those whose voices now bombarded the air in whoops of eager belligerence, those who burst through the front entrance, beating aside the man on guard there, bludgeoning him with staves and clubs, those marauding into the bar area from the rear as well, brandishing crude but deadly weapons of their own, lurching in and out of the lamplight like crazy hallucinations. Male and female. Tattooed. Pierced. Spiked hair. Studded jackets. Ripped jeans. T-shirts bearing obscene slogans. Kids the same age as the quartet of captives but free to do as they pleased.

The Silent Majority's worst nightmare.

It seemed as though the meeting was over. The adults scattered as soon as the invaders appeared, none of them even thinking of standing their ground. Outnumbered and, so to speak, outgunned, it wouldn't have made much difference anyway. They fled towards the doors, the sicker members of the committee yanked and dragged into retreat by their more mobile fellows. Mr Hoskiss was struck a few times about the head and shoulders, Mrs Spears helped on her way by a series of slaps to her rear, but essentially the teenagers were content to let their elders go, hurling only mockeries and insults after them, like stones. Within moments the raiders were in swaggering, exultant and total control of what had once been the Wayvale Conservative Club.

They turned their attention to the four prisoners.

'Cut them loose,' ordered one of the boys. He was tall, well-built, seventeen, a throwback to the glory days of punk rock. He could have played with the Sex Pistols, his blond hair as jagged as a broken bottle, a contemptuous sneer in permanent possession of his features. In the centre of his forehead the letter J had been tattooed; the same letter had been inscribed on both cheeks. Their liberators' leader, Travis assumed.

Certainly his companions obeyed him. A dreadlocked girl promptly dashed forward to slice at Travis's bonds with a knife. To his far left, a boy so smothered with piercings he looked almost as if he was wearing chain mail performed the same service for Simon.

'Looks like we owe you some thanks,' said Travis cautiously. While their rescuers were welcome, part of him could quite understand the adults' response. 'A lot of thanks.'

'You owe me, yeah,' said the punk.

'They were gonna *kill* us.' Mel sounded more offended now than afraid. 'They were actually going to – people you see doing their gardens on summer afternoons. It's unbelievable. You want to be chasing after them and giving them some of their own medicine.'

'We didn't come for them,' the punk said, shrugging. 'Fogeys are nothing now. We came for you.'

And even as the ropes binding Travis fell away, he felt other, invisible restraints tightening around him. 'Name's Travis,' he said, standing. 'Travis Naughton. That's Mel, Jessica and Simon.'

'Jester,' said the punk. 'And these are my people.'

I'll bet they are, thought Travis, as the dreadlocked girl, having released Mel, twined herself around Jester's body. *And some more than others*. 'Well, we appreciate your help.'

'Those lunatics told us we weren't the first,' Mel added, rising to her feet herself. 'They said their previous victims – what's left of their previous victims – are upstairs. Maybe – they might still be alive.'

'Garth,' ordered Jester. Obediently, one of the band – greasy-haired, ferret-faced – left to investigate.

'How did you actually know we were here?' Travis asked.

'Surveillance. Like in the war. We've been watching this place for a while, just waiting to build up enough of a force to make our move and take it. Adults got no right to be here any more.' Jester's eyes glittered like knives caught in the light. 'This part of town belongs to *us* now.'

The old line about frying pans and fires came rather disturbingly to Travis's mind.

'What's the matter with Blondie?' the boy freeing Jessica asked.

211

'Nothing.' Mel put her arms around her friend and helped her up. 'She'll be all right.'

'Looks like she's on a one-way trip to dreamland to me,' observed the boy. 'Not much use to us, J.'

Jester thought for a moment. 'We'll take her along anyway.'

'What?' whimpered Simon. On reflection, he wasn't sure he hadn't preferred the company of the adults. At least they'd *looked* normal and surely, with names like Colin and Nigel and Daphne, they wouldn't *really* have done them any harm. 'Are we going somewhere?'

'You know we are, Simon,' Travis said steadily. 'We're going to Willowstock, to my grandparents'. They're our bags over there.' All for Jester's benefit as much as for Simon's. 'And thanks again for the nick-of-timer but we want to be as far out of town as possible by morning so we really need to get started.'

'I don't think so,' said Jester.

'Excuse me?'

'You getting started. Don't be hasty. Not after the nasty little ordeal you've just been through. No need to race off already, still stressed, is there? Come with us. You won't believe where we're living. Get some sleep, some hot food inside you. Chill for a bit.'

'Thanks, but—'

'Travis, mate, I *insist*.' And of course, Travis's group was presently even more of a minority than the adults had been. 'Besides, I have a little proposition for you all . . .'

'Hot food sounds good to me, Travis,' Simon urged, with an eye on the blade that had severed his bonds.

'I don't know . . .'

'You owe me,' Jester pointed out casually. Before Travis

212

could respond, Garth returned from his expedition upstairs, looking decidedly paler than he had when he'd set out: he shook his head with finality. 'Looks like you *really* owe me,' Jester said.

Travis had no choice. 'OK,' he said reluctantly. 'We'll come with you.'

Until the Sickness, the Landmark Hotel had been the premier place to stay in Wayvale. Behind its stylish modern façade were over a hundred elegant rooms and suites, a health club and spa, a bar, a lounge, and two award-winning restaurants – all of which, however, really needed staff and electricity to be experienced at their best. In the absence of both, the hotel was little more than a shadow of its former splendour, a gloomy ghost. Since the weekend, business had been sort of slow.

'We did find some guests,' Jester informed Travis and his companions as he led them into the lobby, 'but they were in no state to check out. We shifted them all to the upper floors. I wouldn't go up there if I were you.'

'I see the Landmark has a new kind of clientele now,' Mel noted.

The lobby area, the lounge, the bar, were all infested by kids dressed in dark colours who looked like a larger breed of rat. Most, to be fair, seemed happy enough to be here, gathered around lamps and playing cards or chatting or simply staring numbly into space, lesser versions of Jessica, no parents around to tell anyone that it was way past their bedtimes. Many, though, were trying to get to sleep, curled up on chairs or on the floor, perhaps because with sleep might come forgetfulness.

213

A number of older teenagers, conducting themselves more aggressively, more like guards than anything else, seemed to be patrolling the premises, possibly due to the presence of a third distinct grouping under the Landmark's roof, a largely younger element who huddled together, bewildered at best, fearful at worst, not really understanding the convoluted series of events that had ultimately deprived them of their former homes and delivered them to this sumptuous yet soulless surrogate instead. Snatches of laughter could be heard from various places but so could sobs.

'How have the mighty fallen,' commented Jester coldly. 'A week ago the people who ran this hotel would have called the cops if the likes of me had even passed by the front doors. Garth here used to scavenge through the scraps left outside the kitchens for food, didn't you, Garth? But a week is a long time now there's the Sickness. *We* run the place now. The Landmark is going to be our base of operations.'

'What operations?' said Travis.

Jester appeared not to have heard. 'The ovens are gas so all the while we're being supplied we can still light them. You can eat later. We're bringing stuff in from foraging expeditions – food, lighting, whatever we need. That's ongoing. What we need most of all, though, is people. *Our* kind of people.'

'So are we your kind of people?' Mel said.

'You're sure mine,' grinned Garth suggestively.

'Oh, please.' Even the Sickness, Mel thought, didn't change everything.

'That's what we need to talk about,' said Jester. 'Come through to my office.'

Which turned out to be the manager's office, though Mr

214

Leonard Evans, as the nameplate on the door read, was unlikely to be returning to work to reclaim the room for himself. Jester lounged behind the desk while Travis's group sat a little more warily in front of it. Garth, the dreadlocked girl and a couple of others leaned against the wall by the door. Taking no chances, Travis realised.

'You want a drink?' Jester offered, indicating a cabinet to his right. 'There's all sorts in there. Whisky, gin, vodka, a bottle of that blue stuff they use in cocktails for the rich and famous. I reckon there'll be a lot of that going to waste now that the rich and famous are pretty much extinct. Serves 'em right, too, I say. I'm not wasting my time shedding a tear for the death of the haves. When they were alive they didn't give a toss about us.'

'Kids?' Travis said.

'The have-*nots*. That's who we are, Travis, mate.' Jester smiled. 'All of us who saved your lives, me, Garth, Kelly, all of us. We're society's dirty little secret. The kids nobody wanted. The homeless. The runaways. The street kids. Those rejected and abandoned by their parents, neglected and ignored by social services, tossed into care like prisoners into jail. A generation lost.'

'Things were all right for me,' said Garth from the door, 'until my mum took up with a new boyfriend and he moved in. He made it pretty damn clear she had to choose between him and me. She chose him. I've been living on the streets ever since.'

'My dad used to be a member of that club we rescued you from,' said the girl with dreadlocks. 'For all I know he might still be. I haven't seen him in a year – not since he took offence at the company and the hours I was keeping and threw me out.'

'My olds thought they could lay down the law, force me to do what they wanted so I thought, stuff that . . .'

'My dad abused me and nobody would listen. I had to get out, I *had* to . . .' Travis noticed Mel wince.

'And my own example.' Jester. 'Passed from one care home to another like a parcel nobody wanted to open. Spending my childhood in loneliness and fear. Learning quickly never to show those feelings. Learning to repress them, to cover them up in case they made you seem weak. Laugh and joke instead. At everything. I became an expert in laughter. That's why they nicknamed me Jester. But I was learning other things, too, about politics and power, anarchy and revolution. I read books. I dreamed. And when I couldn't stand it in so-called care any longer I did a runner to the streets, became Jester for real. And I'm laughing for real now, too, because street kids might have been the lost generation once but now we are most definitely found. The world has turned upside down and those who were at the bottom are now at the top. Our time has come.'

'I'm not sure I'm with you,' Travis said.

'No?' Jester was sceptical. 'Then let me make myself clearer. Your friend Jessica, for instance. Her present condition – caused by the shock of her parents' deaths as well as the collapse of the world she's known. Am I right? She did have parents, of course, two of them, married. Right again? And they loved her, didn't they, and they loved each other, and they owned two cars and bought Jessica nice clothes and all the latest gadgets and gave her everything she wanted and they went to Florida for their holidays . . .'

'OK. OK.' Travis resented the scornful manner in which Jester was – with a somehow belittling accuracy – sum-

216

marising Jessica's life. It had been a good life. It wasn't her fault that Jester and so many others born to inadequates undeserving of parenthood had been denied one like it. He saw that Mel evidently felt the same. 'You don't have to go on.'

'So I'm right, though,' Jester gloated. 'More or less.'

'You're trying to turn Jessie into a cliché,' Mel protested. 'But she's not a stereotype. She's herself and there's no one like her.'

'At this moment in time,' Jester said, perusing the vacant, expressionless face of the blonde girl, 'I'm sure that's true. But the point I want to make is this. With adult authority removed, kids of our age are going to become the new leaders. But *which* kids? It won't be the likes of Jessica here, in a trance or out. Their upbringing will have been too soft, too weak, too middle-class. They'll be too traumatised by the loss of their parents to look after themselves, let alone plan and organise for others. They'll be no use to anyone. Case in point' – gesturing dismissively at Jessica – 'no offence intended.'

Maybe not intended, Travis thought. *But taken*.

'No, it's people like me who hold the future in their hands, street kids like me. Do you know how hard it is to survive on the streets?' Mel guessed, not too sympathetically, that it must be very, very hard. 'You don't *know*,' Jester scoffed, 'but you're going to find out. Everyone is going to find out. Because thanks to the Sickness, the streets have become the world, and those who are used to the struggle for survival will shape it, those of us who have had no choice but to become strong and self-reliant already. We have no families to mourn – we left them behind us long ago. We have no adjustments to make.

217

Street kids are better equipped to take charge now than anybody. And that is precisely what I – we – intend to do. For the first time ever, those who were powerless will truly seize power. Welcome to the revolution.'

'But what are you going to do?' Travis sat forward. 'With the power.'

'Our *operations*,' Jester grinned. 'First, we have claimed ownership of this part of town – as I told you – and we will remove from it any surviving adults and any kids unwilling to accept our rightful role as leaders. Then we will begin to rule our territory.'

'Who for?' Travis demanded, more confrontationally now. 'Assuming you can get that far, Jester, who will you rule *for*?'

'Travis,' Simon cautioned him in a sickly voice, 'I don't think now is the time for a political discussion.'

But his friend persisted. 'For everyone? For the good of all?'

'*Trav*.' Even Mel hissed at him to be quiet.

But Jester burst into laughter, mocking and malicious. 'For everyone? Of course not, Travis. We'll be putting ourselves first. We'll be ruling for our own benefit. Like the adults' governments always did. After years of skulking in alleys and shelters, of being disowned and denied, it's the least we deserve, the very least.' The punk's features hardened again. 'And if you're our kind of people, you'll agree with that. You'll want to join us. I'm *inviting* you to join us. That is my proposition. Work with us. Be part of our movement. Help us claim the world in the name of the dispossessed.'

Travis sat back and shook his head. He'd known his answer all along. It was the only answer he could give. 'No.'

'Travis,' groaned Simon.

Jester frowned. 'I think I must have misheard.'

'You didn't: I said no. You're not interested in the dispossessed, Jester. You're only interested in what you can get out of them. A community founded on that basis won't last – it can't last – and I want nothing to do with it. Answer's no.'

'So's mine. A big, fat, in-your-face no.' Mel leaned over and planted a wet, supportive kiss on Travis's cheek.

'I won't ask Little Miss Middle Class what she thinks,' Jester said icily. 'What about you?' To Simon.

Who was fearfully aware of Travis and Mel's expectant stares on him. All of Simon's life experience so far had taught him that the wisest course was always to agree with those who were stronger than you, that by doing so you minimised the risk of ending up hurt. That same experience had taught him nothing about siding with friends against an enemy, however strong, primarily because Simon Satchwell had never had friends. So far. 'N-no,' he mumbled.

'Speak up,' growled Jester.

'No. I don't want to – you know . . .' And when he saw the relief, the appreciation, the *respect* in Travis and Mel's eyes he could have cried. Or maybe it was simply terror bringing the tears.

'So,' said Travis briskly, 'if that means we're done, it's thanks again but we ought to be leaving. If we can just have our things . . .'

'I think,' mused Jester, 'you should stay a little longer.'

At a glance from their leader, the other teenagers moved in menacingly towards Travis's group. They still carried the makeshift weapons they'd used at the Conservative Club.

Travis rose to his feet regardless. 'We said no. We meant no.'

'Ah, but "no" was the wrong answer,' Jester said, and tutted.

Mel stood too. 'Are you threatening us?'

'Threatening? Hardly.' The punk seemed offended at the suggestion. 'I'm giving you an opportunity. To come up with the *right* answer. Garth, Kelly, the rest of you – take our guests somewhere quiet where they can have a bit of a think. The honeymoon suite might be nice for them.'

Simon was hauled from his chair but found enough courage to protest. Jessica would have been manhandled too if Mel hadn't stepped in to protect her first. 'You put your hands on either of us, pal,' she warned ferret-faced Garth, 'and you'll find out what it's like surviving in a post-Sickness world with broken fingers.'

A glare from Travis had the same deterrent effect on a leather-jacketed youth about to grab his shoulder. He redirected his gaze to Jester. 'Why is this so important to you? There are only four of us. You've got ten times as many kids with you already. Why can't you just let us go?'

'Because if I let you go now, you'd have defied me and got away with it,' said Jester. 'I can't have that, Travis, mate. What leader can maintain his authority if he lets those who defy him get away with it? No, you're staying. And if you've got any sense, which I think you have, you're changing your minds.'

'And what if we don't?'

'Then, Travis, mate, you'll wish we'd left you to the tender mercies of the fogeys. We'll talk again in the morning. And you'd better have the right answer for me. For all your sakes.'

The honeymoon suite boasted a four-poster bed, not that its

four prisoners had any interest in sleeping arrangements. Garth, after some eyelash-fluttering cajoling from Mel, agreed to leave them an oil lamp, so at least they could see each other in the gloom. Travis preferred to slump beyond its rim of yellow light. Darkness matched his mood.

'What's up, Trav?' Mel probed, having laid Jessica down on the four-poster. 'Or is that a stupid question?'

'Nothing you say is ever stupid, Mel.' Travis smiled faintly.

'Mm. Compliments. You want to throw in a declaration of undying love there as well before we face the executioner tomorrow?'

'Mel, don't joke.' Simon shuddered. 'It's not a laughing matter. I know bullies when I meet one, believe me, and this Jester means what he says. We're in serious trouble.'

'Then we'll seriously get out of it. Won't we, Trav?'

'It's not just what happens to us that worries me,' Travis sighed.

'Speak for yourself,' Simon muttered in the background.

'It's Jester's whole agenda. Power for its own sake. *Ruling* – he uses the word "rule" like he wants to be king or something, a dictator. Dictating to kids. Exploiting and intimidating children. He's no better than the adults at the club. All of them settling old scores, giving in to violence. Like savages. They've lost their way.'

'OK,' Mel said. 'You're right. But what can we do about it?'

'We mustn't lose *our* way. We mustn't become like Jester or Hoskiss. We have to remember what it is to be human. And we have to find others who want to remember that, too.'

'We're not gonna find them here, Trav,' Mel said.

'No.'

221

'Listen, though,' Simon interrupted. 'I've got an idea. I mean, when Jester comes for us in the morning, why don't we just tell him we *have* changed our minds? Make out we're onside, that we agree with him. Keep breathing. Then, later, you know, we can just sneak off and head for Travis's grand-parents' place as planned. What do you think?'

'Could work, Simon,' Travis admitted. 'But one problem. I'm not supporting a thug like Jester, not even in – jest. No way. When he comes for us in the morning, we won't be here.'

Travis crossed to the window. The honeymoon suite was on the third floor. Staring down was like peering into a deep well, with bone-cracking concrete waiting at the bottom. Jumping for it was out.

'Maybe we could tear the sheets from the bed into, like, strips and kind of knot them together and lower ourselves down that way,' Mel suggested. 'They do it in movies.'

'Sadly, we're not living in a movie.' Travis turned towards the door. 'There's only one way out. The way we came in.'

'But Garth and that kid with the piercings are standing guard.'

Which was why, several minutes later, Mel was tapping speculatively at the door. 'Garth,' she whispered, her face close to the wood, 'are you there? It's me, Mel.'

'Shut up.' A gruff response from the corridor outside.

'But Garth, I want – I need to talk to you. Please. Pretty please.'

'If you want something to eat, forget it. Jester's orders. You might think smarter on an empty stomach.'

'Oh, Garth,' Mel breathed, hoping for seductively husky rather than croakingly sore-throated, 'I don't want food. I want *you*.'

222

Was it possible to actually *hear* a gulp? If so, Mel did. 'Me?'

'*You*, Garth. And I know you want me, too. Let me out. We can be together.'

'I can't.' Dread and desire competing for control. 'Jester said—'

'Jester doesn't have to know.'

'But before, in the office' – the boy's voice closer now, the two of them a door's thickness away from a kiss – 'you told me to keep my hands off.'

'It's called playing hard to get,' Mel improvised, 'and I'm bored with it now. I'd rather play – *other* games. You-and-me kind of games. And we can't do that if I'm in here and you're out there.' And heavy breathing. Surprising how the sound of that could travel. 'Are you alone?'

'Sid's with me.' The pierced guy.

'Can he hear us now?'

'No.'

'So get rid of him. We don't want him to see . . .'

'See what?'

'How'd you like to find out?'

A pause. Mel glanced worriedly across to a grinning Travis who nodded, indicating that she was doing fine.

'How do I know this isn't a trick?' Garth back again. Mel could almost see him licking his thin, ferrety lips. 'If I unlock the door, how do I know your mates won't try to rush me?'

'They're asleep,' Mel lied, 'and they're not my mates, not any more. I like *you* now, Garth. Anyway, you're armed, aren't you? Mm, a boy who's good with a weapon turns me *on*.'

'Wait. Wait a minute.' Audibly eager now.

Mel heard him barking orders at somebody, presumably his pierced partner. She only hoped they were the right kind of orders. When Garth resumed by instructing her to stand back from the door, she knew they were. A thumbs-up to Travis and Simon sent them scurrying into the bedroom and out of sight.

The key in the lock. Door and frame parting with the reluctance of lovers.

'Oh, *Garth*.' Mel passing through.

Her stare fixed itself on the boy's, though she could still make out, in the corridor lit by a single lamp placed on the floor, that the two of them were indeed alone. Wherever Garth had sent his comrade, she trusted he'd be a while coming back.

'Thank you. *Thank* you,' she pouted as Garth locked the door again. He was using a pass key. That made matters easier. The short iron bar he was also holding, like a cosh, did not.

'Yeah, you *can* thank me, baby.' The ferret features trying to look manly and mature. Failing dismally, but what the heck.

'Oh, I *want* to thank you.' Mel flung her arms around the boy's neck and thrust her body, her lips, against his. She couldn't afford to hold back now.

'. . . Blimey . . .' Garth was almost smothered.

'Do you know how I'd *really* like to thank you, big boy?' Mel teased.

'No.' Gasping. 'How?'

'Just like this.' Mel's knee was thin and bony. It wasn't a portion of her anatomy to which Garth might immediately be attracted. But she let him feel it anyway. Very, very hard.

The ferret face registered pain and surprise in equal measure. As he doubled up, Mel swung him round, hammered his head against the wall. Then his expression was limited to pain. Mel didn't stop, didn't dare let up. Garth's nose kind of burst at the third or fourth impact, blotting the paintwork with blood. The cosh slipped from his hand. Mel retrieved it, felt both afraid of it and empowered by it. Her gorge and a sob rising in her throat together, she brought the bar down on Garth's spiky-haired skull. Not hard enough. Even as he subsided slowly to the floor his twitching hand groped blindly towards her like a lizard's tongue. Clenching her teeth, Mel struck at him again. At last, unconsciousness.

Knocking someone out was another thing that looked easier in the movies.

Gladly, Mel dropped the cosh. Hastily, she grabbed the key.

Travis and Simon were waiting just inside the door with Jessica between them. Simon was also carrying the lamp.

'I did it. I – hope I haven't killed him.'

Simon grunted. 'Let's hope you have.'

Travis gave possession of Jessica back to Mel and knelt by the crumpled guard's side. He felt for a pulse. 'He'll live,' he reassured the goth girl. 'But he'll have one hell of a headache. And he might well need a nose job. You did good, Mel.'

'Wasting time on him,' muttered Simon, panicking. 'If we're caught again *now* . . .'

'We won't be.' Travis snatched up the lamp in the corridor. 'Fire exit and three flights of stairs and we're out of here.'

'What about our bags? Our supplies?'

'Jester'll have to send them on, Mel. Let's go.'

'Shouldn't we take Garth's cosh with us?'

'Mel, you want to use it again, feel free.'

She left the iron bar where it was.

225

They'd have done better in the stairwell had they been favoured with greater light or not been encumbered by a catatonic Jessica. Even so, they reached the ground-floor fire exit without any sign of pursuit. 'Let's hope it's not locked or anything,' Travis said. Lamp in one hand, with the other he pressed down on the bar across the door.

Which *wasn't* locked or anything. The teenagers emerged into an alley at the rear of the hotel. 'Jester's previous lodgings,' Mel remarked. They dumped the lamps. Now they needed the dark.

'. . . Thank you thank you thank you . . .' Simon clasped his hands together and lifted his eyes to the night.

Then they heard the shouts, the fury in the shouts, spilling out from the Landmark's main entrance into the surrounding streets, reverberating down the stairwell behind them.

'There's our cue,' said Mel.

They ran. Away from the voices. Other than that, direction didn't matter. Only swiftness mattered. Only establishing as much of a head start as possible. Maybe Jester's people wouldn't spot them. Maybe they'd be fine.

Maybe the world would be back to normal tomorrow.

'There they are! I see them!' As the fugitives broke cover, the roars of a mob became the cries of pursuers.

Not far away, the headlights of a parked car blazed into life.

Travis pelted down the middle of the road, glanced back over his shoulder. Two dozen or more street kids zeroing in on them. Impossible to identify Jester but he was certainly there. He'd want to punish personally and severely so public an affront to his authority as an escape attempt. Likely he'd get his chance. Simon was just about keeping pace with

Travis, but Jessica was hopeless. Mel was holding her hand and had her running, but the blonde girl was doing so without urgency, without any survival instinct.

Jester and his gang were closing.

'Come on. Come *on.*' Travis slowed to grip Jessica's other arm and to speed her along with him. She stumbled and almost fell.

'She can't go any faster,' Mel protested, as if Travis was at fault.

'She'll have to.'

'She *can't*. You'll . . . leave us. You and Simon go, Trav. They won't hurt us. We're girls. But you . . .'

'Not an option.'

Simon was almost jumping up and down, torn between fleeing and staying, between self-preservation and solidarity. 'Please. Travis. Mel. We can't wait.' He could hear their pursuers' words now. They weren't intended for a family audience.

He could hear the car, too – the large silver Volvo, gleaming in the dark, that suddenly seemed to appear from nowhere, accelerating manically towards them from behind the street kids. It would have ploughed right through the youths if they hadn't leaped and dived out of the way. Headlights dazzling them, the vehicle squealed to a halt only yards in front of the fugitives.

'What the hell . . . ?' Travis squinted against the glare.

The driver was poking his baseball-capped head out of the window.

'Yo, Naughton, Morticia. Fancy a lift?' yelled Richie Coker.

EIGHT

'Richie?' said Mel.

'Coker?' said Travis.

Simon said nothing.

Yet the bully was beckoning. 'Well, if you're gonna get in, get *in*. We haven't got all night.' Behind the Volvo, Jester and his supporters were on their feet again, their mood not improved by their close encounter with the tarmac. 'Doesn't look like we've got all *minute*. Come *on*. I'm not hanging around to be massacred by these morons.'

It had developed into a night, Travis reflected grimly, of very few choices.

'Let's move,' he snapped, jerking Jessica towards the car, Mel alongside her.

'But Travis . . .' Indignant protest in Simon's voice.

'Simon, there's no *time*.' Travis was already bundling the girls into the back seat.

And Simon knew that Travis was right. It was just that when he looked at the heavy, brutish features of Richie Coker he didn't see a rescuer, he saw a tormentor. But he was cramming himself up against Jessica even as Travis scrambled into the front passenger seat.

'Accelerator's the one on the right,' the brown-haired boy prompted.

'You don't say,' said Richie Coker, grinning.

The first fists pounded on the rear window. Fingers groped for the door handles – and were nearly torn off as Richie stamped his foot on the gas and the Volvo surged forward, so suddenly that everyone was thrown back in their seats. Not that they cared. Their transport's speed reduced their pursuers to impotent threats and lobbed chunks of concrete that fell harmlessly short. Richie took a left – in a manner that would have failed him his driving test – and put Jester out of sight, if not entirely out of mind.

'Hey, Simes,' he called back cheerily, 'shouldn't you be tucked up in bed with a hot-water bottle by now?'

'Shut up,' Simon whined. 'Shut *up*. Tell him, Travis.'

'What?' Richie huffed. 'Is that any way to talk to the guy who's probably just saved your sorry lives? Where is the gratitude?'

'Yeah, thanks for stealing a car, Richie,' put in Mel. 'Though I guess you've had a lot of practice.'

'How come you were outside the Landmark in the first place, Richie?' asked Travis.

'Yeah. If you'd been *in*side with those goons we wouldn't have been surprised,' Mel said. 'Scumbags stick together.'

'If you want to know,' Richie said, a hint of defensiveness in his voice, 'I was tossing up whether to join that lot or not.'

'Yeah, they beat up on people,' Simon said bitterly. 'You'd have fitted right in.'

'But, Simes, when I heard more about this Jester guy and what he was planning and that kind of stuff, I thought, this guy's a loony. Teaming up with him might be more trouble than it's worth. I was parked in the street, thinking should I, shouldn't I, when I saw you four being marched inside. I knew Mr Self-Righteous here wouldn't stick with Jester for long so I waited for you to come out again. Took longer than I thought. You pissed Jester off in the end, though, Naughton, huh?' Travis declined to answer. 'Anyway, thought I'd help you out. Richie-to-the-rescue kind of thing. For old times' sake.'

'Yeah. Well. Thanks,' Travis said grudgingly. 'But these are *new* times now. No more smart remarks at Simon's expense. No more bullying – full stop.'

'Don't push your luck, Naughton – don't start trying to tell me what to do. You owe me.'

'That's just what Jester said. I didn't listen to him, either.'

'You piss me off, I stop the car – and you get out, all of you.'

'There's a nice big parking space available by the kerb just there, Richie. If you feel like pulling over.'

'No. No. I was just saying. You're all right. For now.' And this time it wasn't defensiveness in Richie's tone, but something else. If the speaker hadn't been Richie Coker, Travis might have suspected it to be fear. 'I've got the wheels. I might as well drive you – where?'

Mel leaned forward. 'We're going to Wil—'

'Out of town.' Travis cut her off. 'Just get us out of town, Richie.'

'Without a please?' Richie Coker grunted. 'What happened to your manners, Naughton?'

But he drove on anyway. Through streets where the only light flickered yellow in the flames of burning cars and buildings, streets that slithered with dark and secret movements, like snakes. One road was too dangerous to negotiate, the buildings on both sides ablaze like a scene from the Blitz.

Another was physically impossible to traverse, blocked by vehicles that had tried earlier to retreat from Wayvale but had failed. They were now almost all either alight or already reduced to the cremated shells of their former glories; a sickly, stomach-churning reek rose from the cars and vans that smelled – and the occupants of the Volvo didn't want to think about it – more like burned meat than scorched metal and incinerated fabrics.

Occasionally other cars flashed by, usually large or expensive or both, usually packed with joyriders flourishing bottles and whooping, cheering, trying to tempt the Volvo into a race or to intimidate it by seeming to threaten to ram it before they lost interest and zigzagged away as if the vehicles themselves were inebriated and unable to proceed in a straight line. And sometimes the group passed kids on foot. Some of them gave chase, either begging for help or displaying naked, inexplicable hostility.

'Don't stop,' Travis instructed, 'for anyone. Don't even slow down. There's nothing we can do here.' Richie didn't need to be told. He didn't even stop for the girl with the screaming baby in her arms who suddenly appeared from nowhere directly in front of the car. He swerved, missed them, resumed the journey. 'There's nothing we can do here,' Travis repeated, as if defending himself against unvoiced criticism. 'Not now.'

Eventually they gained the outskirts of Wayvale. Clearly the authorities had attempted to impose quarantine as they'd announced. The road out of town was guarded by police cars and military vehicles which now stood redundant and unoccupied like pieces on a chess board in a game that would never be played. The barriers that no doubt were to have been erected were stacked up on the roadside. For some strange reason, Richie crept slowly past these relics of the old order, as if he was driving a hearse on its way to a funeral; the teenagers barely breathed. Only when they were through and beyond did the group utter a collective sigh of relief. Richie pressed down again on the accelerator.

They stopped at a vantage point overlooking the town where, a lifetime ago – last week – lovers might also have come to get away from the mundane concerns of everyday life, perhaps to plan their futures together. They probably hadn't bargained for the Sickness.

Everybody got out of the car except Jessica.

'Hey, Jessica, sorry about gatecrashing your party.' Richie, willing to build bridges. 'Too much cheap cider. It goes straight to— Hey, what's the matter with Blondie?' Leaning inside the car where she sat silently staring into space.

'Get away from her, Richie.' Mel pulled him back, cracking his head against the car roof as she did.

'What's the matter with *you*?'

'You keep away from Jessie,' Mel warned, 'or it'll be what's the matter with *you*. Understand?'

'Actually, no.'

'All right, Mel,' Travis intervened. 'Richie might as well know.' To the best of his ability, he explained Jessica's condition.

'Too bad,' Richie responded, unable to repress a leer. 'But if she wants help getting undressed for bed, you know, I'd be willing to pitch in.'

Mel snorted with contempt. 'That's your level, isn't it, Richie? You make me sick.'

'Let's just go, Travis,' urged Simon from behind the other

boy, a wary, distrustful eye on his former persecutor. 'We don't want anything to do with yobs like Richie.'

'Simes, old mate,' Richie protested aggrievedly, 'I'm hurt. And here was I thinking we were friends.'

'No, you weren't,' Simon retorted.

'No, you're right. I wasn't. But I was thinking, go *where*? Where are you all gonna go? On foot? And what with? You don't look very prepared, Naughton, and you're in charge, yeah? I'd have expected better from you. I mean, you must have been a Scout once, right? Good deed every day. Dib dib dib. All that shit.'

Travis smiled wryly. 'We had to part company with our packs back at the Landmark, but we'll get by. There'll be places we can find food, clothes, whatever. Plenty of goods in the shops.'

'Yeah, but why put yourself out' – Richie winked, going round to the back of the car – 'when I've got everything you want right here.' He opened the boot. Unlike in Joe Drake's car, petrol cans were about the only commodity the storage space *didn't* contain. Food, drink, blankets, clothes (boys', at any rate), candles, lamps, tools, a whole range of other items.

Travis had to concede – though he didn't show it – that the bully had chosen his supplies wisely. 'And you're willing to share your little haul with us, Richie – is that what you're saying?' He sounded sceptical.

'Sure,' Richie nodded, and slammed down the boot lid. 'On one condition.'

'Don't listen to him, Travis,' implored Simon. 'You can't trust him.'

'What's the condition?'

'Wherever you're heading – 'cause I'm betting you've got somewhere in mind – I come with you.'

'What?' A demand Travis hadn't anticipated.

'You heard. I join up with you.' And for a moment again, beneath the bully's bravado, Travis sensed an unexpected vulnerability. 'Me and you – like a team.'

Mel gave a scornful laugh. 'You? Richie, I'd sooner team up with Darth Vader.'

'Tell him we don't want him, Travis.' Simon. 'Tell him it's out of the question.'

'Why don't you use your brains instead of your mouths?' said Richie Coker. 'You need me.'

'Exactly how?' Travis said non-committally.

'I've got skills you're gonna need.'

'Yeah?' Mel scoffed. 'Extorting dinner money from children isn't a talent that's likely to be much use from now on, Richie.'

'You'll need muscle, though, won't you? Someone who can handle himself when the going gets tough. I don't see Simes being much of an asset when it comes to a fight. You neither, Morticia. And it *will* come to a fight sooner or later – you know that, don't you, Naughton?' Travis's silence suggested he might well do. 'And I can hot-wire cars. I *know* about cars. Shit, I've been stealing them since I was twelve. Which gives us wheels. And I know a few other tricks besides. You don't need guys who play by the rules now, Naughton. You need guys who know how to break 'em. And I'm the only one on offer.'

'Are you listening to him, Travis?' Simon asked in horror. 'Tell me you're not.'

'Trav? What are you thinking?'

Travis turned away from Mel, gazed back at the panorama of the town where he'd been born. Wayvale was ablaze in scores of places, like an animal slowly dying of countless wounds. Surviving the aftermath of the Sickness was going to be painful and difficult. So, it seemed, were the decisions that would have to be made in order to secure that survival.

'If it's all the same to you, Richie,' he said, 'the three of us'll vote on it.'

'Democracy,' Richie remarked. 'A bit pre-Sickness, isn't it, Naughton?'

'Richie Coker said a word with four syllables in it. Astonishing!' Mel marvelled mockingly.

The bully smiled wryly. 'I'll go and wait by the car.'

'A vote?' Simon complained as his nemesis moved away. 'What are you talking about, Travis? What do we need a vote for? Surely none of us want Coker around, do we? Not after all he's done in the past.'

'I know what you're saying, Simon,' Travis acknowledged, 'but he does have a point. None of us can hot-wire a car, for example, can we? Richie can teach us how to do it. He's big. He's right about fighting – there'll be other Jesters out there for sure. Joe Drakes. Maybe worse. And your objections, Simon, I sympathise. Coker was a thug and a bully – might still be – but what he's done *is* in the past, and the world he did it in is also pretty much in the past now. It's burning behind us. We *could* use him, but it's not for me to force the issue one way or the other. So let's vote. Simon?'

'No. No Richie Coker.' With unusual vitriol in his voice. 'Absolutely not.'

'Mel?'

Who couldn't look at the bespectacled boy. 'Sorry, Simon.

I don't like it – I don't like *him*. In fact I loathe him and everything he stands for, but I have to vote yes. At least for the time being.' After all, Richie wasn't the only one who'd done bad things before. And his presence would free her up to devote more time to Jessica. 'But if he steps out of line *once . . .*'

'OK, OK. So I get the decider.' *Terrific*, Travis thought bleakly. *Which way would Dad vote?* Trouble was, his father wasn't here. Travis was on his own.

'Travis, *don't . . .*' pleaded Simon.

But he did. He had no choice. 'Richie's in,' he said reluctantly. 'I'm sorry too, Simon, but bottom line is that what he might be able to bring us is too valuable to lose. We do need him – or someone like him. But he needs us, too. Don't forget that. That'll give us a hold over him.'

'Holds, yeah. Richie's good with holds,' Simon snorted bitterly. 'Around your neck was one of his favourites, I remember, as he forced your head down the bog and pulled the flush.'

'Simon, I realise this is harder for you to accept than it is for Mel or me, but think about it. If we're going to make things work, we're going to have to win over guys like Richie Coker.'

'Change him, you mean? Reform him?' Simon shook his head. 'You won't do it, Travis. Scumbags like Coker don't change. They can't. Bullying's in their blood. You promised you'd stand up for me against the likes of Coker, Travis, and first chance you get you let me down. Thanks for that. Thanks a lot.'

Travis felt Mel's hand squeeze his shoulder as Simon stalked off petulantly. But if the effect was meant to be comforting, he had to tell her – it didn't work.

*

Linden thought she was dreaming the squeals. She somehow felt it was right that if her troubled sleep was going to be haunted by dreams at all, they should be of horror. The frantic unzipping of the tent, the fearful voices whimpering her name, maybe she *hoped* they were imaginary, that if she simply lay there without responding they would eventually dissolve back into silence. But the small hands shaking her – they were real, the knees digging into her, the terrified eyes she saw when she opened her own.

'Linden, Linden, wake up!'

'I *am* awake.'

It was the little girl Juniper clambering over her. She recognised the voice rather than the face in the murk of her mother's tent.

'You've got to get up. You've got to come out and speak to it. Tell it to go away.'

'What are you—? Juni, tell *what* to go away?'

'The *eye*.'

'What?' Rather more harshly than she ought, she pushed Juniper off her and towards the tent flaps. Her mother came first. Linden felt Fen's brow. It was burning. But the woman was still alive, still breathing, though raspingly, as if each intake of air was torture. There could still be a chance. Linden didn't want to leave her even for a moment.

But, 'Linden, the *eye*.' The children needed her.

She hadn't changed her clothes before going to sleep. In fact, lying alongside her mother she must have just succumbed to exhaustion without realising it. So crawling out into the clearing with the time past midnight wasn't a problem. In the moonlight, however, the children's expressions betrayed that they at least thought *something* was. The ghostly

237

features of Juni, her younger sister Rose, little Willow and the boys River and Fox – five frightened gazes fixed on her. The children were aged between six and twelve.

Their little hands clutched at Linden's for reassurance.

'What's going on?' she said, a tetchiness in her tone of which she was immediately ashamed. She was addressing kids who were either already or about to become orphans. On the other hand, of course, so, it was likely, was she.

'It's looking at us, Linden.' From Juniper.

'The *eye* . . .'

'. . . One eye, floating . . .'

'. . . And it won't go away. It *won't*.'

'Make it stop looking at us, Linden.'

'An . . . eye?' The older girl struggled to make sense of the children's words. 'I don't – you must have been dreaming, that's all. Having a nightmare.'

'We can show it to you,' Juniper insisted. 'It's in the forest. It might listen if you tell it to go, Linden.'

The small hands dragged her to the edge of the dark woods.

'But what is it you think you saw? *All* of you?'

'An eye,' repeated River. 'But not like our eyes. Just one. And bigger, like a football. And it glitters. And it doesn't blink.'

'And it *hovers*,' Juniper said. 'In the air. I saw it when I got up to go to the toilet. I woke the others. We all saw it. There, Linden, *there*.' Pointing, jabbing her finger into the darkness with utter conviction.

But nothing was there, nothing untoward. Only trees and undergrowth, blackened into tentacles and lurkers by the night.

'It's gone. The eye's gone.' Juniper voiced the relief that all five children felt. Their grip on Linden relaxed.

'There, you see?' Taking advantage of the altered situation. 'You imagined it. There was never anything here in the first place, no floating eye. You dreamed it.' Though the inquiring part of Linden was not at all sure how it was possible for each of the children to experience the same dream. 'Nothing for you to worry about.'

'Thanks, Linden.' Juniper sounded emboldened. Momentarily. 'But what if it comes back?'

Strangely, it suddenly seemed to Mel as if she'd never left Wayvale after all, never left her own house.

She was standing at the top of the stairs and at the foot of them her dad was lying and he was broken and dead. Outside, Travis and Jessica were calling her name. 'Mel! Come on, Mel!' They wanted to move on. They wanted her to go with them. So did she.

She descended the staircase.

And her dad seemed to have been dead a long time. His body appeared stiff and pale, as white as if in death the flesh had taken on the hue of the bone beneath. He couldn't frighten her any more, or hurt her. He was in the past and her friends were calling.

She had to join them or they would leave her behind. She had to step over her father's corpse.

Mel lifted a foot to do so.

Her father seized it. His lifeless limbs worked. His dead eyes stared.

'You'll never be free of me, Melanie,' he said. 'Never.'

Which was when she woke. She was in the back seat of

239

Richie's stolen Volvo. Jessica, still sleeping, was propped up against her. Simon was in the front, blinking stupidly at her without his glasses. There was daylight in the country lay-by where they'd pulled off the road last night.

'Mel? You OK? You cried out.'

'I'm fine, Simon, thanks. In an end-of-the-world sort of way.' But would her father return to torment her *every* night? Was that what was meant by a guilty conscience? 'What time is it?'

'Coming up to eight.'

'Yeah? Any idea what day?'

'Friday. Yesterday was Thursday.'

'Was it? Maybe we should appoint you Keeper of the Calendar, Simon. Eight o'clock on a Friday. We should be on our way to school.' Mel smiled faintly. 'If only, huh?'

Taking care not to disturb Jessica, Mel slid out of the vehicle. Among the nearby trees where they'd opted to kip down on some of Richie's blankets – 'We'll let the girls have the car,' he'd said, 'all three of them' – Coker and Travis were already awake and Travis had managed to light a fire. Richie's baseball cap was in place on his head as usual: Mel wondered whether he actually slept in it.

'Hey, here she is.' The bully grinned. 'I always wanted to see what you look like first thing in the morning, Morticia.'

'Better than you, Richie,' she retorted. 'And it's Mel. If we're gonna have to put up with the dubious pleasure of your company, you may as well get our names right.'

'Whatever you say, *Mel*,' replied Richie. 'And it's good that you're up. Just in time to make us some breakfast.'

She snorted disdainfully at that. 'You'd choke on it, Richie.'

'How'd you sleep, Mel?' Travis said.

'I've had better nights . . .'

'And could have again, you play your cards right.' Richie winked sleazily.

'. . . But I guess any sleep is better than none.'

'What about Simon and Jessica?'

'Jessie's still out of it. Simon's awake but I think he's happy staying where he is for now. I reckon he might have a problem with the people over here. Or should I say *person*?' Directing a glare pointedly at the boy in the baseball cap. Mel sat down by the fire – next to Travis. 'So what now?'

'We get something to eat. We do whatever else we need to do while we're here . . .'

'Good job I remembered the Andrex, Mor— Mel, huh? Though maybe to preserve stocks we'd better use both sides.'

'You're gross, Richie,' Mel declared, but with a twitch of amusement at her lips.

'Thank you.' Travis frowned. '*Then* we drive on to my grandparents' place.' It had been his idea to rest up for the night once they'd put Wayvale a fair distance behind them. 'Another eighty or ninety miles to go – we should be there by lunchtime.'

'Unless we run into trouble,' Mel said apprehensively.

'Yeah,' Travis conceded. 'Unless that.' Though it wasn't the journey that was really troubling him, but what they – he – might find at the end of it. Grandma and Grandad miraculously alive and well – or two more bodies? It astonished him that he – and the others, too, with the exception of Jessie – were evidently still able to function pretty much as normal, despite the devastating emotional blows that they'd all suffered, despite the grief and the death and the horror.

There was an ongoing struggle, he thought, in the soul of the individual, between giving in and going on, between defeat and defiance, submission and survival. Within everybody there was a spark, an instinct, a will to live. They had to nurture that spark. When they founded their own community, they would have to fan it into a flame and make it burn in the hearts and minds of each and every member. They had to inspire with hope; they had to provide post-Sickness life with meaning and value and purpose. Without those things, Travis knew, the human race was doomed.

'. . . Lights are on but there's no one home. Hello? Trav?'

'Sorry, what?' Mel had obviously said something he'd missed. 'I was, uh, miles away.'

'Willowstock already, huh? I was asking, now that we've got a moment to stop and think, do we *really* reckon that all the adults are either . . . gone or about to – you know. *All* of them? In the *world*?'

'It's nearly impossible to comprehend, isn't it?' Travis acknowledged. 'It's almost as though our minds are too small to accept the truth.'

'I reckon Richie's is too small, full stop,' Mel said, goading Coker. But for once the subject of her barb didn't respond. He was staring broodingly, distractedly into the fire.

'Maybe the Sickness didn't turn out to be so virulent in other countries, those with smaller, more spread-out populations,' posited Travis. 'I don't know how we can find out or how that could necessarily help us – in the short term – even if we do.' He shook his head. 'We're used to a 24/7 world. We're used to satellite reports of breaking news events beamed into our front rooms from all over the globe. We're used to incalculable amounts of information at our fingertips, at the click of a mouse. We're used to knowing just about everything about just about everybody. And now we know crap. And I don't see how that's going to change.'

'Maybe we'll find a computer that works,' Mel said. 'Or a radio or something. A transmitter. Maybe we'll be contacted by adult survivors in bunkers in America. You can't say for sure that we won't.'

'No. You're right, there might be bunkers,' Travis replied. 'Protected installations. Controlled environments. There might even be some in this country. Maybe all we'll have to do is find one – or be around for one to find us – and every-thing'll be fine. But the trouble is, Mel, we have to plan for the maybe-*nots*. From what we've seen, and until we know for sure otherwise, we're going to have to move forward on the basis that the adults are out of the equation. That it's just us.'

'I reckon you're right, Naughton.' Both Travis and Mel were surprised that Richie should suddenly choose to con-tribute to the discussion, and in an unexpectedly sober tone. 'The other night, something happened. The authorities were desperate then.' He told them about the rounding-up on Wayvale Rec – everything except, of course, how he'd man-aged to escape at Lee's expense. (No need to let on that so far during the Sickness he hadn't quite lived up to his hard-man reputation.)

A long, gloomy silence ensued.

'So that's why it was either join up with Jester's group or get out of town,' Richie said finally.

'And join up with ours,' Travis added. 'Safety in numbers. Fair enough. But what about your family, Richie? What hap—?'

'Uh-uh, Naughton.' Richie cut him off sharply. 'I don't

want to know what happened to your family – more than I do already – and it's none of your business what – well, anything about mine. They're dead, right? Let's just leave it at that.'

Mel looked at him curiously. She'd never considered the possibility that Richie Coker even *had* family, let alone feelings about them, an emotional life. Bullies couldn't feel hurt, could they? 'What I want to know,' she said, 'is how a disease can only infect adults. It can't be natural, can it? You know, I mean like malaria or typhoid or something.'

'My grandad said he thought it was a biological weapon,' Travis said, 'or the result of an accident in a biological research lab. I think he was right. The virus as a weapon of mass destruction. I think the Sickness was engineered to attack only certain people, adults. There must be something about the genetic make-up of fully grown human beings that's different from those of us who are younger and that can be targeted, exploited, I don't know.'

'Is that possible?' Mel asked, doubt in her tone.

'Hello? Morticia? The bodies piling up *prove* it's possible, don't they?'

'But I still say, why? So it's biological warfare. OK. Why not kill everyone? Why develop a disease that's harmless to children?'

'Because everybody likes children?' Richie suggested lamely.

'Because children aren't a threat,' Travis exclaimed as realisation struck him. 'You're one side in a war, right? You want to beat the other. There are going to be civilian casualties in any conflict these days – that's inevitable – but you don't want to wipe out the enemy's entire population. Who are you going to rule over if you do? You just want to smash their armies and

244

destroy any chance of an organised resistance after you, I don't know, after you invade their country or whatever. And you want to keep the risk to your own forces as minimal as possible. So you don't engage on the battlefield in a conventional Battle of Waterloo, D-Day landings sort of way. You attack with biological agents, the Sickness, and you kill all those who might be able to put up a fight – the adults – and leave alive all those who are too helpless to oppose your advance anyway, the children. That's it. War over. Then you just march in and take control without any danger whatsoever.'

'Naughton, you ever thought of writing books for a living?' Richie wondered. ' 'Cause don't. Nobody'd ever believe 'em.'

'That's a horrible idea, Travis,' Mel shuddered.

'But plausible,' he said, defending himself. 'If you were ruthless enough to put it into practice.'

'Anyone *that* ruthless I don't want to meet.' Mel paused. 'And Trav, what happens when *we* turn eighteen or twenty or whenever? Are we all gonna catch the Sickness then, too?'

'Good question, Naughton,' Richie agreed, remembering the words of Terry Niles. '*In four years or so, if you last that long, you'll be me.*' 'How you gonna get out of that one?'

'Any surviving adults – scientists – they'll have developed a vaccine by then. Or we'll have developed a natural immunity ourselves – we're resisting infection now, aren't we? Maybe our system, our genes, DNA, maybe they'll just adapt. It's irrelevant exactly how. We'll survive. *Some*how. We have to believe that or we may just as well give up now.'

'So you think it's worthwhile getting some breakfast down us?' Richie said. 'Suits me. I'll go and fetch some food.'

As he crossed back towards the car, Mel sprawled full-length on the grass and groaned expansively. She gazed upwards at sunlight cascading like golden water over leaves and boughs. 'How can it still be beautiful, Trav? The day, I mean.'

'Because it is, I suppose.'

'Oh, that's cracking.' She closed her eyes and laughed hollowly. 'That's major philosophical insight. *Because it is, I suppose*. And you were doing so well on the Sickness, Travis.'

'What I mean is, when my dad was killed I thought the world would end. I didn't think it could survive without him in it. I *wanted* it to end, Mel. I wanted the sun to stop shining and I wanted darkness and storms and cold winds and I wanted rain to fall for ever. To mark Dad's passing. To show that he was important.'

Mel sat up again. 'Trav, I didn't mean to . . .'

'No, it's all right.' He smiled at her and it was. 'Let me – I wanted the world to be as heartbroken, as miserable as I was. But it wasn't. It didn't change. The sun rose, the sun shone. At first I was upset by that. It made me angry. I thought it meant that Dad didn't matter, that none of us mattered. But it didn't mean that. I don't believe it did. It meant that life mattered more, life itself, the life in us and around us and everywhere. It meant – means, Mel – that life has to go on. The day my dad died. Today. Every day. Maybe now more than ever. That's why *we* have to go on too.'

Her arms were around him before he'd even finished. 'Trav, we will,' Mel promised, holding him to her. 'We will.'

The nature of the accommodation in the settlement facilitated matters. Sleeping bags into body bags. As simple as that, and as heart-rending. No dawn greeting ceremony was held that morning. Instead, at first light Linden visited every tent and

246

zipped up the dead. And the dead were in every tent. No adult had survived the night. At some point, her mother too had passed away while she, Linden, had been sleeping. She'd been woken to deal with the ridiculous nightmares of the kids, but had failed to be conscious when her mother had needed her most, when she could – should – have said goodbye. She felt guilty, ashamed, on top of her grief. It wasn't good.

But she'd given Mum a belated farewell now. There was nothing left to keep Linden in the forest. Others, however, seemed perhaps to have different ideas.

A clutch of bereaved under-twelves clustered around the ashes of a fire that had not been relit. They were sobbing, which Linden could understand. But they were also looking at her, *to* her, their limpet stares clinging to her every move, watching her hungrily, desperately, demandingly. Possessively. Linden could understand that, too. She was the oldest survivor among the Children of Nature; leadership had devolved to her with the adults' demise. She understood the logic but she didn't have to like it.

She was afraid of it.

She'd closed Oak's eyes last of all. Maybe she'd imagined it but she'd felt his Sickness-scarred expression was puzzled rather than peaceful or pained, as if he couldn't quite come to terms with the tragedy that had befallen both himself and his followers, as if he was baffled why his beloved Nature should turn so mortally against Her staunchest advocates. He'd been wrong, Linden knew. Oak had been mistaken all the way down the line. But at least he'd had the courage of his convictions and the strength to lead. She didn't. She wouldn't be able to cope. All she wanted was someone to hold her so she didn't feel so *alone*.

Where was Ash when she needed him?

She joined the younger ones by the fire. Their craving eyes, searching for a parent substitute, imposing the role on her, compelling Linden to be what she was not.

'Well . . .' she said.

'What are we going to do, Linden?' Juniper first. Then the others, as though a dam of voices had been breached. 'What are we going to do? . . . I want my breakfast and a cup of tea . . . Help me put my clothes on, Linden . . . My mummy won't answer me. My mummy's all red . . . You're our mummy now . . . You'll look after us, won't you, Linden? . . . Help me, Linden. Help me.'

They were around her, a swarm. They were pawing at her, overwhelming her, suffocating her. She couldn't breathe. She couldn't think. She wanted to shout. She wanted to scream. She wanted to shake off their thin and questing fingers and strike out and . . .

She had to get away.

'Listen, all right? Listen to me. Listen, listen, *listen.*'

She couldn't stay here. She had to get away.

The children listened. Little Willow sucked her thumb as Linden had seen her do when her mummy was telling her a story.

Willow's mummy, yes. Not Linden. Linden wasn't related to any of these ragged urchins. She bore no responsibility for them.

'Let's have a big breakfast,' she said. 'Let's light the fire and have a— But we need fresh wood to light the fire, don't we? Who can collect some sticks so we can light the fire?' The little hands shot up. 'Good – then off you go, then. Into the forest. Collect as many twigs and stuff as you can. There'll

bc   there'll be a prize for whoever collects the most. And
I'll . . . I'll help, too.'

She probably hadn't needed to add the last sentence. In
young minds, 'prizes' was as potent a concept as 'parents'.
The children scattered into the undergrowth to forage for
firewood.

I've done it, Linden thought. *I've fooled them. Given myself an
out. Hurrah.*

She walked slowly and steadily into the woods. At first.
And if any of the little ones had paused in their work long
enough to notice her they might have wondered why Linden's
gaze was fixed directly ahead rather than on the ground,
where experience told them most of the best firewood was
normally to be found. They might have commented on the
strange kind of glaze over her eyes, too. But none of them
even saw her. Which, oddly enough, failed to make her flight
any easier for Linden.

An act of cowardice was still – and always would be – an
act of cowardice, whether it was witnessed by others or not.

And as Linden penetrated more deeply into the forest her
pace increased. A step became a stride. A stride quickened
into a sprint. She was running. Before she knew it, Linden
was running. When the children returned to the camp with
their firewood they'd be in for a bit of a shock.

But she couldn't help it. She couldn't stay. She'd always
planned to leave. The children were not her responsibility.

If she kept telling herself that, sooner or later she might
even start to believe it.

Travis's group were about twenty miles from Willowstock
when they chanced across the accident. So far this morning

249

they'd made good time, stopping only at an isolated country petrol station to fill up with fuel: Richie knew how to pump the precious liquid up from its storage tanks manually. The petrol station itself had been deserted. In fact, they'd seen nobody since their hasty departure from Wayvale.

Until now. The girl in leather – sixteen, seventeen – was definitely a someone. She was waving them down vigorously with both hands, had been from the moment they'd rounded the bend onto this long, straight stretch of road, hemmed in by trees on both sides and by rising ground to the left as well. She seemed grateful for the appearance of a vehicle in working order. Given the condition of the two cars behind her, one of which was certainly a write-off, the group in the Volvo wasn't exactly surprised.

'What do you want to do, Naughton?' Richie said.

'Stop, of course. We're not in Wayvale now.' In the front passenger seat, Travis couldn't believe the question. 'Out here we can make a difference – and she needs help. There's been a crash, can't you see?'

'Can't see any bodies,' Richie observed, braking gradually nonetheless. 'What I *can* see, those cars are practically nose-to-nose across the whole road.'

'You mean it's some kind of amateur roadblock?'

'I mean we haven't got much choice but to stop, whether or not we've got a chick in distress wiggling her hips at us. Stop or turn round.'

They were virtually upon the accident now. The girl in leather was rushing towards them with relief.

'Turn round,' Simon suddenly piped up from the rear. 'Coker, turn *round*.'

'Simon?' Mel regarded him curiously.

'Simon, what's the matter with you?' Travis glanced back.

'I don't *trust* this.'

'And here's a thing,' said Richie. 'I agree with Simes.'

'Well, you don't make the decisions, Coker,' Travis snapped. 'And there's no debate on this one. We don't just abandon people who need help.'

It was too late, anyway. The girl was at the open window. 'I'm so glad,' she babbled. 'I'm so glad someone's come at last, glad you've come.' Reaching in to touch Travis's hair and shoulder as if to check he was real. 'Please. Quick.' Opening the door herself, plucking at his sleeve. 'You've got to come. All of you.' Gesturing to the crashed cars. 'Please.'

'OK. What happened? Tell us what—?' But the girl was flitting away from Travis back towards the vehicles. Halfway out of the Volvo, he turned to the others, who hadn't yet moved. 'Well, come on. You heard her. Turn the engine off, Richie.'

'Yes, sir, Mr Samaritan, sir.' Richie obeyed. 'Just hope you know what you're doing.'

'Travis!' Mel called after him exasperatedly. But by the time she'd clambered out of the car Travis had joined the girl in leather.

'We shouldn't stop for anyone,' Simon complained. 'Town or country doesn't matter. We've got ourselves to think about.'

But, with the exception of Jessica, everyone was now out on the road. Mel noted that the windscreens of both cars involved in the crash had shattered – so where was the glass that ought to be glittering on the tarmac?

Travis was standing beside the damaged vehicles. He peered into both of them. Empty. 'No other . . . What happened?' He glanced at the roadside. 'Where are the others?'

'What others?' said the girl in leather innocently.

'The other driver. The others involved in the accident.'

'Oh, there hasn't been an accident,' the girl said, as if he should have known.

Suddenly, from the screening woods on either side, multiple engines roared into life. Not cars, though, Travis judged. Motorbikes.

'What's—? You don't need help?'

'*I* don't,' giggled the girl in leather. 'But *you* do.'

Travis heard Mel shouting his name and whirled in time to see the half-dozen Harleys tear out from among the trees, cutting off any possibility of retreat back along the way they'd come, their riders hostile and leather-clad. 'Naughton!' Heard Richie too and a cry from Simon as further biker types emerged from their hiding places on foot. Male and female together. A gang.

Travis cursed. Seemed he was making a habit of blundering into ambushes. But that wasn't the worst of it.

The shotgun that a grinning pock-marked thug was pointing square at his chest – *that* was the worst of it. 'You even *breathe* out of turn, kiddo, and you get a hole between your ribs as big as the one between your ears.'

NINE

Travis raised his hands, more in a bid to defuse the situation than in actual surrender. 'We don't want any trouble.'

'Sure you don't,' said the pock-marked youth. 'People staring down the barrel of a shotgun rarely do.' Travis saw that his immediate adversary was not the only member of the biker gang who was armed. Mel, Richie and Simon were also surrounded by shotguns. 'But that's OK. We don't want any trouble either. So there won't be any as long as you're sensible and obey the rules.'

'The rules?' Derisively.

'Do whatever he wants, Travis,' came Simon's advice. Travis bridled at it – but, on the other hand, if he'd listened to the bespectacled boy's fears earlier . . . How come doing the right thing so often turned out wrong?

'*Our* rules, if you want to get picky,' said Pockmarks.

'And you are—?'

'They call me Rev.'

'Not short for Reverend, surely.'

'What?'

'He's trying to be funny, Rev,' said the girl in leather. 'Let's find out how funny he can be with his kneecap blown off.'

'Rev as in what we do to our bikes' engines,' Pockmarks explained. 'We're bikers, see, kiddo, and because we're bikers,

253

in this present state of national emergency we've taken it upon ourselves to be the – what did you say the word was, babe? – the *custodians* of the Queen's Highway.'

'Roaring down the Queen's Highway just like a streak of lightning,' the girl in leather expanded helpfully.

'It's an important job,' said Rev, 'and we need to be financed to carry it out. So this road has been – what was the word, babe? – *designated* a toll road from now on. And guess what? You guys are the first to pay the toll.'

'You want money? Is that what this is about?'

'Do I look stupid to you, kiddo?' Rev wanted to know. Travis thought it wise not to tell him. 'Money's worthless now, we know that. But goods aren't – food and stuff. You must be travelling with supplies.'

'What's the toll?' Travis said.

'Everything you've got. Boys, collect payment.'

The shotguns swivelled towards Richie, who was holding the car keys. 'Wait . . .' One over-eager biker couldn't. The butt of a gun jabbed Richie violently in the stomach and he went down, his breakfast all but coming up to meet him. If the same fate or worse might not also have been about to befall him, Simon would have smiled.

'Don't fight them, Richie. It's not worth it,' Travis called.

The former bully already knew *that*. His 'Wait' hadn't been uttered from aggressive resistance, in a 'Wait, don't come any closer or else' sense, but had been intended to precede the rather more conciliatory 'Don't hurt me, here are the keys.' Grovelling on his knees and retching, however, the keys wrested from his grasp, Richie supposed that it wouldn't do any harm for Do-Gooder Naughton to believe he'd been prepared to make a stand. If they both survived the next few minutes. (If?

254

Richie would. There was always the option of changing sides.)

Rev's fellow bikers had the boot open and were emptying it with enthusiasm.

'There's no need for this,' Travis said. 'If you'd have asked, we'd have shared.'

'*Shared?*' Rev hooted with laughter. 'Where do you think you are, kiddo? Back at school?'

'Hey, Rev!' yelled a thug from the Volvo. 'There's a blonde chick in here in some kind of coma or something.'

'Must be the company she keeps,' sniffed the girl in leather, running an unflattering gaze over Travis.

'Is that it, then?' he said stonily. All their provisions were heaped on the roadside. 'Can we go now?'

'Nah. That Reverend crack, kiddo. Didn't show respect to the – to the . . .'

'Custodians,' the girl in leather reminded him.

'– The custodians of the Queen's Highway. For that, you can't go forward. Have to go back.'

'Hold on a minute, you creep.' Mel for one seemed intent on going forward and was prevented from storming up to Rev only by several guns shifting their attention from Richie to her. 'We've paid your stupid toll.'

'It's OK, Mel. It's all right,' said Travis soothingly. 'There are other roads to where we want to go. This one's a dead end anyway.' He fixed his gaze on Rev. 'Can we at least have our keys back?'

'Give 'em the keys,' Rev ordered. 'It's been a pleasure doing business with you, kiddo. Pass this way again, maybe we can do some more.'

'Don't hold your breath,' said Travis.

*

255

At least nobody criticised him *openly* over stopping for the girl in leather. But, Travis sensed as they drove a different route towards Willowstock, his companions were *thinking* he should have known better, shouldn't have taken the chance. Even Mel. Had he been naive? Maybe. But for laudable reasons, surely. To help the girl. To do what Dad would have done. But then, would he have been quite so keen to play the hero if the unfortunate on the roadside had been male rather than female? Was doing the right thing some kind of ego trip for him? Certainly, his decision had jeopardised the others' safety. But what would the long-term effect on people be if you had to start thinking ambush before you thought accident, if you assumed everyone you met *couldn't* be trusted rather than that they *could*? Society – any community, even the family – was built on trust. If trust was lost, Travis thought, in the end everything else of value would be, too.

'We're here,' Richie announced. 'Willowstock.'

The woodland fell away and the village was revealed, its single street ahead. The shop where Grandma used to buy Travis a bag of 'bits', his own selection of sweets from old Mrs Stickings's glistening glass jars of goodies. The pub that Grandad would sneak off to of an evening when he thought Grandma wasn't looking. The surgery where he'd had to be taken to see Dr Parker that time a bug had bitten him and his knee had swelled up like a balloon. Willowstock, the context for so many cherished childhood memories, all those stays at his grandparents' cottage over the years.

Today's, Travis feared, would be the last.

'Where to from here?' Richie asked, slowing the car to a crawl as they approached the village.

Back, Travis dreamed. *Back into the past*. Back into the old world, where his memories were real and alive and everything was certain, safe.

'Crap!' Richie cried, braking abruptly.

Something had struck the windscreen, chipped it. A stone.

'What the hell?' Mel joined in. So did other stones, skimming across the bonnet, bouncing noisily off the doors. The attack was coming from the right. 'Look!'

The culprits were easy to spot. A handful of ragged urchins in the shadow of the wood, none of them looking older than eleven or twelve and the youngest perhaps only five or six, hurling with abandon whatever missiles they could find.

'This what you call a welcoming committee in these parts, Naughton?' Richie was out of his seat belt, half out of the car, bawling: 'You brats are asking for it, you know? I'm gonna ram these stones down your throats!'

'That'll be right,' Simon muttered. 'They *are* all smaller than him.'

Travis grabbed at Richie. 'No, you don't, Coker. They're only kids.'

'Yeah,' retorted Richie. 'So was Genghis Khan once.'

'A role model of yours?' Mel wondered.

'Get lost, Morticia. We could have crashed.' But he made no further advance towards the children. As soon as he'd threatened to, they'd retreated into the forest in any case. 'Who the hell do they think they are? The sons and daughters of Robin Hood and his Merry Men or what?'

'They probably don't know *who* they are,' said Travis. 'Or what they're doing. They're probably traumatised. Get back in the car, Richie.'

'Trav, we ought – we really ought to do something,

257

though.' Mel stared after the children. 'About the little ones, I mean. They won't be able to fend for themselves, will they? Not for long, anyway. What's going to happen to them?'

'We *will* do something.' Travis was aware he sounded unnecessarily short-tempered. Must be the stress of being so close to his grandparents' place. 'We'll help them. We'll protect them. But we can't do that yet. We need a base, a home, and older kids first, establish a community that can work. *Then* we can start looking after the tinies.'

'Sometimes, Naughton,' said Richie, back in the driver's seat and pretending to be deeply moved, 'you really bring a lump to my throat.'

'I'll bring a lump to your *face* if you don't shut up and start driving, Coker.' Travis glared. 'Grandma and Grandad live in a lane on the other side of the village. I'll tell you where to turn.'

'Trav, are you all right?' Mel leaned forward to squeeze his shoulder.

He shrugged her concern away along with her hand. 'I'm fine. I'm fine. Just – let's get there.'

They'd have passed on, of course. Like both his parents had now. Like everybody's parents. Like Uncle Phil. They couldn't be alive. Impossible. Why was he even allowing himself to think that way? It was ludicrous. He had to face up to reality. Reality was the Sickness.

And *yet*.

His grandparents' cottage was the same as ever. The pristine thatch. The whitewashed walls. The perfect little garden, meticulously tended. The garden path, always swept. The front door, green, and the matching garden gate, painted from the same pot – Travis had helped Grandad do the job

258

but 'The boy's got more paint on himself than he has on the door, Grandma.'

Richie parked the car and switched off the engine. 'End of the line,' he said.

And it was the same as ever. But not *quite* the same as ever.

The garden gate was open (and Grandma always kept it closed). The front door was open, too, a bit, ajar, but there was no caller on the doorstep, no reason for the door not to be—

Someone was inside. Inside his grandparents' cottage. Someone who shouldn't be.

Travis was out of the car, racing to the door, oblivious to Mel's voice behind him.

'Grandma!' he was shouting. 'Grandad!' Their names brought tears, brought fury, brought grief.

There was a girl on the sofa in the parlour. An *intruder*. She was stumbling to her feet and looking dazed as if she'd been asleep and had been rudely awoken. An *intruder*. Shabby dress, reddish hair cropped short. Looked like a pixie. Wasn't. *Intruder*.

Opening her mouth. 'I—'

Travis wouldn't let her lie to him.

He smashed his fist into Linden's jaw so hard she fell back onto the sofa and the blood sprayed from her lacerated lip.

'Great shot, Naughton,' said Richie admiringly from where he stood in the doorway.

Mel pushed past him. 'Travis? Oh, my God.'

'What are you doing here?' Travis was screaming at the redhead, on the brink of assaulting her again. 'What are you *doing* here?'

'Trav, get a grip.' Mel clamped her arms around him, tried to pull him away from the cowering, frightened girl.

'I'm sorry,' Linden whimpered.

'Who do you think you are? This is my grandparents' house. My *grandparents*'.'

'I'm sorry.'

'Where are they? Answer me. *Where are they?*'

'Upstairs,' said Linden.

Instantly the blood drained from Travis's face, the rage from his expression. 'Get off me, Mel,' he said tonelessly. She felt his body go slack in her embrace like a man who'd just died and she wanted to keep holding him because of it. But she did as he told her. Without another word, he turned and left the room, Richie and Simon awkwardly making way for him.

Travis found his grandparents where he probably should have looked in the first place. Their little bedroom with the slanting ceiling and the fine view across the fields to the forest beyond. He remembered gazing out of the window once as a very small boy and declaring in wonder: 'You can see the whole world from here, Grandma, the whole world.' And his grandma might have kissed his hair as she'd had the habit of doing and she might have said: *'You*'re the whole world to me, Travis.' He liked to think so, especially now.

Grandma was lying next to Grandad in bed. They'd been covered up but Travis twitched the sheet back. He was a relation confirming the identity of the deceased. At least, beneath the circular crimson scars of the Sickness, their true faces seemed peaceful, at rest. How he hated the physical legacy of the disease, marring loved ones' features – like Death doodling.

'Too late,' he murmured. 'I'm so sorry.'

'Trav?' Mel, hesitantly. She'd followed him upstairs.

He ignored her – knew she was there but pretended otherwise. There wasn't space in his pain for anyone but himself right now. He was down the stairs again, out of the door, into the garden. He felt the warmth of the sun, gazed up into the blemishless blue of the sky, breathed in the scent of burgeoning spring flowers. Insects hummed their tuneless music. He thought back to what he'd said only that morning to Mel: that life had to go on, no matter what. Somehow, it had seemed an easier idea to believe in then. But then, sometimes it was easier to give comfort than to accept it. It occurred to him there'd been no rain since the advent of the Sickness. Either Nature was going all out to drive home the value of continuing life. Or else a storm was brewing.

'Travis.'

Guess who. 'Mel, are you stalking me?'

'Kind of. It's all right to be upset, you know. You don't have to hide anything. Not from me.'

'I knew they'd be dead – really. How could they not be? But still' – Travis turned to her and it didn't matter that she could see his tears – 'God, Mel, I wanted them not to be.' She cuddled him, consoled him with her actions because she didn't have the words. 'I thought they were our last chance, could have been our final connection to the world of the adults. But they're gone, too. It really is down to us, Mel.'

'I know. And we'll be all right. We trust you, Trav.'

His brow suddenly creased in confusion. 'Hold on, I'm just – Grandma and Grandad were covered up, *both* of them. How . . . ?'

'*She* did it,' Mel said. 'The girl you . . . She's called Linden. She did it. She told me after I followed you downstairs. She thought the cottage was empty, broke in looking for a place to

261

rest and found your grandparents. She covered them, made them look, well, more dignified.'

'She did that for them?' Gratitude swelled in Travis's heart. 'And I thanked her by giving her a fat lip.' And shame.

'Nobody's going to blame you for losing it just for a moment, Trav.'

'I am.' Travis breathed deep, sought to regain his self-control. Losing his temper like that, no matter what the provocation, actual or perceived . . . he'd never have made a police officer. 'We'd better get Jessica inside. Then I think I have some forgiveness to beg. And, Mel – thanks for the stalking.'

The others were still in the parlour. Simon had found a box of tissues and was dabbing at Linden's bleeding lip with one of them. Richie had found a bottle of lemonade and was swigging from it thirstily. 'Seconds out, round two,' he announced as Travis, Mel and Jessica entered.

Travis darted him a warning glance. He left Jessica to Mel, crossed to the sofa. 'Linden,' he said. 'Mel said your name was Linden.'

'Linden Darroway,' the girl confirmed.

'I'm Travis Naughton.'

'They told me.'

'Well' – kneeling on the floor in front of her – 'I want to thank you and I want to apologise, and I don't quite know which to do first.'

'I don't deserve either. I know I shouldn't be here.'

'We're glad you are, baby. More chick to go round,' said Richie, leering. 'Three babes. Two boys. Simes doesn't count.'

'Oh, you're so funny, Coker,' Simon snorted.

'Don't listen to Richie, Linden,' Travis advised her. 'More nostrils than brain cells. Thank you for tending to my grandparents. I appreciate that more than I can . . . well. And I'm sorry I didn't give you a chance to explain yourself when I just steamed on in. I'm really sorry I hit you. That was inexcusable. It's not me. I don't know what I can do to make it up to you, Linden, but if there is anything, anything at all, just say it.'

The girl's hazel eyes brightened. She smiled. It was the first smile from Linden Darroway that Travis had seen, and maybe it was because he was so close to her, crouched at her feet, or maybe it was because, since striking her, he felt a kind of responsibility towards her, or maybe it was something else, but he found himself hoping this first smile would not be the last. 'There is – actually, there is something,' she said.

Travis warmed to the sound of her voice, too. 'What? Anything.'

'She wants to take a free shot at you, Naughton,' laughed Richie. 'It's only fair.'

'Simon was saying you plan on setting up some kind of community. Let me join, Travis? Let me stay with you.'

'Linden,' Travis said, and he nearly reached out to touch her. 'You've got it.'

There was more than enough food in the cottage for their immediate needs, and a good supply of candles and matches. Tomorrow, Travis said, they'd go into Willowstock and see what else they could scavenge. But for the moment it would probably be better for them to rest, now that they'd found a place where it was safe to do so.

Over a meal that evening stories and experiences of the

Sickness were exchanged. Linden's revelation that she'd belonged to the Children of Nature delighted Richie: he'd always subscribed to the general belief that hippie chicks were easy. He thought it might be worth establishing whether there was any toothpaste in the bathroom – that old Coker charm might soon get a chance for a run-out.

Travis was more interested in Linden's encounter with the soldiers, linking it with the incident on Wayvale Rec in which Richie had been involved. (The boy in the baseball cap had expanded his valiant role in said incident for the purpose of impressing Linden, who was struggling to repress her admiration for him, he could tell.) Maybe the army, the authorities – the *politicians* – had known all along how deadly the Sickness was going to be, maybe because it *was* an artificially engineered biological weapon that for whatever reason had escaped into the atmosphere and become like the Reaper himself, impossible for human beings to cure, contain or control, the agent of inevitable death.

Even if all that was true, Simon didn't understand how one outbreak – a single accident or act of sabotage in a scientific installation somewhere – could have infected the whole world so quickly and so comprehensively. Contagious was contagious – but *this*? Mel speculated about terrorist attacks at key points around the globe that could have activated various biological weapons simultaneously. True, unless the terrorists were under eighteen, which was not out of the question these days, they'd have perished too. But in the age of the suicide bomber and with the prospect of however many virgins awaiting the righteous martyr in Heaven – 'More than you'd find round my way,' Richie muttered – such a possibility could not be ruled out. Maybe they'd never know for certain what had caused the Sickness, Travis mused. Maybe it was better not to know.

Fascinated, Linden watched Mel feed a docile Jessica. Linden felt something close to envy. 'I wonder if Jessica knows how lucky she is,' she said.

'You call being reduced to a zombie lucky?' Mel objected.

'I bet your Children of Nature pals were out of it all day, every day,' said Richie, grinning. 'Pick the right kind of mushrooms from those woodland glades and you're away, yeah?' He winked conspiratorially at Linden.

'I'd get that twitch seen to if we ever find a doctor,' she said coolly and dismissively. 'I didn't mean she's lucky because of her condition, Mel.'

'Mel knows that, don't you, Mel?' Travis said, seeking to defuse any argument.

'I meant, she's lucky having friends, people who care about her enough to keep her with them and look after her even though she's . . . withdrawn. I know some who wouldn't.' Linden was thinking of Ash.

'That's what friends do. They look out for each other.' But Mel was flattered nonetheless.

'And we'll do the same for you now,' promised Travis. 'You're one of us now, Linden. You can rely on us.' He smiled at the russet-haired girl, hoping for a response in kind.

But she looked away. She didn't want to. Had to. There was something so compelling about this Travis Naughton's eyes, yet at the same time they turned you in on yourself and made you ask yourself difficult questions. 'I don't deserve to be one of you,' she said.

'What do you mean?'

'You take care of each other. You take responsibility for

each other. There were children in my care, much younger than me, the other survivors at the settlement, and I should have taken responsibility for them but I didn't. I couldn't – not on my own, not just me. I'm not good on my own.' Shyly – and daring a glance Travwards: 'I ran out on them. I abandoned them.'

'Is the tallest one a girl about twelve, with kind of beaded dreads in her hair?' Mel asked, describing the oldest of their earlier assailants.

'That sounds like Juniper, yes, but how . . . ?'

'Then you don't need to worry just yet,' Mel said.

'We saw them,' Travis explained. 'They threw stones at the car.'

'If it wasn't for me wrestling to keep control of the wheel we could have come off the road and everything,' boasted Richie.

'We'll find them again. Once we're settled and know where we're going. And Linden,' Travis said gently, 'whatever you did or didn't do, it was under the kind of pressure none of us ever imagined we'd have to face. Don't be too hard on yourself. You were alone, too. Well, that's one thing we've put right. You're not alone now.'

'No,' said Linden, her gaze drawn almost magnetically back to Travis after all. 'I guess I'm not.'

'Good. And you know what? Simon? I've just thought of a job for you. *If* Grandad hasn't got rid of it.'

Travis found the battered old short-wave radio languishing in the cupboard under the stairs among mops and brooms and aprons, bottles of cleaning fluid and piles of unfashionable shoes. Carrying it as carefully as if it was a crown, he bore it to the candlelit dining-room table where Simon was waiting.

'Grandad used to spend hours listening to this,' Travis said. 'So did I, sort of. Whatever Grandad liked to do, I liked to do. He could pick up stations from all over the world. Let's just hope the batteries haven't run out.' He switched the radio on and was rewarded by a crackle of static. 'No, we're in business.'

'What business?' said Simon. 'I'm not in the mood for music.'

'It's not music I want you to find.' Travis extended the radio's telescopic antenna to its full length. 'It's information. If any adults *are* still alive, if anybody's organising anything, they might also be broadcasting and with this we might be able to pick up their signal, get an idea what the situation's like in the States or Europe or London. Maybe the BBC are still going. We might even hear the voice of Natalie Kamen again.'

'Who?'

'Don't worry about it. This dial, Simon, you tune it with that.'

'I know how to work a radio, Travis,' said Simon indignantly.

'Sure you do. That's why I want you to take charge of it.'

'Take charge?' The bespectacled boy liked the sound of that. At school, his customary role as life's loser had meant that nobody had trusted him with anything, not even the teachers. (Except that earnest young woman with the round glasses and the CND badge who insisted on being called 'Ms' – she'd lasted less than a term.)

'It's vital we find a station if we can. We need to learn as much as we can. Communications, Simon, that's your job.

Find us a contact.' Travis paused. 'You know, I couldn't trust Richie with this.'

'No? I thought you and Richie Coker were best mates now, Travis.' Resentfully. 'Your vote let him in.'

'We need him for some things. For others, we need you.'

Travis Naughton needed him. Simon felt a rare flush of pride, his loyalty refreshed. 'I won't let you down, Trav.'

'I know you won't, Simon. Shout if you find anything.'

He left the other boy twiddling with the dial. Linden was standing in the doorway. In the semi-darkness, Travis hadn't noticed her there before.

'That was a nice thing to do,' she said as she fell in step with him.

'What?'

'Make Simon feel like he's important, like he matters.'

'He *does* matter.' They entered the parlour, which was empty. 'Do you know where Mel is?'

'She's taken Jessica up to bed. Looks like we've got one of the spare bedrooms and you boys have got the other. Single-sex sleeping arrangements.'

'Right.' Travis would have made for the stairs, only Linden was somehow in his way.

'Aren't you going to ask me how my lip is?' She pursed both of them as though she was blowing a kiss.

'How . . . how's your lip?' Travis could see that the bleeding had stopped but Linden's jaw would be bruised for a few days. He could see something else besides: her mouth lifting closer to him.

'It doesn't hurt now,' the girl said. 'Touch it if you like. You'll see. Put your finger on it. Or, if you like . . .'

'Naughton, your grandad wouldn't have left any fags lying

268

around, would he?' Richie barging in. 'I'm dying for a smoke.'

' 'Fraid you're out of luck,' said Travis, using the interruption to bypass Linden. 'Unless you want to try puffing on a candle. I'm going up to check Jessie's all right.'

'Excellent,' said Richie. 'That leaves just you and me, then, babe.'

'Correction, bonehead.' Linden bypassed him in turn. 'That leaves just you.'

But the whole group – minus Jessica, of course – came together again when Simon called out that he'd found something, a signal. *Someone was broadcasting.*

'It's American,' he jabbered excitedly. (Simon Satchwell, the centre of attention – and in a good way for once, not the public victim of a bully's cruel prank.) 'I thought it was first off because of the accent and then the guy, the announcer guy, he said he's sending from New York City, from Brooklyn Heights in New York City. It's really faint even with the volume turned up full and there's a lot of interference and the signal kind of fades in and out . . .'

'Well, if you shut up we might be able to hear it,' grumbled Richie.

'*You* shut up, Coker,' Mel snapped. 'You've done a good job, Simon.'

Because there was an eagerness in all five faces, including Richie Coker's. They were gathering close around the radio in the flickering candlelight, leaning in to detect even the slightest syllable. Travis felt his heart pounding with painful anticipation, with more than anticipation, with a need, a yearning that was almost spiritual, a desperate hope that someone who could save them was out there. He wondered whether the others felt the same. It was likely. The radio transfixed them all. *Please please please*, Travis prayed silently.

The broadcaster's voice was the first disappointment. Not the President. Not an army general. Not even Arnold Schwarzenegger. A boy younger than his audience.

'. . . Hear me . . . I don't know if anyone can . . . this is . . . Rothwell in Brooklyn . . . Todd Rothwell . . . broadcasting until my batteries run . . . dead like everything . . . like New York City . . .'

'Where's the rescue plan?' Richie demanded restlessly. 'Don't care who this guy is. When are they coming to rescue us?'

'Quiet, Richie,' Travis admonished, though the other boy's frustration was understandable. He shared it. Mel slipped her hand into his. Linden noticed.

'. . . You can see it from here, I want to tell you . . . somebody should tell the world if the world can still hear . . . Manhattan is burning . . . fires blazing to the East River . . . inferno, impossible to . . . Empire State Building is aflame . . . much smoke, the sky's black with smoke . . . oh, I shouldn't be here, I shouldn't be seeing this . . . my older sister left with . . . we had to get out of the city before . . . the city's burning, Manhattan is . . . stay with Mom and Dad, I couldn't leave them, I'll never . . . oh, God, and the bodies, the things I've seen . . .'

'Turn it off, Simon,' Travis said quietly.

'But' – Simon didn't like to think he'd failed – 'it's a signal.'

'It's the wrong signal.'

'. . . Stay with Mom and Dad for ever . . . keep broadcasting . . . batteries . . . Todd Rothwell . . .'

'Turn it off.'

270

Reluctantly, as if in admission of defeat, Simon switched the radio off. The group sat in lonely, ashen-faced silence. The candles guttered feebly, like a distant echo of flame. Halfway across the world, New York City was burning. Every city was burning. And above them the skies were black like the dirt of a grave.

'Tomorrow, Simon,' said Travis. 'We'll try again tomorrow.'

'Mel? Mel . . .' The voice was thin and querulous, so faint that in one way Mel was surprised it had woken her. But not in another.

It was Jessica's voice.

'Jessie?' Who was sleeping beside her on the bed in the dark cottage bedroom. A thrill of excitement set Mel's heart racing. 'Jessie, you've come back to us.' She reached out to touch her.

The man's hand grabbed her first. 'Not Jessie. And I never went away.' It was her dead father alongside her instead and blood was frothing at his lips.

Which was when she woke for real. Which was when she realised that someone *was* holding her arm. Linden Darroway, kneeling by the bed, roused from her mattress on the floor.

'You OK? You were crying out in your sleep.'

'I'm fine. I'm fine.' Her assertions too defensive to convince. She glanced to her side. Jessica slumbered on, safe in the sleep of the innocent. Mel wished she knew how that felt.

'A bad nightmare, huh?' whispered Linden.

'Is there such a thing as a *good* nightmare?'

'Want to talk about it?'

271

Maybe. Maybe she should confide in someone. A problem shared and all that. It couldn't be Travis. She feared that Travis would somehow be disappointed in her, or even suspicious, if she told him the truth of how her father had died. But what about Linden? 'Thanks, but I don't think so.' *No. Not yet.*

'OK.'

'I'll just — just try and dream sweet dreams. Thanks, though.'

'OK. Can I ask you something, Mel?' Sure she could. 'You and Travis.' Cautiously.

'Yeah?'

'*Is* it you and Travis? I mean, are the two of you *involved*?'

'You mean are we boyfriend–girlfriend?'

'Yeah.'

'No.' And, even in the dark, Mel thought she saw Linden smile. 'Travis and I have known each other for years. We're close. But the old just-good-friends cliché? That's us. For real. Why? Are you interested in Trav? Even after he punched you out? Great first meeting.'

'Interested?' Linden mused. 'Could be. He's not with Jessica?'

'Trav and Jess are the same as Trav and me. You've got no competition, Linden, but let me tell you this. Travis is a special guy. If you hurt him, you'll have an enemy, and I don't mean Trav.'

'I'll never hurt him,' Linden promised. Later, she'd remember that.

The girls lay back down to sleep. *So Nature's child has her eyes on Travis, does she?* Mel pondered. *Lucky old Trav.* He deserved to have someone to hold in his life, now more than

272

ever. But then, didn't everyone? She was sleeping in her underwear but leaned over to her jeans slung across a bedside chair. In a pocket, the photograph. She couldn't make it out in the dark, obviously, but she didn't have to. She could describe every detail perfectly from memory, and simply handling it felt good, felt like hope. Everybody deserved somebody. Two smiling girls, their arms around each other, their whole lives ahead of them. As they'd been once. As they would be again. 'Wake up, Jessie,' Mel breathed, drawing comfort from the print between her fingertips. 'Please wake up.'

'You know, these taste better without milk than with,' said Richie next morning, scooping cereals out of their box and cramming them directly into his mouth.

'Just as well,' observed Mel, 'bearing in mind any milk we might get hold of now'll be halfway to becoming cheese. Even if it wasn't, I reckon one look at you'd be enough to turn it sour, Richie.'

'Travis,' said Linden, 'do you think we'll ever taste milk again?'

'Sure.' Travis was emphatic, 'We'll just have to learn how to milk the cows ourselves, that's all. Don't worry. We'll get milk. One way or the udder.'

Linden laughed – a little too loudly.

'Don't expect Richie Coker to put his hands on any cow,' warned the boy in the baseball cap.

'Why not, Big Man?' teased Mel. 'Saving yourself for the bull?'

Richie scowled and was glad that Satchwell wasn't around to enjoy his moment of humiliation. Simon was already back on the radio in the dining room, attempting to locate broad-casters a little more constructive than Todd Rothwell had been. Richie got up and stomped to the door. 'Thought we were supposed to be breaking into the village stores this morning, anyway. Sitting around making smart remarks, Morticia. Better get your bums in gear or some other losers will have cleaned it out.'

'Doesn't he have a way with words?' Mel sighed ironically.

'Unfortunately, though,' admitted Travis, 'he's right. Let's go.'

Leaving Simon and Jessica at the cottage, the other four drove into Willowstock. The Volvo still had plenty of fuel in the tank. 'We can siphon the stuff out of other cars if we need more, anyway,' Richie said. They parked outside the shop on double yellow lines. Mel thought it was probably the first time in her life that she'd have been happy to see a traffic warden. Miraculously, the shopfront was intact. On the other hand, given the average age of the village residents and the consequent lack of young people who might have survived the Sickness, perhaps it wasn't so surprising.

'Don't knock it, Naughton,' said Richie when Travis mentioned this. 'Easy pickings for us. Now, do you want to make like the crim and kick the door in or shall I?' Travis declined the honour. 'Thought so. You stick to milking cows, Naughton. Leave the real work to the real men.' Winking at Linden, Richie smashed open the door. 'Hello? Shop? Anyone serving? Looks like not. Looks like we're gonna have to help ourselves.'

Linden hung back as the others ventured inside. 'Travis, while you're loading up the car, I just want to pop over to the doctor's.'

'Why? Something wrong with you? Need an examination?' Richie offered with a leer.

Linden ignored him. 'Only when a − a friend and I were here the other day, there was still a receptionist there, a woman who hadn't yet caught the Sickness. She was pretty much out of it and I can't believe she's still there now but − it'll only take a minute to check . . .'

'Fine.' Travis nodded approvingly. 'Only Richie or I had better . . .'

'I'm on it, boss,' volunteered Richie.

'. . . Go with you. Just in case.'

'I'm on it. Lead the way, babe.' The leer seemed to have moved onto Richie's face to stay, like a squatter.

'*Less* than a minute,' Linden said, revising her estimate.

Though the nature of her companion seemed less relevant after they'd entered Dr Parker's surgery. Mrs Wilson was no longer there. Neither were the medical records that she'd been shuffling on the desk. But unlike the fate of the woman, Linden knew what had happened to them. The ashes in the scorched and blackened waste-paper bin were the final remains of the medical histories of all Dr Parker's patients − probably those of Travis's grandparents were among them. Mrs Wilson's final act as a receptionist, and why not? Even if Dr Parker was still alive himself, he'd have no further need of records. Only death certificates.

'Said you were here the other day − with a friend,' Richie probed. 'A *boy*friend?'

'None of your business, Richie,' said Linden scornfully. 'But you do remind me of him.'

'Yeah?' Richie thrust out his chest.

275

'Yeah. *He* was a creep, too.'

'Ah, don't be like that, babe.' Advancing on Linden – it took more than an insult, or even several, to deter Richie Coker. 'I know you don't mean it. I know you like me.' Kind of pinning her against the desk. 'I know you want me.' Resting his meaty hands on her shoulders.

'You don't know anything, Richie,' Linden said contemptuously. 'But you'll soon learn.' And she kicked him hard on the shin, slipping past him as he doubled over with pain. 'Take that for Lesson One,' she called back from the door. Darting into the street, she was grinning, almost laughing (wishing it had been Travis's hands on her) . . .

Juniper stood about a hundred yards further down the road, grave and silent, observing her.

Humour ebbed from Linden's heart. How easy it was for guilt to stage a comeback. 'Juni? Juni! Thank God.' Still running but not towards the shop, Travis and Mel. Towards the little girl. 'I was coming back for you. I'm here. I've found some friends. Juni, wait!'

Because the little girl didn't seem prepared to listen to Linden. Perhaps she didn't believe her. No need to wonder why. But things were different now. Linden wasn't alone. She had Tr— she had the others.

But Juniper had disappeared around the side of the last house on the street. From there it was only a short distance to the forest, cutting across the field, and if the girl reached the woods before Linden could catch up with her she'd get away for sure. Linden increased her speed, pounded the pavement, rounded the corner of the last house herself.

Came to an abrupt and arm-wheeling halt with a cry as if teetering on the edge of an unexpected cliff. Only she wasn't

276

looking down. She was looking up. Eight feet or so from the ground.

An eyeball hovered in the air.

The kids, Juniper and the others, they hadn't lied to her. The eye they'd seen in the night. Seemed it appeared by daylight, too.

It was exactly as they'd described it. Football-sized, or perhaps a little bigger. Beach-ball-sized. Either way, you wouldn't want to kick it, however. It glittered because its globe's skin was steel, except for a circular panel at the front that looked very much like the lens of a camera, the iris of an eye. Observing Linden. Assessing her.

She sucked in her breath. What the hell was it? And did she really want to know? Fearfully, she began to back away, silently, as if to make a sound might tempt the eye into some undesirable activity.

She only screamed when Richie slammed into her from behind.

'Well, what are you doing just standing here?' the boy complained. His momentum nearly knocked them both to the ground in a tangle of limbs.

'Richie. Look!'

'What?' He was peering in the right direction but was registering nothing remarkable.

The eye had vanished.

Linden asked tamely: 'Did you see it?'

'Did I see what? I saw you charging off down the street like you were in the Olympics or something. I know I might have come on a bit strong, considering we've only just met and all, but doing a runner like that's a bit much . . .'

Vanished. As if it had never existed. What if it hadn't?

What if the airborne eye had been only a figment of Linden's overwrought imagination?

'So what am I supposed to have seen?'

'Juniper. One of the Children of Nature. A little girl.' Best, perhaps, to keep the strange metal globe to herself for the time being. She didn't want to look stupid in front of Richie Coker.

Who frowned in confusion. 'You said "it". Did I see "it"?'

'Her. Did you see *her*? Juniper. Wearing that ridiculous baseball cap all day's affecting your hearing. Juniper was here. I ran after her. Not fast enough.'

'How is a girl an it?'

'*Her*, Richie.' Linden dragged him by the sleeve back into the street. 'Anyway, she's gone now. Forget it. Let's go and help Travis and Mel.'

'You're weird, Linden,' Richie said. 'But don't let it worry you, 'cause you know what? I like weird.'

An endorsement which, as she glanced behind her to innocent house and empty sky, made Linden feel absolutely no better whatsoever.

Once the Volvo was loaded up with all the provisions it could carry, they headed back to the cottage. Simon was at the gate. As soon as he saw them he yelled and waved wildly.

'Something's wrong,' Mel warned automatically. 'What if it's Jess?'

'No, no,' Travis corrected her. 'Looks like something's *right*.'

'Maybe Simes has taught himself to knit while we've been out,' Richie joked.

Linden wondered whether the boy in glasses might not have seen a steel globe like an eyeball floating by.

In fact, Simon had news concerning the radio. Good news.

'I picked up this signal,' he enthused. "They're broadcasting from a school. Not a crappy old bog-standard comp like Wayvale. A public school. The Harrington School. They've still got electricity there and hot water and they're organising. They want people to join them. *We* could join them.'

'Join a bunch of upper-class twats?' snorted Richie. 'I'd sooner take my chances with the likes of Jester.'

'Hey, you know where the door is any time you want to leave, Richie,' said Mel. Richie didn't move.

'It was still kids you heard, though, Simon?' Travis asked. 'Not adults?'

'It was a boy's voice, yeah, but he sounded – I don't know – reliable. Like you could believe him. Like you could trust him.' *Like you, Travis*, Simon thought, *at least until you recruited Richie Coker*. 'He said they're transmitting from their own studio at the Harrington School and they'll be broadcasting every hour on the hour. We've got about ten minutes until the next one.'

'Did he say where this Harrington School is?'

'Said it's just outside a village called Otterham.'

'That's only about twenty, twenty-five miles away,' Linden said.

'Yeah, I looked it up. Your grandad had a map of the local area, Travis. It's on there. Twenty-three miles, I reckon.'

Travis nodded approvingly. 'That's good, Simon. You've done well.'

Simon flushed with pride.

'You'll still need a driver, though, won't you?' Richie put in.

'Let's not get ahead of ourselves,' Travis said. 'Let's listen to their next broadcast first.'

Which began punctually on the hour. 'This is the Harrington School calling. This is the Harrington School calling whoever can hear us. Please listen. Even if you've never heard of us – you probably never *have* heard of us, but it's in your interest to listen to this appeal. Your interest and ours.' Simon had been right: a boy's voice, perhaps a boy even younger than the teenagers in their group. But he'd also been right about the tone of that voice, Travis felt. Somehow it inspired confidence. 'Before the Sickness, Harrington was a private boys' school, but those days are gone. Now we want to provide a home for anybody, for everybody – boys, girls, whatever age you are. We want to forge a new beginning, form a new community, one equipped to help us survive in the difficult times ahead, and we want all of you tuning in to this to be part of it. We need you. If you can hear us, you can join us. Harrington is going to be a safe refuge, a sanctuary for those of us who've suffered because of the Sickness, a place where we won't have to suffer any more. The school's nickname used to be The Castle – you'll see why when you get here.'

'Taking a lot for granted, this kid, isn't he?' grunted Richie.

'Shut up and listen, Richie,' scolded Mel.

'We've got plenty of accommodation, plenty of room. We've got our own generator, which means electricity for lights, for hot water. We're transmitting from our own multimedia studio, which means we'll be able to hear if and when the authorities begin to organise again. We've got land, extensive grounds. We're gathering livestock. We've got everything we need to give ourselves a chance to form a viable community but we still need people, people willing to help, people willing to combine their talents and abilities with ours for the good of all. We have to work together. We have to be strong –

together. This is the Harrington School calling. We need you. If you can hear us, you can join us . . .' The voice went on to provide details of the transmission's timings and the school's location, as Simon had already outlined.

'Well?' he asked eagerly at the conclusion. 'What do you think?'

'Sounds sort of promising, doesn't it, Trav?' said Mel. 'Safety in numbers and all that.'

'Kid sounded like he had a plum in his gob if you ask me,' muttered Richie, scowling. 'They won't want us, whatever he says. They're only after spoiled brats whose daddies were stockbrokers or judges or something. *You* can forget it, Linden. It'll be drawbridge up at the castle for you. Drop-outs don't go to posh schools.'

'Having an alternative kind of upbringing doesn't make you a drop-out, Richie,' Linden snapped defensively. 'So *you* can drop dead. I'm as good as anybody.'

'Trav?' Mel looked at him expectantly.

Travis had been impressed by the broadcast, even a little beguiled by it. Predictably. It was sending out a message that he could have written himself. The whole purpose of their exodus from Wayvale was to find a place for the establishment of a community that would preserve and uphold the values of a civilised society, that would strive, as the Harrington boy had said, for the good of all. Travis had thought that place might be Willowstock. Perhaps, instead, it was Harrington.

But words were only words. They could be used to lie as easily as to tell the truth. He'd allowed himself to be duped twice over the last couple of days. Three strikes and it could be game over.

'I think,' he said, 'it's worth checking out. This Harrington School's so close that it'd be foolish not to. We go over there. We see for ourselves what they're offering. We decide what to do. But we go with an open mind.'

'When, Travis?' Linden said, a slight reluctance in her voice. 'When do we go?'

'Twenty-odd miles,' Travis said and then shrugged. 'Why not this afternoon?'

'Yeah, actually,' said Simon, with a weak smile, 'that twenty-three miles, that's the shortest distance from here to Harrington. Trouble is, if you take that road – I suppose I should have said this earlier . . .'

'Said what, Simon?' Travis asked, frowning.

'It takes us right through Rev's roadblock.'

Richie returned with a black Land Rover, a hatchback, its high sides glistening in the afternoon sun, its shape as square and as pugnacious as a boxer's jaw. Travis remembered seeing an ad for this model on TV once, in another world, where the sight of a vehicle racing down hills, cruising across streams and gliding over treacherous off-road terrain like it was a motorway was supposed to be enviably aspirational. Not much point in casting a car as a status symbol now. The four-wheel drive might come in handy, however. Both the front and the rear of the vehicle were defended by tough, sturdy bumpers. They might have need of those, too

'Wouldn't it be simpler if we just made a detour?' Mel had asked a few hours earlier. 'Miss the bikers' precious little stretch of road out altogether. It might take us longer but a quiet life does have its attractions, you know? Shotguns in my face, they tend to make me nervous.'

'We could do that,' Travis had admitted grudgingly, 'but I don't like letting a yob like Rev think he's got the better of us.'

'Trav,' Mel had persisted, 'he won't know. But no, wait! Don't tell me.' She'd nodded, anticipating what he'd been about to say. '*You*'ll know.'

'Is proving a point worth maybe risking our lives, Travis?' Simon had ventured.

'If it's an important enough point, Simon, always.'

'We don't need to take any risks anyway,' Richie had said. He had been listening to the conversation kind of sulkily. Satchwell praised by Travis like he wasn't in actual fact a whimpering, whingeing waste of space. Hippie chick doing a fine job of keeping her raging passion for him, Richie, to herself. And now the prospect of joining up with a bunch of stuck-up snobs with double-barrelled surnames who were probably so puny they made Simes look like The Rock. But maybe he'd seen a chance to raise his own profile.

'What do you mean, Richie?' Travis had said.

'If we had the right vehicle, I'm reckoning we could smash through their crummy roadblock, no trouble. Save time. Put Biker Boy in his place.'

Simon had blanched. 'There's no need for that, Travis. We can go round. Richie's just trying to make himself look good.'

But Travis had been tempted. (His father wouldn't have gone round, not this time.) 'What kind of vehicle did you have in mind?' he'd said.

Now he knew.

Mel helped an unresisting Jessica into the back of the Land Rover. Everyone was in the lane outside the cottage, ready to depart.

'Saw it in some dead guy's drive,' Richie explained confidentially, gratified to note that it was old Simes's turn to look sulky again – the pecking order something like back to normal. 'It wasn't doing anyone any good there so I swapped it for the Volvo. Even found the keys in the guy's kitchen. He's gonna need a new back door, though.'

'All those breaking-and-enterings really coming into their own now, Richie, huh?' Mel commented acidly.

'You sure you don't want to load up the car, Travis?' Linden asked him, almost as if she'd be grateful for the delay.

'No need. Not yet. If we like Harrington, we'll be able to drive back and pick stuff up later. If we don't, we'll be coming back anyway. And if we run into Rev, roadblock or not, it might make sense to be travelling light. But don't worry, Linden. We're going to be fine.'

'I'm not worried.' She paused. 'Not about Rev. From what you've told me about him, he's nothing.'

'So – something's on your mind.'

'It's Harrington.' Linden wrinkled her brow. 'What if – miracle of miracles – Richie's right? What if they *are* all rich kids there? The kind of people I've grown up with, they won't be that kind of people. I'm not sure I'll be able to . . . fit in, I guess. I won't know what to do. I'll look stupid. What if they all look down on— Travis, why are you laughing?'

'Because, Linden,' said Travis, smiling, 'you're making me laugh.' And he couldn't help it this time. He did reach out for her. He snaked his arm around her shoulders and he hugged her to him. To reassure her, of course. Nothing more. 'You won't look stupid. How could you ever look stupid? You look . . .' Her deep hazel eyes raised to his. Her perfect elfin face. 'How could you ever look stupid? And nobody'll ever look down on you, either, Linden, or they'll have me to answer to.'

'Do you mean it?' said Linden.

'Oh, yes,' said Travis.

'Then we'd better get in the car with the others.'

As if to emphasise the point, Richie pipped the horn.

His companions' impatience, however, didn't stop Travis from gazing back at the cottage. Linden watched his expression sadden. 'Travis?' she said.

'It's all right. I'm ready. Just thinking what I've got to do back here, however it goes at Harrington.'

'What's that?'

He turned to her and the pain in his eyes made her heart ache for him. 'Bury my grandparents.'

With the moment almost upon them, Richie was beginning to have second thoughts. Talking the talk was all very well, but then you were expected to walk the walk. And right now Richie's legs felt like water. The roadblock was almost upon them. His muscles could scarcely muster the strength to keep pressure on the Land Rover's accelerator. His hands felt clammy on the wheel. At least Hippie Chick couldn't see the apprehension that was making his face go pale.

'We're nearly there.' Bloody Satchwell putting his oar in. 'I recognise this bit of road. I think the next bend . . .'

'We don't need a bloody commentary,' Richie growled. 'I know where we are.'

The thick foliage on both sides of the road, perfect cover for lurking bikers. The rising ground to the left. The bend and Richie braking slightly to round it safely.

'We might be all right,' Simon said. 'They might have moved on.'

They hadn't.

'Heads up,' warned Travis in the front passenger seat. Déjà vu. The two crashed cars blocking the road, almost nose to nose. The narrowest of gaps between them, not wide enough for any vehicle to pass through.

The girl in leather begging dramatically for help.

'Doesn't she get time off for bad behaviour?' Mel quipped.

'She hasn't seen this car before. Doesn't realise we've seen *her* before. Gives us an edge,' Travis said with grim intent. 'Richie, make the most of it.'

Not the brake this time. 'Ladies and gentlemen, please fasten your seat belts. We're in for some turbulence.' The accelerator. And no more talk. Richie thrust his foot down. Surprisingly, his foot did what he wanted it to. Unsurprisingly, so did the Land Rover.

Its big wheels tore up the tarmac. Richie zeroing in on the opening between the cars, the one impossible for them to pierce. (Unless, of course, they *made* it wider.) The girl in leather's ardent appeal weakening, the truth dawning on her that it wasn't being heeded. Shouting to the trees as if they might like to offer some assistance instead. Standing her ground as if daring the oncoming vehicle's driver to flatten her into the road.

She could stand there all day and it wouldn't make any difference. By now Richie's eyes were closed.

'Here we go!' cried Travis.

At the last second, before the girl in leather threw herself to the side and out of the Land Rover's hurtling path, she recognised its occupants. Travis saw awareness of their identity in her eyes. He was *glad*.

286

Both wings of the Land Rover rammed into the sides of the obstructing cars. The impact of the collision jolted everyone violently – Jessica's head and limbs shook as bonelessly as a puppet's. The percussive clash and rending of metal. The squeal of rubber on road. As the speed of the moving vehicle and its size and its weight and its pile-driving bumpers bulldozed the smaller vehicles aside, powered past them and into open space again. Whoops from the girls. A triumphant shout from Travis.

Time for Richie to open his eyes as if he'd been in control all along. 'We made it. I knew we'd make it. I told you. Who's the driver? Who's the man?'

'If you mean you, Richie, then you'd better keep going.' Satchwell. Shouldn't the little turd just shut up and be grateful?

But Richie looked in his mirrors, saw what Simon meant. Seemed he hadn't done with walking the walk quite yet. Half a dozen motorbikes were already in pursuit. Each of the machines was carrying a pillion passenger as well as a rider crouched low over the handlebars. Each of the pillion passengers was toting a shotgun.

'Oh, shit,' groaned Richie Coker.

Rev wasn't giving up his toll without a fight.

TEN

'What do we do? What do we do?' Richie probably wasn't aware he was screeching.

Travis swivelled in his seat so he could see the enemy more clearly. Too clearly for his liking. The bikers already seemed to be gaining as the road narrowed and the forest gave way to hedgerows. Rev himself didn't appear to be among their pursuers. Travis didn't plan on slowing down to check for sure. 'We've got to outrun them. Richie, keep your eyes on the road and your foot on the accelerator. Everyone else' – as the guy riding the pillion on the nearest machine raised his gun to fire – 'keep your heads *down*.'

Just in time. The rear window shattered. The cries in the car were no longer exultant.

'Shitshitshit.' Was now the time to think about a change of loyalties, Richie wondered? If he stopped and handed over Travis and the others to Rev, would he himself be forgiven? Maybe. But maybe not. He reckoned he might have burned his bridges on this one. Pity there wasn't a real bridge behind them that they could destroy to cut the bikers off.

A second and a third shotgun blast peppered them from the rear, wounding only the Land Rover's metal.

'Eyes on the *road*, Richie,' Travis reminded him.

'When some bastard's shooting?'

'Everyone all right?' Apparently. 'We need to make our-selves even more of a moving target, make it difficult for them to get a bead on us.'

'OK. OK. I'm on it.' Richie swung the steering wheel crazily, sending the Land Rover veering, careering wildly from side to side. Scratches to the paintwork from the hedgerows were the least of their problems.

'And we should have a right turn coming up. Make sure you stay on the road.'

'We're being shot at and you're talking right turns? What about let's just get the hell out of here?'

'We're heading for Harrington,' Travis insisted. 'I won't let Rev stand in our way.'

'Those posh kids are gonna love us.'

'They're getting closer, Trav!' said Mel as another blast of shotgun pellets struck the Land Rover's body.

'If they weren't idiots they'd be firing at our tyres,' said Simon.

'If they weren't idiots they wouldn't be with Rev,' Travis remarked. 'But you've just given me a great idea, Simon. Linden. Mel. The spare wheel on the back' – the hatchback model was equipped with a spare attached in that position – 'what's it looking like?'

The girls dared to peep through the jagged hole where the rear window had been. 'It's kind of round, Trav, and it's kind of made of rubber.' Mel.

'It's half hanging off, Travis.' Linden.

'Is it looking like it could come off entirely?'

'Any second.'

'Excellent. Because somebody's gonna have to reach out and *pull* it loose. The bikers are skittles and that's our ball.'

'You're kidding, Travis, right?' Mel again, from sarcasm to stupefaction.

'Wrong.'

'But that's . . .'

Unbuckling his seat belt. 'I'll climb over.'

'*I'll* do it.' Linden volunteering, up on her knees on the back seat already.

Travis twitched a smile. 'Be careful, Lin. Mel, Simon – anchor her. Hold on to her legs. I mean tightly.'

'How come I never get the good jobs?' Richie moaned.

'Keep swerving,' Travis ordered. 'They mustn't be able to hit Linden.'

'They won't.' Richie kept swerving. The tyres squealed. It was like riding a waltzer at one of those old travelling fairs. Cries from the rear as Linden's legs nearly followed her upper body through the gaping window.

'Hold *on* to her!' Travis yelled.

And she was squinting in the wind as she half dangled out of the Land Rover. The bikers were dark shapes in her vision and not her only concern. If Linden wasn't careful, she'd impale herself on the broken glass that jutted like a miniature mountain range from the window's frame. An explosion at her ear came as a violent reminder that their pursuers would prefer to injure her themselves first. *Kill* her. The threat drove her on. The bolts that secured the spare wheel in place were already terminally damaged by shotgun fire. Her fingers clawed at the wheel itself, prised at it fiercely. She didn't want to die – didn't intend to die. In a world of death, Linden wanted to live.

The wheel came away suddenly. 'Done!' she bawled and was hauled back inside as the bikers fired futilely at her again. For the last time, in fact.

They had more to worry about now

The wheel bounced against the tarmac, spun up like a maddened and oversized frisbee. The first biker tried to zigzag out of its way. Wasn't quick enough. The tyre slammed into him head-on, propelling him backwards and causing his machine to rear up into the air. Both riders were spilled sprawling to the road while their bike crashed to earth beside them, skidding sideways in a scorch of sparks, a second obstacle for the remaining pursuers to contend with. A second casualty, a bike pitching over its riderless counterpart and bucking off its riders like a stallion in a rodeo.

'Richie!' Travis alerted. 'Right!'

And virtually at right angles, the way to Harrington opening up ahead of them. Their own turn to panic as with scarcely any reduction in velocity Richie pulled desperately on the steering wheel to force their hurtling vehicle into the new road. The tyres gripped the surface screaming, as precariously as the fingertips of a climber hanging from a precipice. But they did their job. They held, even as everyone was thrown unceremoniously to the left-hand side of the car. Which was more than the third of the bikes managed, its attempt to take the corner too sharply depositing both itself and its riders in the hedge.

A larger lead re-established. The hunting pack reduced by half. But undeterred.

'Why don't those suckers just know when they're beaten?' Richie wailed.

'Because they're not. Not yet. But we might be in for reinforcements,' Travis said. 'Look!'

Ahead of them now, a private drive that turned off from the public road and meandered through pleasant, peaceful woodland. A drive guarded by a stone gatehouse, evidently unoccupied but reassuring nonetheless. The entrance to the drive marked by twin concrete pillars, a nameplate in bronze on one of them.

'It's Harrington!' Simon yelled gleefully. 'It has to be!' Not that he exactly had time to read the confirming nameplate as Richie raced the Land Rover past the gatehouse and through the woods.

'So we're here. So are Rev's goons.' Mel watched nervously as the final three bikers began to close in once more. 'We got anything else to throw at them, Trav?'

'Try insults, Morticia. You're good with those,' Richie said.

'Travis!' Linden suddenly gaped, staring beyond Richie, pointing. 'The Castle!'

Glimpsed above the trees like some magical ideal, turrets and what appeared to be battlements complete with crenellations like a series of giants' teeth. A fortress prepared to repel all attackers.

Another shotgun blast. But not from behind them this time, not from the bikers. From in front. The boy in grey trousers and a grey blazer – and a *tie* – stepping out from concealing foliage. He'd taken aim. He'd fired. The leading biker flung up his arms as if to surrender but it was too late for that. The bike left the drive and smashed into an oak.

Its two companions braked smartly, unsure how to adapt to meet this sudden and unexpected turn of events.

More boys in grey emerging from the surrounding undergrowth, running up the drive, some of them armed with shotguns or air rifles, while others – were they carrying bows and quivers of arrows? Richie, a glazed, disbelieving expression on his face, looking ready to plough on through the ranks

292

of the newcomers. Travis clamping his hand on the steering wheel. 'Might be better to stop, Richie,' he said.

'Trav!' Mel yelled, though she wasn't sure whether in horror or delight. 'Are you seeing what I'm seeing?'

She was seeing the pillion passenger of the crashed bike struggling to his feet and clinging on to his weapon. Then she was seeing him drop it, clutching instead, just before he fell forward, at the feathered shaft of an arrow that had somehow buried itself between his shoulder blades. She was seeing a further flight of the missiles arcing through the air, embedding themselves with unerring accuracy in the bodies of Rev's followers, reducing their numbers to one. Finally, she was seeing that lone surviving biker turn his machine round and retreat even faster than he'd advanced. Cheers from the forces in grey.

'I saw,' said Travis. 'Better turn the engine off, Richie.'

The Land Rover was surrounded by teenage boys in school uniform. Travis's group was an object of interest for most of them, though those in the car could also hear a 'Good shot' and a 'Well done, Piers' exchanged among the archers and the marksmen who'd disposed of the invaders.

'It's all right.' A ginger-haired boy with freckles addressed the refugees. 'You can get out now. It's perfectly safe. You're among friends here.' With a hint of superciliousness, as if he was twenty years older than them rather than maybe a year or so younger.

Nonetheless, the first part of what he'd said was certainly true. 'OK.' Travis led the way. Apart from Jessica, everyone stepped down from the Land Rover, clustered together. 'Uh, hi. I'm—'

'Hello. Good afternoon.' Another boy hailed them, a lad

293

of about sixteen or seventeen, striding purposefully towards them from the direction of the building they'd sighted. His hands were clasped behind his back and though he wore a grey uniform like the others his tie was exclusively blue rather than striped blue and yellow as those of the rest were. If Linden and Mel had been asked, they'd have had to concede that he was handsome in an aristocratic way: athletic, features perfectly proportioned, green eyes, hair a mass of tight blond curls. Travis might have been reluctant to use the word 'handsome', but the boy did remind him of the likeness of a Caesar he'd once seen stamped on a Roman coin.

'Well, you fellows certainly know how to make an entrance.'

'Is this guy for real?' muttered Richie.

It seemed he was. His schoolmates parted respectfully to make way for him. 'Luckily,' he said, beaming, 'we know enough to be on our guard here. Leo' – he addressed the boy with freckles – 'who's in charge of this afternoon's watch?'

'Hinkley-Jones,' reported Leo dutifully.

'Well, I think vigilance of that quality merits a commendation, don't you? Send Hinkley-Jones to see me when the watch is over.' Returning his attention to Travis's group. 'And before we go any further, I suppose I'd better introduce myself. I'm Antony Clive, Head Boy. Welcome to Harrington.'

It wasn't quite a castle, of course. More likely the Harrington School's founders had simply been influenced by medieval motifs, perhaps in an attempt to enshrine concepts of honour, courage and chivalry in the very brickwork of the institution as well as ingraining them in the minds of its students. The architecture certainly made a statement: the sheer, proud walls with their rows of pointed Gothic windows like lead and glass shields, the bulwarks of the circular towers at the building's corners, the crenellated roof that had so impressed Linden, the great open arch that led into the lawned quadrangle.

'There used to be two huge doors here made of solid oak,' explained Antony Clive, escorting Travis and everyone but Jessica through the arch. The blonde girl remained in the Land Rover. 'Then one of our previous headmasters, Dr Amory, had them removed. "There should be no barriers in Harrington," he's reputed to have said, "and no closed doors. The education we offer here should be open."'

'I'm all choked up,' grunted Richie.

'Open, yeah,' Mel said sceptically. 'To those who can pay ten grand a year, right?'

Antony Clive regarded the skinny girl with her black hair and her black clothes with amused interest. 'Actually – Melanie, did you say?'

'Mel.'

'Actually, Mel, Harrington's fees are closer to eighteen thousand pounds per annum, and my own interpretation is that Dr Amory was talking more about open minds than open access. For you, though, I'm sure he'd have made an exception.'

'Head Boy fancies you, Morticia,' whispered Richie in her ear.

'You could do with the doors back again now, though, couldn't you?' said Simon, with a pointed glance at his baseball-capped companion. 'Help keep the undesirables out.'

'We can defend ourselves,' Antony Clive assured him. 'I believe you've already witnessed considerable evidence of that.'

Travis was surveying the quadrangle. Whatever purpose it had served pre-Sickness, its role now seemed to be as a car park. Several rows of vehicles were stationed on its grass.

'Carburetti is in charge of our transport operations,' said Antony Clive, following Travis's gaze. 'His father is – was – a car designer in Italy. Perhaps your Land Rover could supplement our fleet.'

'We haven't said we're staying yet,' said Linden. 'Have we, Travis?'

'Linden's right,' Travis admitted. 'We heard your broadcast. We were in— We weren't too far away. Thought we'd better come over and take a look. I'm sorry we brought trouble with us and we appreciate you pretty much saving our lives – obviously – but none of that means we've decided to stay. Not yet.'

'I quite understand.' Antony Clive didn't appear perturbed in the slightest. 'You need time to make up your minds, to consult with each other. That's perfectly acceptable. No pressure. We need people, as you heard, but only willing volunteers. What say I accompany you to the dormitories, leave you there to have a shower and a rest – we've got hot water, remember – and then perhaps show you round. You can decide whatever course of action you wish to take after that. Fair enough?'

'Sure,' said Travis.

'Thought you lot only had cold showers,' remarked Richie.

Antony Clive appraised him coolly. 'Sometimes,' he conceded. 'But even a cold shower is more hygienic than no

296

shower, as I'm sure *most* of us would agree.' And he sniffed as though scenting a rather unpleasant aroma in the air.

Simon laughed.

Antony turned his back on Richie dismissively, allowing the bully to become the target of undisguised glares from Travis and Mel. Not from Hippie Chick, though, which encouraged him. And he'd get Satchwell back for that laugh soon enough. But first . . . 'Please.' The rich kid was ordering them around. 'Follow me.'

There were two quadrangles, in actual fact. The main building of the Harrington School formed a straight-sided figure of eight around them. The second courtyard featured – absurdly, it seemed, given the calamities of recent days – a duck pond, complete with resident fowl bobbing about on the water in serene indifference to the incalculable losses among the human population. Mankind to them had always been limited to the several small boys who fed them three times a day – who were feeding them stale bread and crumbs of biscuits even now.

'Isn't that a bit of a waste of food, under the circumstances?' Mel asked.

'Romeo and the others help keep up morale,' Antony said.

'Romeo and the others?'

'The ducks. They're named after Shakespearean characters. Have you heard of Shakespeare?'

Mel stared into the Head Boy's confident, maybe condescending green eyes. 'Sure. I heard he was dead.'

'Guess Romeo and his mates'll make a tasty main course themselves one day, though, huh?' said Richie, grinning sardonically.

'I don't think so,' Antony said. 'At Harrington, we tend not to eat our pets.'

As they entered the school and made their way upstairs towards the accommodation wing they saw more of the community's population, all of them looking purposeful and occupied. Most were teenagers and most were boys – those dressed in uniform were almost certainly Harrington students – but their numbers also included a few younger children and some girls. Oddly, many of these also sported one or more garments that were part of the school uniform, despite the fact that the blazers in particular were often too large or too small for those wearing them.

Antony chuckled when he saw the new arrivals staring. 'We don't force people to wear Harrington uniform,' he said, 'except for Harringtonians themselves, of course, who at present do still account for the majority of our community. But we have a large stock of uniforms in housekeeping and our first recruits simply slipped on a blazer or a tie by choice. Others have tended to follow their example. It's not compulsory but we encourage it. Uniform fosters unity, creates a sense of belonging and togetherness, reduces difference and promotes equality. As Head Boy I think these are values worth preserving and I intend to do so.'

'You won't catch me wearing your poncey bloody uniform,' declared Richie.

'No, somehow I don't think it would suit you,' Antony agreed cryptically, 'Richard.'

(If Satchwell laughed at Richie again he'd be laughing with a broken nose.)

'How many people have you already got here?' Travis asked.

'Forty-two. Twenty-five of us are Harringtonians, the rest have found their way to us over the last couple of days. Only seven girls so far, I'm afraid. We need girls . . .'

'That's what all the boys say, right, Linden?' quipped Mel.

'If you choose to join us, of course, taking into account yourselves' – glancing speculatively from Mel to Linden and back again – 'and your poor friend, that would make ten.'

'You can add up, Antony, I'll give you that,' Mel said. 'That's eighteen grand a year well spent.'

Travis saw Antony smile. Mel was the first of the group to call him by name. 'I know forty-two isn't exactly a big number but wc hope to expand. We *have* to expand. Hence our radio appeal.'

'Don't be so hard on yourself,' Travis said. 'You're doing well.' *Better than me*, he thought with more than a trace of envy. Antony had mustered a group seven times larger than Travis's own and seemed to have them all united, all sharing a common purpose and pulling in the same direction. Travis's own little band had been formed largely by accident and had stayed together so far almost in spite of each other. And he'd had the arrogance to consider himself a leader. It wasn't Linden who should be worried about feeling inferior and unworthy to enter Harrington – it was himself. 'This is . . . you're doing an amazing job.'

'Thank you, Travis,' Antony said graciously. 'I appreciate that. And I think, if you stay, together we can – but I said no pressure, didn't I? I think I'd better leave you alone for a while. Julie' – to a girl in a Harrington tie who was passing in the corridor – 'could you show Mel and Linden here to the girls' dormitory, please? We've made one of the dorms girls-only, of course.' Julie was more than willing, but Mel preferred to fetch Jessica in first. Antony approved. 'Julie can go with you and then, after I've directed your male friends to

299

a boys' dorm and you've all freshened up, perhaps we can talk further.'

'They won't be playing cricket on *that* pitch any more,' predicted Simon. 'I mean, I'm not an expert on the laws of the game, but I don't reckon allowing half a herd of cattle to chew up the square is one of them.'

He was leaning against the windowsill in the twelve-bed dormitory where Antony Clive had left them and gazing out across the Harrington School's grounds (and the radio message had been spot on – they *were* extensive). Simon had got back from the communal bathroom first, largely because he'd contented himself with a wash rather than a shower. He'd claimed that was because he only needed a wash, but the real reason was that he hadn't wanted to strip off in the presence of Travis and, more importantly, Coker. The bully already had plenty of ammunition with which to humiliate him; Simon didn't see the point in voluntarily supplying Richie with more. 'Always knew you didn't quite measure up, Simes' – that would be the least of it. So he'd sought the welcome privacy of the dorm again as quickly as possible. His two companions were only just rejoining him now.

'Cattle?' snorted Richie. 'Load of bull, Simes, old mate.'

'Think again, Richie.' Travis crossed to the window. 'Get those milking fingers ready. And how good are you with shears?'

'What?'

Sheep. Where the first fifteen and first eleven had used to play. Harrington's sports fields had been converted to agricultural use. Rickety fencing had been erected around the cricket and rugby pitches to pen in half a dozen cows and ncarly twice as many sheep. If the animals really wanted to they could probably stage a mass break-out any time they liked, but grass was grass on a farm or within the grounds of a former boys' public school, and they seemed happy enough to graze where they were.

'Livestock,' Travis observed admiringly. 'They're on the way to self-sufficiency. A good supply of fresh water.' In the distance, beyond the fields, the silver ribbon of a river. Other, more modern buildings than the main school could be viewed from the teenagers' vantage point as well: a sports hall, a theatre.

'Deadstock, too,' said Richie darkly. 'Don't forget them.'

And something that looked like a cemetery over towards the trees. Markers for sure, crosses carved from wood rather than marble, the raw brown earth of freshly dug graves. Maybe nine or ten of them: Travis felt uncomfortable counting.

'Who do you reckon they've got buried there?' Simon asked nervously.

'Probably adults who died here from the Sickness,' Travis said. 'Teachers who stayed with the kids until the end.' He thought of Mr Greening, doubted that 'Gestapo' would have met the same terrible fate if he'd been employed at Harrington rather than at Wayvale so-called Community College.

'What about kids who said no to the jolly old Head Boy's offer to stay?' suggested Richie, only half joking. 'Jester, Rev, and Antony Clive completes the set?'

'No. Way off.' Travis dismissed the idea. 'I think he's on the level.'

'Why? Because he's got wealthy parents and wears a tie?

Just 'cause he's posh don't make him perfect, Naughton. Think of those fine, upstanding citizens at the Conservative Club who wanted to slice you up. Most of them probably went to a poncey bloody school like this.'

'I know what you're saying, Richie,' Travis acknowledged. 'But I don't base my judgements on a person's background or past. You should know that. I haven't made my mind up *what* I think yet, but I have to admit, I'm finding the set-up here pretty attractive so far.'

'Me, too,' agreed Simon. 'I think we can trust Antony Clive, Travis.'

'Well, if *you* think so, Simes, let's sign up for a fitting for those poncey bloody grey blazers right now.'

'Try one of the ties, Richie,' retaliated Simon. 'With any luck it'll strangle you.'

'All right, all right,' Travis cut in. But the two adversaries would probably have gone on sniping at each other regardless had an eager knock at the door not been followed immediately by the entrance of an excited Mel, Linden lagging behind her.

'Travis,' the first girl enthused, darting over and embracing him. 'Something amazing's happened.'

'We woke up and it was all a dream?' Simon muttered, his gaze still drawn to the graves.

'It's *Jessica*.'

'She's recovered?' Travis's heart surged.

'Not . . . exactly. Not quite. But she's going to. She will now, Trav, it's just a matter of time.' Mel's optimism was adamantine. 'She recognised me. Just now. That's why we had to come and find you. She was sitting on a bed and I was on the other side of the room and I just happened to glance across at her and she was watching me, Trav.' She widened her gaze to include Richie and Simon in her glad tidings as well. 'Jessica's eyes, they were focused on me like they haven't been focused on anything since . . . well. And she recognised me, I could tell. She knew who I was. And her lips, they weren't just . . . she was on the point of smiling, maybe even speaking. You saw it, didn't you, Lin? I called Linden in case I was imagining things – but you saw it too, didn't you? Jessica's getting better.'

'I saw it, Mel,' Linden confirmed, though with a lack of conviction which to Travis implied that her words were expressing sympathy rather than truth. 'It was . . . amazing.'

'Where's Jessica now?' Travis asked.

'Still in the dorm. Lying down. The moment . . . well, it didn't last. But next time it will. Or the time after that. Jessica's going to get better, Trav – isn't that fantastic?'

'Sure, Mel.' Travis smoothed long black strands of hair out of her shining eyes and felt like a father humouring his naive daughter. Jessica might arguably be in a castle now, but he no longer had any faith in the story of Sleeping Beauty. 'Sure.'

'Oh, I do apologise. Am I intruding at an inappropriate moment?' Antony Clive stood in the doorway.

'No,' beamed Mel. 'It's a *good* moment. I was just telling Trav and the others – our friend, Jessica, her condition's improving.'

'Well, that *is* good news. I'm pleased for you.' His eyes on Mel, his tone sincere. 'Ah, for all of you.' Scratching his blond curls in sudden awkwardness. 'Ah, but in future, if you elect to remain with us here at Harrington, of course, you mustn't, um – girls and boys aren't actually allowed in each other's dormitories, night or day. That's the rule. I'm sure you can

303

understand why. Decorum, you know. We have to uphold certain standards.'

'Of course we do,' Mel said with sarcasm in her voice. Just when his first few words had started her warming to Antony Clive at last, he had to go and not only spoil their effect but deflate her positive mood entirely with his prissiness about rules. (*How totally like a boy.*) 'We'll try not to let you down again, boss.'

'I'm sorry.' Antony appeared pained. 'I didn't intend to embarrass . . . I'm not . . . I should have informed you sooner.'

'Don't worry about it, Antony,' said Travis.

Richie mumbled: 'Thought in these places it was the other *boys* you had to worry about.'

Scanning the group, Antony Clive seemed to sigh. 'Perhaps it's time for you to make your decision.'

They completed their introduction to Harrington. The Great Hall, where everybody dined at long tables most of which were now redundant, particularly the one set high on a raised platform to watch over the rest, the one traditionally occupied at mealtimes by the masters. The housekeeping area, where girls had adopted those duties – the cleaning, the laundry – formerly discharged by women, proving only, Mel huffed disapprovingly, that, like children, sexism seemed immune to the Sickness. The library with its shelves of books that had already outlived generations, which Antony nominated as the most important room in the school. 'We'll need two qualities to enable us to survive,' he said. 'Courage and knowledge. The first we have to find in ourselves. The second we can find here. From books we can learn how to tend our livestock, grow crops, make bread, keep the generator going. Everything.' Richie commented that he wasn't much of a reader; nobody seemed surprised.

And Travis had been right about the graves. Antony confirmed who was occupying them when the group had adjourned to the headmaster's study, a large room of leather chairs, rugs on the floor and Impressionist paintings on the walls. A little different from Dr Shiels's office at Wayvale Comp, Travis thought.

'When the Sickness came,' Antony said, 'Dr Stuart gave permission to both staff and boys, anyone who felt it was the right thing to do, to leave Harrington if they wished to return home. The day boys did, of course, last weekend, but a number of boarders stayed, including myself.'

'Why?' Mel was baffled. 'Didn't you want to be with your parents?'

'My parents are in South America. My father is on the staff at the British embassy in Buenos Aires. They phoned me on Monday to tell me to remain in Harrington until they could catch a flight home. Whether they managed to or not I suppose I'll never know. They never came. I've not heard from them since and now . . . I doubt I ever will.'

'I'm sorry, Antony,' Mel said shamefacedly.

'We all are.' Travis. And, for once, even Richie was prepared to at least *appear* sympathetic.

'Thank you. I appreciate . . . thank you. As for the masters, a handful of them, including Dr Stuart himself, elected to stay. They helped us to organise, to prepare for life after the Sickness. Even as they were dying one by one they thought only of us. The last time I spoke with Dr Stuart he told me,

"Harrington is not a school, but an ideal, an aspiration, the promise of a more enlightened, more civilised way of life." He told me, "Be true to the ideal. Never let it be lost. Be true to the values that Harrington has bred in you and bring them to others." That is my purpose as Head Boy. It's what I vowed to do.' Antony's green-eyed gaze flickered to the window. 'Dr Stuart lies with his colleagues now, but he will be remembered.'

'So your new community, Antony,' said Simon, 'it's going to be like a school?' He wasn't sure he relished that idea. Schools to Simon had always been less about teachers and students than bullies and victims. It was not an arrangement to which he wished to return.

'Not quite.' Antony smiled faintly. 'Though education will obviously be a vital factor, learning from the past to face the future. No. What I have in mind to establish is a community built on traditional English virtues, the principles on which Harrington was founded. Truth. Honour. Decency. Integrity. Self-restraint. Generosity. Fair play. The strong caring for the weak. Christian values.'

'You what?' Richie's reserves of sympathy for the blond boy's loss were clearly exhausted. 'All sounds a bit bloody poncey to me, mate.'

'I realise that in much of the country these are values that have already fallen into disrepute,' Antony remarked tartly. 'But the society that connived in the collapse of proper standards and traditional morality has itself now fallen. We are living in a new world. We have a chance to make it a better one.'

'I don't disagree with that, Antony,' said Travis. 'But it's not going to be easy. We've already met plenty of guys – those bikers who were after us, for a start – who aren't motivated by decency or fair play, whose only interest in the weak lies in intimidating and exploiting them. They'll see something like Harrington as a threat. They'll move against you.'

Antony nodded, his expression determined. 'I know that. You're right. But the school's motto is "Avoid the Easy Way". Nothing of true value can be achieved quickly. And, as I believe I have already pointed out, we are more than capable of robust self-defence.'

'You mean you can kill people,' Richie said pointedly.

'If and when necessary, yes. I make no apology for that. Archery was one of our games options at Harrington and we've learned well. Many Harringtonians also have experience of shooting with their fathers . . .'

'Pheasants or peasants?' inquired Richie.

'. . . And we've collected a number of firearms from the surrounding farms. We may be seen as enemies by bikers and brutes – I can live with that – but we shall certainly not be considered easy prey.'

'What about those bikers you . . . saved us from?' ventured Linden.

'Leo is arranging their burial,' said Antony. 'Leo Milton, my Deputy Head Boy. Ginger hair and freckles. You've already met him.'

'Sure,' said Travis. 'Bit young to be second-in-command, though, isn't he?'

'Another of our little mottos here: nobody is too young to take responsibility,' said Antony. 'But I've talked too much. You know something of Harrington now and I still know so little about the six of you. Where are you from? How did you find your way here?'

Travis filled Antony in on all that had happened to the group from Wayvale and the blond boy listened intently. He seemed particularly intrigued by Jester and his thinking.

'Odious though he sounds, he has a point, of course. The hardship of life on the streets may well perversely prove an asset in the present battle to survive. But it's not an advantage unique to the homeless. The boarders here at Harrington, including myself, we've had to learn independence and self-reliance as a matter of course, too. We've had to cope without our parents, our families. It's a tough regime. We're as equipped to lead in the post-Sickness world as the likes of Jester, and we have more enlightened reasons for doing so. A society cast in Harrington's image will be a better place in which to live than one modelled on Jester's.' He surveyed the new arrivals. 'Would you agree? Travis? Mel? Simon?'

'If you put it in those terms, it's difficult to *dis*agree,' admitted Travis.

'Then stay with us. Help us make it happen. We need you, people like you. I . . .' Antony's voice almost faltered. 'You remarked before that Leo Milton is rather young to be Deputy Head Boy. It may have escaped your notice, but I'm a year young to be Head Boy, too. I'm only in Year Twelve; the Head Boy should be selected from Year Thirteen.'

'Nobody blah too young blah responsibility blah,' observed Richie.

'Colin Matheson was our real, properly elected Head Boy,' Antony confessed. 'But his parents came to pick him up last weekend. One of the final things Dr Stuart did was to appoint me to the position in Matheson's place. I'm not . . . I've held the job less than a week.'

'We wouldn't have known, Antony,' Mel said encouragingly.

'And – well, I know what I believe. I know what Harrington should stand for. But I have to accept that we Harringtonians have led privileged lives thus far. I can't draw on the experiences that all of you can bring us, your knowledge of what's happening in the outside world. Courage and knowledge. You can provide our community with something that we're missing. You have to help us. I'm appealing to you. Please. You must stay.'

The moment of truth, Travis thought. 'Can we . . . decide among ourselves, Antony?'

'Of course. Of course. I'll be outside. Let me know when . . . let me know.'

'So,' Travis said when the study door had closed behind Antony Clive, 'it's simple enough. Do we become part of the Harrington community or do we not?'

'What do *you* think, Travis?' Linden asked cautiously.

'You need to ask?' Richie gave a laugh. 'Naughton's set his sights on becoming Deputy Head Boy Mark Two – can't you tell?'

'Have you, Travis?' Simon seemed concerned.

'I've set my sights on what's best for us,' said Travis, glaring Richiewards.

'And?' Linden prompted again.

'*And* . . .' When his father had said that unless good men were prepared to stand up for what was right evil men would have their way, he'd meant individuals, Travis knew. *Nobody is too young to take responsibility*. But the same imperative was also true for larger groups. The new communities would need to be strong to resist the Jesters and Revs of the world. Dad had worked closely with colleagues for the greater good. He'd been a police officer, part of an organisation larger than himself from which he'd drawn help and support. It sometimes required more than an individual to make a difference. '*And*,' Travis said, 'I think it's right for us to join Harrington.'

'What did I tell you?' Richie snorted.

'Me, too.' Mel. 'OK, I think Antony's a bit of a prat but he's a well-meaning prat and he can't be blamed for being the product of his class. And, yes, it's all a little bit "I say, good show, old chap", a bit snooty, but they've got a good place here, a big place, and people, and direction. Plus – maybe it's coincidence and maybe it isn't – it's only since we arrived here that Jessica's shown any sign of recovery. *So*, I think we should stay.'

'I agree,' said Simon. So it was a school. It wasn't like Wayvale Comp. It was a school where Richie Coker and his attitudes were likely to be sidelined. If Simon got lucky, his nemesis might even leave of his own accord or be shown the door by Antony Clive. The possibility almost made him smile. 'Safety in numbers.'

'It's good being part of a group,' said Linden. 'But you can only really belong if you've got something in common with that group. In some ways I'm not sure I have here. This is the kind of place the Children of Nature despised. They'd have called it reactionary, conformist, elitist. My mum would have died before . . . well, you know. Though I didn't fit in too well with the Children, either.' She fixed her gaze on Travis. 'I'm not sure whether I trust Antony, Travis, but I trust *you*. If you want to join Harrington, so do I.'

'Thanks, Linden,' said Travis.

'Oh, cosy. Oh, barf.' Pacing the study restlessly, Richie

pretended to throw up. 'Well, I think we're bloody mad if we stop here. I think these upper-class dorks don't have a clue what they're doing, not really. They've been spoiled and pampered all their lives and they reckon life's just a game, survival's just a . . . Fair play. Playing by the rules. What a load of shit. There *are* no rules. There's no one left to make them. Jester and Rev and guys like that, they're gonna come and they're gonna roll right over this place and they're gonna burn Clive's precious Harrington School to the ground just like Joe Drake and his mates did with Wayvale. And if we're not careful we'll be in here when it's burning.'

'I'm sure *you* won't, Richie,' Mel said contemptuously.

'Don't look down your nose at me, Morticia. I want to save my own skin, sure. Don't you want to save yours? Even if it is kind of pasty? And you've got a better chance of survival if you just keep a low profile, say yes to whoever's in charge, and absolutely *never* risk your life for something as useless as beliefs. You know what martyrs are? Yeah, I know. So I turned up once for an RE lesson. Martyrs. They're dead guys who the living get all misty-eyed over once in a while and then forget about while they go on living. This place stinks of martyr to me.'

'Is this a roundabout way of saying you're leaving, Richie?' said Travis.

Simon praying, *Pleasepleaseplease*.

'Leave and go where?' Richie stopped and stared out of the window. Darkness was descending. 'Back to Wayvale, maybe?'

'You can't go back, Richie,' said Travis. The dream of his father was in his mind. 'You have to go forward. Or you'll be lost.'

311

'Naughton.' Richie shook his head incredulously. 'You are so *full* of it. But you're not getting rid of me yet. I'll stick around – until I get a better offer. Wouldn't want to abandon my old mate Simes, now would I?'

Simon met the bully's arrogant grin with a fearlessness he could not have managed a week ago. And the key word was *yet*, he reassured himself. They wouldn't be getting rid of Coker *yet*. But soon. It had to be soon. Simon would find a way.

Travis called Antony back in. 'How many people did you say you had here again?'

'Forty-two,' said the Head Boy.

'Forty-eight,' Travis corrected him.

The next day was Sunday, which at Harrington meant morning service in the chapel, a Bible reading, a hymn sung from the school-issued hymn book, the Lord's Prayer. Everyone was expected to attend, apart from those on the early watch; everyone did attend apart from Richie, who declared disdainfully that he'd never been inside a church in his life and that he'd no intention of starting now.

After the brief service Antony drew Travis aside. There was something he wanted to show him, something they'd found while scavenging for supplies at a nearby farm, something the Harringtonians couldn't explain. Perhaps the new arrivals might be more successful. Travis agreed to the expedition immediately, though Mel declined when she was invited to join the boys, preferring to walk Jessica around the grounds. Linden was keen, however, to be with Travis and agreed to come along for that reason rather than because she was particularly interested in the nature of this mysterious

312

object that Antony refused to describe in advance. Simon joined the party too, for reasons of his own. Richie was nowhere to be found.

Leaving Leo Milton in charge, the little group drove off, accompanied by two archers and a third boy armed with an air rifle. They chose cars from the range available in the quad, Antony, Travis, Linden and the rifleman opting for a nippy Nissan, Simon and the archers following in a Renault.

Their weaponry was probably unnecessary. They saw neither person nor vehicle during the short journey to their destination, no sign of other human life.

'But it's never wise to take chances,' said Antony.

'Another one of Harrington's many mottos?' Travis teased mildly. Antony was driving, Travis sitting alongside him. 'I have to say, we're impressed by what you've already managed to achieve – aren't we, Linden?'

In the back seat Linden agreed. Though she was less impressed by the barrel of the air rifle, which seemed to be developing a disturbing inclination to prod her in the ribs as if she was under guard and could expect to be executed at any moment. 'Excuse me,' she said to its owner. 'Could you point this thing somewhere else, please? It's making me nervous.'

'I mean compared to us,' Travis was continuing, 'just virtually running around the country, you *know* where you're going. I'm envious, Antony.'

'I wouldn't be.' Antony smiled ruefully. 'It's been handed to me on a plate so far. The school's a perfect site for a community, that's true, but it's not as though I had to search for it. As Head Boy I've inherited a ready-made following who respect and accept my authority without question. But they'd respect and accept *any* Head Boy. What if it's only the status they're responding to and not me personally?'

'I'm sure it's you, Antony. You can tell they're not just going through the motions.'

'Can you? I hope so. I just feel I haven't been tested yet. Unlike you and your group, Travis. You've engaged with the destructive element more than once already. As you've raised the subject, I don't mind admitting I'm a little envious, too. Of you.'

Coincidentally, envy was an emotion also being experienced by at least one of the occupants of the car behind. Simon interpreted his presence in the Renault as a kind of demotion, an erosion of the position he imagined he'd held with Travis. Travis had promised to be his friend, his protector, but constantly now he seemed to be turning to others and overlooking Simon. Ignoring him. Jessica and Mel, he didn't mind them. Travis had known the girls for longer, they'd done things together for years – he was bound to be closer to them. But if it wasn't bad enough allowing Richie Coker into the group, now there was this Linden bird too, and she clearly had the hots for Travis and was wheedling her way in with him – and he was *letting* her. But, again, OK. Linden was a girl. That was different from a male friend. Maybe Travis fancied her back.

But there was absolutely *no* excuse for the preferential treatment that he seemed to be giving Antony Clive. Sitting alongside him up ahead like they were old pals, kindred spirits or something. They'd only just met. Simon wasn't happy. His own loyalty to Travis was unrivalled – so why didn't Travis want him in the same car? It wasn't often that Simon listened to anything Richie Coker said (other than 'Give me your dinner money or else') but the crack he'd made yesterday, about Travis wanting to be Deputy Head Boy, Simon felt there was a ring of truth in that. What if Travis *did* allow himself to be sidetracked into the running of Harrington? What if he was tempted to forget his first friends, his real friends, and his promises to them? That wouldn't be fair. That wouldn't be acceptable. Simon thought he'd better keep his eye on Antony Clive.

A left turn and a road spattered with dried manure took them to the farm. They parked by its ramshackle outbuildings and got out. The place was deserted.

'Our cows came from here,' Antony said. 'We were *going* to go through the house, too, but—'

'Something got there before you,' finished Travis softly, and whistled in wonder.

A hole had been blasted right through the middle of the farmhouse, gaping like an astonished mouth. It was some twenty metres across. The roof directly above the massive cavity was sagging but hadn't quite yet collapsed inwards. Tiles had slid from it to shatter on the ground but, considering the damage done to the brickwork generally, precious little debris littered the surrounding area. It seemed to Travis that a missile of some description must have struck the building like a bullet entering a body. He said as much.

'A most appropriate simile,' said Antony. 'As you'll see.'

The hole in the farmhouse's back wall matched that in its front for size but not for height. The exit cavity was lower, suggesting a trajectory angled from above. Something had fallen at great velocity, pierced the house and ploughed into the earth beyond. Hence the ragged, shallow crater in the garden, the stony soil that had erupted at the moment of impact and that had shattered every window at the back of the house. There was more than enough rubble here to compensate for its absence out front.

And in the crater, the cylinder.

'What the hell . . . ?' exclaimed Travis, staring.

'Give or take an expletive,' Antony said, 'precisely.'

The cylinder was black and metallic and it glittered like a devil's smile. In fact, its surface's ebony glossiness seemed to be constantly shifting, fluctuating, independent of the natural light playing on it, flowing as if dark waters were perpetually washing over its surface. The object was ten metres or so long and rounded at each end; its diameter was perhaps three metres. Remarkably, the collisions it had suffered appeared to have damaged the cylinder not at all – not even a dent, not even a scratch. The most startling aspect of the thing for Travis, however, was that it was clearly an artefact, a device. Not a meteor. Not any kind of natural phenomenon. Man-made. But *which* men? And why?

'I'd rather hoped *you* might be able to tell *us*,' said Antony after Travis had asked these questions aloud. 'I'd rather hoped you might have seen an item on the news or something that possibly explained it. A government probe into areas known to be infected by the Sickness, perhaps. It has a serial number of some kind on it.'

'What?' Travis was so absorbed by the cylinder that he failed to notice Linden's face growing paler all the time.

'Jump down and see. It's quite safe – well, as far as we can tell, to be fair. You'll see it. On the side nearest us. And feel the thing, too.'

Travis stepped out over the lip of the crater and let himself drop down beside the cylinder. To steady his landing he reached out to touch the object. The metal was iceberg-cold, like the inside of a freezer, like outer space. Like death. He withdrew his hand with an involuntary cry.

'Travis?' A concerned Linden.

'It's all right. It's just . . .'

'Freezing?' supplied Antony.

'Yeah. On a warm day.'

'The external temperature doesn't seem to affect it. The cylinder's felt that cold since we found it a few days ago. It's too heavy for us to move so it could be totally solid. There's certainly no trace of any hatch or mechanism for activating an opening. On the other hand, if it doesn't contain anything, what purpose can it possibly serve?' Antony shrugged in defeat. 'We've no idea how long it's been here, but almost certainly only since the Sickness or I'm sure we'd have heard of it.'

'Be careful, Travis,' Linden said again as he examined more closely the device's sleek and smooth casing.

'It's OK. It's OK.' He found Antony's serial number marked on the metal, though to call it a number was to define the word very loosely. What Travis was studying was a series of symbols, as utterly unintelligible as a foreign language. *A foreign language.* 'Hey, what if this is written in Chinese or Korean or Arabic or something? You know, from a country that doesn't like us. We talked about the Sickness being a ter-roris— No, can't be. They had the Sickness in Iran and everywhere too. I did see that on the news.'

'If those symbols *are* language,' said Antony, kneeling at the edge of the crater, 'it's not a tongue ever taught at Harrington, which one has to say rather narrows it down. Perhaps, if not a serial number, some kind of scientific coding?'

'Could be. Simon?' Travis waved him over. 'You're the boffin. Any ideas?'

'Ah, actually' – flushing, his big chance to prove his worth to Travis – 'I'm not . . .'

'I suppose it could have something to do with the eye I saw.'

Everyone suddenly turned towards Linden. 'The what?'

She smiled sheepishly. 'There was this floating ball thing, like an eye. I saw it in Willowstock. The children at our settlement saw it, too, before then.' Falteringly, 'I . . . should have mentioned it earlier, I suppose.'

'Yeah, I suppose you should,' Travis said, a touch of disappointment in his voice. He climbed back out of the crater. 'Mention it now.'

Linden told her companions everything she could. 'I didn't believe the kids at first,' she concluded, 'and then, when I did see it myself, so briefly, I thought I might have imagined – thought it was a hallucination. I didn't want to make myself look stupid, like some kind of nutter, not when I'd just met you, Travis, and everyone else, so I kept quiet. But now. This. I'm sorry.'

Antony for one recognised sincerity in her eyes. 'It's all right, Linden. We quite understand, don't we, Travis?'

Travis might have seen the same honesty if he'd condescended to meet her gaze at all. 'Sure. You've told us now, anyway.' But he felt certain that any of Antony's fellow Harringtonians would have informed him of such an encounter immediately. It hurt that Linden hadn't trusted him. 'Not that your information's much help right now. Instead of one mystery, we've now got two.'

'Sorry, Travis.' Linden tried again but his back was to her.

'Yeah. Don't worry about it. Shouldn't we be getting back to Harrington, Antony?'

Though perhaps Linden didn't have *too* much to fret over, Simon thought a little resentfully. She still travelled back in the same car as Travis.

They might have discussed the cylinder and the eye further once they'd returned to the school, possibly considering whether the two devices might be connected somehow. But events at Harrington were about to alter their priorities.

Antony saw them first. A white van parked in front of the school as if a plumber had called to check the pipes. A Vauxhall family saloon, lacking the family. A pair of Harley Davidson motorbikes. Around the vehicles, a milling crowd of armed Harringtonians, Leo Milton prominent among them. 'It appears that we may have attracted some more new recruits,' the Head Boy said cheerfully.

'I wouldn't bet on it.' Travis's tone was grim. Mel and Richie were part of the group, exchanging what, reduced to mime by distance, still seemed to be angry words with several youths in leather, one or two of whom Travis recognised. A girl he'd last seen sprawling on the road. A thug with a pock-marked face. 'That's Rev.'

It was then that both boys noticed the white flags hanging from the bikes' handlebars.

'What's he here for, Travis?' Linden leaned forward nervously.

'Not to wish us well, that's for sure.' The blue eyes narrowed. 'You wanted a test, Antony. You might want to be careful what you wish for in future.'

'They're here under what appears to be a flag of truce,'

Antony observed, pulling up just behind Rev's vehicles. 'We're honour bound to listen to what they have to say, at least.'

Leo Milton had rushed over even before they'd climbed out of the car. 'Am I glad to see you, Clive. We have a situation here. Visitors.'

'So why haven't you invited them inside? Extended the traditional Harrington hospitality?'

'Perhaps,' suggested Leo Milton, 'you'd better hear what they want first.'

Mel darted across to Travis and threw her arms around him. Anxiety flickered in her eyes. '*Trav.*'

'I know. Don't worry. It'll be fine.' He glanced towards the Head Boy of the Harrington School. *As long as Antony knows what he is doing.*

The two groups met by the bikes in the shadow of the castle. Leather jackets and blazers.

'Kiddo.' Rev's grin was more like a sneer as he regarded Travis. 'Good to see you again.'

'Can't say the feeling's mutual.'

'Don't waste time on *him*, Rev.' At her leader's right hand, the girl in leather snarling.

'You're right, babe. We've been kept waiting here for an hour for the Head Boy to come back. Which of you proper young gentlemen is he?'

'I'm Antony Clive.' Stepping forward, offering his hand. Which wasn't taken. 'As Head Boy of the Harrington School, I'm pleased to meet you.'

Rev chuckled. 'Can't say the feeling's mutual. I'm Rev. You killed five of my guys yesterday.'

'They were trespassing on private property yesterday,' said

Antony bluntly. 'They were armed and posed a threat to our community.'

'You think anyone gives a toss about private property any more, rich boy?'

'I doubt whether some people ever cared very much about anything,' Antony responded archly. 'Rev.'

'I don't believe it. Would you believe it?' A sudden interruption from one of the biker's lackeys who so far had been lurking in the background. He pushed his way to his leader's side. Then he pointed at Linden and laughed, not warmly. 'Lin.'

Linden's blood ran cold. 'Ash.'

'You know this chick, Ash?' asked Rev, grinning.

'Just a bit. Actually, just about every bit.' Rev and the rest of his entourage found that amusing. 'You could say we were close.' Ash embraced a phantom figure in front of him and puckered up. 'I'd say about *this* close.'

Linden stared at the ground in humiliation, willing a deeper crater than the one that the cylinder had made to open up and swallow her whole. So she wouldn't have to be aware of Travis's quizzical, confused eyes looking at her, the pity in Mel's. 'Way to go, hippie chick.' The gloating in Richie's.

Ash was enjoying himself. 'We were Children of Nature together, weren't we, Lin? But that was then. Which lucky lad's getting close to you now?'

'Shut up, Ash.' How could she ever have liked him, let him touch her, let him . . . ? His body was squat and ugly. His features were stupid and slow. She'd been told that love was blind – but did it have to be retarded as well?

'I know you, Lin. There's got to be someone. You don't like lonely.'

'Shut up.' A lucky escape. Ash had found his rightful place with Rev and his rabble.

'Let me tell you, any of you blazer boys here, if you think you're up to it, she's—'

'Shut,' growled Travis, 'up.' Fists clenched. Blue eyes burning. Linden saw that. Her heart leaped. 'Or I'll make you.'

'So *you*'re the one,' sneered Ash.

'Kiddo, why am I not surprised?' Rev said. 'But you, Ash, do like he says and shut the hell up or *I*'ll make you. We didn't come here to talk chicks. Business, Antony Clive. Our dead. How you're gonna – what's the word?'

'Compensate,' supplied the girl in leather.

'Yeah. How you're gonna compensate us for our loss. 'Cause we don't want any bad feeling. We don't like bad feeling, not when we're almost like neighbours.' Rev's eyes glittered. 'We don't want to fight.'

'That's just as well,' observed Antony, 'given that you appear to be rather significantly outnumbered.'

Rev chuckled. 'Listen to this guy.' Adopting a mock, effeminately upper-class accent. '*Rather significantly outnumbered*. Well, believe that if you like, rich boy, but we've got people joining us all the time, people wanting to be custodians of the Queen's Highway. This isn't all of us.'

'This isn't all of *us*, either,' said Antony, realising why Leo Milton had wisely kept the bikers from entering the school building and perhaps gaining a truer assessment of their strength.

'It doesn't matter,' declared Rev, ' 'cause like I say, we don't want to fight. Not if we can sort our little problem out peacefully.'

'I'm willing to negotiate.'

322

'He's *willing to negotiate*. Listen to this guy. OK, here's the terms. You killed five of my guys but that's all right. We've got more where they came from – plenty more. Put it down to an accident. I mean, you didn't deliberately set out to provoke us. But someone did. Someone provoked us bad, provoked me, showed me no respect – me, a custodian of the Queen's Highway – and they need to be taught a lesson. So we want them. And that's how you're gonna compensate us, rich boy. You hand them over, we leave, and everybody's happy.' He turned to Travis. 'You're coming with us, kiddo. And your little friends. Ash, you might even get lucky again. Though not for long.'

'Nobody,' Antony intervened, 'is going anywhere with anyone unless they are willing to do so. Travis?'

'You have to ask?'

'One must always be clear in matters of diplomacy,' said Antony. 'And can I take it that Travis speaks for you all?' This time he'd spoken even for Richie. 'Then I'm afraid that our negotiations are concluded.' Making quote marks in the air with his fingers: 'Rev.'

'You what?'

'Would you like it in writing? Can you read?' Travis watched Antony with mingled relief and gratitude. Not that he'd ever doubted him, not really. And yeah, he did look a little like the Caesar on that coin. 'The Harrington School welcomes any who seek shelter within its walls, and we'll surrender no one to vermin such as yourself. Your request for compensation is denied.'

'Don't get smart with me, rich boy. Don't be so hasty, neither. For *your* sake.' Rev's mood was swiftly darkening. 'Let me just – if you *don't* do what we want and give us kiddo and his mates, then we'll come and get them and we'll take them by force, and we'll crush anyone who stands in our way. You hear me, rich boy? We'll burn your little playschool to the ground.'

'You can try,' said Antony.

'OK. OK.' Rev snorted. 'Have it your way. But I'm still gonna give you one more chance. 'Cause you talk nice. We'll go now but we'll be seeing you again at – when? – dawn tomorrow. Dawn. And if you give kiddo here up to us then, fine. Everybody's still happy. But if you don't, let me tell you, rich boy, it *won't* be fine.' The biker stabbed his finger at Antony's chest. 'It'll be war . . .'

ELEVEN

That afternoon, Travis went to see Antony in the headmaster's study. The blond boy was alone, sitting in the headmaster's chair, staring out distractedly across the grounds towards the graves by the trees.

'Antony?' Travis had to speak before the other teenager seemed fully aware of his presence. 'I thought we'd better talk.'

'Did I do the right thing with Rev?'

'You did the right thing. I'm just not sure that *we* have.'

'I don't follow.'

Travis frowned, troubled. 'Maybe we shouldn't stay here, my group. Maybe we should just get out now while Rev's mustering his forces or whatever. If there's gonna be a battle tomorrow, it'll be over us, and whether we win or lose . . .'

'We'll win,' stated Antony.

'Whether we win or lose, there'll be casualties. Kids, young kids who maybe don't really know what they're doing, or why, they'll be risking their lives for us, for people who two days ago they weren't even aware existed. What if some of them are killed tomorrow? For us. I'm not sure that's something I want on my conscience. It might be better for us to go.'

'You can't go. You're needed here.' Antony stood up.

'Harrington, what I'm trying to found here, it mustn't simply be a place, just bricks and mortar. It has to be spirit, too, and belief. It has to mean something, to symbolise our faith in the future, an ordered, civilised future, where right and wrong don't only still exist but still *matter*. That's what we'll be fighting for tomorrow, Travis, not for you and the others alone but for a way of life, *our* way of life, and that's worth any sacrifice. Don't leave now. You've only just found us. Now find the strength to stay.'

'Antony, I'm not sure . . .'

'If we don't make a stand here, Rev and all the others like him will have their way.'

Travis felt his eyes sting. The old words, rephrased for new circumstances: words his father might have said. He thought of his father. Dad, the knife wound in his chest, gasping out his final breaths in a street where people walked. He remembered once again. *I want to be like you, Dad. I'll do what's right. I'll make my stand. I promise.* And now, perhaps, his time had truly come.

'Your Dr Stuart knew what he was doing when he made you Head Boy, Antony. I'll give him that.'

'You mean—?' Hopefully.

'We'll stay,' said Travis.

Linden was waiting for Travis in the corridor. 'Hi,' she said.

'Hi.'

She looked nervous, uncertain, almost as if she half expected Travis to hit her again. He suspected he knew why. 'Ah, Travis? I wanted to say thanks. For speaking up for me with Ash.'

'No worries.' He wasn't pausing to chat, was striding off

down Harrington's long corridors towards the dorms. Couldn't have said why. Didn't really need to be going there. Linden was almost having to run to keep pace with him. 'I don't approve of anybody making comments like that about a . . . a friend of mine. 'Specially not when the guy making the comments is such a patent creep.'

'You're right. Ash *is* a creep.'

Travis halted abruptly. Linden practically collided with him. 'So why did you—?' Hurt in his eyes, perplexity. 'Nothing he said was untrue, was it?'

'I wish it was. I wish I'd never known Ash.'

'But I guess, living with the Children of Nature, not exactly a wide choice of boyfriends, yeah?'

'You could say that,' admitted Linden, though she'd rather Travis hadn't spoken with that kind of hard, sarcastic edge to his voice.

'And, of course, you had to have a boyfriend.'

'It wasn't . . . It was the Sickness. Everything was falling apart. Everyone was dying. I needed someone to be there for me and Ash was. Yes, he was taking advantage of me. I can see that now but you can't see everything at the time, can you? Nobody's perfect, are they?' Travis didn't appear to be prepared to agree with her any time soon. '*I*'m not, anyway, and I needed comfort, I needed to know that I was alive, to *feel* that I was alive. If that makes me weak, well. We can't all be strong, Travis.'

And part of him wanted to enfold her in his arms, stroke her hair, kiss her cheek, her lips, her neck. But another part of him visualised the grinning Ash doing those same things, smearing her body with his fingers, and Linden liking it. And still another part of him wanted to tell her it was all right,

327

everything was all right, that it didn't matter that she'd kept the existence of the flying globe secret, didn't matter what she'd done in the past or who with, none of that mattered because when he was around her he felt— But another part of him didn't feel, couldn't bring himself to feel. The part he'd trained since his father's death to protect him from feelings and keep him safe.

'Why are you telling me all this, Linden?'

'I wanted to explain. Why me and Ash happened. So you didn't think I was . . .'

'Whatever you did before we met is none of our business.'

'Our?'

'The group. You're one of the group now.'

'But I don't just want to be one of the group, Travis. I want to be . . .'

'What?'

'It doesn't matter.'

But it did. And they both knew it.

Outside, against the window-pane, the first sound of rainfall, like a hundred beating hearts.

Richie listened to the rain as he stood on the landing in the night. Its relentless hiss reminded him of the audience response to the appearance of the villain in that pantomime his mum had taken him to see that Christmas, a million years ago. In the show the villain had worn black in order to identify himself to the hard-of-understanding. These days villains wore hooded sweatshirts and baseball caps – hey, and guess what *Richie* was wearing. But the weather's jeers weren't prompted by his entrance. They seemed to him to be in anticipation of his exit.

328

If he was going to do a runner, the time was now.

He'd dressed and had stolen out of the dorm while every-one else was sleeping. He was at the top of the staircase now: nothing to prevent him descending it, creeping into the quad, liberating one of the cars and getting the hell out of there. The watch was posted, of course, but if Richie Coker couldn't sneak round the back of half a dozen dozing snobs then he didn't deserve to save his skin. And abandoning Naughton, Morticia, Simes, Harrington itself, that was the only way to do it for sure.

He reckoned.

OK, so Antony Clive had a plan of defence ready for the morning, and they all now knew their role in it and, to be fair, it just might work. The key word, though, was *might*. 'Might' always implied the possibility of 'might *not*', and 'might not' would leave them – him – at the mercy of Rev and his gang of morons. *Would*. For certain. Not good enough.

And why should Richie Coker put himself on the line for a rich kid like Clive and a do-gooder like Naughton anyway? He hadn't signed up to fight Rev or anyone else. Why should he risk his continuing health for the greater-good kind of crap they kept jabbering on about, like they were in church or something? There was nothing greater in life than yourself. You had to look after number one.

Which, being the case, maybe he should think about stay-ing where he was, after all. What if the good guys (according to themselves, anyway) *did* win tomorrow, *did* give Rev and his bikers a bloody nose? It could be a sweet set-up here, Richie had to admit. A nice little number. An easy life. If he fled, he'd be on his own. He didn't like the sound of that.

Another sound. The door of the girls' dorm opening.

He didn't want to be seen. He didn't want questions asked.

Moment of decision. And it still might not even come to battle, but if it did he only needed to keep his head down, out of harm's way. He could manage that. Let the others engage the enemy, face the gunfire. He could slip out quietly in defeat or emerge from hiding in victory with lies of bravery on his lips. Either way, he'd make damn sure that Richie Coker was OK.

Decision made. When Mel padded barefoot to the top of the staircase too, she had no idea that Richie had been standing there only seconds before. Neither did she detect the closing click of a door along the corridor. In her defence, there were other things on her mind.

Rev had visited her dreams tonight, or for a moment she'd imagined so. He'd advanced menacingly towards her, wearing a helmet that somehow covered his entire face, his legs swinging stiffly from the hips, as though they'd lost the habit of natural movement. She'd realised why when he'd reached up and removed his helmet. It hadn't been Rev at all. 'I'm coming for you, Melanie,' her father had threatened. 'You can't hide from me.'

She cried out when the hand touched her shoulder.

'Ssh! You'll wake the whole place. It's only me.' Linden.

Mel masked her embarrassment with anger. 'What do you think you're doing – creeping up on someone like that in the middle of the night?'

'You don't expect me to draw attention to myself in *this*, do you?' Linden and Mel had both borrowed nightdresses from the selection garnered from the surrounding area and stored in housekeeping. Linden's choice – an ankle-length winceyette number that had probably last seen service during the Blitz – was perhaps a little unfortunate. At least it served to lighten the mood.

'Lingerie to linger in,' Mel giggled.

'I heard you talking in your sleep again. It didn't sound like a pleasant conversation. Saw you get up. Another nightmare?'

'I needed the loo. Is that all right with you?'

'The loo's the other way. Mel,' Linden dared to ask, 'what happened to your dad?'

'Nothing.' Trying to dismiss the other girl's concern. 'Apart from the fact that he died. But then, whose dad didn't?'

Linden wasn't deceived. 'There's more to it than that, though, isn't there? You kept repeating his name like you were frightened. Of *him*. You kept warning him to stay away. It's your dad giving you the nightmares, isn't it? You can tell me, Mel. I won't tell anyone else, I promise. I want to help.'

Mel hung her head, her long black hair spilling down her front like ink. 'You can't help,' she sighed, too exhausted by the dreams to fend off Linden's persistence. 'What's done is done.'

'What – *is* done?' Linden ventured.

'My dad's dead, yeah. But the Sickness didn't kill him. I did.'

'I don't believe you.' Shocked but certain. 'You *can't* have.'

'Oh, you could call it an accident. You could call it that if you were looking for excuses. Let me off lightly. We were on the stairs at home, see. Dad was already infected, weak, well on the way to . . . And I was ahead of him, going up to check on my mum, and he was behind me and he grabbed me. He *grabbed* me, his hand was on me and this time it was one time too many and I turned and I swung my arm and I kind of

331

shook him off but – he lost his balance and he fell. He broke his neck. Died. At the bottom of our stairs.'

Linden's gaze narrowed. 'I don't understand. Why—? What do you mean, *this* time when he grabbed you?'

'Oh, he was keen on grabbing, was Dad.' Mel's eyes blinked furious, guilty tears. 'He used to do it a lot. He used to hit me. A lot. So when I saw him, when he was dead, I was glad. I was *glad*. Glad that my own father was dead. So I deserve to suffer, don't I? And he'll make sure I do. Every night. In my dreams.'

'No, he won't. He won't.' Linden put her arms around Mel, comforted her. 'Not now you've told someone. You've been bottling all this up. *That's* been the problem. You've let the . . . accident gnaw away at you inside like what happened was your fault but it wasn't, was it? You didn't push him, did you?'

'No, but . . . I think I wish I had.'

'You don't. Not really. That's just guilt and there's no need for you to feel guilty. From what you've just said your dad's to blame, if anyone. You did nothing wrong.'

'I didn't do very much right, though, either,' Mel said mournfully. 'That's what Travis would say. Reason why I haven't told him. I let my feelings get the better of me. I didn't think.'

'That can happen,' said Linden. Her eyes seemed to be looking beyond Mel, as if she was seeing the past rather than the present. 'And when it does, we can all make mistakes, make fools of ourselves. All of us.'

'That guy Ash,' Mel guessed sympathetically.

'Yeah.' Linden focused again on her companion. 'Him.'

'Scumbag ex-boyfriends. Abusive fathers. We could do without males altogether, I sometimes think.'

332

'I wouldn't go that far.' Linden remembered with distaste Ash's hands on her, his lips, wondered with excitement what it would be like to feel *Travis's* hands on her, *his* lips. He did like her. She knew he did, sensed the attraction. It was only going to be a matter of time.

'I'm glad I've told you about my dad, Linden,' Mel said.

'I'm glad you trusted me enough to tell me.' Linden smiled. 'And something else Travis said: whatever we've done or haven't done, we've been under intolerable pressure. Trying to cope with the consequences of the Sickness, no wonder we've all gone a little crazy here and there. But that phase is almost over now, Mel. The old world's finished. Whoever we were in it, whatever we did, it means nothing any more. Whatever baggage we carry from it – guilt, regret – we have to cut it loose. We *can* cut it loose. Tomorrow Rev is gonna come and we're going to fight him – and Ash – and if we win we'll be able to start again, start afresh, renew ourselves like Mum used to say Nature does.' Linden's hazel eyes shone on the landing in the night. 'If we win tomorrow, Mel, everything's possible.'

Dawn came, though it was difficult to tell precisely when. The rain that had teemed down all night still tumbled like hard stones quarried from the grey pit of the sky. The little glimmering brightness was the colour of slate, as if the day hadn't fully made up its mind whether to appear or not. Light and darkness contended, neither certain of supremacy.

One of the watch, a boy whose voice had not yet broken, reported to Antony, Travis and Leo Milton in the headmaster's study that a delegation from the bikers was approaching the school on foot. Three in number, two males and a female, unarmed and bearing white flags. 'Then we'd better go and meet them,' said Antony. The Harringtonians were equipped with their own flags of truce this morning, cut from sheets.

It had been decided that Travis, as a representative of the group at the centre of the dispute, should accompany the Head Boy and his deputy for any final parley with Rev. Together, they made their way along the corridor, out into the quad, crossing to the arch. They moved with purpose but without haste, their expressions fixed, determined, betraying no hint of anxiety or apprehension. Antony had stressed that their comrades should perceive only reassuring resolve and morale-boosting confidence in the faces of their leaders as they passed by. Fear, like the Sickness, was contagious.

In common with every other door and entrance into the school, the arch was now defended by barricades – desktops nailed together into timber shields and propped up by slanting poles – constructed by boys in the woodwork room. By themselves these barriers were hardly impregnable, but they also served as protection for the Harringtonians with shotguns who were ready to stand behind them and fire at any biker reckless enough to ride within range.

The barricades were parted to let the three boys through. 'Good luck, Clive,' somebody said.

Travis glanced behind him. Most of the school's defenders had gathered in the dripping quadrangle. All were armed in some manner, the elite marksmen with guns or bows, the rest with more primitive staves or clubs. The lads in the woodwork room had been busy. Briefly, Travis saw Mel and Linden, who gave him a smile and an encouraging kind of half-wave. They'd be a team during the assault if – when – it occurred. That was good. They could rely on each other; neither would let the other down.

Which, of course, was the idea. Antony had organised the defence of the school building itself on the principle of friendship teams. 'Like some of the armies in ancient Greece,' he'd explained. 'If you're fighting side by side with a close friend, someone you love, you'll battle harder to ensure the survival of you both than if you're placed alongside a total stranger. Pairs of friends as far as possible – that's how we'll do it.'

Assuming that they were on amicable terms, Antony had originally partnered Simon and Richie. But neither of them were having that: they'd had to be matched with other Harringtonians instead. Travis hoped that Simon would be all right. He looked for him in vain – and then the barricades were being pushed to once more and he had to focus his attention on what lay ahead.

Rev. Ash. The girl in leather. Awaiting the Harrington deputation a hundred yards away, their leather jackets glossy with rain.

'This Rev fellow's not going to compromise, is he?' said Leo Milton. He didn't seem to be entirely disappointed.

'No,' Travis agreed tersely. 'He's not.'

'So why are we simply going through the motions?'

'Because a civilised society is based on rituals, Leo,' said Antony. 'And this is one of them.'

They marched towards the enemy.

'Morning, Head Boy, Little Head Boy.' Rev appeared to be in a breezy, swaggering mood. 'Morning, kiddo. Not a good day for it, is it? So I won't hang about. Rain'll spoil your posh blazers.' Antony and Leo were wearing full school uniform.

'Are you and your little gang coming with us, kiddo, or are we coming to you?'

'Nothing has changed since yesterday,' said Antony.

'I told you, Rev,' snapped the girl in leather. 'This is a waste of time. Let's get on with it.'

'We attack, rich boy. No mercy,' Rev warned, with a grin.

'Mercy is a moral concept,' said Antony. 'I wouldn't expect it from you. *Iacta alea est.*'

'You what? You disrespecting me?' Rev's grin became a glower.

'It's Latin. It means "the die is cast". If you want a battle, Rev, you've got one.'

'Excellent,' enthused the girl in leather.

'I'm coming for you, kiddo.' Rev.

'I'll be waiting.' Travis.

'Hey,' said Ash, 'and tell Linden I'll be seeing her soon, yeah?'

'Guess we won't be needing these no more.' Rev threw down his white flag, trod it into the dirt.

Both sides turned their backs on each other. 'That die,' Travis muttered, 'well and *truly* bloody cast.'

Before they'd even reached the arch Antony was punching his fist into the air. The signal for the Harrington School's plan of defence to be initiated. The barricades were hauled open again and twenty uniformed students jogged through, almost half the community's total fighting strength. Each boy wielded either a shotgun or a bow. A spare firearm was given to Leo Milton.

'All right, you know what to do. Be true to the spirit of Harrington. Good luck.' Antony clapped his deputy on the shoulder. 'Good luck, Leo.'

'Thank you, Clive. You, too. And you, Naughton.'

Travis returned the sentiment with feeling before Leo Milton and his force dispersed among the undergrowth and the trees. 'You think the plan'll work, Antony?'

And with just the two of them present, Antony finally allowed his features to show his doubts. 'We'll know soon enough,' he said.

Already, beyond the grounds and snarling like wild beasts at the bars of a cage, the roar of engines revving.

Richie heard it in the library where, though he'd scarcely ever read a book in his life, he was stationed, along with a curly-haired kid called Digby – first or last name, Richie had no idea. Didn't care, neither. So long as the boy wasn't called Simon. Digby had an air rifle and a sense of mission: 'We're so lucky to be placed here, Coker. We've been trusted with a weighty responsibility. The books must be protected at all costs.' At all costs to Digby – Richie was happy to accept that, but at none to himself. Let the pompous twat shoot from the window; Richie was keeping his eye on the door.

And already the engines' volume was escalating as vehicles so far unglimpsed trespassed onto the grounds of Harrington.

Mel and Linden, with fire extinguishers in their hands, heard it in the cold stone corridors. A little sexist, perhaps, but it had been decreed that girls should not become actual combatants in the forthcoming fray unless absolutely unavoidable. Their job was to put out any fires that might be started by Rev. 'I just hope Jessie's going to be all right,' Mel said, worried. She'd left the blonde girl sleeping in the dorm, oblivious to the imminence of violence.

And already, Rev's phalanx of vehicles was closing in on the school, racing into view, ripping forward through the rain.

Simon saw it from the vantage point of Harrington's upper floor. He'd been sent there with a first-year boy, Giles somebody, who was renowned both for fleetness of foot and eagleness of eye. Too young to be on the front line, his task was to monitor the course of the battle and relay to Antony in the quad intelligence about where the school's defences might need reinforcement. Simon had not initially been flattered to be teamed with such a youngster: by association with Giles he might appear to be unfit to fight – the club he'd been given seemed puny and pathetic. But now he was changing his mind. As he saw it, he wasn't a coward. But constant persecution had taught him to anticipate pain with dread. And pain seemed to be coming to Harrington.

Rev's forces included motorbikes, of course. Maybe a dozen, maybe more (Giles was counting them). Rider, passenger, guns. (And bottles? Was that a glint of glass in the pillion rider's possession?) But that wasn't all. The bikers had diversified into other forms of transport. Cars. Vans. Larger vehicles. *Not so easy to stop with bows and arrows,* Simon realised with horror. A single-decker bus grinding up through its gears at the rear. *Not so easy to stop at all.* It looked like the attack was going to be pressed in two waves: cars, then bikes. Giles thought so, too. 'I'd better go and let Clive know the numbers,' he said, sprinting off. 'Stay here, Satchwell.' This last was unnecessary. Simon had no intention of straying. Wide-eyed, he watched the struggle unfold beneath him.

The Harringtonians were keen to engage the enemy. Shotgun blasts crackled from their various hiding places among the trees, flashes in the grey. Arrows streaked across the dingy sky. But unlike the hapless fatalities of the other day's skirmish, this time Rev's followers were prepared for attack, returning fire themselves through their cars' windows. An archer, frustrated as his shafts snapped as feebly as twigs against the bodywork of the oncoming vehicles, broke cover to find a better aiming point. Gave the enemy the chance to do the same. Cried out as a bullet smashed into his chest. Thudded to the earth. Writhed in agony on soaking grass. Thirteen years old. A boy rushing to his aid never saw the shot that hit him. His stare had been fixed on his fallen friend and now he dropped bleeding beside him.

Elsewhere, successes. The white plumbers' van caught in a crossfire as it sped towards the school. Two of its tyres exploding. Veering out of control. Crashing into an oak head-on. Its driver learning belatedly and painfully why wearing a seat belt is always a good idea. Momentum took him through the windscreen but not through the tree trunk. His passengers spilling out, now vulnerable to Harrington's archers. A short distance away, a solitary brave marksman exposed to full view as a Peugeot hurtled towards him, splintering its windscreen with a single blast, scurrying for safety only when the car, out of control, failed to avoid a hefty fallen bough that tipped it up onto its side, the vehicle then skidding onto its roof, wheels spinning uselessly in the air.

So successes, yes – but few and far between. Even on the saturated ground with the wet causing their tyres to slip, Rev's forces quickly got behind the main body of Harrington's fighters, flashed between them, effectively bypassing the natural cover provided by the terrain. An archer, fleeing one battered old estate, catching a glancing blow from the wing of another. Someone pausing to reload not permitted the opportunity as a bullet shattered his hand. Someone else pinned with his back to a beech – and, shortly afterwards, as he slid to the ground, his blood dribbling down the tree after him, as if seeking to return to the vein it had bled from.

The Harrington line breached in several places, the bikers and the bus not even committed yet, the defenders' discipline failed. Fit and wounded together, the boys stumbled into retreat. No sign of Leo Milton to stiffen their flagging will.

Behind the arch's barricades, Travis glanced uneasily at Antony Clive.

'All right. Open up!' the Head Boy yelled. 'Let them in!'

The survivors scrambled into the quad, their comrades deterring the vehicles' pursuit with sustained gunfire. Not that the enemy seemed too bothered about breaking through, Travis thought. The cars steered left and right in turn to circle round the school.

And now the second wave of the assault. The bikes themselves, with Rev at their head.

From a first-floor window Simon was reminded of Native Americans besieging a wagon train in old westerns, only this time bows and arrows had been the weapons of the beleaguered. The attackers were employing different missiles. He realised now what the bottles were for. Filled with a liquid that was not water. Rags stuffed into their necks, set alight.

'What are they?' little Giles gasped beside him.

'Molotov cocktails,' Simon quailed. 'We're going to need those fire extinguishers.'

'I'll tell Clive.' And Giles was off again.

'Believe me,' Simon murmured, 'he'll know.'

The first of the petrol bombs, hurled from the cars, exploded harmlessly against the walls. But the bikes raced closer to the school, towards its more vulnerable windows, not all of which could be guarded. The smashing of glass as

Molotov cocktails fireballed into Harrington, igniting drapes and desks and timber floors.

Mel and Linden heard another girl scream. They sprinted in the direction of the sound, lugging their extinguishers. Just as well. The waiting room for visitors to the school, its window a jagged, screaming mouth: several of its chairs were ablaze. Two of the youngest members of the Harrington community, a boy and a girl, each of them under ten, cowered on the floor.

'I've got this, Lin. Look after them.' Mel sprayed foam at the fire.

'It's OK. It's gonna be OK.' Linden soothed the children, but her thoughts were with Travis.

Who was gaping in horror as the bus was finally given something to do. It was being aimed directly at the arch, flanked by several bikes. Several minus one, as a bullet from the Harringtonians made its mark.

'It'll break through,' Antony predicted. 'Nothing we've got can stop it.' Already in possession of his own gun, he snatched up a similar weapon discarded by one of the wounded. 'You know how to use this, Travis?'

'Now's a good time to learn.' He took hold of the shotgun. He thought of a drowning man grabbing a straw.

The bus was looming larger by the second. It was a Number 143 to Otterham. Had kind of lost its way. And its driver. He was bailing out while he could but he must have wedged the accelerator down somehow because the bus wasn't slowing, if anything was increasing its speed and . . . 'Scatter!' cried Antony and everyone did and Travis dived onto the grass and glanced behind him and the bus was barrelling, bludgeoning through the flimsy barricades, the impact

341

launching its wheels into the air, its roof scraping the underside of the arch. It slammed to the ground again, its back end swinging round so that side-on it screeched across the quad. Towards Harrington's own stock of vehicles. 'No!' wailed Carburetti. But words were never terribly effective at arresting a body's motion.

Bus collided with cars. Fuel in all of the tanks. A mighty explosion shook Harrington as a volcanic whoosh of flame erupted skywards.

The fire could be contained, though, Antony reasoned. It couldn't damage the school itself. They could let it burn itself out. The fire wasn't the problem.

The problem was the bikers scorching into the quad in the wake of the bus. The bikers howling with perverse delight. Rev sniffing triumph in the stench of burning petrol.

But the Harringtonians weren't beaten yet. The school motto. *Avoid the Easy Way.* They'd done that all right, and now would come their reward. 'Leo,' Antony breathed.

And in the grounds, among the broken arrows and spent cartridge cases and crashed cars and bodies, down from the trees where they'd hidden in the branches until now, jumped a dozen uniformed Harringtonians. Nodding in grim approval, Leo Milton led them running towards the school.

Simon saw them, of course, realised that the final stage of Antony Clive's defence plan was in operation. The pincer movement. The bikers lured in close by a mock retreat. Their own options to withdraw then curtailed by gunfire from Leo Milton's fresh and fully armed Harringtonians, the best shots in the school. So far, so good. On the other hand, Simon had heard the explosion, too – the very stones had seemed to shudder – and little Giles had not returned from the quad.

342

Maybe he was hurt somewhere. It wasn't over yet. So what should he, Simon, do? Though he'd been assigned this position on the upper floor, its tactical usefulness was clearly at an end. What should he do?

The same question was occurring to Richie Coker.

'Save the books! Save the books!' Digby was shrieking from the window through which he was shooting pretty much indiscriminately. No wonder he wasn't out there with Leo Milton. Yeah, and if he'd been on top of his job maybe a Molotov wouldn't have smashed through one of the other windows and set fire to the Psychology and Sociology sections of the library.

Small loss there, Richie thought. But he sprayed the shelves with foam from his fire extinguisher anyway. He'd sooner deal with this kind of fire than the alternative.

But Digby was raving on and on. 'Put your back into it, Coker. We have to save those books.'

'The guys who wrote this shit are dead. They're not gonna care.' *Or to put it another way, piss-for-brains*, Richie fumed silently, *shut your upper-class mouth.*

And maybe someone was listening. At the window Digby kind of gurgled, spun round to face inwards, his shotgun clattering to the floor, blood streaming from his forehead where a biker bullet had grazed him. He slumped against General Fiction T-Z.

The flames doused and the deliberations of Freud and Jung preserved for posterity, Richie felt annoyingly compelled to at least check on the health of his unwanted partner before abandoning his post. Unconscious but alive, Digby would need to put his Harrington shirt and that poncey blazer in the wash when he recovered – if Rev wasn't in charge by then.

But *he* wasn't dead. Good. If necessary, now Richie could claim that he'd left the library to find Digby medical help – a mission of mercy rather than an exhibition of cowardice. Time to keep his head – and the rest of him – well and truly down.

Richie bolted from the library. He did not turn towards the quad.

Where circles were developing within circles. It was impossible to make out Rev's expression on the bike he shared with the girl in leather, but Travis wagered it wasn't quite as gleeful as it might have been a minute ago. The bikes had poured into the quad and were roaring around the bonfire of bus and cars, but by doing so they'd allowed themselves to become surrounded by a ring of focused, determined Harringtonians. With weapons. Deploying them. The whistle of arrows. The crackle of gunfire. Rain and flame. Antony yelling: 'For Harrington! For Harrington!' Travis feeling the recoil shiver through his body as he pulled the trigger of his own shotgun, as if teenager and weapon were one.

The tide turning.

But some of the bikers had already gained access to the school building. Mel and Linden heard their voices, expletives like artillery shells, hurtling down the corridor towards the waiting room. The younger children heard too, and began to whimper.

'Stand right there.' Slamming the door shut, Mel positioned them in the middle of the room so that the eye of anyone entering would immediately be drawn to them. 'Trust us. You'll be all right. Me and you, Lin, either side.' Of the door. Fire extinguishers raised above their heads. You could make a weapon out of anything if you set your mind to it.

344

Of course, both girls might still have preferred the enemy to pass them by.

They didn't.

The door burst open. Two figures in leather jackets burst in. Saw the kids. Hyena grins.

Down swept the fire extinguishers in heavy blurs of red. Mel's cracked her target on the skull, flooring him at once. His companion reacted a little more quickly, or perhaps Linden was slower than her friend to lash out with violence at boys. Either way, he flinched his head back in time to avoid the blow that only dashed the gun from his grasp.

'Damn.' Linden stepped forward to renew her attack. *'Damn.'*

'Lin,' groaned Ash.

'Actually, I should be glad I've seen you, Ash,' spat Linden. 'I've got something for you.'

She swung the fire extinguisher up and round and a second kind of red sprayed out as steel connected with flesh and bone. Ash's nose had never exactly been his best feature. It certainly wouldn't be now.

And circles within circles. As the vehicles looping around the walls sped past the front of the building they were coming under fire from Leo Milton's reserves. The best shots in the school.

The driver of a Vauxhall having been disabled, the car hurtled blindly beyond Harrington's corner turret and ploughed finally into a tree. A Ford, fresh from a showroom somewhere, the price still taped to its rear window, screeched and slid to a sudden halt, its three occupants leaping out. Under pressure from Leo's gunfire, one of them had fumbled with a Molotov cocktail on the back seat. A lit Molotov cocktail. They hit the deck just as the Ford blew up, the fuel in its tank joining in the pyrotechnics. Just as well the price-tag burned: no salesman could secure such a sum now. And the car behind failed to avoid its incinerated comrade. More of Rev's followers compelled to take emergency measures in self-preservation. Their appetite for further battle going up in the flames of their vehicles. Hands going up, too – in sur-render.

And what should Simon do? He should fight. He *wasn't* a coward and now he could prove it. He could put his days of victimhood behind him once and for all. He raced towards the stairs that would lead him down to the quad. Stopped abruptly. Someone was bounding *up* the stairs that would lead him *away* from the quad. Someone wearing a baseball cap. Simon darted into a doorway so that he wouldn't be seen. *This* was an unexpected bonus. Richie Coker, the hard man, Richie Coker who could handle himself when the going got tough. Simon squeezed his bony hands into fists. Seemed that when that happened, some of the tough (self-proclaimed) really *did* get going. Backwards. And as fast as their legs could carry them. Richie was fleeing in the direction of the dorms. Travis wouldn't be impressed by that; neither would Antony Clive. At last, Simon realised ecstatically, he had leverage over Richie Coker.

Excited, invigorated, he charged on down to the quad.

On arrival there his heart swelled further. They were going to win. Rev was going to lose. Even against the backdrop of blazing vehicles that much was obvious. Fighters were down on either side but the handful of remaining bikers were being picked off by the Harringtonians. Their circle was imploding, like a noose being tightened.

Simon spotted Giles. Close by. Limping, his hand pressed against a tear in his trousers, a gash in his thigh.

A bike heading straight for him. Rev and the girl in leather on it.

'Giles!' Simon reacted instinctively. (He wasn't a coward.) Flung himself at the younger boy, winded himself as they collided, as his weight and momentum propelled them both out of the machine's path. They rolled on the grass and were safe. Luckily, Simon's glasses had stayed on.

Travis saw Simon's act of courage. Pride for his friend and anger at Rev clashed in his heart. The biker's leader was in retreat now, racing towards the arch and the grounds beyond – towards the Queen's Highway, no doubt.

No *way*.

Travis fired his shotgun. His aim was off. He missed bike and riders but Rev swerved anyway. His front wheel struck a broken shard of barricade. His back wheel lifted off the ground. Rev and the girl in leather, with cries of desperate terror, were catapulted onto the concrete. Somehow, Leo Milton was there to confiscate their weapons. And Rev's fall had signalled complete capitulation among his followers.

Travis ran to the arch where the biker and the girl in leather grovelled. Through it he could see a few beaten vehicles evacuating at speed, Harringtonians guarding disconsolate and defeated prisoners. It was over for them. But not quite for him.

He jabbed his gun against the back of Rev's neck. 'So, coming to get me, were you, Big Man? Told you I'd be waiting.'

'Don't shoot me, kiddo. Please.' Pock-marked and bleating, blubbering. The custodian of the Queen's Highway.

'Get up. On your feet.'

Rev scrambled to oblige. 'Whatever you say. Whatever . . . I don't want no trouble.'

Travis smiled thinly. 'People staring down the barrel of a shotgun rarely do.' He was aware of Antony and Leo by his side, of hush and expectation. He wouldn't even have to aim from this range. And he thought of the children who'd fought for Harrington this morning with the rain falling and who were dead and wounded now because of Rev. And he thought of their parents and wondered whether they'd be proud of what had happened here today, were they themselves still alive. He thought of Mum at home in emptiness and silence. He thought of Dad. Someone like Rev, in Rev's image, had killed his dad. Could have been Rev's own actual father. Maybe. It was possible. Whatever Travis chose to do now, Rev would deserve it. And what would Dad do in his son's place?

'Don't kill me, kiddo. Please. I'm *sorry*.'

All it would take, a contraction of muscles in a single finger.

'Travis?' Antony's restraining voice. But then, Antony's father hadn't been stabbed to death in the street by a thug with Rev's face.

Then again, Antony's father hadn't left him an example, an ideal to live up to. Inspiration. Travis had made one stand today. He could make another.

'I'm not gonna kill you, Rev, as long as you're sensible and obey the rules.'

'The rules?'

'*Our* rules, if you want to get picky. Correct me if I'm wrong, Antony, but we want you out of here, scumbag. You

348

and your morons. We want you off Harrington land now and we don't want you coming back – not ever. Don't even *think* of coming back.'

'Travis is perfectly correct,' added Antony. 'Because next time we'll be even stronger.'

'Don't worry,' Rev muttered. 'We won't be back. There'll be easier pickings in other places.'

'Then why are you still here?' Travis snarled.

'It's OK, kiddo,' the biker promised. 'We're gone.'

And soon, for once true to his word, they were.

Antony delegated Leo Milton and a group of armed Harringtonians to escort the vanquished bikers to the main road. Travis watched Rev's depleted force, denied their machines, trudge into the distance until the foliage obscured them. He sighed and stared around him. The various fires were burning themselves out – even the conflagration in the quad would die down eventually – and though plenty of windows had been smashed the damage sustained by the building was essentially superficial. The school still stood.

Despite their victory, however, nobody seemed in jubilant mood, Travis included. There'd been too much blood and pain for that – and loss. The cemetery would be expanding. Then there were the living casualties to take care of. Minor injuries would heal themselves – they'd have no choice – but a number of the defenders had suffered more grievous wounds. Oliver Dalton-Booth, who pre-Sickness had planned to become a doctor, was going to have his work cut out for him.

And what about Travis's friends? With Antony organising

the medical effort, he crossed the quad to where Simon was leaning shakily against the wall. 'You OK?'

'Still standing, Travis.' With a weak smile. 'I think.'

'You weren't standing just now, Simon. I saw what you did. *Out*standing.'

'He saved my life,' declared little Giles. 'I'll never forget it.'

'I'll make sure you won't,' joked Simon.

Travis patted his shoulder admiringly. 'If only the kids at school had been here to— have you seen Mel and Linden?'

'No. They were on fire-extinguisher duty, I think. Travis . . .' As the other boy broke into a run.

'Get your friend to Dalton-Booth. I'm going to find the girls.' Shotgun still in hand. A rogue biker might yet be at liberty in the school.

There were two of them in the waiting room, lying senseless on the floor. He recognised the one with the broken nose. A pair of the younger children huddled nearby. Linden's arms were around them both. 'Travis, what's happening?'

'It's done. Are you OK?' Glancing pointedly at the prostrate Ash.

Linden nodded. 'Are you?'

'Where's Mel?'

'She went to check on Jessica. She was worried that if any of Rev's gang had got to the dorms Jessica wouldn't be able to—'

A strangled cry from the upper floor. Mel.

Travis was sprinting instantly for the stairs, Linden right behind him. Taking them two at a time. If something had happened to Jessica. If something had happened to Mel. Still carrying the gun. Smashing open the girls' dorm's door.

Mel was embracing Jessica as they sat on her bed, clasping

350

the blonde girl frantically, rocking her to and fro, half sobbing, half laughing. And Jessica was hugging her in return. Mel's face could not be seen; it was buried in her friend's shoulder and screened by her own jet hair. But Jessica's could, and there was confusion in it and bewilderment and fear but all that was good. There was *awareness* in it, life. The green-eyed stare fixed entreatingly on Travis and he almost shouted. But his throat was clogged with an emotion beyond expression.

Jessica had to speak herself.

'Trav, where are—? What's . . . I don't understand. I've had such a horrible dream.'

TWELVE

'The last thing I remember,' Jessica said, and her voice was barely more than a whisper, 'the last thing I remember as being real, was seeing my parents . . . gone. Seeing them in bed, with the Sickness. I knew Dad was infected but Mum had seemed all right, she'd seemed healthy. It must have taken her by surprise, taken her quickly. They didn't have a chance. And I saw them lying there, not moving, not answering me, and I knew what had happened, that it was all real, they were dead, but I didn't want it to be real, it was too much, too much pain. I couldn't bear the reality of the Sickness. I refused to accept it.'

'It's OK, Jessie.' Mel was again sitting on the bed alongside Jessica, an arm around her shoulders. Jessica had dressed. 'You don't have to go through this if you're not up to it. She doesn't have to tell us, does she, Trav?'

Who was also in the dorm, together with Simon, Richie, Linden and Antony. 'Of course not,' he said comfortingly. 'We're just glad you're back with us, Jessica, whole.'

'No, but I want to tell you. I *need* to,' the blonde girl insisted. 'Because I don't know exactly what happened then, don't know the medical terms for it if they exist, but suddenly, looking at my parents, I seemed to be falling away from them, not physically but mentally, I suppose, inside my own head. I felt myself falling into a deep, dark place where everything I saw was like shadows on a wall and where none of it was true or actual so none of it could hurt me, because I couldn't bear to be hurt any more. It seemed to me then that if I stayed in that dark place I'd be hidden and I'd be safe. No one would see me. No one could hurt me. I wanted to stay there. Seems I did. For nearly a week? While you got me here from Wayvale?'

'Do you remember anything of the past few days?' Travis asked gently.

'In blurs. Like nightmares. I remember being out in the night and running. I remember faces I'd never seen before, twisted faces passing in front of my eyes. I remember hearing voices – yours, Trav, and Mel's – but not understanding what they were saying.'

'So what . . . what do you think's made you recover now? There's got to be a reason.'

'Who cares what reasons?' Mel said. 'Jessie *has* recovered, that's all that matters. And we're so, so glad.' Kissing Jessica extravagantly on the cheek.

'I don't know. I think' – the blonde girl's brow furrowed in her effort to understand – 'maybe it's just time having passed or leaving Wayvale or arriving here. But I heard what you've told me were gunshots, and I heard explosions, and they kind of – I don't know – they somehow broke into the dark place where I was, broke down its walls. Made me see what was real again. Woke me up. Maybe I was just ready to recover.'

'Prob'ly finally realised what you were missing with me around,' boasted Richie.

'That was certainly a surprise,' Jessica admitted wryly.

'You're enough to make anyone want to retreat to a deep, dark place, Richie,' snorted Mel.

'But you could have left me,' Jessica said, 'couldn't you, Trav, Mel? You could have given up on me and left me behind.'

' 'Fraid not,' said Travis. 'I told you on your birthday, Jess. I'll always be around for you if you need me.'

'Me, too,' echoed Mel, a little resentful that Travis had got in there first.

Jessica closed her eyes and nodded. 'Thanks.' Opened them again. 'And it seems I've got some new friends to meet as well. Linden. Antony.' She smiled shyly at them both. 'Some catching-up to do. More change, Travis, hmm?'

'You've plenty of time, Jess. Keep taking it easy for now.'

'But Mum and Dad are still gone.' Jessica sighed deeply. Her shoulders sagged. 'I'll never see them again. Or my house. Nothing can bring back the life I had, can it?'

'That's true,' said Antony. 'Sadly it's true. But we have hopes for a new life here. It won't be the same as the way we lived pre-Sickness, but it can still be good, fulfilling. Jessica, your friends recruited you to Harrington by association, as it were, during your illness. I hope, now that happily you're well again, you'll choose to stay with us of your own free will, to help us bring our new life to pass.'

And despite the tears she couldn't hold back, Jessica Lane smiled. 'I'd like that.'

Antony returned to his theme later, strolling across the grounds with Travis towards the cemetery. The clouds had cleared away and the sun was belatedly shining.

'Now is the time,' he said. 'While our defeat of Rev is still in the forefront of our minds. While the bonds forged between us in battle are strong. We've fought for what we believe in. Now we have to translate those beliefs into practical achievements, into improving our daily lives.'

'That shouldn't be difficult.' Travis nodded towards the playing fields. At some point during the bikers' assault the animals had been spooked and had broken through the fences. They hadn't wandered far, however, and most had now been rounded up again. Boys were working on repairing their pens.

Antony paused, gazed back at the Harrington School appraisingly. The fires were all now extinguished. The clean-up operation had begun under the supervision of Leo Milton. Tomorrow they were going to begin replenishing their transport pool, with luck locating a pick-up truck or similar vehicle to remove the burned-out cars and bus from the quad to a spot selected for them in the woods that had never been renowned for its natural beauty.

'It's a straightforward matter to restore wood and glass and stone,' the Head Boy observed. 'People are a little more difficult to replace. Human resources are any organisation's most valuable asset, and right now ours are stretched to the limit.'

'Casualties,' Travis acknowledged as they walked on again. The final count had been made. Eight members of the community dead, seven boys and a girl. Many more temporarily incapacitated through their injuries; at least one boy that Oliver Dalton-Booth doubted would survive, given Harrington's present lack of medical supplies and its would-be doctor's lack of training and experience. 'Not that I trust Rev as far as I could throw that blasted bus he hit us with, but I *do* think he's unlikely to attack us again. Not for a while, at any rate. He'll need to regroup, too.' Fatalities among the bikers, the bodies abandoned on Harrington soil, had been double those suffered by the defenders, while Ash and his hapless companion, once they'd regained consciousness, had seemed only too delighted to be accompanied off the school's premises. Ash hadn't dared to mention Linden at all.

'There might be other Revs,' Antony said thoughtfully. 'We need to assume that there will be. Other trials. Whatever's worth defending will always be subject to attack.'

'I just love those Harrington Thoughts for the Day,' Travis said, grinning.

'You used to be able to see them scrawled on desktops. In our school, that was what qualified as graffiti.'

'You're kidding, right?'

'How very perceptive of you, Travis.' Antony smiled, too, though not for long.

They reached the graves. Several new pits had already been dug. Their tenants were waiting to move in. Antony stared sombrely into the dank black earth.

'James Harris, he's going to be buried here. He was in love with a girl he met in France last summer. He tried to write letters to her in French because apparently she didn't speak a word of English, but foreign languages were never his strong subjects, either. Goodness only knows what was in those letters. There, next to him, that plot's reserved for David Yardley. Superb cricketer, D.G.J. Yardley. I remember him once scoring a winning boundary off the final ball of the match. He was lifted shoulder-high by his team-mates and paraded around the ground like a trophy. Right over there –

where the cows are grazing.' Antony sighed. 'Into their graves like children sent early to bed.'

But, turning to his companion, Antony's resolve was absolute. 'I know the people buried here, Travis, our "casualties", and we can't bring them back, but I want no more deaths, no more graves. And the only way we can ensure that is to expand, to increase our numbers and make ourselves too strong for any Rev or gang of thugs to even consider an attack. We need more people. Now. We can't rely on our broadcasts alone any longer. We can't rely on people finding us. We have to find *them*. We have to be proactive.'

'What do you have in mind?'

'Something of a recruitment drive,' Antony said. 'Beginning tomorrow.'

They consulted maps and they drew up schedules. They chose to avoid towns of any size, not only because lack of manpower necessarily limited their ambition but also to minimise the risk of exposure to disease. Their first sweep for new blood would be confined to villages in the surrounding area and it would be controlled, organised, systematic. Harrington would be renewed.

Because they themselves were recent arrivals, and the oldest so far to join the community, Antony proposed that Travis's group should take a leading role in this 'vital undertaking', as he put it. Richie Coker, however, retorted that he was having nothing whatsoever to do with this 'total waste of time' – as *he* put it. Until it was pointed out to him that the alternative was grave-digging duty for Rev's late allies: the unalluring combination of dead bodies and hard physical work almost miraculously transformed Richie into the most eager of volunteers. Jessica could have been excused duties if she'd wanted to be, to allow her time for recuperation. She didn't want to be. She wanted to join the others, to get out and about, to feel herself fully alive again. 'Are you sure?' Antony asked her. She was. She was also pleased that he'd asked. Antony Clive seemed a very nice boy.

So in cars newly pressed into service, Travis too now cautiously at the wheel, they travelled out into the silent villages, searching for life. In Otterham several children emerged from their houses and followed the sound of engines as if entranced by the music of the Pied Piper. In Midvale the tiny village school yielded a teenage girl who'd been playing teacher and mother combined to three children under ten. In Brimley Green a pair of brothers were coaxed out from a corner shop they'd been ready to defend to their last breath because it had belonged to their parents.

The quest wasn't always successful. Some youngsters that they glimpsed simply ran off before they could be persuaded otherwise; occasionally they were warned warily to keep their distance or were threatened, inevitably by small roaming gangs of teenage boys. But most of the survivors they encountered, particularly the younger kids, proved only too happy to join them, relieved to be offered somewhere to belong again.

The Harrington population began to grow.

On the third day, Linden begged Travis to be allowed a detour from their route. 'It's Juniper and Fox and little Willow, the others, the kids I ran out on. I have to see if I can find them and put things right. They might still be at our settlement in the forest. I need to go and find out for sure, Travis.'

'Of course you do.' He held her hand.

'I can go on my own if . . .'

'Of course you won't.' And he squeezed it.

'But what if they're not there?'

'They will be, Linden.'

And they were. All five children. More ragged and runny-nosed than ever now – thinner, too, of course – but essentially in good health. Not recognising Travis or even Richie as the occupants of a car they'd once stoned. Overjoyed to see Linden again – even Juniper, who made no mention of fleeing from her in Willowstock the other day. The older girl also thought it wise to bypass the subject. She was too thankful at being able to hug the children once more and to know that this time she had the strength and support to do right by them.

Some of her gratitude she reserved for Travis – most of it, actually, expressed in the kind of gaze she'd never bestowed on Ash. It wasn't only about bringing her back to the camp.

'So this is how the hippies live?' Richie screwed up his nose in disgust. 'Lived.' Several of the shelters and tents had collapsed since Linden's departure; those inside did not appear to object. 'You can stick your eco-shit if you ask me.'

'Trav.' With a wince of horror, Mel directed the boy's attention to what had been a tent but was now little more than a khaki mound, the canvas torn, shredded, as if by claws, as if by teeth. The Sickness didn't affect the animals of the wood. And animals had to eat.

Travis's face darkened. 'Richie, go back to the cars and fetch the spades.' Along with shotguns, an assortment of tools was standard equipment in every Harrington vehicle.

'Spades? What the hell for?'

'We're going to bury as many of these people as we can.

We're going to bury Linden's mum and these kids' parents at least. So they know they'll be at peace. So they won't be mauled in the night.'

'Get real, Naughton.' Richie doubted that Jessica and Simes would be much help. 'If I'd wanted to dig graves, I could have stayed at the school.'

'*Do* it.' Travis's eyes flashed threateningly. 'Or I'll bury *you*.'

And by now Richie knew when it was unwise to argue with Travis Naughton. 'Easier ways to impress Hippie Chick,' he grumbled as he slouched off on his errand.

They worked in short shifts and dug one large if shallow pit. In it they laid the bodies of Fen Darroway and the parents of the younger children. Into the soil. Into the earth. The living forest all around them. A fitting final resting place for the Children of Nature.

'We'll come back later,' Travis promised. 'Do the same for the others.'

'Travis, what this *means* to me.' Linden held his left hand in both of hers. 'I can't tell you, but I'll show you. You've helped me through this morning. I want to help you through this afternoon.'

'This afternoon?'

'When we get to Willowstock.'

And Travis performed his final duty for his grandparents as he'd vowed to do. They dug the grave in the garden so Grandma and Grandad could still be close to everything they'd loved. Even Travis would not be very far away.

'Do you want to say anything, Trav?' Mel asked softly when it was done.

'What is there to say? I loved them and they're gone. We've lost so much, all of us. But not everything. Not each other.

Not our lives. I suppose we never had much control over our lives before now. We were only kids. Adults ran things. Adults told us what to do. The adults built the past but the past is over. The future's just starting, and the future is ours to build.'

Antony met with Travis and Leo Milton in the headmaster's study first thing on Friday morning. Antony was keen on maintaining the chronological discipline of days and dates. The calendar was a symbol of humankind's ambition to structure and organise time itself, he believed; its inherent sense of progression was central to the planning and realisation of great enterprises. If Harrington was ever to lose track of the day or the month or, eventually, the year, then that would be an admission that the future had no meaning and only the present moment mattered, and that, Antony suggested, would mean they had become savages. It was not going to happen while *he* remained Head Boy. Today was Friday, the twenty-fifth of May.

'I'm afraid I have some bad news, Travis,' Antony confessed, 'though some good news, too.'

'What's the bad news?'

'Our recruitment drive is going to have to be put on hold.'

'What? Why?' Travis glanced from Antony to his deputy and back. 'It's been successful, hasn't it?'

'Too successful, I'm afraid, as Leo has brought to my attention.'

Leo. Was that a smirk playing around the freckled boy's lips? Travis recalled the hint of condescension in the deputy's tone when first they'd arrived at Harrington. 'Too successful how?'

'I'm quite in agreement with Clive's general intention to

encourage individuals to join us – you're doing a splendid job in that regard, Naughton.' Why did Leo insist on the pointless formality of surnames? 'Additional mouths, however, require to be fed and, given our current level of food supply, if we enlarge our population any further we will struggle to cope. It would not be to our benefit for Harrington to go hungry.'

'Hard to argue with that,' Travis admitted, though he kind of felt he wanted to. There was something in Leo Milton's attitude that irked him. Good job Richie wasn't here. 'Couldn't we up our food supply?'

'You mean increase it?' Leo Milton asked fussily.

'Yeah. Up it.' *And up yours*, Travis thought.

'In time,' Antony said. 'We'll sow crops. We'll improve our animal husbandry, add chickens, pigs, rear then slaughter and eat our livestock. In time we'll become as self-sufficient as possible. But for now we're dependent on supplies brought in from surrounding shops and supermarkets. With more people requiring more provisions, as we exhaust our closest sources we'll be compelled to forage ever further afield. Journeys will take longer, require more petrol, possibly more vehicles. We must be careful not to overreach ourselves.'

'In any case,' Leo Milton threw in, 'Harrington was always a select institution.'

'It's not about selection, Leo,' Antony admonished. 'It's about survival.'

'Of course, Clive.'

'Presently we have sixty-four members in our community,' Antony said. 'If anyone else arrives seeking refuge here, we can hardly in conscience turn them away. But from now on, and for the foreseeable future, we cannot afford to continue

362

actively seeking out recruits.' The Head Boy shrugged. 'I'm sorry, Travis.'

'No. I can see what you mean.' And he did. He'd just sooner not have seen it in the company of Leo Milton. The ginger-haired boy's involvement in Antony's decision smacked just a little of putting the upstart in his place. 'So I guess I'm out of a job.'

'Yes and no,' Antony said, earning a surreptitious sideways glance from his deputy. 'That's the good news I wanted to talk to you about. At least, I rather hope you'll consider it to be good news. Both of you. I haven't told Leo yet.'

'Cue drum roll?' wondered Travis.

'We do now have sixty-four residents at Harrington and more than half of them were not students here. Therefore, I think it might be sensible to appoint a second Deputy Head Boy with specific responsibility for those members of our community who are new to us. And by appoint, I really mean invite. Travis, I think we have much in common. I think we've already proved we can work together. If you want it, the position's yours.'

'If I—?' Deputy Head Boy. Maybe it was ridiculous to use such terms post-Sickness, but it was a kind of promotion nonetheless. Recognition. Dad would have been proud. 'I'm honoured, Antony. And I accept.'

'Excellent. I'm very pleased.' Shaking hands warmly. 'Of course, you'll also be working closely with Leo from now on. I'm sure the two of you will get along famously.'

'I'm sure we will, Clive.' Though Leo's handshake was a little cooler than the other boy's.

'Famously,' said Travis. And, of course, he hadn't taken the job simply in order to see that flush of resentment spread

363

across Leo's already rather pink complexion. That was just a bonus.

'And one other matter. I thought perhaps we ought to hold a small social event tomorrow evening in the Great Hall. Music. Dancing. That kind of thing. Give everyone a chance to celebrate what we've achieved so far. After the nightmare we've lived through, remind ourselves that we are still allowed to enjoy ourselves. What do you think?'

'Antony,' said Travis approvingly, 'let the party begin.'

But it felt strange.

Partly, of course, because Travis had never been to a party ('social event') in a Great Hall before. The ambience was kind of different to the cramped front rooms where he was accustomed to drinking and dancing and chancing his arm with girls. He found the space intimidating, even lit by candles as it was tonight to create a more intimate atmosphere. The haughty stone walls and the windows (those that had survived Rev's rampage), stained-glass like the ones you saw in churches, they didn't seem designed to encourage pleasure. The music, too, was unlikely to trouble the charts. Four Harringtonians with violins playing jigs; the girl from Midvale borrowing one of the school's acoustic guitars and warbling through a set of standards. But Travis supposed that the actual nature of the music wasn't the point: there were tunes, and melody was sufficient.

In any case, the bottom line was that it all felt odd and *he* felt uncomfortable, because he was also haunted by guilt. Guilt that he might laugh, that he might feel the urge to dance, to ask Mel or Jessica – or Linden – to dance with him. Guilt that he might, even for a moment in the candlelight and to the strumming of old songs, forget that his mother was dead, his grandparents were dead, that countless millions of people were . . . Would it be wrong to laugh again? Would having a good time be an insult to the memory of those who'd perished, a betrayal – or a tribute? How long were they required to grieve for the lost past?

Not long for the younger children, it seemed, the likes of Juniper and Willow. They were up on the floor where the tables had been cleared back already. They were clapping their hands, shrieking, trying to keep pace with the Harrington string quartet. Little kids – Travis supposed they were more resilient, more adaptable. In young minds reality and fantasy blended and merged. The Sickness and the monster under the bed were the same. They would have loved their parents (he hoped), but they wouldn't have known them, not as people, not as individuals, and those you don't know you're more likely to forget. It was their generation who would be the true survivors.

'Hey, Trav.' Mel. She was sitting on a bench with Jessica. 'You're reminding me of that horse joke.'

'What horse joke is that?' He sauntered across to them.

'You know. Horse goes into a bar. Barman says: "Why the long face?"'

'Hm. Stay sat down. A stand-up you ain't.'

'You do look kind of glum, Trav,' put in Jessica. 'I know we all feel the same but . . .'

'You have to make the effort. Like we have,' Mel grinned, indicating the girls' clothes. 'Party wear or what?' The idea of exclusive ownership of one's wardrobe was beginning to seem a little pre-Sickness. The clothing that was being imported to Harrington from shops and houses was heaped in communal piles, boys' and girls', and people just helped themselves to whatever fitted and suited their taste. Jessica's outfit was preposterously frilled and louder than the music, and even Mel had opted for a rather more flamboyant look than was usual for her, though she did persevere with her traditional black.

'You look great. Both of you,' Travis said with sincerity. 'And I don't just mean the clothes. Actually, I don't mean the clothes at all.' Jessica returned to something like full health, Mel happier because of it – there were things to be grateful for.

'What about me, Travis?' Linden behind him. 'How do I look?' In a simple white dress, short. Bare legs. Seemed that Linden had left the more rustic fashions favoured by the Children of Nature well and truly behind her.

Travis felt his blood rush. 'Out of ten? Twenty. At least.'

'Does that mean that if I asked you to dance you'd say yes?'

'Ask me.'

'Would—'

'Yes.'

Linden giggling, Travis smiling, they joined the under-twelves on the floor. And OK, she might have giggled once with Ash, maybe other boys, too, but they weren't here now and they wouldn't be. Travis could ignore them. He could block them out of his mind. He really wanted to. And it was OK to have a good time; he couldn't help himself after all. And russet was suddenly Travis's favourite tint of hair, hazel his preferred colour of eye, Linden's hands the hands he most wanted to hold, and her body, when it came into sinuous contact with his own . . . Things to be grateful for.

366

From the margins of the Hall, Antony watched Travis and Linden start to dance and was glad. Meant the way was clear for him to approach Mel himself. He could have done so already, of course, if he hadn't permitted nerves to delay him. What was there to be nervous about? The words were simple enough: 'Melanie, would you like to dance?' Six words. Not too many to remember. And in English. But it wasn't what *he* was intending to say that was the problem but what Mel *might* say in response. A single word, possibly: 'No.' Rejection was not pleasant. If only he had more experience of girls like Mel – though the fact that she was so different formed a large part of the attraction. That mass of black hair, the clothes – the goth look, he believed it was called – the sharp eyes and the sharper tongue, the confidence to stand up for herself, a contrast to the designer-clad sophisticates with whom Harrington students normally socialised. Actually, truth be told, if only he had more experience with girls of *any* description. Antony could talk politics and philosophy all day long, but when it came to expressing his emotions, where he came from that wasn't really done. It would be safer, less awkward, not to ask Mel to dance at all. But then, he *was* Head Boy of the Harrington School and he lived by its precepts. *Avoid the Easy Way.*

'Hi, Antony.' Mel smiled at him. That was good.

'Hello, Antony.' Jessica, too. Jessica Lane, he thought she was called.

'Ah, evening. And how are you feeling this evening, Jessica?' Curry favour by inquiring as to her friend's health first.

'Better. As well as can be expected, I suppose. At least I know where I am. Thanks for asking.'

'Yes, well, um . . .' Enough with the preliminaries.

'Do you sleep in that thing, too?'

'Excuse me?' Mel was peering at him with amusement in her eyes. What did she mean?

'Those things, I should say. Your blazer and tie. Do you ever take them off, Antony, or are they, like, part of you, like a kind of second skin or something? This is supposed to be a party and you're dressed like it's double history.'

'Don't be horrible, Mel,' chided Jessica.

'I'm not being horrible. I'm just asking questions.'

'Ignore her, Antony,' said Jessica. 'I think you look very smart.'

'Yes, well, um . . . Melanie, would . . .'

'Mel,' corrected the goth girl.

'Mel, would you like to dance?'

And she wouldn't. She wasn't going to. The way her eyelids flickered involuntarily and the twitch of her lips, smiling but falsely smiling because she didn't want to hurt him unnecessarily. But however many words she was preparing to say they all boiled down to one. 'Oh, Antony, it's sweet of you to ask but I don't dance. With anyone, really. Especially not tonight. I just want to sit here with Jessie and watch. Make sure she's all right.' Rubbing her friend's back.

'I *am* all right,' Jessica protested mildly. Looking up at Antony: '*I*'d . . .'

'Of course. Of course.' After rejection, retreat. A.s.a.p. 'Have a pleasant evening is what I really wanted to— I'd better, um, circulate. See you later.' Humiliation complete.

'You were a bit rude, Mel.' Jessica scolded her friend once Antony was out of earshot.

'What are you talking about? These public-school types

368

have got skins as thick as their daddies' wallets. And heads, some of them – though not Antony, I'll admit.'

'You should have danced with him since he'd plucked up the courage to ask. *I* would have done if he'd asked *me*.' Following the blond boy's disappearing form with wistful eyes.

'That's 'cause you're a better person than me, Jessica Lane. But we've always known that.' Mel squeezed her. 'I'd sooner sit here with you.'

'That's fine,' Jessica said tetchily, shrugging her shoulders free of Mel's arm. 'But you don't have to prop me up. I can stand on my own two feet again now, or haven't you noticed?' Seeing hurt crumple Mel's face. 'Sorry. Sorry. I didn't mean to . . . after all you've done for me. It's just, I don't know, boy asking girl to dance, it's just reminded me.'

'Of what? Are you OK?'

'You know where we were two weeks ago tonight, what we were doing? We were at my house, celebrating my sixteenth birthday. Two weeks ago. That's all. The length of a summer holiday. Where's everybody who was there now? How many of our friends are even still alive? Mel, what are we going to do?'

And this time, when Mel put her arm around her, Jessica did not object.

Meanwhile, over by one set of doors: 'Morticia knock you back, Tony?' taunted Richie Coker.

'It's Antony,' the Head Boy corrected him frostily. He looked at Richie, propped up against the wall and swigging lager from a can, with open hostility. 'Kindly refrain from calling me Tony. And I have no idea what you're talking about.'

'Whatever. And I think you have. But see, the trouble is,

Tony, Morticia's a real girl, and real girls need real men, you know what I mean?'

With a snort of contempt, Antony turned away from Richie and strode towards the far side of the Hall. Richie laughed and raised his can in mock salute. That took the upper-class prat down a peg or two. Tonight was turning out better than he'd expected. Course, the beer helped. Beer always helped. And this can was empty. No worries. There were more in the room next door. Harrington's age limit for the consumption of alcoholic beverages had been set by Tony Clive and that Ginger Milton for special occasions like this at only fourteen. They had some sense, after all.

Richie slouched into the adjacent room where the drink was kept. It was almost empty. Everyone was in the Hall either bopping or gassing – both wastes of time when you could be boozing – except for the one sad loser always to be found in the kitchen at parties, even if a room hung with maps of the world didn't quite qualify as a kitchen.

'Simes, me old mate, how you doing?'

'I was doing all right.' Simon's lip curled. 'All of a sudden, though, I've got this really pressing urge to throw up. Why do you reckon that is, Coker?'

'Tut, tut, Simes.' Richie wagged a cautionary finger. 'Wouldn't have talked to me like that back home. Wouldn't have dared.'

'Things have changed since we were "back home", Coker,' said Simon.

'Don't you believe it.' Richie grabbed a fresh can of beer, yanked at the ring pull. 'You're still on the outside looking in 'cause nobody really wants you, Simes.'

'That's not true.' Defensively, as though it might be.

'I told you that your do-gooding mate Naughton wanted to join the snobs' club, didn't I? And what is he now? Deputy Head blah in charge of blah? Naughton's not interested in you any more, Simes. He's moved on, left you behind. No one's interested. You're on your own in an empty room.'

'So are you.' Trying not to think of Travis and Antony, or Mel and Jessica, or Travis and Linden, or any friendship pairs where two was company and the third – the crowd – was always himself. 'No one's bothered about you either, Coker. No one likes you, and they'd like you even less if they knew what I know. They'd want you out if they knew that.'

'And what *do* you know, Simes?' Richie asked casually, almost in a friendly way.

'Your mercy dash for Digby,' Simon gloated. 'I just happened to see it. I guess you didn't find Dalton-Booth up in the dormitories, though, bearing in mind everyone had been told he was going to be treating any wounded in the Great Hall. But I expect you spent a long time looking. I'm sure Travis and Antony would be delighted to hear about your commitment to the cause.'

'So you saw me, Simes, huh?' Richie nodded, grinned, placed his can of lager on a table. 'You're gonna tell tales on your old mate Richie.'

'Not if I don't have to. We can keep it a secret, just between the two of us, as long as you – well, as long as you promise to leave me alone from now on. No more treating me like I'm some kind of dirt on your shoe. That's the deal.'

'That's the deal, is it?' Richie glanced towards the door, which was closed. 'Guess you don't really give me any choice, do you, Simes, old mate?' And Simon was half in the process of shaping a triumphant smile on his lips when

Richie's forearm smashed like lightning against his windpipe and Richie's weight shoved him back against the wall and Richie's heavy, ugly features scowled and snarled at him from only inches away. 'Forget it, four eyes. Forget it, you useless piece of shit. You think you can get the better of me, Satchwell? You couldn't get the better of a slug.' Slamming Simon repeatedly against the wall. 'You're a loser, a waste of space. You were born worthless and you're still worthless and you always will be. Weak and worthless, Simes, you hear me?'

'Rich . . .' He heard. 'Can't . . . can't . . .' *Breathe*, he wanted to say.

And suddenly Richie was releasing him, stepping back. Simon crumpled to his knees, coughing, massaging his injured throat.

'Here's the deal, Simes,' Richie sneered. 'Nothing changes, not between you and me. If I want to beat you up a little bit, if I get bored – and I get bored real easy – if I want to torment my own pet victim from time to time, I will. And you'll put up with it like the pathetic retard you truly are. And you won't tell Naughton about it or no one. And you'll never mention where you *think* you saw me going during the battle, either. Or else, Simes, whatever they do to me, throw me out or whatever, before I go I'll make you wish you were old enough for the Sickness to have got you. You hear me, Simes?'

'I . . . hear . . .' Choking out the words, tears of frustration and impotent rage streaming down his cheeks even after Richie had left the room with his beer, left him on his knees. Again. Always on his knees. *Bastard. Bastard.* And he'd been deluding himself, deceiving himself. He'd been indulging in make-believe. New beginnings? Fresh starts? Simon Satchwell valued? Nothing ever changed for Simon Satchwell. Never had. Never would. Richie was right. Simon had been born worthless and without worth he would remain. There was no way out and no one could protect him. Not even Travis.

Who was laughing in the corridor at that very moment, Linden leading him by the hand away from the Great Hall, past a grinning Richie Coker.

'Where are we going? Is this kidnap or what? If you didn't want to dance any more we could have sat with Jessica and Mel.'

'Uh-uh. I'm feeling kind of greedy tonight, Trav. I want you to myself.'

'Well' – Travis wrapped his arms around her, kissed her in the dark corridor – 'it looks like you've got me.'

'I'm glad. Because there are things I want to make up to you, Travis.'

'What do you mean?' *Things to be grateful for.*

'Letting you down over the eye. I should have told you about it as soon as I saw . . .'

'No, that was me not wanting to look foolish in front of Antony . . .'

'And Ash.'

'And *that* was me being unfair and unreasonable and jealous. Forget Ash.'

'I have. I want to prove to you that I have.'

'Mm-hm. And how are you planning on doing that, Ms Darroway?'

'I'll show you. Come with me.' Taking his hand again. Leading him on again.

'Where are we going?' Grinning.

'To the dorms.'

And then not grinning. 'Why?'

'That's where the beds are.'

Not grinning at all. Pulling his hand away. 'Wait a minute.'

'Wait? That's just the point, Trav. I don't *want* to wait. I want to show you what you mean to me.' Gazing at him imploringly. She didn't like to be alone. 'I want to be with you.'

'But – I . . .' Was he really going to turn her down? Why? 'But we've only known each other for, you know, a week. That's not . . .'

'Look what's happened in that week, Trav,' argued Linden. 'And the week before that. This is a new world now. We can be new people. We don't have to think about waiting and dating and playing games and worrying what others might think. The old conventions. They're gone. We can do what we feel and there's nobody older to carp or criticise or point a moralising finger.'

'That's true, Linden.' And he *was* going to turn her down. And he knew why. 'But just because we *can* do something, that doesn't mean we ought to. I don't believe in moralising but I do believe in morals, values. That's why we fought Rev. That's why we're here. And I don't believe – being with you – tonight, now – would be right. Not for either of us. Sorry, Linden.'

'Me, too. Don't you like me, Travis?'

'It's because I like you – *really* like you – that I don't want to rush. I want to get to know you better, not just hop straight into bed. You're worth more than that, Linden. We both are. Do you – can you understand that?'

374

He *did* like her. She'd been right. It was only going to be a matter of time. 'You really are nothing like Ash, Travis,' she said. 'I understand – reluctantly. But does this at least mean we're kind of like boyfriend and girlfriend?'

'I think it does.'

'And we can still, like, can we still kiss?'

'I thought,' said Travis, 'you'd never ask.'

And they kissed. They kissed rather a lot.

In fact, they only darted back into the Great Hall when they heard the music stop and Antony begin to deliver his speech. His rallying call. Standing on the platform where once Harrington's masters had stood, a symbol of order and continuity. Harrington's masters, now dead.

'. . . We've worked hard to earn ourselves this evening and we deserve it. One night off. One night to pause and reflect on everything that we've achieved. Defeating Rev and his bikers was a baptism of fire. Not for the Harrington School as such – this building has stood for almost three hundred years. Thousands of boys and young men have been educated within its walls. Myself, you, Leo, Oliver, Giles, the rest of you who were privileged to attend as students pre-Sickness, we're the last of our kind. The days of Harrington as a school are over. What we witnessed in the battle against Rev was the birth of something else, an evolution. People coming together from far and wide, male and female, from all social back-grounds, uniting to battle a common enemy, united by faith in a shared ideal, the belief that in this place a future can be built that will be civilised and decent and good. A future worth living for. A future of which we can all be proud.'

Cheers and applause from Antony's audience. Travis glanced at his companions, at Linden and Jessica and Mel and Simon. Yes, and even at Richie Coker. They'd made it this far. They'd made it from an end to a beginning.

Things to be grateful for.

'So. *So.*' Antony signalling for quiet, gradually getting it. '*So*, I have an announcement to make. Harrington will no longer be called a school. I'd like to propose a toast instead to a new, more appropriate name for what we're establishing here together. The Harrington Community.' Antony raised his glass. 'I give you – the Harrington Community.'

'The Harrington Community!' The words resounded among the assembly as everyone followed suit and lifted up their glass or can or whatever it was they were drinking from, and everyone cheered again and applauded some more and certain people broke into a stirring rendition of the school song. So nobody heard the boy's shrill scream. Not at first. Not until he brought it with him, bolting in absolute terror into the Hall.

Then there was confusion, anxiety, fear. Then there was silence.

'What on earth—? Roland?' Antony tried to calm the traumatised boy.

Roland Garrick. One of the watch.

'Outside! *Outside!*' All he could cry.

'Rev,' Travis growled vengefully, racing for the doors. The girls, too. Antony, Leo Milton – everyone racing for the doors. 'He's come back. Dammit, he's come back.'

He hadn't. It wasn't Rev.

The light, silver like the stars, dazzled them as they spilled out into the quad. They staggered blindly for several seconds as their eyes adjusted. Travis was thinking, *Headlights. This must be how a rabbit feels staring into the headlights of the car that will kill it.* The screams on either side of him, from all around him, a sudden plague of insanity.

'God, Travis!' Linden clutching his arm, gazing up. Everybody gazing up. Into the night. Into the midnight sky. Travis gazed, too.

And at once he felt the panic rising in him, the incomprehension, the fear, the overwhelming, soul-destroying sense that reality was all too much for him, too much to bear.

He'd never seen such craft before and yet he had. In countless science fiction movies. Whooping in his cinema seat as aliens brought apocalypse to Earth. Aliens in armadas of obliterating, invincible spaceships. Titanic. Terrifying.

And they were here, now, overhead. This was what they truly looked like, because the ships had set the heavens ablaze with unearthly fire and in it they were revealed. Skyscraper-high, made of a metal forged in furnaces galaxies distant, silver and searing. Shaped like sickles, like scythes, the mighty arcs of their crescents hundreds of metres across. Scimitar edges like blades for cutting, blades for reaping in fields where the crop is ripe for harvest. The engines in the ships' under-bellies burned like white suns and the hum of their power caused the ground to tremble beneath Travis's feet. But at the same time there was a coldness about the alien craft, the glacial temperature of deep space.

Linden was gripping him more tightly but there was nothing he could hold on to. Just when Travis had thought they'd established some semblance of control again, found direction and hope, came a crushing reminder of his helplessness, his ignorance. His mind reeled and the world seemed to spiral around him. Nothing was right. Nothing was as he'd imagined it to be.

They'd been wrong from the beginning.

As above them the night continued to throng with space-ships. He couldn't count them. He couldn't begin to. Spaceships spreading across the entire planet. Spaceships blotting out the sky.

And, to Travis's petrifying, paralysing horror, *descending*.

To be continued in
SLAVE HARVEST

About the Author

Andrew Butcher was once an English teacher but now devotes his time to a ragtag group of orphaned teenagers fighting a desperate resistance against alien invaders. He lives in Dorset with an unfeasibly large comic collection.

For more information about Andrew Butcher and other Atom authors visit www.littlebrown.co.uk

SCOTT WESTERFELD

MIDNIGHTERS

BOOK ONE

The Secret Hour

12:00 A.M.

THE SILENT STORM

Jessica woke up because the sound of the rain just . . . stopped.

It changed all at once. The sound didn't fade away, trickling down into nothingness like rain was supposed to. One moment the whole world was chattering with the downpour, lulling her to sleep. The next, silence fell hard, as if someone had pushed mute on a TV remote control.

Jessica's eyes opened, the sudden quiet echoing around her like a door slam.

She sat up, looking around the bedroom in confusion. She didn't know what had woken her – it took a few seconds just to remember where she was. The dark room was a jumble of familiar and unfamiliar things. Her old writing desk was in the wrong corner, and someone had added a skylight to the ceiling. There were too many windows, and they were bigger than they should have been.

But then the shapes of boxes piled everywhere, clothing and books spilling out of their half-open maws, brought it all back. Jessica Day and her belongings were strangers here, barely settled, like pioneers on a bare plain. This was her new room, her family's new house. She lived in Bixby, Oklahoma, now.

'Oh, yeah,' she said sadly.

Jessica took a deep breath. It smelled like rain. That was right – it had been raining hard all night . . . but now it was suddenly quiet.

Moonlight filled the room. Jessica lay awake, transfixed by how strange everything looked. It wasn't just the unfamiliar house; the Oklahoma night itself felt somehow wrong. The windows and skylight glowed, but the light seemed to come from everywhere, blue and cold. There were no shadows, and the room looked flat, like an old and faded photograph.

Jessica still wondered what had awakened her. Her heart beat quickly, as if something surprising had happened a moment ago. But she couldn't remember what.

She shook her head and lay back down, closing her eyes, but sleep wouldn't come. Her old bed seemed uncomfortable, somehow wrong, as if it didn't like being here in Bixby.

'Great,' Jessica muttered. Just what she needed: a sleepless night to go with her exhausting days of unpacking, fighting with her little sister, Beth, and trying to find her way around the Bixby High maze. At least her first week at school was almost over. It would finally be Friday tomorrow.

She looked at the clock. It said 12:07, but it was set fast, to Jessica time. It was probably just about midnight. Friday at last.

A blue radiance filled the room, almost as bright as when the light was on. When had the moon come out? High, dark clouds had rolled over Bixby all day, obscuring the sun. Even under the roof of clouds the sky was huge here in Oklahoma, the whole state as flat as a piece of paper. That afternoon her dad had said that the lightning flashes on the horizon were striking all the way down in Texas. (Being unemployed in Bixby had started him watching the Weather Channel.)

The cold, blue moonlight seemed brighter every minute.

Jessica slid out of bed. The rough timbers of the floor felt warm under her feet. She stepped carefully over the clutter, the moonlight picking out every half-unpacked box clearly. The window glowed like a neon sign.

When she looked outside, Jessica's fingers clenched and she uttered a soft cry.

The air outside sparkled, shimmering like a snow globe full of glitter.

Jessica blinked and rubbed her eyes, but the galaxy of hovering diamonds didn't go away.

There were thousands of them, each suspended in the air as if by its own little invisible string. They seemed to glow, filling the street and her room with the blue light. Some were just inches from the window, perfect spheres no bigger than the smallest pearl, translucent as beads of glass.

Jessica took a few steps backward and sat down on her bed.

'Weird dream,' she said aloud, and then wished she hadn't. It didn't seem right saying that. Wondering if she were dreaming made her feel more . . . awake somehow. And this was already too real: no unexplained panic, no watching herself from above, no feeling as if she were in a play and didn't know her lines – just Jessica Day sitting on her bed and being confused.

And the air outside full of diamonds.

Jessica slipped under her covers and tried to go back to sleep. *Unconscious* sleep. But behind closed eyelids she felt even more awake. The feel of the sheets, the sound of her breathing, the slowly building body warmth inside the covers were all exactly right. The realness of everything gnawed at her.

And the diamonds were beautiful. She wanted to see them up close.

Jessica got up again.

She pulled on a sweatshirt and rummaged around for shoes, taking a minute to find a matching pair among the moving boxes. She crept out of her room and down the hall. The still unfamiliar house looked uncanny in the blue light. The walls were bare and the living room empty, as if no one lived here.

The clock in the kitchen read exactly midnight.

Jessica paused at the front door, anxious for a moment. Then she pushed it open.

This had to be a dream: millions of diamonds filled the air, floating over the wet, shiny asphalt. Only a few inches apart, they stretched as far as Jessica could see, down the street and up into the sky. Little blue gems no bigger than tears.

No moon was visible. Thick clouds still hung over Bixby, but now they looked as hard and unmoving as stone. The light seemed to come from the diamonds, as if an invasion of blue fireflies had been frozen in midair.

Jessica's eyes widened. It was so beautiful, so still and wondrous, that her anxiety was instantly gone.

She raised a hand to touch one of the blue gems. The little

diamond wobbled, then ran onto her finger, cold and wet. It disappeared, leaving nothing but a bit of water.

Then Jessica realized what the diamond had been. A raindrop! The floating diamonds were *the rain*, somehow hanging motionless in the air. Nothing moved on the street or in the sky. Time was frozen around her.

In a daze, she stepped out into the suspended rain. The drops kissed her face coolly, turning into water as she collided with them. They melted instantly, dotting her sweatshirt as she walked, wetting her hands with water no colder than September rain. She could smell the fresh scent of rain, feel the electricity of recent lightning, the trapped vitality of the storm all around her. Her hairs tingled, laughter bubbling up inside her.

But her feet were cold, she realized, her shoes soaking. Jessica knelt down to look at the walk. Motionless splashes of water dotted the concrete, where raindrops had been frozen just as they'd hit the ground. The whole street shimmered with the shapes of splashes, like a garden of ice flowers.

A raindrop hovered right in front of her nose. Jessica leaned nearer, closing one eye and peering into the little sphere of motionless water. The houses on the street, the arrested sky, the whole world was there inside, upside down and warped into a circle, like looking through a crystal ball. Then she must have gotten too close – the raindrop shivered and jumped into motion, falling onto her cheek and running down it like a cold tear.

'Oh,' she murmured. Everything was frozen until she touched it, like breaking a spell.

Jessica smiled as she stood, looking around for more wonders.

All the houses on the street seemed to be glowing, their windows filled with blue light. She looked back at her own house. The roof was aglitter with splashes, and a motionless spout of water gushed from the meeting of two gutters at one corner. The windows glowed dully, but there hadn't been any lights on inside. Maybe it wasn't just the raindrops. The houses, the still clouds above, everything seemed to be incandescent with blue light.

Where did that cold light come from? she wondered. There was more to this dream than frozen time.

Then Jessica saw that she had left a trail, a tunnel through the rain where she had released the hovering rain. It was Jessica shaped, like a hole left by a cartoon character rocketing through a wall.

She laughed and broke into a run, reaching out to grab handfuls of raindrops from the air, all alone in a world of diamonds.

The next morning Jessica Day woke up smiling.

The dream had been so beautiful, as perfect as the raindrops hovering in the air. Maybe it meant that Bixby wasn't such a creepy place after all.

The sun shone brightly into her room, accompanied by the sound of water dripping from the trees onto the roof. Even piled with boxes, it felt like *her* room, finally. Jessica lay in bed, luxuriating in a feeling of relief. After months of getting used to the idea of moving, the weeks of saying good-bye, the days of packing and unpacking, she finally felt as if the whirlwind were winding down.

Jessica's dreams weren't usually very profound. When she was nervous about a test, she had test-hell nightmares. When her little sister was driving Jessica crazy, the Beth of her dreams was a twenty-story monster who chased her. But Jessica knew that this dream had a deeper meaning. Time had stopped back in Chicago, her life frozen while she waited to leave all her friends and everything she knew, but now that was over. The world could start again, once she let it.

Maybe she and her family would be happy here after all.

And it was Friday.

The alarm rang. She pulled herself from under the covers and swung herself out of bed.

The moment her feet touched the floor, a chill ran up her spine. She was standing on her sweatshirt, which lay next to her bed in a crumpled pile.

It was soaking wet.